KT-447-860

Maggie Hope was born and raised in County Durham. She worked as a nurse for many years, before giving up her career to raise her family.

Also by Maggie Hope:

A Wartime Nurse
A Mother's Gift
A Nurse's Duty
A Daughter's Gift

MAGGIE HOPE
Molly's War

EBURY
PRESS

3 5 7 9 10 8 6 4 2

First published as *The Marble Clock* in 2001 by Piatkus Books
This edition published in 2013 by Ebury Press, an imprint of Ebury Publishing
A Random House Group Company

The Random House Group Limited Reg. No. 954009

Addresses for companies within the Random House Group can be found at:
www.randomhouse.co.uk

A CIP catalogue record for this book is available from the British Library

ISBN   9781785031939

To buy books by your favourite authors and register for offers visit:
www.randomhouse.co.uk

The Random House Group Limited supports The Forest Stewardship
Council® (FSC®), the leading international forest-certification organisation.
Our books carrying the FSC label are printed on FSC®-certified paper.
FSC is the only forest-certification scheme supported by the leading
environmental organisations, including Greenpeace. Our
paper procurement policy can be found at
www.randomhouse.co.uk/environment

Printed and bound in Great Britain by Clays Ltd, St Ives PLC

To my aunt, Mary Walker, one of the Aycliffe Angels, who worked in the Royal Ordnance factory there. Also my uncle, the late Sergeant Joseph Howe, Croix de Guerre.

Though this book is a work of fiction I drew heavily on their experiences during World War II to create the atmosphere and background material.

Chapter One

1938

'Sing as you go and let the world go by . . .'

The high, sweet voice of Gracie Fields rang out over the clatter of the sewing machines on the factory floor and the girls in the long line on the belt bent over the cloth racing under the needles, singing along with her.

Molly Mason finished yet another side seam and flung the pieces in the bin at her side. She hardly lifted her head to look as she picked up two more pieces and deftly fitted them under the needle. Enid Parker, the line overseer, was nearby, walking up the line collecting the bins of finished work to take to the next line where the shoulder seams were sewn.

Molly's fingers were a blur. She could sew this simple straight seam over and over, barely thinking what she was doing. Neither did she hear the wireless for she was thinking of clocking off time and if she would make her bonus this week. Oh, she needed it, it was the only way she could afford new winter shoes. The toes of her stockings were still damp and gritty because it had been raining at seven-thirty when she'd walked to the bus which took her to work and her old shoes let in the water.

Consequently, it was a minute or two before Molly realised that the music had stopped. She looked up in surprise. It was only a quarter to five, there were fifteen minutes left of the working day.

'We are going over to our news room at Newcastle for an important announcement,' said the radio announcer's plummy disembodied voice. The girls looked at each other. Had the war started after all? But what about Chamberlain's visit to Munich? Peace in our time and all that? The thoughts raced through Molly's head while her fingers holding the cloth stilled on the machine.

There was a crackling noise from the wireless and all heads turned to the set, which was on a shelf on the wall above their heads.

'This is John Grage, speaking from Newcastle. News is coming through of a major mining disaster,' said another voice suddenly and Molly's heart plummeted. It's not likely to be Eden Hope, she told herself, we're miles from Newcastle, even as the voice continued: 'There has been an explosion at Eden Hope colliery, a mine near Bishop Auckland in County Durham.' There was an audible intake of breath along the whole of the line. 'A number of miners are trapped behind a roof cave-in. We are not at present able to ascertain the number of casualties. Further bulletins will be issued as more news comes in.' After a moment the music started again, not Gracie now, more solemn, classical music.

Enid Parker was standing by Molly, one hand on the pieces bin. 'Your dad works there, doesn't he?' she asked, in an interested, conversational sort of tone. Molly stared at her.

'Mine an' all,' Joan Pendle chipped in from the next machine. One or two other voices joined hers. 'My dad's off shift, thank God,' someone else said.

Mine isn't. No, he's not. He went to work this morning when I did. We left the house together, walked down the street, parted at the bus stop. For a second or so Molly didn't know whether she had spoken aloud or not but then she realised the voice was in her head. The scene this morning ran through her mind. They had walked in silence as usual, Dad and her, a companionable silence, though.

'Doesn't he?' Enid repeated, and this time Molly heard her. She nodded, but still didn't speak. She had a feeling of unreality. Maybe this was just a dream, a nightmare. The classical piece was finished and Gracie was singing again, about her aspidistra.

Molly's dad liked that song, always hummed snatches of it while he was shaving. She shook her head. No, nothing could have happened to him, of course not. This was the first year he was back at work, the first year after the long lay-off of the depression years. The depression which had killed her mother, or so he always said though the doctor maintained it was meningitis. The depression which had sent Harry, her brother, into the army to escape from it. Harry was in India now, he and his mate Jackson.

Dad's hands had been too soft when he went back to work; they had blistered and bled and he had suffered intensely with them at first. Molly had treated them with methylated spirits to harden them. The cuts had healed now, in their place calluses. And Dad was bringing in a proper wage now, held his head high, even joked and laughed as he used to do. He was changing back from the dour, silent man he had become after her mother died.

The manager, Mr Bolton, came on to the floor. The girls turned back to their work as he spoke to Enid Parker. Molly looked down at the piece in her hand but she was moving so slowly she never actually got it under the needle. Then suddenly all was quiet, the power had been switched off.

'Righto, girls, you can go now,' Enid called though it was only five to the hour. There was a buzz of conversation as the women bustled about, collecting their bags, going to the cloakroom for their outdoor things. But it was subdued. There was no light-hearted relief that the day was over, just solemn glances at the girls from Eden Hope.

'Your dad will be all right, I expect,' said Enid. 'Go on now, Molly, the factory bus is going five minutes early, you don't want to miss it.' The floor was almost empty. Joan Pendle hadn't waited for Molly even though they were next-door neighbours. But then, thought Molly, with that twinge of hurt puzzlement which she always felt when the girl ignored her, Joan wouldn't wait for her, they had never got on.

All the way home on the bus there was a ball of dread in the pit of Molly's stomach. It was no good telling herself that her dad stood a good chance of not being caught in the fall – after all, the mine employed 700 men, there were different levels being worked, why should it be the one where Bill Mason was working? It was no use. When at last the bus reached the village and stopped close by the pityard gates, Molly was first off to join the knot of people standing there.

'Any news?' 'Which face?' 'How bad is it?' the new-comers questioned, but before they could be answered there was a buzz of activity around the shaft. The driver of the green Union ambulance which had been waiting by the offices drove forward.

'They've got someone out alive!'

The cry went through the crowd, hope springing up in them all. Molly closed her eyes and prayed then tried to be glad that it was Mr Morley they were taking out of the cage, Mr Morley who lived in Eden Terrace. It was his son Jackson who was in India with Harry. Mrs Morley slipped through the gate and ran to the stretcher, went in the ambulance with him.

'His back,' the murmur went through the crowd as they made way for the gate to open fully and the ambulance to drive off. 'His back and face cut open. His bonny looks will be gone now.' The Morley men were famous for their good looks.

A few minutes later the manager appeared, a list in his hand. The crowd fell silent, watching him intently. He spoke to someone in an expensive suit who looked incongruous in the pit yard. 'The owner,' the whisper went round, and everyone gazed at this alien to their community. The man nodded and the manager, Mr Hill, walked towards the group by the gate. Halting, he cleared his throat before beginning the roll call of the dead. William Mason's name was halfway down the list.

'You get a good night's sleep, lass, and you'll feel better.'

'I'll try, Mrs Pendle.'

Molly closed the door after her neighbour and turned back to the empty house with a sigh of relief. She was grateful to Ann Pendle who'd done all she could for her in the days leading up to the mass funeral in Eden Hope Methodist Chapel, even gone to the inquest with her beforehand. (Accidental death, the coroner had said.) Ann had brought her broth afterwards which Molly had politely accepted but couldn't eat.

This was the first time she had been on her own since the disaster. It was very quiet, the only sound the ticking of the marble clock which stood on the high mantel over the mantel frill which Mam had embroidered before she died, three years ago now. Molly's thoughts touched on that and skimmed away. Not now, she wasn't going to think of that now. Rising from her chair by the fire, she picked up the rake and pulled small coals from the shelf at the back of the fire on to the flames, banking it as her father had always done before bed. She turned the mat away from the range just in case anything spat out, seeing in her mind's eye Dad doing it. She turned the key in the back door lock and climbed the stairs to bed.

'I'll not be able to sleep,' she said aloud, more to break the silence which was so profound she could almost hear it than anything else. Dad had been the noisy one, always whistling or humming something. 'Little Old Lady' or 'The Lambeth Walk' or that Fred Astaire song from *Top Hat.* He liked keeping the wireless on until last thing at night or until the accumulator batteries ran down and had to be taken to Eldon to be recharged. Except when he was on night shift. That was it. Molly would pretend he was just on night shift. Illogically she was comforted by that. Her restless, rambling thoughts shut off and she drifted into sleep.

There was a letter from the manager of Eden Hope Colliery when she came downstairs next morning. It had a crest on the envelope and on the top of the single sheet of paper the words *Hope Estates*, all curlicues and fancy lines.

Dear Miss Mason,
    On behalf of the owners and management of Eden

Hope Colliery, I wish to convey the Company's deepest sympathy for the loss of your father in the tragic accident which occurred last week.

The Company will pay in full any funeral expenses. As Mr Mason had no dependants, being a widower with grown-up children earning their own living, there will be no compensation payable according to law. However, the Company is prepared to offer you £25, without obligation, to help you with removal costs.

If you have any questions concerning the above, you may call at the colliery office at your convenience and I will endeavour to answer them.

Molly stared at the letter, uncomprehending. There was an unrecognisable scribble for signature. She felt no alarm but was dimly aware that she would have to do something about this. Go to see Mr Hill, that was it. She glanced at the clock. It was nine o'clock, she could go today, Friday. If she didn't she would have to put it off until Monday and she was going back to work then. She had to, they wouldn't keep her job open forever.

Glad of something positive to do, Molly put the letter down on the table. She stirred the fire and grey ash fell through to the box underneath. There was a hint of red so she added a few sticks from the box by the fire, raked cinders on top and a few good lumps of coal. Then she filled the kettle and put it on the gas ring.

Ten minutes later, sipping milkless tea, she picked the letter up again and read it through once more. Three hundred pounds was the usual compensation for a miner killed in the pit; she knew that, had heard the men discussing it. It had not occurred to her that she was no longer a dependant because she was working at the factory. And in the back of her mind she had known she would have to move, that the house would be wanted for a working miner, oh, yes, she'd known that. But she had put off facing the knowledge until after the funeral; hadn't been able to think beyond that.

The tea tasted acidic on her tongue, churned in her stomach. She would have to eat something, she thought, and found the heel of a loaf, buttered it and spread on blackcurrant jam. Methodically, she chewed and swallowed, chewed and swallowed. She was not angry or upset at the letter, just felt disconnected, as though it was happening to someone else.

She felt vaguely angry at Harry, her brother. He was three years older than she was and should have been here to see to things. But, no, he was in India. India! He probably didn't even know yet that Dad was gone. Though how could he, she hadn't written to him? She was being unfair, she knew it.

Sighing, Molly rose from the table and cleared away the breakfast things. She washed and dressed in her grey costume, the Sunday one, the only one she had really. There was nothing for it but to wear her old shoes, she hadn't got into West Auckland for last week's pay yet. She brushed her straight brown bobbed hair and clipped it over her right ear with the tortoiseshell slide which Mam had bought for her years ago when she was still at school. She didn't have another. As an afterthought she pulled on her velour hat with the brim and gazed in the mirror of the press. Did it make her look older? She decided it did. Picking up her handbag, imitation leather and cracked now but all she had, she went out of the door and down the yard, turning to where the black path led off, a shortcut to the pit used by generations of miners.

'It is the agreed policy of the Owners' Association,' said Mr Hill. 'I'm sorry, I'm afraid it is all I can do.' He looked away from the slight young girl sitting before his desk. She reminded him of his own daughter, away at the Friends' School in Great Ayton now, and the comparison made him slightly uncomfortable. The two girls were of an age. He dropped his eyes before Molly's direct gaze and walked to the window, staring out across the yard to the stack of new pit props just come from Norway.

'You have a brother in the army, don't you? Have you written to him yet?'

'He's in India,' said Molly. 'Won't have got the letter yet. In any case, he can hardly get back from there by next week, can he?'

The manager coughed, bit his lip, sought for a handkerchief in his trouser pocket and held it to his lips to conceal a momentary shame. But there was nothing he could do. He turned back to the desk.

'Take the cheque, my dear,' he said. His tone, which had been business-like up until then, sounded softer. 'I'm sure someone in the village will take you in. Or why don't you get a room closer to your place of employment? Think of the bus fare you would save.'

He meant to be kind, she knew. He had sounded almost fatherly. And Molly couldn't bear it suddenly. She jumped to her feet, picked up the cheque and stuffed it in her bag though she would rather have stuffed it down his throat.

'Don't worry about me, Mr Hill,' she said. 'I'll manage fine.'

'Got a plan, have you?' he asked, relief showing in his face. 'Oh, good, you –' He broke off as she turned on her heel and hurried to the door, banging it shut behind her. Oh, well, he thought, he certainly didn't need to worry about that little madam. That was all the thanks one got for trying to be kind.

Molly began to walk back along the path. Oh, Dad, she cried silently, what am I going to do? On impulse she cut off to the side and made her way to the cemetery, to the fresh-turned earth of the new graves. The flowers were already beginning to wilt, she saw, even the large wreath of white lilies which had come from the owners. Her own bunch of dahlias was lasting better, she thought, and bent to straighten a large sunshine-yellow head. Dad had loved his garden, the dahlias were his pride and joy. He had grown these himself. She bent down and moved the bunch into a more prominent position, pushing the lily wreath to one side. There was going to be a big memorial one day, there was a subscription fund already.

'Dad?' she said tentatively. 'Mam?' For she was laid in this grave, too, though there was no headstone. It was something Dad had been going to do once he was back at work. 'As soon as we're back on our feet, pet.' Though, of course, that couldn't happen now.

After a minute or two Molly became aware that it had started to rain. She walked away, slowly at first then briskly, out of the cemetery and down the path to the houses. There was no sense in catching pneumonia on top of everything else. And besides she had work to do, a new life to arrange.

'Don't let the buggers get you down,' Dad was always saying, and by heck, she'd be blowed if she did.

Chapter Two

Harry marched smartly out of the Adjutant's office and stopped abruptly on the edge of the verandah. He stared out over the dusty parade ground, the officer's voice still echoing in his ears, though the words hadn't sunk in, not yet.

'It's ruddy hot,' he observed to no one in particular. Even though it was barely eight o'clock in the morning, the air shimmered with heat. The sky glared white above the roof of the barracks on the opposite side of the square. Suddenly Harry's shoulders slumped and he looked at the paper in his hand, an official communication from headquarters.

No matter how often he read the few typewritten words, they told him only the bare fact that Dad was dead, killed in the pit. He stared in front of him, seeing not the parade ground but the pithead buildings at Eden Hope; smelling not the heat and dust and multifarious smells of India but soot and engine oil and damp coal.

The day when he was thirteen and had first gone down in the cage with his dad returned vividly to Harry's mind.

The steep drop, and the feeling of having left his stomach somewhere up there in the light. Then trembling dread as he had followed his dad to the coalface, ducking when his father said duck, too late once or twice so that he had banged his head on low-slung battens; a dread he had tried valiantly to hide because that day he was finally a man, a miner like his dad.

Not that he had worked in the pit for long. Six months after that day he had been laid off, never to go down the mine again as the depression of the thirties bit deep into the coalfield. He remembered the day he'd joined the army as a boy soldier at sixteen, along with Jackson Morley, his mate at school and his marra in the pit. At least it was employment and money in his pocket.

All those years Dad had fretted to get back down the pit. And now the pit had got him. Harry couldn't believe it. He wiped his brow with a khaki handkerchief, adjusted his hat and started out over the parade ground. He was halfway across it before he thought about young Molly. She was on her own now. God, and she was just a kid! There were no relatives left at home; his mother had been an orphan, and Gran, his father's mother, had died before Mam. Harry halted, thinking about going back in to see the Adjutant. He had to get home, he realised desperately.

Then he saw Jackson come to the door of the barracks, lifting his hand to shade his eyes as he looked over towards Harry. He'd talk it over with Jackson, the only one who would understand exactly because he came from Eden

Hope too. There was still time before he had to go on guard duty at the main gate.

'Your old fella? No! Are you sure?'

Jackson Morley stopped buttoning his tunic and stared at Harry. Shocked, he thought of Bill Mason, his cheeky, lopsided grin so like Harry's and wavy black hair only just touched with grey. A man so full of life couldn't be dead, it had to be a mistake.

'Here, read it,' said Harry and thrust the piece of paper into Jackson's hand. He studied the few words written there. No ambiguity, no room for doubt. Bill Mason was gone, poor beggar.

'But what about Molly? What will she do?' Little Molly, only fifteen when they had left England. Bonny little Molly. Jackson was going to marry her when she grew up – that was what he'd always told her, jokingly of course.

'I'll have to try for home leave,' said Harry. 'The Company won't let her stay in the house on her own, there's nowt so sure.'

'No,' Jackson agreed. 'But she'll be taken in by somebody in Hope, you know she will. Folks'll rally round.'

'It's up to me, she's my sister,' said Harry. 'I must try to get home. I'm off to see the Adjutant again.'

'I'll walk over there with you.' Jackson bit his lip. 'Oh, man,' he said, 'I'm right sorry.'

'Aye.'

The Adjutant, Lieutenant Carey, was just coming out of the office.

'Private Morley,' he said, 'I was about to send for you.' He had a paper in his hand similar to the one he'd given Harry and Jackson's heart sank to his boots. He cast a quick glance at Harry.

'I'll wait here,' said his friend.

Five minutes later, Jackson came out of the office. 'Dad was injured,' he said, 'he's in hospital. Come on, I've asked to see the Colonel, we can ask for home leave together.'

They waited around the verandah for ten minutes before being summoned into the office only to be told that home leave was unlikely to be granted.

'I'm sorry, men,' said the Colonel, a dapper little man with steel-grey hair who, in spite of the heat, looked as though he had never sweated in his life. 'With the situation as it stands at the moment – well, you have my sympathy, I'm sure, especially you, Private Mason, for the loss of your father. But after all your sister is an adult, she is not dependent on you, is she?'

'She's sixteen, sir,' said Harry. 'And we have no other relatives.'

'Sixteen? Well, there you are. Earning her own living, I presume?'

'Yes, sir.' Despair ate into Harry. Outside a Sergeant-Major began to bark orders; there was the sound of marching feet. Harry opened his mouth to ask what the Colonel would do in his position but the habit of deferring to a superior officer was too strong. He merely stood to attention and stared straight ahead.

'Well then, request for compassionate leave denied.' The Colonel turned to Jackson. 'I hope your father recovers, Private Morley. However, your request is denied also, for the same reasons. You men have to realise these are troubled times. We have to be constantly on the alert. A number of our men have problems at home but this is the army. We must all do our duty.' He nodded a dismissal and the two men from Eden Hope marched smartly out of the office.

'I'll put in for a transfer to the Durham Light Infantry,' said Harry as they walked over the parade ground.

Jackson glanced at his friend; Harry's face was set, his eyes steely. 'We both will,' he agreed. 'I'm fairly sure war is coming, no matter what Chamberlain says. The Durhams will have us, I don't think the Colonel can stop that.'

'It's my bedroom, Mam, and I'm not sharing it! Especially not with that toffee-nosed Molly Mason. Let her find somewhere else to live.'

'But, Joan, in simple Christian charity . . . You know her mother was my friend.'

'Aye, well, Molly isn't mine and I want nothing to do with her. Or her good-for-nothing brother!'

'That's it, isn't it? It's because Harry jilted you?'

'He did not! I didn't want him!' shouted Joan. 'Don't you go saying he jilted me . . .'

Molly, just about to turn into the back gate of the Pendles' house, paused, clearly hearing the raised voices. She flushed, hesitated for a moment, backed away from the gate and leaned against the coalhouse wall. The sun shone brightly, low on the horizon this December day, blinding her. She closed her eyes tightly.

'Are you all right, pet?'

The concerned voice was that of old Tom Bailey who worked in the lamp cabin at the mine and lived in one of the older, single-storey cottages on the end of the rows.

Molly did her best to summon a smile. 'I'm fine, Tom,' she mumbled.

He leaned on his stick and gazed at her with faded but shrewd blue eyes.

'Aye, well, you don't look fine to me,' he pronounced. 'Still . . . I was right sorry about your dad, Molly. A grand man.' He coughed and she looked away quickly, her eyes filling. 'Aye,' he said and went on, his stick tap-tapping and his pit boots ringing on the cobbles.

'Pull yourself together!' Molly said fiercely, her words loud in the empty house. She had run back into her own kitchen and closed the door, wiped her eyes and blown her nose. She had to plan her next move. She could ask Mrs Morley, she supposed, but though Jackson was Harry's friend she didn't know his mother all that well. Mrs Morley was a woman who kept herself to herself. No doubt one of the other families would take her in but she couldn't offer much for her board, her usual wage was only

12/6 even with bonuses. Now the pit was working there were single miners coming in and they took up most of the spare rooms in the village. The mining folk had been poverty-stricken during the long slump and were struggling to pay back debts even now.

Taking a pencil and piece of paper from the press drawer, she wrote a 'room wanted' sign. She could ask the paper shop to put it in the window, she thought. In the end she left it lying on the table while she put on her coat and hat and, picking up her bag, went out for the bus into Bishop Auckland.

She met Mrs Pendle at the door. 'Look, Molly,' she said. 'Don't you think it would be a good idea to get a place near the factory? Think of the bus fare you'd save. The thing is, pet, I don't think I can take you in. I've thought about it and it's not fair to ask Joan to share her room . . .'

Mrs Pendle was the picture of embarrassment. Molly decided to take pity on her.

'Just what I was thinking myself,' she said. 'In fact, I'm going there now. Do you want anything brought from Bishop? I'll be going through.'

The relief showed on Ann Pendle's face. 'Eeh, no, I don't think so, ta, not today.' She put out a hand and laid it on Molly's arm. 'I think you're doing the right thing, I really do. Get away . . . that's best.'

'Ta-ra,' said Molly, walking off for the bus. Ann Pendle looked after her as she strode purposefully up the street. Waiting at the bus stop at the end of the rows, she calmed the butterflies of panic in her stomach by counting the number of people who crossed over the street rather than walk by her, averting their faces, pretending they hadn't seen her.

Molly sighed. Oh, she knew they weren't unfeeling, the trouble was they were *too* feeling, just didn't know what to say to her. But most of them had been to the funeral, had paid their respects. The trouble was there were so many bereaved in Eden Hope just now, misery was all pervasive. They wanted to get back to normal. And everyone wasn't the same, she thought, remembering old Mr Bailey.

In Auckland the wind blew down Newgate Street, built on the line of the old Roman road and providing no corners for shelter. In Hardisty's, the greengrocer's and florist's, there was a Christmas tree in the window, strung with coloured lanterns and tinsel. Christmas? When was that? she thought vaguely. Not that it mattered. Christmas was nothing to her now.

Lockey's bus for West Auckland and St Helen's Auckland was standing waiting, only a few passengers already aboard. Molly sat at the back on her own and stared fixedly at her hands so that no one getting on the bus could catch her eye and talk to her.

'Where are you going, love?' asked the conductor after waiting patiently for her to look up.

'Oh, St Helen's.'

'Tuppence ha'penny return.'

He took a ticket from his board and handed it to her, and went off whistling to the front of the bus. Molly looked out of the window, seeing nothing until the line of new factories came into view, built on the site of an old colliery. The bus stopped right beside the clothing factory. She got off and walked in.

'I'm afraid you'll have to wait, the wages aren't made up until four,' said the girl behind the desk. She looked uncomfortable. Of course she had heard about the disaster and Bill Mason being one of the dead. Molly felt like telling her not to worry, she was fine, everything was fine. And everything would have been if it wasn't for the leaden feeling somewhere inside her.

'I'll come back,' she said instead, and went to look in the newsagent's window to see if there were any single rooms to let at a price she could afford. Or even some live-in digs, with a family.

The newsagent's was closed for dinner, which surprised Molly, she hadn't realised it was after twelve. But there were cards in the window. She took her indelible pencil out of her bag and jotted addresses down on the back of the envelope she had received from the mine manager. Peering through the window, she saw it was twelve-twenty-five. She didn't have a watch, that was what her dad had been going to get her for Christmas, he'd promised her.

Molly walked along to the fish and chip shop. She should eat, she told herself. But the line of girls from the factory made her shrink inside herself and the smell of the grease took away any appetite she had. Instead she turned and walked down a side street.

Adelaide Street – that was the first address on the envelope. It was cheap too, only 8/6 a week, and she'd have no bus fares to pay. Cheaper than any of the others. When Molly saw the house she was heartened. The lace at the windows was clean and white and the front door step scrubbed and sand-stoned. She lifted a hand to the shining brass knocker. The door was opened by a girl who looked to be about twelve, wearing a green gym slip and cream-coloured blouse and over them a pinafore that was much too big for her. Her hair was tied back severely with a length of green tape.

She stared at Molly through thick-lensed glasses with large, nervous eyes.

'What do you want?' she asked baldly.

'I've come about the room,' said Molly, and smiled to show she was friendly and harmless.

'My dad's at work,' said the girl. 'And I have to go back to school in ten minutes.'

'Well, can I come in? When does your dad get in from work? Where's your mother?'

'I haven't got a mother and Dad doesn't get in until four o'clock.'

Molly looked at her and after a moment the girl opened the door wide, revealing a passage with brown linoleum polished to a gleaming finish. There was even a length of carpet in the middle and a side table. Oh, yes, Molly liked the look of this house.

'I'll leave my name, shall I? I can come later. Four o'clock, did you say?'

The girl looked even more nervous and glanced about her hesitantly. 'Er, I haven't got a pencil,' she murmured.

'I have, I've got one here,' said Molly. Taking charge, she walked past the girl and wrote her name swiftly on a piece of paper torn from the envelope, laying it on the table. She looked around her. The door to the living room was open, there was a smell of beeswax. 'I'll be back tonight,' she said. 'By the way, what's your name?'

'Betty. Betty Jones.'

'I'll see you later, Betty.'

By, thought Molly as she walked off, that girl's as timid as a mouse. But she felt some fellow feeling with the poor kid. After all, she hadn't been much older when she had lost her own mother.

The line outside the fish shop had disappeared, the factory only allowed thirty minutes for dinner. Molly went in and bought a penny bag of chips and walked along to where the Gaunless stream ran alongside the road. She sat on a low wall by the water and ate the chips. Already she was feeling slightly better. With luck she would get the lodgings at a shilling or two less than she had expected to pay. Nice, clean lodgings an' all.

Chapter Three

'I'll be back at work on Monday, I promise, Mr Bolton,' said Molly.

'Yes, well,' he answered, standing up to show that the interview was ended, 'I hope you are. You understand I have every sympathy with your position, my dear, but I can't keep your place open any longer. We have a lot of orders to fill and there is a national emergency.'

'Yes, Mr Bolton.'

Molly left the factory, her wage packet safely tucked away in her bag. He hadn't *looked* very sympathetic, she thought to herself, but as though he wanted rid of her so that he could get on with his work. She took deep breaths of the clean cold air as she walked outside. The atmosphere in the office had been hot and stuffy despite the winter weather.

She would have liked to have told Mr Bolton where to put his job, she thought rebelliously. She'd had every intention of starting on Monday anyway but he'd implied, by his tone at least, that she was slacking, the tone of a manager who knew there were plenty more where she came from. But Molly's innate caution had stopped her from rising to the bait. During the long depression she had seen what being out of work did to people. Too many friends and neighbours had been broken by it.

Molly turned her collar up against the bitter wind and walked over the road towards the streets on the other side. She would pass the time until four by looking at the other houses with rooms to let.

It was half-past four when she stood once more outside the door of number 44 Adelaide Street and knocked. Her feet ached and her stomach felt empty, reminding her that a bag of chips was all she had eaten since breakfast. This time the door was opened by a thin little man in a suit, his meagre hair smoothed flat against his skull and shining with Brylcreem.

'Good afternoon,' Molly began, 'I've come about the room, I –'

'Aye, I know, our Betty told me a lass had been looking. Come on in then,' the man said impatiently. 'Don't stand there on the step for all the neighbours to gawp at. I won't have them gossiping about me and my doings.'

A bit surprised, Molly glanced about. The street was deserted, not a soul in sight, but she stepped inside the passageway obediently. He opened a door to the left and went in, motioning her to follow. There was electric light. When he switched it on the harsh glare showed her a square room with an empty grate, a brown leather three-piece suite shining with polish, and a sideboard with nothing on it except for a picture of him with a woman holding a bouquet of flowers. The Joneses' wedding picture she presumed. There was a faint smell of damp; obviously the room was not lived in.

'Sit down, sit down,' he said, and Molly sat on the edge of the sofa, knees together, handbag clutched nervously in her hands. I've nothing to be nervous about, she told herself firmly and lifted her chin. Mr Jones took up a stance, legs apart, hands on hips, before the tireless grate and stared at her over the top of rimless spectacles.

'Now then, young lady,' he said, rather in the tone her old headmistress had used when confronting a recalcitrant pupil. 'I haven't much time, my tea's nearly ready. You want to rent the room, do you?'

'Yes, please,' said Molly, though she was beginning to wonder if she did. But only one of the other houses on her list had been as clean as this one and it had been 1/6 extra per week.

'It's 8/6 a week, including breakfast but not including evening meal. You can use the kitchen to cook your own food for that. But mind, I won't have anything which stinks the house out. Let's say between five and six? We'll leave you to it for that hour.'

'That will be all right,' said Molly, perking up a little. She hadn't realised the price included breakfast. Perhaps if she ate a good breakfast she wouldn't need much during the day. His next words disillusioned her on that score.

'I'll leave bread and margarine and jam out for you

before I go to work. I leave the house at six o'clock every morning. Now, I suppose you want to see your room?' He was already leading the way out of the sitting room. Molly got to her feet and followed him meekly up the stairs.

It was quite a large bedroom at the back of the house. A single bed stood in solitary splendour in the middle of an expanse of highly polished linoleum. It was covered with a white cotton bedspread. But there was a dressing table in the corner with a plain wooden chair in front of it, and in the corner a cupboard. Mr Jones opened the cupboard door and showed Molly a row of hooks with a shelf above. 'You can put your things in here,' he said, and turned and stared fiercely at her. 'I can't abide slovens,' he snapped. 'I won't have things laid about, do you understand?' Without waiting for an answer he went on, 'That'll be two weeks in advance, you can move in when you like. Seventeen shillings, please.'

'Is there a fire?'

He looked affronted. 'If you must have a fire, you'll have to find your own coal. I don't hold with fires in bedrooms. I can't have you using electric either, I'm not made of money. It's a coal fire or nothing. An' you'll have to see to getting the chimney swept yourself an' all.'

Molly hesitated. She looked about her. There were floral curtains at the window and a tiny cast-iron fireplace with a paper fan in the grate. But there was a key in the lock; she could shut herself in at least. She wouldn't have to see a lot of Mr Jones. And if she hated it she could always move out. 'I'll take it,' she said, and fumbled in her bag for her purse. 'I'll be back with my stuff on Sunday, I have to work Monday.'

'I won't have the place cluttered up, mind,' he warned. 'And I don't know about Sunday. Me and Betty go to Chapel on Sunday, ten o'clock service. Are you Chapel?'

'I'll be bringing just a few things,' Molly insisted, thinking that for two pins she would tell him what to do with his room. 'I will be cleaning it after all. And since you ask, yes, I'm Chapel.' Not that she'd been to service much since Dad died, she thought dismally.

'Aye, well. Just mind what I've told you,' said Mr Jones, and marched off down the stairs leaving her to follow.

Molly caught the bus back to Eden Hope, it came along just as she approached the stop. She sat staring out of the window, wondering if she had done the right thing. Maybe not, she thought, chewing on the corner of a thumb nail. As she had walked down the stairs in Adelaide Street the door to the kitchen was open. She had smelled boiled cabbage and overdone meat.

'Haven't I told you to keep this door shut, you gormless fool? The place will stink of food,' she'd heard Mr Jones snap as he banged the door to behind him. She thought she'd heard a muffled cry too but was letting herself out of the house by then.

Molly caught sight of her reflection in the darkened window of the bus and put her hand down on her lap. It was years since she'd chewed her thumb, Mam had always been telling her off about it. Suddenly she felt such an intense desire for her mother, her father, Harry, any of them, that it cut into her like a knife. She blinked, blew her nose, and stared fixedly out of the window. The bus had just stopped. Shildon, she thought, it's Shildon. She forced herself to think of that. Home of the railways, most of the men hereabouts worked in the wagon works. There were Christmas lights in the windows of some of the shops, shining out on to the pavement. What was she going to do to celebrate Christmas? Suddenly she dreaded the thought of it. Her first Christmas on her own. Oh, Harry, where are you? she thought sadly.

'Fares, please.'

The conductor had to say it twice before it registered with Molly.

'Sorry. Return to Eden Hope Colliery,' she said. The bell on his ticket machine tinkled. She put the ticket in her bag, alongside the return ticket she had got on the bus from Bishop that morning. Oh, well, she would use both of them up, she supposed. But there was a frighteningly small amount of money left in her purse, she would have to dip into her £25 soon. And she couldn't afford to do that too often.

Ann Pendle looked up at Molly, arrested by the sudden look of desolation which had crossed the young girl's face. 'You do understand, don't you, Molly?' she asked yet again. Ann felt guilty. She knew she should have made more of an effort to get her family to accept the girl, at least for a while. For the sake of Molly's mother at least. But it was Joan . . . she had loved Harry Mason since she was a tiny girl. Her face had always lit up when she saw him. If he had smiled at her, talked to her, she had been in seventh heaven. Ann had felt her daughter's pain when Harry had jilted her. She'd tried to comfort her but Joan would not be consoled. Harry had tried to let her down lightly, told her that she wouldn't want to be tied to him when he was going away for years perhaps. But she couldn't forgive or forget.

Well, I have my own family to think of first, Ann told herself.

'You'll be all right in West Auckland? You've got nice clean digs, haven't you?' she asked for the third time.

'I'll be fine,' said Molly. Her mind was on other things, like the brass poker stand in the form of a prancing horse which had been displayed on the hearth ever since she could remember. And the marble clock, a wedding present from her grandparents to her parents. She touched it with her fingers. The marble was smooth and cool. It ticked away as loudly as it had done ever since she could remember.

'Granma took out a Universal club for it, two an' six a week it cost her,' Mam used to say. She had loved that clock. Maybe Molly should take it with her to West Auckland. She tried to visualise it on the meagre mantelpiece in the room in Adelaide Street but her imagination failed her. Still, she would take it, she couldn't just let it go. It was part of her life.

'The flat cart's here,' Ann announced. By the gate the horse snorted, nodding its head up and down with a jangling of brasses. The second-hand dealer from Shildon had arrived.

Molly had a kind of numb feeling as she stood by the window and watched him carry things out and place them by the cart. Her dad's wooden-ended bed with the rose carved in the middle of the head. Harry's cheap black iron bedstead and her own. The bundles of bedclothes, the press, a chest of drawers. Even the best of the clippy mats. She been given £11 for the lot. Well, it could keep her for a month and buy a pair of winter shoes, at least.

Ann Pendle tied a knot in the string round the box of kitchen bits and pieces and stood back as Mr Robson, the second-hand dealer, came to the door.

'That's the lot,' she said.

'Righto. I'll get loaded.'

Mr Robson glanced at Molly's white, set face and looked away again. He felt sorry for the lass but business was business. He went through these scenes almost every day and couldn't be constantly thinking of the tragedies which usually went before.

'I'll give you a hand,' said Ann, and picked up a box. It didn't take long to load the cart and Molly stood watching as her home was dismantled around her.

'Where's the marble clock?'

She started at Mr Robson's question. 'I'm not selling the clock, I'm keeping it,' she replied firmly. 'I told you I wasn't selling the clock.' Her heart beat wildly. For a minute she thought he would insist on taking it. He couldn't, could he?

Mr Robson pursed his lips, opened his mouth to say something then thought better of it and nodded acquiescence. Taking a wallet out of his inside pocket, he counted out £10, hesitating as he considered deducting £1 at least for the clock. But he didn't. He added the £1 to the pile of notes on the table, reckoning he must be going soft in the head.

The house seemed strange, empty as it was but for the few things Molly was taking with her. Ann Pendle looked around at the patch of unfaded wallpaper which had been behind the press. She had forgotten that the roses on it had once been that particular shade of pink, the trailing ivy so darkly green. She took Molly by the arm.

'Howay, pet,' she said, 'you're coming round to us for a bite of dinner.' She couldn't let the lass go off without her Sunday dinner. After all, Joan was out today, off visiting her aunt, so couldn't object.

Chapter Four

'Only six more shopping days to Christmas,' the voice on the wireless boomed out between records. Enid Parker, walking down the line handing out fresh batches of dress parts to be sewn, grinned.

'To tell you the truth, I could do all my shopping in one go on Saturday. All I need is the money, I'd soon make the time,' she said.

There was a murmur of agreement from the girls on the line. Molly bent her head over her machine, slickly slipping the seam to be sewn under the needle, throwing the two pieces into the box beside her and picking up yet another two pieces of navy blue rayon cloth.

Shopping? she thought. She hadn't even thought about shopping. But then what shopping did she have to do? There was no one but Harry to buy for. Harry! With a sense of shock she realised she hadn't sent him a Christmas present, nor even a card. He wouldn't get it now. Usually she sent one weeks before Christmas. Still she would go into the town tomorrow and get something, send it at the main post office.

Her fingers busy as ever as she bent over her work, Molly's mind wandered off on to thoughts of her brother and his friend Jackson. Where were they? Why hadn't she had a letter since Dad died? Irrational though it was, as well she knew, she felt resentful that he wasn't here but at the other side of the world. He should come home, really he should.

The air was filled with the tinny sound of the wireless, the volume turned up. Christmas carols resounded off the walls, the girls singing along with them. Only the bright and brisk carols, of course, it wouldn't do to have slow, melodic ones. The BBC was well aware that bright and breezy music was needed in factories to push production levels as high as possible. The threat of war had ended the depression, there was leeway to make up.

The threat of war . . . People said that Chamberlain had ended that with the Munich Agreement but the fear still lurked. Molly shivered, she didn't want to think of it. Harry was a soldier. If there was a war . . . Her thoughts stopped there, she couldn't bear to go on.

Luckily the whistle blew just then, the wireless was switched off, the power to the machines stopped and the room was suddenly silent but for the chatter of the girls as they rose from their machines in relief, stretched, picked up bags and tin boxes holding sandwiches and walked out to the canteen or over the road to the fish shop.

One or two of them smiled uncertainly at Molly as they passed, still uncomfortable with someone who had been so savagely bereaved. Joan Pendle, though, didn't even look her way as she went out, surrounded by her cronies. Joan knew how to keep people about her. She was a pretty girl with fair hair and blue eyes, and a curvaceous figure with big breasts she liked to show off under tight sweaters.

Molly wanted to ask her what the people were like who had got the Masons' old house. Was it a big family or just a young couple? Did they look after the place? Was the man a gardener and would he keep the long narrow strip of garden trim? Dad had been a gardener. He'd loved his flowers, had a special trench where he grew his prize leeks, winning a prize for them at the club last year. But of course she couldn't ask. Sighing, Molly picked up her bag and followed the rest of the girls out of the room.

She didn't go into the canteen. That was one blessing of living in St Helen's Auckland, she only had to cross the road and walk along to Adelaide Street to be back in her lodgings. She saved money there. Mr Jones was always out at work during the day and Betty didn't mind her boiling the kettle for tea. In fact, Betty was usually glad of a cup herself, so long as the spoonful of leaves came from Molly's caddy. Mr Jones kept a strict watch on his own.

Over the days since Molly had come to Adelaide Street, she and Betty had become quite friendly, though the girl was still reserved and quiet. Today they sat at the kitchen table eating fish paste sandwiches. Molly finished hers and picked up her cup, holding it with both hands and leaning her elbows on the table. She was grateful for the warmth

of the cup as it seeped into her chilly fingers and sipped at
it slowly. Ten minutes before she had to go back to work.
Her thoughts strayed back to Harry, wondering what she
could get for fifteen shillings including the cost of postage
to India. Not much, she suspected.

'By, it's cold today,' Betty volunteered suddenly, and
Molly forgot about the problem of Harry's present as she
looked properly at her companion for the first time. With
a shock she realised that the girl was pale – well, she was
always pale but now she was even more so. Yet even as
Molly gazed at her a pink flush began to suffuse her
cheeks. It wasn't a healthy flush, though, Betty looked
decidedly feverish. There were shadows under her eyes
and her hand trembled as she held the cup. The sandwich
on her plate had only one bite taken from it.

'You look poorly,' said Molly in concern, berating
herself for not noticing as soon as she came in.

'I'm all right. Just a bit of a cold, I think. Any road, I
have to go back to school,' the girl replied, and started to
stand up before sitting back down abruptly. Her eyes had
a glazed look about them.

'I don't think you should,' said Molly. All of her
attention was focussed on Betty now. She looked really ill,
shivering uncontrollably. The girl tried picking up her cup
but tea slopped into her saucer and she put it down again.

'I'm bad,' she admitted. 'I have to go to school, though,
what would me dad say if I stayed at home?'

'He would likely tell you you'd done the best thing,'

said Molly firmly. 'Look at you, you're not fit to go out.'

'He'll play war with me if I don't go to school,' whispered Betty. 'I have to go.'

'No, don't –' said Molly, but she was too late. Betty had stood up again and promptly fallen to the floor. Molly rushed around the table, her heart beating rapidly in alarm. She bent over the girl, put her arm under her shoulders, patted her cheek. 'Betty!' she cried. 'Oh, please, God! Please, make her wake up!'

Betty moaned and opened her eyes and Molly breathed a prayer of relief. The linoleum was icy. She had to get the girl upstairs into bed, there wasn't a fire on in the house. Mr Jones believed it was a waste of money during the day when there was no one in.

Molly bit her lip as she sat on the floor, supporting Betty's limp form. She had had a fire in her room the night before, just a small one, perhaps there was still some lingering warmth. If only she could get Betty up the stairs.

'Come on, pet, let's have you,' she said. 'You must help me, I've got to get you into bed.'

'Dad says it's pure laziness to . . .' Betty began but Molly interrupted her.

'Never mind what your dad says, he's not here now,' she cried, exasperated. 'Do you think you can walk upstairs if you lean on me? I promise I won't let you fall.'

'I'll try.'

It was a struggle, Betty twice faltering and clinging to Molly, almost bringing them both tumbling down the stairs. But eventually they were on the landing. Betty turned towards the tiny boxroom which was her bedroom but Molly stopped her.

'No, I think you'll be better in my bed,' she said. 'It's warmer there.' By this time Betty was past arguing. She allowed herself to be led into the warmer room and put to bed.

'Thank you,' she murmured, lying back on the pillow, her eyes closed and face as white as the pillowcase once again. She was shivering uncontrollably by now. Molly gazed at her and bit her lip. She had to get back to work, couldn't afford to take the afternoon off which would mean she'd have to break into Harry's Christmas box money to pay her rent.

'How do you feel now?' she asked, and Betty opened her eyes briefly, attempted a smile.

'Warmer.'

'I'll get the doctor,' Molly said, but Betty became agitated. Her eyes flew open in alarm.

'No!' she cried and her breathing became laboured until she was gasping for breath. 'No, me dad will have a fit if you do,' she managed to say.

'All right, all right, I won't,' Molly said hastily. 'Don't get upset, it's bad for you. Lie quiet, man, will you? I'll get you a hot water bottle. I think you've got the 'flu, though.'

She rushed downstairs and found an ancient stone hot water bottle under the sink, heated water and filled it.

Upstairs once again, she wrapped it in her own woollen scarf and put it at Betty's feet.

The girl was quieter now, her breathing seemed easier, she was dropping off to sleep. Maybe she would sleep herself better, thought Molly. She went to the fireplace and, using her own precious store of coal, lit the fire. Oh, to think that she should actually have to count lumps of coal! It was the only thing they'd always had enough of in Eden Hope; the miners' coal allowance had been delivered every third week there. Heaps had been dumped on the pavements outside the back gates, a familiar sight, waiting to be shovelled into coal houses. She pictured it in her mind – the street winding upwards, stepping out carefully into the road to avoid the coal – and wept inside. The emotion took her by surprise. What a thing to be nostalgic about!

Molly blinked rapidly, closing her mind against the memory. She looked at the meagre fire she had built, sighed and added another small shovelful of coal. So she would have to do without a fire for the rest of the week. Well, it wouldn't hurt her, *she* was healthy enough.

Molly looked at the marble clock, perched slightly precariously on the narrow mantelshelf above the fire. It was one o'clock already, the line would be starting up in the factory soon. She went back to the bed. Betty was sleeping. Maybe Molly could just go back to work. After all, Betty's father would be home in three hours, wouldn't he? She felt the girl's forehead, which was hot and dry, tried to feel for a pulse but couldn't remember where to find it.

Betty moved, turned over on to her side, seemed to settle into an easier sleep. Molly decided to go back to work. The girl would probably sleep for hours, sleep herself better. She tip-toed to the door and down the stairs and let herself out of the house.

At three o'clock she was back. She hadn't been able to concentrate on the work at all, had actually spoilt two pieces and Enid had been very annoyed, even when Molly had told her the reason.

'You'd best go back then and make sure the lass is all right,' the charge hand had finally said. 'Mind, Mr Bolton will dock the time off your wages. He might fine you for these pieces an' all. I don't know, Molly Mason, if you're going to take on the woes of all and sundry and let them affect your work, you're not going to be much good to anyone, are you?'

'No, you're right,' she had agreed humbly. 'I wouldn't normally, but she's only thirteen and in the house on her own, she's got no mother.'

'Away with you then, if you have to,' Enid had said, her voice edged with bad temper, and Molly had left while the going was good.

It was very quiet as she let herself into the house. Betty must be asleep, she thought, and took off her shoes before climbing the stairs though the cold from the thin cotton carpet seeped straight through her lisle stockings and her toes curled against it.

'Betty?' she murmured from the doorway. There was

no movement from the bed. The fire was nearly out, the room chilly. Molly moved quietly to the grate, tried to poke the flames to life with as little noise as possible. Ash fell with a plop into the box beneath, a small plume of smoke rose. She added a couple of sticks, blew on the ashes until the sticks crackled then put on a couple of lumps of coal.

Tip-toeing to the bed, Molly looked down at the still figure. 'Betty?' she said. Then louder, 'Betty?'

Oh, God! Betty was so white and still, her eyes not properly closed. She looked as though she wasn't breathing. She had pushed back the eiderdown which Molly had brought from Eden Hope. Molly put a hand on her shoulder, her bare arm. Don't let her be dead, she prayed. There was some slight warmth there, of course there was. Betty couldn't really be dead. By heck, I'm getting morbid, Molly berated herself, and pulled the eiderdown up around the girl's neck, tucking it in. She patted her cheek. 'Betty!' she cried, loudly now. 'Betty!' And she stirred, opened her eyes, tried to sit up.

Molly was weak with relief. 'Oh, Betty, you scared me half to death,' she said, laughing almost.

'My throat hurts,' whispered Betty.

'Wait, I'll get you a hot drink,' said Molly, and ran downstairs to the kitchen. She put on the kettle and rummaged in the press for Ovaltine, cocoa, anything.

'What do you think you're doing, young woman?'

Molly hadn't heard the door opening and was startled

when the angry voice spoke right behind her so that she almost dropped the packet of cocoa she was reaching for.

'Oh, I'm so pleased to see you –' she began as relief flooded through her.

'Aye, I bet you are. I caught you nicely, didn't I?' Mr Jones was angry. His narrow nose quivered pinkly, his lips were moist with spittle. 'Going through my press, eh? I suppose you've already been through all the drawers. Well, you can just pack your things –'

'Shut up! Just shut your flaming mouth!' Molly shouted, all the worry and agitation of the past few hours finding release in fury. 'Do you think I want your measly groceries? You're nothing but a mean old . . .' She bit off the rest of the sentence, forcing herself to calm down as her eye fell on the cocoa and she remembered Betty.

'Don't you speak to me like that,' Mr Jones began, but Molly broke in, her voice quieter.

'Betty's poorly. I think she needs the doctor.'

'What, Betty is? She's never bad. If this is just some excuse, I'll soon find out.'

'It's no excuse. She's in my bed upstairs. I put her there because it's warmer. This house feels like an igloo.'

'We'll see about that! A daughter of mine in bed during the day . . .'

Molly watched in disbelief as he marched up the stairs with the air of a teacher about to sort out a recalcitrant pupil. The kettle boiled and she made the cocoa, adding milk and two spoonfuls of sugar from her own supply. Putting on her shoes, she followed him up to her room.

He was standing by the bed, looking stricken. Molly glanced at him and went round the other side with the cocoa, putting it down on the night table. Betty was lying with her eyes closed, her mouth slightly open, breathing fast in shallow breaths which barely raised the covers. She was unconscious.

'I'll get the doctor,' Molly said.

'No, I'll go. You look after her, will you?'

The man's manner had changed completely. He seemed to have shrunk, gazing at Molly in appeal before turning and running for the door. She heard the front door bang and then there was silence but for the laboured breathing coming from the unconscious girl in the bed.

Chapter Five

'National Emergency!' said Harry, his voice full of disgust. He sat on his hunkers in the typical miner's resting position in the poor shade of a sparse bush. 'Isn't that just like the army? There could be a war in Europe any day and the powers that be think we should stay in India playing war games because of the National Emergency!'

Jackson leaned back against a dusty rock, his long legs stretched out in front of him, his helmet tipped slightly forward to shade his eyes from the ever-present and pitiless glare of the sun. He grinned but there was no real amusement in his face.

'And wouldn't you think they would have had the two best soldiers in the entire British Army back there ready to defend old Blighty to the death? That would frighten old Hitler to death, wouldn't it? He'd think twice before –'

'Aw, shut up, Jackson, this is nowt to laugh at. What about our Molly? Poor lass, in that house all by herself. Why, man, she's just a kid, isn't she?'

'I'm far from laughing, Harry. I just don't know what we can do about it apart from what I've already done. We

can't just desert. How the hell would we get back anyway
if we did? I've asked my mam and dad to keep an eye on
her. I'm sure we'll be going home soon at any rate.'

Jackson stared grimly out at the dusty road, flanked with
rocky outcrops. The platoon was strung out along it, taking
what shade they could from the rocks as they ate their hard
biscuit and bully beef, drank sparingly from their water
bottles. There would be no more water until they got back
to camp in six hours' time, five if they were lucky.

'Let's have another look at that letter, lad,' he said, and
Harry rummaged in his top pocket and pulled out the well-
thumbed sheets of cheap ruled paper. Jackson read it
through, though he practically knew it by heart. Mind, she
was a plucky one was Molly, he thought. This had been
written very soon after her father's death; the pain of her
loss was clear to see in every sentence and yet she had tried
to soften the blow for Harry. She'd written it must have
been instantaneous, their dad hadn't suffered, though the
writing wavered a bit here. She'd asked if Harry could
come home, but told him not to worry if he couldn't.

*'I can manage fine, you know, I'm working at the
clothing factory now, Mrs Pendle is very good too.'*

There was a round water mark right at the bottom of the
page, though. Jackson fingered it. It had to be made by a
teardrop.

'I asked Mam to write back and tell me how she's
getting on,' he said as he folded the sheets up carefully and
handed them back to Harry. Jackson chewed on his bottom

lip. 'We won't be long, you know, they will be sending us back,' he went on as he rose to his feet, lifted his helmet and wiped his brow before settling it firmly back on his head.

'Right then, you lot,' he called along the line of men. 'Let's be having you. We have to make camp before dark.' Jackson had only recently been promoted to corporal and Harry to lance-corporal. There were a few muttered grumbles which the men considered obligatory but they got to their feet readily enough and the column set off down the dusty track.

There was post in from England when they finally arrived at the gates, just as the sun sank beyond the hills in the distance and dark descended with startling suddenness. Nothing for Harry but a letter from Mrs Morley, Jackson's mother. He skimmed through it then handed a page to Harry.

. . . Molly Mason, poor lass, you were asking about her. She had to get out of the colliery house, you know. The pit's working full strength and it was wanted, the gaffer said. He's a hard manager that one. Any road, as to Molly, I can't keep an eye on her because she's left Eden Hope. According to Ann Pendle, she's got a room over West Auckland way, near the clothing factory.

I would have taken her in, I would, Jackson, but with your dad the way he was after the accident I didn't realise till she'd gone. But likely she'll be better off not having to take the bus to work and no doubt she'll be sending word to Harry. Ann Pendle had a Christmas card from her . . .

Harry handed the page back to his friend, saying nothing, thinking that this was the first time Molly hadn't sent him a card and a present in time for Christmas.

'She'll be all right, I know she will. Right as rain once she gets over the first few weeks,' said Jackson, and Harry nodded.

But later, as Jackson collected his soap and towel and headed for the showers, he wondered about Molly. What sort of a Christmas had she had? Lonely, he dared to bet. She was a lovely lass but didn't make friends easily. She was quiet, reserved, had been since the death of her mother. Surely they would get their orders to go back to Blighty soon? He had lied when he'd told Harry he thought Molly would be fine. In fact, he felt anxious about her.

A strange sort of Christmas, Molly thought as she stood at the window of her bedroom and gazed out over the street. The familiar feeling of unhappiness was lodged in her chest. 1939. She hoped it would be a better year than 1938 had been for her but somehow she didn't feel very optimistic.

At least the holiday was over. Like Christmas, the celebrations had been subdued this year. She looked over to where her gas mask lay in its cardboard box on the bed beside her sewing basket. She was making a waterproof cover for it out of an old macintosh. It had been half-finished since Dad had died, now she was getting on with it at last. She drew the curtains across the window and went over to the bed. Picking up her needle, she threaded it and began to sew.

She had stayed in her room over Christmas, apart from Chapel on Christmas morning. But the congregation was strange to her; only a few people and the minister had spoken to her, wished her a Merry Christmas. She had come home afterwards and locked herself in her room, putting on the wireless which she had brought from Eden Hope quietly, not wanting to disturb Mr Jones.

Her needle faltered. If only Betty were still here they might have been friends. But she had gone into hospital with pneumonia and not come back. Instead she had been sent to the sanatorium high in Weardale. A shadow on the lungs, the doctor had diagnosed. It had come to light in the hospital and a good thing too, he'd said. He had said a lot of other things, such as the girl was too thin, almost under-nourished, it was a miracle she had survived pneumonia. She was still very ill. Even if Molly could have afforded the fare, Betty wasn't allowed visitors.

Molly sighed and decided to play some music now, patiently twiddling the knobs on her radio until the crackling subsided and the sound of a dance band came out. They were playing a Noel Coward tune. What was it called? But there was a knocking at the door, loud over the music. She went to it but didn't open it. Somehow she disliked being in the house alone with Mr Jones now Betty was away, always felt uncomfortable.

'Yes? What is it?'

'Turn that damn' thing off, will you? I'm off to my bed and I want to sleep, not listen to that racket all night!'

'Righto. Sorry, Mr Jones.'

Molly switched off the wireless and stood for a minute, curling her bare toes against the cold linoleum. She might as well go to bed too, she thought, and began tidying away the sewing things. The fire was almost out anyway and she couldn't afford to use any more coal.

In bed she picked up her library book from the night table and opened it. It was a Sherlock Holmes mystery. She would finish it and then be able to change it tomorrow. The branch library at West Auckland only opened three days a week.

She was on the last chapter when the knocking came again. Startled, she jumped out of bed and pulled the coverlet round her.

'What is it?'

'Put that light out, do you think I'm made of money? The electric's dear enough without wasting it. Any decent lass should be asleep by now any road.'

Molly sighed. 'Righto. Sorry, Mr Jones.' Snuggling back under the bedclothes in the dark, she began to think about looking for different lodgings. Mr Jones wasn't human, she thought. What a rotten life Betty must have had living here alone with him. She was probably better off in the sanatorium. At least she wouldn't have her father carping on at her all the time. And once she felt better, of course, Molly reminded herself with a prick of conscience.

Over the next week or two there was a subtle change in Mr Jones's attitude. Molly was spending quite a lot of her dinner hours looking about for a new place. There were several rooms to rent but all of them were beyond her purse and she was beginning to despair of ever getting away from Adelaide Street. She even thought of going back to Eden Hope to see Mrs Morley and begging Jackson's mother to take her in, if only on a temporary basis. (Oh, why wasn't there a letter from India?)

She picked up the small photograph of Harry and Jackson, resplendent in their new uniforms, arms round each other's shoulders, both smiling out at her with well-remembered cheeky grins. It had been her Christmas present to herself, having the photograph framed. It had been taken by Taylor's, the photographer's in Bishop Auckland, not long before the two men sailed for India.

Molly smiled at it, touched each tiny black and white face with her finger tip. They had always been together like that, the two lads, all through school and starting work together down the pit. The grins were wiped off their faces on the day they were both turned off in the depression. Molly had ached for their despair that day, hoped with them every time they went after jobs, shared their disappointment when work failed to materialise. Cried when they decided to go into the army as boy soldiers.

Molly put the photograph back on the mantelshelf. Dear Lord, she was getting maudlin. She glanced at the marble clock. Five o'clock. It was time to go downstairs and start her meal, Mr Jones should be out of the kitchen by now.

But was not. He was hovering around the sink, doing something with the tap.

'Oh, you're not finished, Mr Jones. I'll come back,' said Molly.

'No, no, lass, come on in, I'm just putting a washer on this dripping tap. But I filled the kettle for you before I turned off the water.'

'Oh . . . er, thanks.' Molly was surprised at this consideration. Even more so when he turned to her, a spanner in his hand, and took a step or two forward.

'Why don't you call me Bart? Here we are, living in this house together, just the two of us. Mr Jones is a bit formal, isn't it?' His smile was unctuous.

'Er . . . yes,' she mumbled, and turned her back to rummage in the cupboard where she kept her few groceries. What was he up to? She felt decidedly uncomfortable now, her face burning as she moved a packet of dried peas aside, looking for the tin of beans which she had decided to have on toast. There it was, she had been looking at it all the time. Grabbing it, feeling all fingers and thumbs with embarrassment, she nearly dropped it as she looked round and found he was still standing by the sink, watching her. She looked down at the tin, pretending to read the label.

'I'll take this up to my room, I can easily make toast by the fire up there.'

The half smile which had been playing round his lips disappeared. 'No, you won't, young lady,' he snapped. 'I won't have the smell of food in the bedrooms.' For a second or two he was back to his old self.

'Sorry, you're right,' said Molly, not sure why she was apologising. She took a small pan from the rack and put the beans to heat on the gas ring by the range. Sticking a slice of bread on the toasting fork, she held it before the bars, glad of a reason to keep her back to him. Formless fears crowded coherent thought from her mind so that the toast was smoking by the time she snatched it away from the fire and the beans were bubbling furiously. She turned off the gas and went to look over her shoulder at him.

'Mr Jones,' she began but he had gone. Relief flooded through her. She scraped the burned bits off the toast and ate her scanty meal quickly, washed up and practically scuttled upstairs. This time she locked the door and put a chair under the door handle too though she smiled wryly to herself as she did so. Nothing has changed, she told herself. It was all in your imagination.

The next day there was no chance of looking for

somewhere else to live, the girls' dinner hour was reduced by half as a rush order came in.

'We're changing over to uniforms, girls,' said Mr Bolton, sounding eager. 'There'll be no slacking, we have to get the order out as soon as possible. Now, anyone who can stay back and work overtime tonight, put your name down on the list I've pinned on the notice board.'

There was a buzz of conversation among the others on the line. Molly heard Joan Pendle's jubilant voice above the rest. 'Now I'll be able to buy that dance dress in Doggart's window. By, it's lovely, an' only five shillings down and a shilling a week. Are you going to the station dance on Saturday night, Enid?'

There was a dance hall next to the station in Auckland, a five-piece band regularly playing there. Molly had never been but she had heard a lot about it from the other girls. For a moment she wondered what it was like to go to a dance like that then dismissed it from her mind. She had more important things to do with her money. Maybe she could even afford different lodgings.

Enid had moved on down the line and the girls were quiet as the wireless started to play and they bent over their humming sewing machines. Molly's thoughts were with the boys, Harry and Jackson. She still hadn't had a reply to her Christmas card or a thank you for the tie pin she had sent Harry. Nine-carat gold it was, with a minuscule red stone in the middle which the shop keeper had assured her was a ruby. Nice and light too, it hadn't cost much to post.

Soon it would be time to find him a birthday present, get it off in good time for his birthday in July.

It was not until six-thirty that evening when she came out of the factory to face a bitter cold wind which seemed to blow in her face no matter which way she turned, that Molly realised she had missed her hour in the kitchen. Cold and hungry, she paused in the lea of the gable end of the house. She could ask Mr Jones if she could use the kitchen now, though she knew he couldn't abide the smell of food in the house in the evening.

Molly was reluctant to ask any favours of him but she was so hungry her stomach felt like a great empty hole. She'd had only had a tomato sandwich and an apple at dinner time. Pausing at the door, she changed her mind about going in and made her way back to the fish shop where the smell of frying fish made her feel dizzy. She spent half her overtime on a piece of fish and a bag of chips. Putting the newspaper-wrapped parcel inside her coat and buttoning it up, she sped back to the house. As she let herself in she prayed Mr Jones wouldn't smell the fish. Luckily there was no sign of him and she hurried up the stairs and into her room, locking the door after her as usual.

She sat on the clippie mat she had brought from home and ate the fish and chips out of the paper, leaning forward to let the smell go up the chimney as far as possible. The fish was piping hot and flaky, the batter crisp and light, the chips done to a turn. Molly enjoyed them more than she had enjoyed any meal since before her father was killed.

The newly lit fire flamed and crackled, started as it was by the outer layers of the newspaper parcel. Warmth crept through her bones. Though it was late spring already according to the calendar, the north-easter still swept down the Wear valley and drew the flames upwards.

Replete, Molly screwed the inner paper into a ball and added it to the flames. She sat back against the chair and gazed at the fire, rubbing her neck which was aching after bending over the sewing machine for such long hours. She was tired. When she had drunk her Tizer she would wash and go to bed early with her book.

Relaxed now, her mind wandered off. She was back in another time, years before, when she and Harry were children and had pinched pea pods from the row in Dad's garden, ducking down out of view of the house to eat sweet, not yet fully grown peas from the pod. She smiled now as she pictured it, the two of them giggling and laughing, thinking they were safe from detection, out of sight of the windows of the house. And there Dad had been, standing at the end of the row, trying to look stern. He had been out and come in by the garden gate.

'But . . . why have you come this way?' Harry had stammered, jumping to his feet, scattering pea pods. 'You always use the back gate.'

'I didn't today, though, did I?' Dad had asked, and the corners of his mouth had twitched. He hadn't really been mad, thought Molly now. Not like Mr Jones would be if he found out about tonight's meal.

'Oh, what the heck!' she said aloud. She had enjoyed it. Jumping to her feet, she began to prepare for bed.

Chapter Six

'HITLER AND MUSSOLINI SIGN PACT OF STEEL.' The headlines were on the board outside the newsagent's window. Molly saw it as she rounded the corner from Adelaide Street and waited for the bus to go by before crossing the road to the factory. She was heavy-eyed this morning, had slept badly after last night's greasy supper. Mr Jones had knocked on her door again after she had gone to bed and she had been startled out of her first sleep. Standing by the closed door she had asked what he wanted. Could he smell the faint aroma of fish which hung in the air?

'Let me in a minute, Molly, I just want to talk to you,' he had said.

'I can't, Mr Jones, I'm not dressed,' she'd replied.

'Aw, come on, do you think I haven't seen a lass in her pyjamas before?'

Molly had stood there, shivering with cold. 'I'll see you in the morning, Mr Jones.'

'Why can't you call me Bart? It's only friendly like.'

'Goodnight, Mr Jones,' Molly had said firmly and went back to bed. She pulled the covers up over her ears, determined not to let him bother her, but despite that her heart beat fast and she was trembling. Was that the door handle turning?

'I'll speak to you in the morning then,' he called.

'Yes.' It was a few minutes before she heard him shuffling away and another hour before she was relaxed enough to sleep after getting up and checking that the door was locked.

This morning she had been late in waking and had had to rush to work without her breakfast. Her landlord had already gone, thank goodness. But, oh, she knew she had to find somewhere else to live very soon.

There was a parcel by her sewing machine postmarked India. Molly forgot all her troubles when she saw it. She didn't even wonder how it had got there, just sat and stared at it, her happiness intensified by her previous misery until she thought she might burst.

The parcel was still there unopened when the power was switched on and the wireless started churning out 'Whistle While You Work' from Disney's *Snow White*.

'Howay now, girls,' Enid shouted, and the line settled down to work, heads bent over machines, khaki cloth whizzing under needles. For the minute it was enough for Molly to keep glancing at the parcel. Its brown paper covering was scuffed and torn in places after its journey halfway round the world. She was eager to open it when the morning break arrived at last. Some of the girls crowded round, curious about it.

'Your birthday, is it, Molly?' asked Enid.

'No.'

Someone offered her a pen knife and she carefully split the paper and opened the cardboard box inside. On top there was a card with a picture of Father Christmas, mopping his brow as he staggered beneath a sackful of goodies under a blazing sun. 'Merry Christmas' was written in Harry's handwriting.

'Blimey!' one of the girls said. 'It's a Christmas present. Nearly six months late an' all.'

'You brought it, didn't you, Joan?' asked Enid. 'Where did you get it?'

She sniffed and didn't reply for a moment.

'Well?' asked Molly.

'It came to your old house a while ago. I just forgot to bring it.' In fact her mother had been on at her over and over to take the parcel for Molly and Joan had only pretended to forget. This morning there had been a shouting match in the Pendle household about it.

'You'll take that parcel to the lass or I'll come with you and take it myself!' Ann had said.

'Aw, why should I have to run about after her?' Joan had retorted. 'If she wants it, she can come over and get it!'

'You'll take it!' Ann had lost her temper thoroughly and thrust the parcel into Joan's arms. 'Get along with you now, and you give it to her, do you understand me? I'm ashamed it's been here so long.'

'All right, all right,' Joan had said in martyred tones. 'I'll take it.'

Now the other girls were looking at her strangely and she didn't like it. It was all that stuck-up Molly's fault. Joan glared at her. She was so like Harry. Her hair and eyes were lighter but she had the same straight nose and firm chin. Joan felt a pang of misery and turned sharply away.

'Oh, get on with it,' she said crossly. 'I'm going to have my tea. I've got better things to do. It'll only be rubbish any road.' And she walked away, not wanting to think about Harry any more.

Joan looked over her shoulder, however, as there was a gasp from the girls. Molly had lifted out a shawl of palest blue silk, edged with a wide fringe. There was another gasp as a matching dolly bag emerged with a picture of the Taj Mahal embroidered in silver on the side.

'Eeh . . . it's lovely!' one of the girls breathed. 'By, you are lucky, Molly.'

Lucky? For a minute Molly's happiness dimmed. Was she lucky after all that had happened to her? She shook her head. No, she mustn't be bitter. It was a happy day, she was lucky to get such beautiful things. Surely such a lovely shawl had never been seen before in Eden Hope or West Auckland?

'Now then, girls,' said Enid, brisk again. 'Get your tea or you won't have time before the break is over.'

The girls moved away and Molly pulled out a letter from Harry. She would save it for the dinner hour, take it back to Adelaide Street and stow the beautiful shawl and dolly bag safely in her bedroom. She was packing it in the box carefully when she noticed there was something else: a letter from Jackson. Her happiness intensified. He hadn't forgotten her. She was so happy she even smiled at Joan.

'Thanks for fetching it in,' she said. 'How is your mother, by the way?' She well knew it would be Ann who had insisted on Joan's bringing it. But in her present mood she could even forgive the long delay.

The second half of the morning seemed interminable but at last Molly was free to pick up the parcel and run over the road and round the corner into Adelaide Street. She was panting as she opened the door and raced up the stairs to her bedroom. Leaving the door ajar, for she knew her landlord wouldn't be in from work for hours yet, she sat on the bed and unpacked the box again, laying the presents carefully on the bedspread. Then she took the letters and went over to her chair by the fireplace and settled down to read Harry's first.

I'm worried about you, petal. I don't like to think of you alone in the house. Travelling to work too. You should watch out for yourself, there are some funny folk about. And can you afford it? You can't be making much money. I've enclosed a money order for five pounds, it's not much but it will help. Let me know if you need any more. I can let you have an

allowance from my pay if you can't manage, as I told
you in my letter.

What letter? Molly wondered. Had there been a letter gone
astray? For a minute she suspected Joan, but no, she
wouldn't do that. And why didn't Harry know she was
living in St Helen's Auckland now? She had written to
him, sent a Christmas present too. Molly shook her head
and read on.

I don't know when we'll be coming back to Blighty
but it can't be long, not with the way things are over
there. In the meantime, look after yourself and eat
properly. You were always too thin, so don't stint on
food. And *don't* go with any lads. You're just a young
lass, remember. And *I* know what lads are like,
believe me. You're my kid sister and I will be back
soon to look after you. Think on it and be a good girl.
You know Mam and Dad would expect it.

Your loving brother, Harry

P.S. I hope you like the shawl, pet. When we come
home we'll find a posh dance where you can wear it.

Molly had a grand bubbly feeling inside her. In one
morning she had gone from black depression, where she'd
felt completely alone and unloved, to a mood of bright
optimism, which had once been her usual outlook on life
but which she hadn't felt since her dad was killed. She

carefully folded the letter and put it back, glancing at the clock. Goodness, she only had five minutes to get back to her machine. It was amazing how fast half an hour could go. Promising herself she would save Jackson's letter until the evening, she rushed back to the factory, completely forgetting that she'd had no dinner.

By six o'clock Molly was light-headed. The noise of the machines and the wireless still rang in her head as she crossed the road towards Adelaide Street. Calling at the grocer's on the main road, she bought a couple of eggs. She would do herself scrambled eggs or an omelette, she thought. Her empty stomach ached almost as much as her head.

Mr Jones was in the kitchen, sitting by the oil-cloth-covered table and reading the *Evening Gazette*. Molly hesitated in the doorway.

'Can I use the kitchen, Mr Jones?' she asked. 'I have to work an extra hour at the factory nowadays and I've just come in.'

'Aye, go on then,' he replied with a grudging sort of sigh. 'I hope you're not going to cook anything smelly?'

'Oh, no, Mr Jones,' said Molly, thinking regretfully of the onion lying in her cupboard which she had been going to put in an omelette. Scrambled eggs it was then.

He sat at the table, looking at her over a pair of reading glasses from Woolworth's. 'I've told you to call me Bart,' he said mildly. Molly smiled vaguely. She couldn't imagine calling him by his first name, not in a million years. And tonight, as soon as she had eaten, she would go to the newsagent's and take the address of another house with a room to let, even if it cost ten shillings or more. She thought of the five-pound money order which Harry had sent with a warm glow of gratitude.

She whisked the eggs, cooked them in a pan on the fire, sat at the table and ate them with bread and butter rather than spend more time making toast. All the time she could feel Mr Jones's eyes on her, though she kept hers on what she was doing. After she had washed up she escaped to her room, looked regretfully at the letter from Jackson and decided to leave it until she came back in. Feeling decidedly better with something in her stomach, she washed her face and combed her hair. This was a good day with the parcel coming and now she was going to find other lodgings, she was sure of it.

Going to her bedroom door, she realised the key was missing. She looked about on the floor, even turned back the rug, but it wasn't there. It wasn't outside on the landing either and it wasn't in her bag. She couldn't remember if she had used it to get in this evening. She racked her memory but knew she had been feeling slightly dizzy then. Everything before she had eaten was hazy.

Oh, well, she would find it eventually, she told herself. Now she had to go before it was too late. It was already seven-thirty and people didn't like callers too late in the evening when they had settled down to listen to the wireless. Molly closed her door and hurried down the stairs.

'Going to the pictures, are you, Molly?'

Mr Jones was standing in the doorway of the kitchen, watching her.

'No, just to see a friend,' she fibbed.

'I'll treat you to the pictures one night, maybe on Saturday,' he said with a benevolent air.

'Hmmm.' Molly couldn't think of anything else to say. She turned smartly and went out of the door. No, you will not, she thought savagely as she walked down the street. If you think I'm going anywhere with you, you're out of your head.

There were two addresses in the newsagent's window. One of them in West Auckland, about half a mile away, the other in Front Street. Molly considered it worth the extra walking distance to be away from Adelaide Street and set off along Manor Road, past the ancient church and over the bridge which spanned the Gaunless river and into West Auckland. She found the house easily enough. It was in a small row of old two-storey houses with elegant Georgian fronts. There was a bell, too. She pressed it and heard it ring inside the house.

'Answer that, Jimmy,' a female voice called and a moment later the heavy front door opened and a boy of about seven poked his head round. He stared at Molly.

'What do you want?'

'Can I speak to your mam?'

He closed the door and she could hear him shouting at the top of his voice behind it.

'Mam! Mam!'

'Who is it, Jimmy? I'm busy with the baby, you know I am.'

'It's a lass.'

'Ask her what she wants,' the woman yelled back at him.

The door opened again. 'What do you want?' he asked again. 'Mam wants to know.'

'I've come about the room. Can I come in?'

The door closed for a moment again as he held a shouted conference with his mother. Then, 'Aye. Howay in then,' he said and Molly crossed over the high step and into a hall with a high ceiling and varnished dado rail, the floor covered with a worn carpet runner, a piece of coco-matting acting as a door mat. There was a smell of meat pudding from the back of the hall; a door which must lead to the kitchen, Molly surmised, stood beside the narrow staircase. The smell reminded her of her mother somehow. A pair of roller skates lay on their sides just inside the door and a shabby pram stood to one side of the hall.

A woman was coming down the stairs, sandy hair like the boy's drawn back from her forehead, cheeks rosy beneath laughing blue eyes.

'Come on in,' she said, striding forward and holding out her hand. 'I'm Cathy Grimes and this tearaway is Jimmy.' Her handshake was firm, her smile friendly. 'After the room, did you say?'

'Yes. I'm Molly Mason. I work at the clothing factory in St Helen's.'

The room which Cathy led her into was large and airy, with a bay window through which rays of a sinking summer sun shone, speckling the air with dancing dust motes. There was a leather suite, shabby and with sagging cushions, an ancient sideboard and corner cupboard. It had a lived-in air, unlike most of the sitting rooms Molly had known. Most mining families spent their time in the kitchen-cum-living room, the sitting room kept tidy for visits from the minister or other important personages.

'Run along and make sure your sister's all right,' Cathy said to her son, reaching out a hand and tousling his hair.

'Aw, Mam,' he grumbled, but went all the same, and Cathy motioned Molly to a seat and perched on an armchair herself.

'You don't live with your family, then?' she asked. 'Not had a fight with your dad, have you?'

Molly's throat constricted. 'No. My dad's dead, my mam an' all.' She coughed, put a hand to her mouth. 'Dad was killed in the disaster at Eden Hope.'

'Eeh, I'm that sorry! Take no notice of my big mouth, love. Look, I'll just get us a cup of tea then we'll have a talk and I'll show you the room.'

'Don't make it just for me,' protested Molly.

'I'm not. Believe me, after seeing to the kids' teas and struggling with the little 'un – he's cutting a tooth, poor bairn – me own tongue's hanging out.'

Molly looked around when Cathy left the room. The wallpaper was faded. In one place there were crayon marks which someone had attempted to wash off. But there were a couple of nice prints on the wall, one of High Force in Teesdale, the water tumbling over the falls in full spate. The other was an engraving of Stephenson's Locomotion No. 1. Cathy came back in with a tea tray as Molly was studying it.

'My man's an engine driver,' she volunteered. 'He's daft on the old engines.' She poured tea and handed Molly a cup and saucer. 'He's away a lot, on the London run. That's why I wanted a lodger, a woman for preference. Company, you know. That and the money, of course. I'd best tell you it's ten shillings a week. We had to spend some to get it ready, you know, it's a new bed.'

'I can manage ten shillings. As I said, I'm in regular work. I'd like it here, I like children.' Molly sounded too eager, she knew she did.

Cathy laughed. 'You haven't seen the room yet! It's in the attic, mind. And when you've been pestered a bit by my lot, you might change your mind about kids. Come on, I'll show you the room.'

There were three flights of stairs and then a shorter one to a door at the top of the house. Inside the room was large and airy, with a dormer window looking out over the green and the roofs of Post Office Square.

'Oh, it's fine,' breathed Molly. It was too: a single bed with a bright patchwork coverlet, even a square of carpet on the floor. There was a wash stand with basin and jug, and a walnut dressing table. There was a gas fire on one wall with a meter by the side.

'I hope you don't mind paying for your own gas? We couldn't afford . . .'

'I'll take it,' interrupted Molly. 'When can I move in?'

Chapter Seven

Molly walked back to Adelaide Street in the gathering
dusk, so happy she had to stop herself from skipping along.
Cathy was very friendly and sympathetic; Molly had found
herself telling her all about Eden Hope and her dad and
Harry, away in the army in India.

'I bet you have a boyfriend too, a pretty girl like you?'
she had said, teasing. Molly thought about Jackson. Not
really a boyfriend, she had been too young when he went
away. But still . . .

'He's in the army with Harry,' she had replied.

Now she thought of Jackson's letter, still unread. It was
something to look forward to, she would read it in bed
tonight. By, it had been a lovely, lovely day. And she was
moving to Cathy's at the end of the week, would give in
her notice to Mr Jones now. It was a load lifted off her
mind.

The house in Adelaide Street was dark, Mr Jones was
out evidently. Well, she would tell him tomorrow. Molly
let herself in and ran upstairs to her room. The door wasn't
quite closed. Had he been nosing around? She shivered,

hating the thought of him touching her things. Closing the door after her, she put the chair under the handle. That should keep him out anyway. And in a few days she would be gone from this house forever.

In bed she opened Jackson's letter. There wasn't a lot in it and he had written similar things to her brother except for the last sentence. *'We'll be home soon, I promise you. Look after my best girl till then.'*

He meant her! He had to mean her. Maybe it was just a saying but he had written she was his best girl, or that was what it meant. Molly slipped out of bed and checked the chair under the door handle. Was it strong enough? She wasn't sure. But maybe she was worrying about nothing. She wouldn't let it spoil this wonderful day. Putting out the light, she slipped under the covers and curled into a ball.

Today she had found a new friend, she thought drowsily. It was almost like being part of a family again. And there had been letters from the two men she loved most in the world and those lovely things from Harry. Everything was going right for her at last. The sun was shining on her, thank God. Molly slipped into sleep.

She was walking along the promenade at Roker, Mam on one side and Dad on the other. They were holding her hands. She had to reach up to them she was so small.

'Look at that, Molly, will you just look?' Mam cried, and she saw a small cottage all lit up around the roof, a light shining from the tiny window. The roof was orange and the walls white; roses climbed over the front door.

'It's a fairy house, Molly,' said Mam, and she was awed and delighted for her mam read fairy stories to her every night before she went to sleep and she knew what a fairy house was. And as she gazed and gazed, a fairy flew round the front of the house, smiled directly at her and disappeared inside.

'Howay, pet,' said Dad. 'We have to get on, the bus will be waiting.' They were on a bus trip to Roker to see the illuminations. But Molly didn't want to go. She tugged away from his hand and hung on to the railing around the little house. So he picked her up and carried her and suddenly she was frightened. It wasn't really her dad . . . no, he was killed in the pit, wasn't he? Who was holding her? Who?

She struggled to wake up and pull away, hit out at whoever it was and rolled out of bed and on to the floor. Dashing for the bedroom door, she tripped on the mat, almost fell, then blundered into something else. A chair? But she managed to keep to her feet and reached the light switch. Her hand on the door knob as the light came on, she glanced over her shoulder and there, just picking himself up from the floor, was Mr Jones, blinking in the light.

She could almost have laughed at the sight of him, his hair all awry and feet bare. He was dressed in a voluminous nightshirt. She had been going to flee out into the street but he looked so pathetic somehow that she stood still and gaped at him.

'What did you do that for?' he asked.

'Never mind that, what are *you* doing in my room? How did you get in anyway?' Molly looked at the chair, lying on its side. That was what she must have stumbled over. She couldn't have put it under the knob the right way, she hadn't even heard it fall.

'Aw, come on, Molly, you know well what I want. A young lass like you, staying in a man's house, just the two of us! Well, tonight's your lucky night, I'm here to give it to you.' He smiled, showing broken crooked teeth. 'Howay, back to bed, it's still a bit cold on a night. We might as well be cosy,' he coaxed, and Molly began to laugh. She couldn't help it. She laughed and laughed until tears streamed down her face. To think she had been nervous, not to say frightened, of this silly little man!

'Come on, I mean it, I'm not just having you on,' said Mr Jones, still not understanding. His tone implied he thought he was doing her a favour, Molly realised, and laughed the more, released tension making her a little hysterical.

'Stop that!' Mr Jones suddenly shouted. He crossed the room and slapped her hard across the face. Molly stopped laughing and stared at him. He slavered slightly, lips wet. 'Now then, come to bed when I say, do you hear?' He had raised his voice, was almost shouting. He caught hold of her arms and dragged her towards the bed.

'No! Don't be silly, I don't want to!' cried Molly, finding her voice and pulling herself free.

'Don't be so bloody coy and come to bed when you're told,' he shouted. 'Don't you realise all the neighbours think we must be at it any road? If you didn't want me you would have gone somewhere else when Betty went into hospital. Now come on, you've protested enough. Come to bed when I tell you.'

'I'm not! I didn't . . . I locked the door and you took the key. You must have forced your way in here tonight, I put the chair up against the knob.'

'Bloody games. I've had enough,' he shouted, and grabbed her again, practically throwing her on the bed with him on top of her. The breath was knocked out of Molly. He wasn't very big but strong enough to hold her slight form down, her arms pinned. One of his hands was clutching at her hair, the other scrabbling at her breast. His face was close to hers. A drop of spittle fell on to her chin. She felt as though her hair was being torn out at the roots, the pain agonising.

'This is what you want, isn't it?' he said hoarsely. 'This is what you've been angling for ever since Betty went to hospital – wiggling your arse at me every time you went past me, looking at me with those big come-to-bed eyes. Well, now you're going to get it, slut! Now . . .'

In a desperate burst of energy Molly heaved and managed to catch him off balance. He fell off her, teetering on the edge of the bed for a second and falling heavily on to the floor. As he fell his fingers dug into her breast and she cried out with the pain.

'Stop that flaming noise!' someone was shouting. There was a banging on the wall. Molly heard it as from a distance. She was too busy scrambling off the bed, grabbing her coat from the hook and covering herself. She stood at the doorway, poised for flight, then realised Mr Jones was saying nothing, lying on the floor beside the bed. Oh, God, had she killed him? Had he hit his head on the fender? No, he was moving, sitting up, groaning. He put a hand to his head and held it there for a moment before getting heavily to his feet.

Molly took a step through the door, the linoleum cold under her bare feet. She was wary of him but he did not look at her as he walked past her, nightshirt billowing round skinny ankles. At his own bedroom door he turned.

'Get out of here, you slut! Take your things and get out. Never mind the rent, I want shot of you.'

'It's the middle of the night!' gasped Molly.

'I don't care what time it is. You can sleep on the street for all I care. Get your things together now or get out without them. Either way, if you're not out of here in ten minutes, I'll throw you out.'

He stood there, holding his head and trying to look dignified, succeeding only in looking ludicrous so that Molly felt a bubble of hysterical laughter rising in her in spite of her predicament. Hurriedly she went back into her bedroom and closed the door, leaning on it and hiccuping with laughter. But it died almost immediately and tears took its place.

She dashed them away angrily and dressed before gathering her things together. She could only take her case, she thought. What about the bits and pieces she had brought from Eden Hope? Dumbly she put the parcel she'd received that morning, the one which had brought her such happiness as she hadn't known for months, in her suitcase. It stuck up a bit, the case wouldn't close properly. She'd have to be careful with it, she told herself. She'd have to leave her other things, her sewing basket and such. She carried the case to the door, paused and looked back. She had no idea where she was going, she realised. Could she turn up on Cathy's doorstep in the middle of the night? No, she rejected the idea. After all, they had only just met.

Going back into the room, she picked up the marble clock from the mantelshelf. She couldn't leave that. With the clock tucked under one arm and her suitcase, which felt as heavy as lead, in her other hand, she went downstairs. Mr Jones was waiting at the door.

'I'll come back for my other things.'

'You will not,' he replied. 'I'll get them myself and put them outside. If they're not gone by morning I'll take them to the tip.'

'You can't! I'll get the polis . . .'

'You'll not, lass. It'll be me that gets the polis,' he said grimly, and gave her a push out of the door and on to the pavement. Molly dropped her case and grasped at the clock to stop it falling. The case burst open. She must not have closed it properly.

A light came on in the bedroom of the next-door house, the window opened and a man stuck his head out.

'What the hell is all the racket about?' he shouted. 'I have to go to work the morn!'

'I'm sorry, Joe, really I am,' said Mr Jones, and Molly was amazed at his change of tone. He sounded conciliatory now. 'It won't happen again. It's this thieving lass I took in off the streets. She's been pinching the wife's things!'

'I have not!' Molly cried, shock and disbelief making her shout. 'I haven't touched anything –'

'What's this then?'

Mr Jones was bending over the open suitcase. When he stood up he had a bangle in his hand. It sparkled in the light from the open door.

'Do you see this, Joe? Do you see it?' He held it up and Joe nodded.

'Aye, I see it. It's that gold bangle your wife was so proud of, isn't it? Why, the thieving little bitch!' He leaned further out of the window and glared at Molly.

'I didn't take it, really I didn't,' she said. She looked from the neighbour's face to that of Mr Jones. He had a nasty little smile playing round his lips; his eyes were filled with vindictive glee.

'You're my witness, Joe. You saw me take it out of the case, didn't you? I knew she had it somewhere, I missed it out of the dressing-table drawer tonight so I tackled her about it. If she'd give it me back I'd have let her off, but she's a hard-faced little slut, you know. Will you watch her, Joe, while I go for the polis?'

Molly was struck dumb. She stood there, her open case at her feet, the marble clock under her arm. She looked down at it. It was one o'clock in the morning. Surely this was just a bad dream? It couldn't really be happening, of course it couldn't. She closed her eyes tight, prayed that she should wake up then opened them again.

Someone had taken a firm hold on her arm. She almost dropped the clock. It was the man from next door.

'Now then, don't you think you can get away,' he snapped. 'I wouldn't be surprised if you'd done this before, arriving here out of nowhere and trying to take honest folk down.'

'I didn't – I haven't!' moaned Molly. Up the street other windows were opening. Some front doors even had people peering round them.

'What's going on, Joe?' someone shouted.

'It's this lass that was lodging with Bart,' he explained, speaking loudly so everyone could hear. Molly felt herself shrinking inside with the shame of it. 'She's been pinching stuff from him, that's what's going on.' His fingers dug painfully into her arm again.

'I haven't! I didn't!' cried Molly, but hopelessly now.

'May the Lord save your lying little soul,' someone shouted piously. 'Make you see the error of your ways.'

'I did nothing!' she screamed, beside herself now with

an anger which rose up inside her and burst out. 'It was him! He got into my bed . . . he . . .'

'Eeh, I tell you what . . .' said a woman from up the street. She came walking down towards Molly, a coat on over her nightie, old shoes thrust on her feet and her hair done up in steel curling pins. 'I tell you what . . . folk like her'll say owt but their prayers. An' who would've believed it? She looked a meek little thing, butter wouldn't melt in her mouth. Aye, but you've been found out, haven't you?' The woman thrust her face close to Molly's. 'You didn't think you would, did you? Lasses like you should have their fingers chopped off, that's what I think!' She folded her arms across her enormous chest and nodded her head to emphasise her words.

'I didn't do it! It was him, he got into my bed!' shouted Molly, and a growl went up amongst the crowd which was now gathering round.

'Will you listen to her? Will you?' one man cried. 'Isn't that what they all say when they're caught? Blame it on the fella. Oh, aye, it must have been *his* fault. Tried to take you down, did he? An innocent little virgin, are you? I just bloody well *bet* you are!'

The crowd murmured agreement, their mood growing ugly. They moved forward, hemming her in. Someone grabbed her other arm, the one holding the clock, and she dropped it.

'Me mam's clock!' she cried, and pushed and shoved, taking Joe by surprise so that he let go of her and she bent down on the pavement, crying over the clock as though the world had come to an end.

'It was me mam's,' she cried brokenly. 'Look at it now, the marble's all chipped. I bet it won't work neither.'

The old woman laughed. 'It's only an old clock,' she said. 'You won't be needing a clock where you're going, me lass.'

'Now then, what's going on here?' a new voice said, and the crowd melted away as if by magic. Molly was left bending over the clock, trying to fix the glass door back on for it had come off in the fall. Miraculously, it hadn't broken. She hardly heard what was being said by the men above her. The door on the clock went back on, albeit a bit crooked. She stood it carefully on the pavement and turned to her suitcase, pushing her things back into it, trying to get them even so she could close the lid. The catch wouldn't work at first. She tried and tried with it and at last it clicked into place. She nearly cried with frustration. She should have a belt round it, she thought, that would work. One of her father's belts, that was it.

The policeman bent down and pulled her to her feet.

'It's no good taking on like that, lass,' he said mildly. 'You'll just have to come along o' me now. I want no fuss, mind.'

'Where are we going?' asked Molly. Suddenly she was exhausted, couldn't fight any more, feeling like a bird in a trap.

'Well, where do you think? The police station in

Bondgate. You can't go pinching things and get away Scot free, you know. A night in the cells will do you the world of good.'

On the pavement, the clock began to chime, its tone sweet and silvery. It chimed six times. 'See what they did,' said Molly, more to herself than the policeman. 'That can't be right. It's not six o'clock, surely?'

'The lass is off her head,' Bart Jones remarked.

'Never mind that. You're coming along an' all, I want a statement from you. You, too, whatever your name is.' He nodded at Joe.

'I have to go to work the morn!'

'Me an' all,' said Joe.

'That's matterless, you're coming down to the station,' the policeman said calmly. 'Come on, the Black Maria's at the end of the street.'

'Why, yer bugger!' said Joe, glaring at Molly. 'I could be fast asleep in bed if it wasn't for you. A fella's just doing his duty and now I'm going to lose a morning's pay for it. What's the world coming to, I ask you?'

'It's the law,' said the policeman. And, picking up Molly's suitcase, led the way down the street.

Chapter Eight

At least she didn't have to worry about where she was going to sleep, thought Molly. She sat on the hard bed in a police cell in Bondgate and looked about her in total disbelief. How could this have happened? The cold struck through the bare stone walls but she didn't feel it; she didn't feel anything. There was a barred window set so high up the wall it was impossible to see through, a metal door with a peephole which denied her all privacy, a battered table and a chair.

'Lights out in five minutes, lass,' a policeman said through the peephole. 'If I were you I'd try to get some sleep.' He sounded quite kindly, she thought, and opened her mouth to appeal to him but he had gone. She could hear his footsteps retreating down the passage.

She looked at the bed. A hard flock mattress. A lumpy striped pillow with no pillowslip. A brown blanket, clean but worn almost away in patches. She took off her shoes, thought about removing her dress but decided against it. She lay on the bed, covering herself with the blanket. Her mind felt blank, she couldn't even think. She stared at the door. The light from the bare bulb in the middle of the ceiling shone in her eyes and she closed them against the glare. The next minute it was suddenly dark, a dense blackness relieved only by bars of lighter grey near the ceiling and coming from the window.

'Dad,' she whispered. 'Oh, Dad.' She needed him here so much but he was dead. And then a moan she hardly recognised came from her lips. 'God help me. Please, God, please.'

She became aware of noises. Someone in the next cell was drunk. He was singing a song from the Great War. 'Mademoiselle from Armentieres', that was it. Someone else, a woman's voice it was, shouted, 'Stop that ruddy racket, will you?' And a policeman walked in heavy boots outside the door.

'Quiet in there!' an authoritative voice shouted and the drunk was quiet for a few minutes then started up again with 'Keep the Home Fires Burning'.

Suddenly Molly was desperate to pass water. There was a lavatory pan in the corner. She got up and went over to it, moving hesitantly in the dark, her hands out in front of her, feeling her way. She sat on the lavatory, finding herself at first unable to use it. There was no seat and the cold of the pottery pan bit into her. At last she managed and made her way back to the bed, stubbing her toe on the leg. The pain was agonising. She fell into bed, pulled the blanket over her head and sobbed and sobbed, shoulders heaving. No one was going to help her, no one at all. She was completely alone. Eventually the storm of crying passed and she fell into an uneasy sleep.

It was morning when she awoke and the cell looked worse in the daylight than it had in artificial light. Molly sat up, disorientated for a moment. Her head throbbed, her throat was dry. A tin mug stood on the table. She pulled on her shoes and went over to it. As she had thought, it held water and she drank thirstily, stale though the water tasted.

A policeman opened the door and came in with a tray which he put down on the table. There was porridge, bread and butter and jam, and a mug of tea, strong and brown.

'I don't want anything,' said Molly. She felt dirty and dishevelled, her dress creased from sleeping in it. The policeman looked at her, considering. He was about the same age as her father, she thought. Did he have a family?

'You should eat something, lass,' he said. 'Howay now. And drink the tea, I put two sugars in, it'll give you strength.'

'I want to wash.'

'All right, I'll bring you a dish of water and a towel. But drink the tea at least.'

He went out, the door clanging behind him. Molly took a spoonful of porridge. It was lukewarm and sweet. She drank the tea because the policeman seemed kind and had told her to. When he came back she washed and combed her hair, rubbed at a mark on her dress with the soapy water.

At ten o'clock, feeling better, she followed the policeman upstairs to the magistrates' court and stood before the bench. The magistrates would let her go, she told herself. Surely no one would believe Mr Jones?

'Remanded in custody until Monday next,' said the chairman.

'Why? I didn't do anything!' cried Molly. The chairman sighed. 'No one ever has,' he remarked to his neighbour, a white-haired lady in twinset and pearls, who nodded sagely.

'You have no fixed address,' he went so far as to explain to Molly.

'But I have. I have a room in West Auckland,' she said eagerly, filled with relief. 'I told the officer –'

'Take her down, Constable,' said the magistrate. 'Bailiff, call the next case.'

As Molly was led away, an old man shuffled in, his eyes bleary with drink, his movements unsteady. He took her place before the bench. The bailiff was saying something about him being drunk and disorderly.

For the rest of the day, Molly sat in her cell, going over and over the hearing in her mind. Mr Jones had appeared an upright citizen, worried to death about his daughter in a sanatorium, allowing Molly to keep on her room out of the kindness of his heart. His neighbour had testified to seeing him bring the bangle out of Molly's suitcase, said he recognised it as once being the property of the late Mrs Jones. The evidence was all against her, Molly conceded,

but it was lies. She'd protested her innocence, told them
that Mr Jones had come into her room and attacked her,
but they had cut her off. 'That's enough of that!' the
chairman had said sharply. 'You can get into serious
trouble if you take that line, my girl.'

'But –'

'Take her away,' said the chairman.

'Have you not got anyone who will testify as to your
good character?' asked the kindly policeman later on.
'Where did you say you come from? Eden Hope? Well,
there must be someone there, surely?'

His name was Constable Hardy and he was the only one
who tried to help her. She learned he came from Coundon,
his father a pitman there. His daughter was a teacher now
and he was very proud of her.

Molly shrank within herself at the thought of asking
Ann Pendle to testify for her. Mrs Morley might have
done, but Molly was too ashamed to ask. She didn't want
anyone in Eden Hope to find out, anyone who had known
her family in better days. But surely when the magistrates
heard the whole story she would be set free, they would
know they had made a mistake? British justice was the best
in the world, her dad had always told her so, and she
believed him.

In the end, Molly decided not to ask anyone from Eden
Hope. She would stand up in court, tell the truth and the
magistrates would have to believe her, of course they
would. She would be set free and would go to Cathy's

house in West Auckland and then, with a room in a decent house and Cathy for a friend, the nightmare would be over.

Wearing a clean dress which Constable Hardy had had pressed for her, and with her hair brushed back from her temples and gleaming almost chestnut in the overhead lights of the court, Molly faced the magistrates once more. Her heart beat so fast she could feel it in her throat and she clasped her hands behind her to still their trembling. It would soon be over and she would go free, she told herself. A disturbance took her attention. It was someone coming in late and sitting down on the Press bench. The chairman of the magistrates frowned down at him.

There was a report in the local paper next day.

Before Bishop Auckland Magistrates yesterday morning, Molly Mason, of no fixed address but previously of Eden Hope, was sentenced to three months' imprisonment for the theft of a gold bangle, value fifteen pounds and ten shillings, from her then landlord, Mr Bartram Jones. Mr Jones said the bracelet belonged to his late wife and was of great sentimental value to him. In sentencing, the chairman, Sir John Hume, made the following remarks to the defendant.

'Mr Jones trusted you in his house and you betrayed that trust and stole from him. I am aware that you are of previous good character and also that you recently lost your father in the mining disaster at Eden Hope colliery. Nevertheless I have consulted with my colleagues and we are agreed that three months in prison could be just the shock you need to force you to see the error of your ways.'

Molly had climbed into the van which was to take her to prison, sat beside a policewoman, did what she was told automatically. It was a nightmare, she told herself, a nightmare which went on and on. And now she was sitting in a workroom with a number of other women, dressed in a stiff grey dress, sewing thick calico bags which the other girls said were to hold gun powder. The sewing machine she was using might have been the first one ever invented. She was in a line not unlike the one in the factory at St Helen's Auckland, but here there was no wireless, the women weren't chattering and laughing or singing along to music. There was just the clattering of the machines, the wardresses walking up and down, and the ache in Molly's fingers from handling the stiff fabric all day long.

Chapter Nine

The troopship nosed its way into Southampton and came to a slow, lumbering halt alongside the quay. A band of marines was playing far below them as Harry and Jackson stood to attention on deck with the rest of their platoon, part of this army of men returning to Britain to defend the homeland.

They were sunburned a dark brown by the Indian sun in contrast to the civilians below, waiting for the gangplank to be lowered and the soldiers to come on to dry land. They had been in transit for weeks, going the long way round by Cape Town rather than risk coming through the Suez Canal and crossing the Mediterranean Sea. There was no war as yet but the threat of it was ever present though some members of the government still thought it could be averted.

The August sun was shining, a pale imitation of what they were used to in India. But to the men on the deck of the ship it was infinitely preferable to what they had left behind in Bombay.

England, thought Jackson. Everything about it was

different. The smells, the feel of the air, the noises. They would be in barracks for a few nights, but next week, always supposing war wasn't declared, they'd be on their way north, with rail vouchers which would take them all the way home. Or at least to Bishop Auckland which was as near as made no difference at all. Two whole weeks at home! Time enough for them to make sure Molly was managing on her own and coming to no harm.

The order to fall out was given, the men were beginning to file down the gangplank, and eventually the recently promoted Sergeant Morley was at liberty to talk to Corporal Mason. They threaded their way through the crowds of wives and sweethearts come to meet their men and onlookers who were simply curious or liked the atmosphere of excitement when a troopship came home.

'Molly's not here,' said Harry. They had searched and searched again, just in case they had missed her in the crowds.

'Oh, come on now, Harry, you didn't expect her to come all the way down here to meet the ship? The train is expensive. And besides, Molly will be at work. She has to make her living, hasn't she?'

Harry nodded. 'I know. But I still looked for her somehow.'

Jackson knew exactly how he felt. He too had felt a moment's disappointment when he had scanned the people meeting the ship and not seen Molly. They couldn't have missed her either. Both Harry and he had been looking and they had keen eyes.

'Five days and we'll be on our way any road,' said Harry as the soldiers came together again and the order rang out to form ranks. A step nearer home, he thought. They marched through the town to their temporary barracks, led by their own regimental band. It was August and the sun beat down on them but to men who had been in India for two years or more the air felt fresh and clean, the familiar scents of England carried on a breeze from the west. Yet it was not quite the same as the breeze which would be blowing down the Wear Valley, straight from the moors, Jackson mused. And five days suddenly felt like an awful long time.

The Northumbria, the Newcastle express train, was packed with soldiers as it left King's Cross and picked up speed as it steamed north. Harry and Jackson sat together in a compartment reserved for non-commissioned officers where they could relax, their kitbags stowed on the rack above their heads. They talked little as the train sped through the northern outskirts of London and on into the dark countryside. They were due in Darlington at five past six in the morning. There would then be a wait of half an hour or so for the local train to Bishop Auckland.

There was little talking among the men, each of them had their thoughts fixed on home and family. Jackson settled down to sleep. The compartment light was dim.

With his long legs stretched out in front of him and his cap over his eyes he took only minutes to drop off, waking only briefly as the train pulled into Peterborough and later on Doncaster. When it arrived in York he sat up, as did most of the others. There was a buzz of quiet talk. They all gazed at the Minster as it fell behind them in the grey light of early morning.

'It has the Taj Mahal beat, mate,' said a burly corporal, and Jackson agreed, grinning, aware that they were a tiny bit prejudiced. He took out his comb and tidied his hair, stroked his chin where he could begin to feel stubble. It didn't matter, though, soon be home. Harry and the others were also tidying themselves up. Jackson looked across and grinned.

'Not long now, mate, Molly will be waiting at the station, I bet.' They had sent a telegram to her and one to Jackson's mother. 'Everything will be all right,' they assured each other, though both had misgivings which intensified the nearer they got to home. It was such a long time since they'd heard from Molly, Harry hadn't even had a Christmas card. But mail could go astray so easily . . .

'Darlington in ten minutes,' said the conductor, sliding open the door of the compartment. 'Next stop Darlington.'

'By, that sounds grand,' a soldier remarked. 'I've been dreaming someone would say that.'

There was no one to meet them at the station at Bishop Auckland. Jackson hadn't expected his mother, not when she had his father at home an invalid, but he had been hoping against hope that Molly would be there. This time he had no words of comfort to offer Harry.

'Let's walk through the woods to Eden Hope,' he said instead. 'It'll be almost as quick as going down the street for the bus. It's no good you going off to West Auckland when you don't know where abouts Molly lives.'

'Righto.'

Newgate Street was a mile long. If they cut across country they could be halfway home before they'd even have got to the bus stop. Shouldering their kitbags, they set off.

The wood was pleasantly cool and the Gaunless flowing through it tinkled and splashed, a sound they hadn't heard often in India. They emerged on to a hill where they could see a number of colliery villages, all clustered round a winding wheel and chimneys. The countryside was green apart from patches of gold where corn was ripening. And, of course, the black heaps by the pits, slag heaps. But even the mineheads were beautiful to the two homecomers, pale smoke curling from the tall chimneys.

They hadn't far to go to Eden Hope and soon Jackson was turning into his own back gate while Harry went on to the house where he had been brought up. Or rather to the house next door to question Ann Pendle about Molly's new address.

'Eeh, I've been looking out for you for hours,' Mrs Morley cried, running to Jackson, her arms outstretched.

He could feel her bones, he thought as his arms enfolded her, she'd lost weight. He realised why when he heard his father's voice, calling weakly from the sitting room. Frank Morley was laid in a sort of large perambulator, more like a wooden box bed on wheels. His back really was broken, Jackson realised. His mother had written to say so but somehow he couldn't believe it until now. His dad was such a solid, strong man, had always been so. God damn the pit, he thought, filled with helpless anger.

'I'm all right, son,' Frank said quickly, seeing the horror which Jackson had been too late to disguise. 'An' we've got the house and a bit of compen to live on, dinna fash the'self.'

Compensation? thought Jackson. No amount of money could compensate for what had happened to his dad. But he smiled and bent over him, almost kissed him but stopped himself in time. You didn't kiss men, not unless they were dying. And he knew his father wasn't about to give in just yet. But he was only a third of the weight he had been. The muscles of his arms, which Jackson remembered as being so powerful, were wasted away, his neck scraggy, cheeks fallen in.

'Why, no, man, I didn't think you were ready to pop your clogs yet a while,' was all he said.

'How've you been doing?' his father asked eagerly. 'Maggie, have you got the kettle boiling? I dare wager the lad'll be glad of a proper breakfast now he's home. He likely hasn't had anything worth eating since he went in't army. Hey, a Sergeant are you now? That's grand!'

As the kettle had been kept on the boil for the last couple of hours and bacon and eggs were already on the table ready to cook, Maggie was soon bustling about, smiling broadly but with suspiciously wet eyes. She looked up as she was breaking an egg into the pan as there was a knock at the door and Harry Mason walked in, his kitbag on his shoulder. Her smile became a look of concern. In the excitement of Jackson's homecoming she had forgotten about the Masons and their trouble. Had Harry heard about Molly?

'Harry, lad, howay in,' she said now. 'How would you like some breakfast? I can soon do enough for two.'

'No, thanks, Mrs Morley,' Harry replied. He wasn't hungry, simply bewildered and upset. The story which Ann Pendle had told him couldn't be true, it was quite unbelievable. Maggie saw he was white as a sheet under his tan.

'Sit down, lad, you look all in,' she said swiftly, pulling the pan off the fire and going to him. Her heart sank. Obviously Ann had told him. She only hoped that cat Joan hadn't been in to add her ha'porth of spite.

Harry put down his kitbag and she led him to an armchair by the fire.

'What is it? What?'

Jackson had come back into the kitchen, alarm making his voice sharp. He gazed from his mother to Harry. Something had happened to Molly, he knew it. Oh, he should have tried harder to get home before now. Both of them should have. No one answered him for a moment.

Maggie thrust a mug of hot strong tea into Harry's hand. 'Drink that, lad, go on,' she said, and stood over him until he had taken a few sips. 'Right then, come on now, you'll both eat something. There's nothing to be done this minute, nothing at all. You can get something in your stomachs and we'll talk about it.'

'What? Talk about what?' Jackson demanded, frustrated. Why didn't they tell him?

'Our Molly is in prison,' said Harry. He looked up at his friend. 'Ann Pendle says so any road.'

'In prison? Don't be so flaming daft!'

It was unbelievable, someone was having them on was all Jackson could think.

'It's true. They said she robbed the house where she was lodging. Took a gold bangle.'

'No!' Jackson said flatly. 'That's a lie, Molly wouldn't rob anybody.'

Harry looked up at Mrs Morley who was standing biting her lip, her face red. 'You knew about it?' he said.

'Aye, I did. Everyone did. I didn't see it in the *Echo* but Joan Pendle made sure we knew. She told anybody who would listen.'

'You believed Molly had done it?' asked Jackson, staring at his mother, and her face went redder still, as though she had been caught out in some wrongdoing herself.

'I . . . I didn't know what to think, that's the God's honest truth, son. That fella was a respectable man, like, and they said his neighbour saw it in Molly's suitcase.' She sighed heavily. 'I blame meself, really. I should have made time to go and see the lass. She was on her own like, must have been hard up . . . I don't know. But your dad was so poorly at the time . . .' Her voice trailed away.

'Well, *I* know!' said Jackson. 'An' Harry does an' all. She didn't do it. We'll never believe it, no matter what anybody says.' Without his meaning it to happen, his voice had risen, emphasising his words.

'Hey, lad, you've only been home a minute and you're shouting at your mother. I won't have it!' his father was calling and Jackson subsided immediately.

'Oh, Mam, I'm sorry. I didn't mean to shout at you, you know I didn't.'

'I know. I know, lad. It's all right.' Maggie looked at the food beginning to congeal in the pan. 'Look, eat this afore it spoils. Howay now, we can't waste good food, we'll be short enough of it if the war comes. Harry'll have a bit an' all, won't you, lad? Please, for me. Then we can sit down and decide what's to be done.'

The soldiers sat at the table and ate the food before them though neither of them could have said what it was they were eating. It was just a matter of getting the meal out of the way. Both their minds were working on how they were going to get to see Molly.

Mrs Morley wheeled the ungainly carriage through and

stood it by the side of the table so that Frank could join in the talk.

'Thanks, Maggie,' he murmured. They were quiet until Jackson and Harry had finished the meal and laid down their knives and forks.

'More tea?' asked Maggie but they shook their heads.

'Well then,' said Harry, sounding more normal as the initial shock wore off, 'I think the first thing I've to do is telephone the prison.' There was a murmur of assent from the others.

'I'll come with you,' said Jackson. The nearest telephone was three-quarters of a mile away, by the post office in the next village.

'Mind, I think it was May or June, you know,' said Maggie. 'Joan Pendle said Molly got three months. She might be out by now.'

'What I can't understand is why they put her in gaol when she had a good character? The lass hasn't done a thing wrong in her life, I dare swear she hasn't,' said Frank.

Maggie flushed. 'They said in the Co-op that it was because she had no fixed address,' she said in little more than a whisper. 'I blame myself, I do. I could have let her stay here but she was gone before I had the chance to say. I thought she was all right, honest I did, Harry.'

'I'm sure you had enough on your plate, Mrs Morley. It's not your fault.' A terrible anger was replacing his initial sense of shock, an anger he kept well under control, the only sign being the white line around his lips and the set to his chin. 'Is it all right if I leave my kitbag here, Mrs Morley?'

'Why, lad, you know it is. An' you can stay here an' all, I'll make a shakey down bed up in Jackson's room. Now, I'll have no arguments, that's what you'll do.'

Harry nodded, he had had no intention of arguing. 'Thanks, Mrs Morley.'

The soldiers crossed over the field to Jordan, the next village, taking the path well worn by the miners and their families. At the phone box they both went in, their broad shoulders squashed against the glass. Jackson looked up the number and they scrabbled between them to find the six pennies the operator asked for.

'Who's enquiring?' the male voice at the other end asked.

'Does that matter?' Harry was exasperated. This was wasting time and they had no more change between them.

'We can't give out information –'

'All right, all right! I'm her brother. I've just returned from India and I have to find her,' he shouted down the phone.

'Steady on, Harry,' Jackson murmured. 'Losing your temper isn't going to get us anywhere.'

'If you hang on a minute, I'll look it up. What did you say the name was? And what was she in for?'

'Molly Mason. She was in for theft, though she didn't . . .'

'Right then, here it is. Molly Mason, age eighteen years. Discharged 20th August. You've just missed her, son.' The man was beginning to sound almost human.

'Your time is up, caller. If you want to continue, please put another fourpence in the box,' the operator butted in.

'But where? Where did she go?' shouted Harry.

'Why, home, I should think, wouldn't . . .' But the line was disconnected.

'I'll get some change at the post office,' suggested Jackson as they eased themselves out of the box. 'Or maybe we should just go to West Auckland and see if she's gone there? After all, she might have got her job back.'

'We could ask Ann Pendle first. Or Joan might be home now.'

'Any road, we'll go back and ask around Eden Hope. Tell Mam where we're going too,' Jackson decided, and they set off back across the field. They walked in silence, each man's thoughts on the young girl and what had happened to her. What might still happen to her if they didn't find her and help her put her life back together. For both of them knew what it could be like for anyone coming out of prison into the small enclosed mining communities. Molly could be in for a rough ride.

Chapter Ten

Jackson and Harry were on the Eden bus bound for West Auckland by one o'clock that afternoon. They could have gone through Bishop Auckland, changing buses in the town, but Mrs Morley advised them to go on the Eden. 'You won't have to change,' she said. 'It'll likely be quicker.' She couldn't do enough to help them, she felt so guilty over Molly. She could have got someone to sit with Frank when the lass was up before the magistrate; she could have gone and backed her up, told the chairman what a good lass Molly had always been. Aye, she said to herself, she could have done. But her thoughts had been centred on her husband, on his pain and looking after him night and day. She had been so tired those first few months after the accident.

'Bring her back with you, Jackson,' she said as the two soldiers went out. 'Bring her back, she can stay with us, I'll find space for her.'

He gazed at his mother for a long moment but it would be cruel to tell her she could have taken Molly in before now, and probably asking too much of her anyway. Maggie looked so careworn, he knew he was being unreasonable even to think it.

The bus passed the old coach house at Shildon which had been the very first railway ticket office in the world, a fact which always gave him a thrill of pride. But today he only wondered where Molly was. Was she in trouble? A nagging anxiety about her had grown inside him ever since he'd heard she had been in prison, innocent, and alone. For he had no doubt at all that she was innocent, he was as sure of that as Harry. But where was she?

At that moment Molly was walking down Newgate Street in Bishop Auckland after leaving the small damp room down by the Wear where she had been living since she came out of prison. She was on her way to the Labour Exchange where she went every morning searching for work. The money from the colliery, the £25 which she had received after her father's accident, had run out, careful though she'd been, eating only one meal a day and that as frugal as she could possibly exist upon. Now she *had* to get work, had to!

She rounded the corner into South Church Road and then again into Kingsway. The bus was just coming in from Eden Hope. She paused for a moment and gazed at it. It came from another world, it seemed to her, the world of her childhood where, even when the depression was at its height, she had felt safe because there was her dad and her mam and Harry.

The bus pulled up, people alighting, Molly hunched her shoulders and bent her head. Oh, she didn't want them to see her, no, she did not!

'Isn't that Molly Mason over there on Kingsway?' a housewife asked her friend. They were off to the store, the Co-op, to see if they could find any tinned food they could afford to buy to stock up against the threat of war, for everyone said there would likely be rationing.

'Is it?' her friend replied, looking, but Molly was gone. 'I felt sorry for that lass all right,' she went on. 'I would have offered her a place wi' me, but she was away afore I had the chance.'

'Aye. Do you know, I saw their Harry in the street the day. A fine upstanding lad he's grown into an' all. I wonder if she knows he's back?'

'Well, we can't go chasing after her. She must know, surely? But if she doesn't, no doubt she'll soon find out. Howay then, there'll likely be a crowd in the store.' And the two women bustled off into Newgate Street.

'There'll be more chance of work for you shortly, especially if the war does come,' the clerk in the Labour Exchange said to Molly. 'Nothing at present.' He looked over her shoulder at the queue: shabby, down at heel, depressing. 'Take this chit over to the cash desk for your money.'

'But I must get something!' she said, desperation making her tone sharp. 'I can't live on the dole, it's not enough.'

'Well, it's all you're going to get,' the clerk said wearily. 'Next, please.'

Already the next person in line was moving forward, nudging Molly out of the way. She took her chit and went over to the cash desk. Eight shillings and sixpence. It barely covered her rent. Out on Kingsway once again, she stood for a moment irresolute. She had tried all the shops in the town the day before, there was nothing there. Lingford's the baking powder factory, too. They had vacancies but when they'd asked where she had been working last and where her references were Molly had backed away. 'Excuse me,' she had said. 'I must go, I . . . I forgot . . .' She'd left the manager looking after her in astonishment. Did she want work or not?

'I'll walk to West Auckland, St Helens at least,' she said aloud.

'Eh? What did you say?' A man was turning into the Labour Exchange. He paused and stared at her.

'Nothing, sorry, just talking to myself,' replied Molly, blushing.

'Aye, well, pet, it's when you begin to answer back that you have to worry,' he said, grinning. He was an older man. His shirt collar was clean but threadbare, his suit shiny with age. His grin slipped a little as he looked into her face, saw the shadows under her eyes, how thin she was.

'Are you all right, pet?'

It was the first time anyone had spoken to her with any

sort of concern for such a long time that her eyes filled and
she had to turn away in case he saw it. 'I'm fine, really,'
she mumbled, and fled down Kingsway and round the
corner into South Church Road.

It was a fine day at least, she thought, as she got her
emotions under control and strode out for West Auckland.
She paused at a butcher's shop in Cockton Hill and bought
a penny dip, a bread bun dipped in the juices from roasted
meat. Once away from the houses and on the open road
she stopped at a stile and sat down to eat it. She had to
force herself to take it slowly, savouring every bite. She
had been so hungry she had felt sick with it, and light-
headed too. She sat for a short while until the food made
her feel better before resuming her journey. She was
approaching Tindale Crescent, close to the factories which
had been built on the site of an old colliery. Not far to go
now. The sun was warm on her face, her spirits lifted.
Perhaps Mr Bolton would give her her job back? After all,
the factory was working full pelt, she knew that, turning
out khaki uniforms for the troops.

Molly was hot and dusty by the time she reached the
factory. She hesitated at the gate, her heart thumping in her
breast as she tried to raise the courage to go in. It had been
one thing thinking about it but now she was actually here
. . . She lifted her chin and went into the reception area.

'Molly Mason!' exclaimed the girl behind the desk.
'By, I never expected to see you.'

'Hello, Alice.' The receptionist hadn't been hostile,

merely surprised, and Molly felt slightly better. 'I'd like to see Mr Bolton, if I may?'

He kept her waiting for half an hour before calling her into his office.

'I suppose you want your job back,' he said with no preamble. He sat back in his chair and stared at her, no expression on his face.

'I would, yes,' said Molly in a small voice. She looked down at her clenched hands. He wasn't going to give her work, she could tell by his attitude. By, she wished she hadn't come back, wished she were anywhere but here.

'I don't know if it would be wise to take you on again.'

'But I'm a good worker, you know I am, I always kept my production up!'

'Aye, I know that. I wouldn't be seeing you otherwise.' He drummed his fingers on the desk, the first and second stained brown with nicotine. She was a bonny lass, he thought, and wondered if there had been hanky-panky in that house when she was alone with her landlord. Maybe he had given her the bangle for favours received and then said she'd stolen it when she would no longer perform.

Molly rose to her feet. 'Well, if you don't want me, I'll be on my way,' she said. She had had enough humiliation, she wasn't going to beg him, not Bolton.

'Hold your horses, woman, I never said I didn't want you.'

Molly paused on her way to the door and looked back at him.

'Where would you live if I did take you back?' he asked. 'No one round here would have you, I'm certain of that.'

'I have a room in Bishop,' said Molly. She was so filled with a mixture of embarrassment and humiliation, she could hardly see straight.

Mr Bolton studied her for a moment. A bonny lass she was. There was no doubt she was a good worker, had always earned her bonuses in the past. And he didn't think the other workers would care that she had been in prison. At least most of them would not. And what would it matter if they did? None of them would want to lose their job. There was the added advantage that she would probably work harder than anyone to prove herself, and keep her head down too. She was just the sort of experienced machinist he needed to fill the government orders. He came to a decision.

'Righto. You can start tomorrow. But mind, you'll have to keep yourself out of trouble.' He stood up and came round the desk to pat her on the shoulder, a move which caused her to jump and back towards the door.

'Thank you, Mr Bolton,' she managed to say, her cheeks flushed yet again. 'I'll be here at eight o'clock.'

Outside she took a deep breath of air, laden with the scent of new-mown grass where the gardener was trimming the lawn in front of the building. She couldn't believe her luck in being taken on again at the factory, had shrunk initially from trying there where she was known.

But now she felt as though a load had rolled off her shoulders. She would be able to keep herself, no more hated dole office.

The afternoon sun was shining along Manor Road. She walked along in the opposite direction to Bishop Auckland with a fancy to see the house in West Auckland where she would have been living now if it weren't for Mr Jones. She felt the familiar twinge of hatred and despair as she thought of him but put it firmly from her mind. This was turning into a good day, the best for ages, and she wasn't going to spoil it. She walked past the entrance to Adelaide Street without even looking down it.

Cathy's house was still there, its windows dusty in the sun. She wondered about her. What had she thought when she'd heard about Molly? That she'd had a lucky escape, could have had a thief in the house? As Molly watched the house from across the street the little boy, Jimmy, came out and picked up the bicycle which had been laid down on the cobbles. He glanced across at Molly and she smiled tentatively but he simply looked at her and pedalled off along the street. Of course, she thought sadly, he had only met her for a few minutes that night.

So had Cathy. Molly had thought of knocking at the door, maybe apologising for not being able to take up the room, telling her the true story. But no, Cathy didn't know her either, it might just embarrass her. Molly walked back the way she had come with a sense of loss which dimmed the happiness of getting her job back.

Next day as she went into work it felt as though she had hardly been away, at least for the first few minutes. She was anxious and therefore earlier than the other girls who worked on the line. Enid was there, though. She said nothing, just allotted Molly a machine. She hung up her coat on the rack in the cloakroom, put her bag with her sandwich box in the small space by the side and waited for the electricity to be switched on. Her machine was at the far end of the line now. When the other girls came in she was sitting with her back to them.

'Well! Will you look what the cat's brought in?' the hated voice exclaimed, the voice she had been dreading ever since Mr Bolton had told her she had got the job. Joan's.

'It's the little sneak thief!'

Molly cringed. She wanted to curl up and die. She concentrated hard on threading her machine needle. The other girls fell quiet. One sniggered in embarrassment.

'That's enough of that! I'll hear no more of that or whoever it is they'll be out on their ear. Now get on with your work.'

Mr Bolton was standing in the doorway. The girls hurriedly sat down at their places on the band, the electricity began humming, the machines zipped away and the wireless came on: Fred Astaire singing 'Dancing Cheek to Cheek'.

Molly felt grateful to Mr Bolton even though she knew he hadn't said it to protect her but to ensure the work went on smoothly. She concentrated on her sewing. She was stitching the bands on battledress jackets, more interesting than sideseams and more complicated too. But Molly soon got the hang of it.

At dinnertime she took her sandwiches outside and sat on the low wall which bounded the factory. The sun was shining and the air felt fresh after the stuffiness and lint-laden atmosphere of the machine room. There were a number of girls doing the same thing. Some of them were laughing and flirting with the male cutters and pressers, Joan Pendle among them. She was smoking a Woodbine, holding it up in the air and gesturing with it, her elbow cupped in her other hand. Molly took care not to catch anyone's eye but looked down at her sandwiches and the apple she had bought on the way to the bus.

There was a burst of laughter from the group of men and girls on the corner, Joan's laughter ringing out over the others'. Involuntarily, Molly glanced quickly over at them to find they were looking back at her and grinning. Joan's expression was pure malice, she thought, flinching. Molly took a bite of fish paste sandwich and chewed doggedly but somehow it refused to go down for ages and when it did she almost choked, coughing and spluttering.

'Get yourself a cup of tea, lass,' one of the men said. He was older, about forty, with kindly eyes.

Joan's jeering voice rang out. 'Don't tell me you're taken in by her big brown eyes an' all, Tom?' She looked round the group, inviting the others to laugh with her.

'Don't be so bloody soft!' he growled, and turned his back on Molly.

She put the remains of her sandwich back in her box and went inside, not to the canteen but to the cloakroom where she got a drink of water from the tap. After all, a cup of tea cost tuppence and she couldn't afford to waste money like that.

All in all, she reflected on her way home at six o'clock that evening, it hadn't been so bad. While she was working on the machine no one had bothered her. Enid had taken the sewn pieces away and left her fresh batches, not speaking to her while she did. But then, Enid was busy. They all were. Only one or two girls actually spoke to her but it was difficult what with the wireless being on and her being at the end of the line. Things would get better, she thought, surely they would? If it wasn't for Joan Pendle . . .

She had a potato to bake for her tea and a piece of hard cheese she'd picked up cheap at the store to grate over it. She washed the potato and put it in the ancient coal oven in the basement of the tumbledown old house which she shared with half a dozen other people down on their luck. While she waited Molly toasted her feet at the fire, glad to be able just to relax. No one was going to make snide remarks here. The fact that she had been in prison wasn't so remarkable in this house; she wasn't the only one.

Sitting in the rickety armchair Molly began to doze, what with her tiredness and the heat from the fire. She awoke with a start when a door banged somewhere in the house and a draught blew in under the kitchen door. Disorientated, she looked round apprehensively, thinking she was still in prison. The horror of that first night was still with her. The loneliness, the feeling of being abandoned by God and everyone else.

She could never go through that again, she told herself. Harry, where are you? Jackson, help me! She was still caught up in the dream she had been having. She saw Jackson running towards her and she was trying to run to him but somehow they never drew any closer no matter how fast they ran. The wall of the prison loomed between them suddenly. She sobbed. It was hopeless. And Harry, Harry was calling to her over Jackson's shoulder, calling her name . . .

Molly woke up properly. She could smell the potato now, it must be ready. Her heart still beat fast and her head throbbed but she was awake and no longer behind the prison wall. She took the cloth which was singed brown with oven marks from the line under the mantelshelf and retrieved the potato from the oven. She was hungry, that was all that was the matter. She cut the potato and grated the cheese on to it and ate. She would feel better when she had her stomach full, she told herself.

She missed the old relationships she had had with her workmates. Though she hadn't been close friends with any of them at least she had felt part of the crowd. Now she was excluded, she thought sadly. But given time, and if

Joan Pendle didn't stir things up too much, she would be accepted again.

Climbing into bed in her damp little room in the basement, she said a prayer for Harry and, of course, Jackson. She had grown used to thinking of them together. She wondered where they were now, yearned to see them. She felt so lonely. She hadn't written to either of them for months, had been unable to bring herself to while she was in that awful place. She was ashamed to, shrank from letting them know what had happened to her, felt degraded somehow.

At first she had been confident that Harry would believe her, Jackson too, surely they both would? But now she had doubts. Had Jackson's mother written to him, told him of the scandal?

Perhaps she had. Maybe that was why Molly hadn't heard from them. Perhaps even they didn't want to know her now. Restlessly she turned over in bed, trying to find a comfortable spot on the lumpy mattress. She must get some sleep. She had to catch the seven-thirty bus in the morning – couldn't afford to miss it. If she lost her job again she didn't know what she would do.

Most of the time Molly couldn't bear to think about what it was like in prison but tonight the memories wouldn't go away. Why were people so hard, so spitefully cruel? It wasn't just the wardresses, who were only doing their job, she supposed. The other women were worse, some of them at least. And then there was Bertha. Oh God,

Bertha! She'd had to share a cell with Bertha. Only for one night but that had been enough. Molly had really reached rock bottom that night. She had fallen asleep from sheer exhaustion and when she woke it was like the night when Bart had put his slimy hands on her. Only this time it was a woman, Bertha.

Molly shuddered, tried desperately to think of something else, anything else. She jumped out of bed and walked the floor, backwards and forwards. Her skin crawled. She could still feel Bertha's hands on her, hear that voice whispering obscenities in her ear. Things she had never heard before, couldn't even comprehend.

Slowly, painfully slowly, Molly regained control of her thoughts, forced herself to push the memories out of her mind. Eventually numbness crept over her, brought on by extreme exhaustion. It allowed her to go back to bed and at last she slept.

Chapter Eleven

'You've both been called back, lads,' said Mrs Morley as they walked into the kitchen. Her voice wobbled slightly with disappointment and apprehension at what was to come.

'What? You must be joking!' cried Jackson, unbelieving.

'No, your mother's not having you on,' his father said, his voice coming through the door from the room beyond. 'It's come over the wireless. All troops to return to barracks. There's a telegram an' all.'

Jackson slumped into a chair, despair rising in him. They were so close to Molly, he knew they were. In another couple of days they would surely find her.

'What are we going to do, Jackson?' asked Harry. He too sounded thoroughly dispirited. But his question was rhetorical. He knew they had to go back to camp. War was coming nearer all the time and they were in the regular army. Jackson didn't even bother to answer, he knew too.

'Have you got any news of the lass?' asked Maggie, as

she had asked every evening when they'd come in from searching the area for Molly.

'Oh, aye, we have,' said Harry. 'We know she started work back at the clothing factory three or four days ago. Worked the first two days then didn't go back.'

'Harry! You asked at the factory three days ago, or Jackson said you did any road.'

'Yes,' said Jackson. 'Evidently we asked only an hour before she was set on. I tell you what, Mam, anyone would think we weren't meant to find her. We seem to keep missing her all the time.'

Maggie sighed. 'Well, howay, lads,' she said, taking the oven cloth from the line. 'Come and eat your dinner. I've made a nice steak pie. I reckon we won't be getting a lot more of them if the war comes what with rationing an' all.'

She served the pie, rich with onion gravy and succulent steak, which had cost more than she usually spent on meat in a week. There were mashed potatoes and vegetables from the garden, the pie crust was thick and savoury, and the men tucked in with a will in spite of their anxiety over Molly, a feeling which worsened as the days went on.

Today they had become desperate enough to knock on doors at random in West Auckland. And they thought their luck was getting better when one woman had said yes, she had seen her.

'Come after the attic room,' she had said. 'A nice lass

an' all, I thought, though that's not what folk said about her, not when she was sent down for thieving. I didn't think she looked the type at all. I was looking forward to having her living here but she never came back. I would have took her in an' all, I don't care what other folk think or say.' Cathy looked speculatively at the two soldiers. 'You her brothers, are you?'

'I am,' said Harry. 'This is my friend, we're both from Eden Hope. Molly didn't do it, you know. She wouldn't, she's an honest girl. Look, if you see or hear from her, will you let us know? This is Jackson's mother's address.' He handed her an envelope, addressed and stamped.

Cathy took the envelope and studied it for a second or two.

'I'll do that,' she said. She bit her lip and hesitated before going on: 'I know that Bart Jones – he's a flaming hypocrite, always was! They chucked him out of the Chapel once, some goings on they hushed up. Now *that* never got told to the magistrates. His own daughter went about like a timid mouse before she went into the sanatorium up Weardale. But there's no justice, is there?'

The men nodded in agreement. They were both silent at first as they walked on to the bus stop. There was no point in knocking on any more doors and it was almost tea-time.

Jackson couldn't bear to speak, in fact, his emotions were so mixed. Anger that the magistrates had taken the word of Bart Jones against a girl like Molly, frustration that yet another day of their leave had gone and they were no nearer to finding her. Worst of all was the anxiety of wondering where she was, if she was all right, always hoping nothing had happened to her.

Now they had to go back to camp without finding her. The order said immediately which meant the overnight train to King's Cross where they would get their connection. Suddenly he'd had enough of his mother's steak pie and pushed his plate away.

'Now then, lad. You have to eat, keep your strength up. Don't you go wasting good food, not after all the years we were short during the slump.'

With an effort he managed to clear his plate. Leaving food was indeed a sin in Eden Hope. And then the two friends had to pack their kitbags and go dashing through the wood to the station at Bishop Auckland, to catch the train by the skin of their teeth.

'I'll watch out for Molly, I will, son, I promise,' Mrs Morley called down the street after them. She stood gazing after them long after they had turned the corner.

'You've had the lad home on leave then?'

Turning, she saw Ann Pendle coming towards her and was just in the mood to give her a piece of her mind.

'Aye, I have,' snapped Maggie. 'The both of them. Not that we saw much of them, mind, they've been out looking for young Molly most of the time. I blame your Joan for most of it an'all, the spiteful little cat!'

'Well! How could it be Joan's fault, eh? *She* never pinched anything.'

'No, and neither did Molly Mason. You should be ashamed, Ann Pendle, an' you her mother's best friend. Your Joan spreading lies about her, just because she was jilted by Harry. If you ask me, he had a lucky escape there!'

'By, you have a flaming nerve, talking like that about my lass! I'll have you know –'

But what she was going to let Maggie know was lost as that lady stalked up her yard and went into the house, slamming the door behind her.

At Darlington, Harry and Jackson found the train full of soldiers returning to barracks and had to settle down on their kitbags in the corridor. Neither of them caring much about it, they sat there and stared at the floor or their boots, occasionally standing to stretch their legs and staring out of the window at the darkening landscape. Jackson lifted his eyes to see Harry, a Woodbine in his fingers, the ash on the end growing longer and longer as he forgot about it. Jackson got to his feet and stood beside him.

'We did all we could,' he said.

'An' not very much, was it?'

'No.' Jackson spoke heavily, feeling defeated.

The train was slowing down as it came into York station. It was crowded with men in uniform and women seeing them off but Jackson stared out unseeingly.

They had gone to Adelaide Street, found the house where Bart Jones lived, but there'd been no one in. The man next door had come out, angry at being woken.

'Can you not let a man sleep when he's on night shift?' he had snarled.

'Sorry, mate,' said Jackson. 'I wonder, though, now you're awake, when does Mr Jones get in from work?'

'He'll be here any minute,' the neighbour had replied. 'Ah, look, here he is now. Now if you don't mind . . .' He went inside and closed the door behind him.

'Yes?' Bart Jones had asked, his head cocked to one side. 'Are you looking for me?'

'We are if you're the man Molly Mason used to lodge with,' said Harry. 'We want to know where she is.'

Bart's demeanour changed. He looked about him before gesturing them closer. 'Aye, I am,' he said. 'An' a sorry day it was too when I let her into my house. Stole from me, she did.'

'You're a liar!' Harry had suddenly yelled at him, and Bart Jones visibly paled and jumped away from the two soldiers. 'My sister never stole a penny in her life! She's just a young lass, brought up right an' all, she wouldn't steal anything.'

'Harry, calm down,' Jackson had cautioned, though his own blood was boiling.

'Aye, you tell him, coming here, threatening a poor chap like me. I've got a bad leg, let me tell you, and if you go

for me I'll have the polis on you, I will!' As if he had been
summoned, a policeman appeared at the top of the street.
'Constable Horton! Constable!' Bart Jones yelled, suddenly sounding more confident. 'These soldiers are
threatening me!'

'What's all the commotion?'

The policeman was middle-aged and portly. He walked
slowly up to them and frowned at the soldiers.

'It's about that young lass what stole from me. You
know, the one who got sent to prison. They want to know
where she is. I'm sure I don't know, I don't want anything
to do with the likes of her again.' Bart sniffed and pursed
his lips in disdain.

'He was saying things about my sister,' said Harry, his
fingers itching to squeeze Bart's throat.

'An' you threatened me! I have a good mind to lay you
in, threatening innocent citizens . . .'

Jackson took a step towards Bart and he hurriedly
backed into the house, ready to close the door on him.

'Aye, well, I'm sure it was in the heat of the minute. We
don't want to be putting our soldier lads in gaol, do we?
Not just now, we might need them,' said the constable
mildly. 'Howay then, lads, time to be away, I think.' He
gave them a friendly nod.

'Aw, come on, Jackson,' said Harry. 'We're going to get
nowt out of him, the dirty little bugger. I suspect he was
sniffing up our Molly's skirts and when she turned him
down . . .'

'I didn't! I never did!' shouted Bart Jones, his head peeping out from behind the door.

'Never mind that,' said the constable. 'Inside wi' you now. An' you two, away wi' you.'

And Jackson and Harry had turned on their heel and marched up the street.

'I didn't expect to find out anything from him any road,' said Harry. 'I just wanted to see the man who put the lass in prison.'

'Aye,' Jackson agreed. 'I think you hit the nail on the head too. That was likely the way it happened, he'll have made up to her.'

'Aye.'

They lapsed into silence. Jackson was thinking of Bart Jones with his hands on Molly and his skin crawled. There were plenty of Bart Joneses out there, ready to take advantage of young girls. Pray God nothing more happened to her before they found her.

He sat down on his kitbag and leaned his head and shoulders against the side of the train. He closed his eyes, unable to get out of his mind a picture of Molly, frightened, at the mercy of men like Bart Jones. Or else in gaol, trying not to show how humiliated she was. For she would have been humiliated. Molly was a proud girl. Even as a little 'un she'd held her head high like a queen.

The train was steaming into Peterborough when on impulse he got to his feet and worked his way to the door through the crowds already on the train and the crowds beginning to get on, most of them soldiers with kitbags.

'Watch it, Sergeant!' a voice protested as he pushed his way out, bumping into a sailor and knocking the kitbag from his shoulder.

'Sorry,' Jackson muttered and jumped down from the train.

'Jackson!' Harry was shouting through the open window of the carriage.

'You go on, Harry,' he shouted back. 'I'll be there in a couple of days. Nothing will happen before then but there's no need for two of us to get into bother. With a bit of luck, I'll find her.'

His last words were lost as the whistle blew and the London train chugged out of the station. Jackson ran over to the opposite platform and jumped on the train standing there, this one half empty. He couldn't just go away like that, war or no war. He had to have another try at finding her.

Molly woke in black darkness. For a moment she thought herself back in prison and fear of the morning overwhelmed her before her mind cleared of nightmares and she sat up in bed. There was the sound of water. Rain was drumming against the small window at the top of the basement wall. There was more, though, not just raindrops. Water was lapping against something, it sounded close. She got out of bed, putting her feet directly into her shoes for the floor was of stone slabs and bitterly cold even at this time of the year. Groping her way over to the light switch, she slipped and almost fell. She was treading in water!

The light came on briefly and went off with a crackle. She had to find the mantelshelf and the candle and matches she kept there, for the electricity here was always going off. The hem of her nightie was wet, she realised, it flapped coldly about her legs. Something else brushed against her legs, something furry. She felt a scream rise up from her throat and forced it down again.

Her fingers closed around the box of matches. She fumbled to open it, almost dropped it, managed at last to take out a match and strike it to light the candle. Lifting it high, she gazed around the room: the dank walls, the steps leading up to the ground floor of the old house, the door with the bottom rotted away and a hole as big as a fist. Water was running down towards her.

Molly jumped on to the bed in a panic as she saw two, no, four, rats thrashing in the water, one of them actually swimming. For a moment she stood on the bed, frozen into stillness, then her brain began working again. She jumped down and grabbed her coat from the hook on the back of the door, lifting the latch.

The door swung open with the force of the water; the passage outside was completely covered. There was no sound but for the rushing of the water, the drumming of the rain, and from a room upstairs a man snoring, oblivious to it all.

'Get up! Get up! The place is flooded!' Molly shouted at the top of her voice. No one answered. She climbed up the stairs and shouted again, 'There's a flood! Wake up – wake up, all of you!'

'What the hell's all that noise?' a man's voice shouted, the landlord's voice it was. 'Has Hitler invaded or what?'

'There's a flood,' cried Molly, 'the river must be up!'

'Aye, well, it does that now an' again down here,' the voice said. 'I'm going back to bed. It won't reach me up here. We'll deal with it in the morning.'

'But what about me?' she screamed.

'Oh, aye, you're in the basement, aren't you? Well, you'll just have to sit it out at the top of the stairs. I'm away back to bed, I have work the morn.'

Molly stared after him as he went back into his bedroom. She heard the springs creak as he got back into bed. Then she ran up and knocked on his door in total disbelief.

'What about me, I said? What about me? I pay my rent!'

'Aye, well, there's nowt to be done about the Wear. I'm not Moses, I can't hold back the waters,' he replied. The bedsprings creaked again, the door opened and he threw out a blanket and pillow. 'I told you, bed down on the landing, will you? And don't disturb me again.'

Someone shouted from the floor above. 'It's all right, go back to sleep!' the landlord shouted back, and closed his door.

Molly stared at the blanket and pillow, neither of them too clean. Then she rushed back down the stairs. The water in the basement was up to the level of her mattress. She waded in and grabbed her underclothes and skirt and jumper, wet though they were. Her teeth clenched against screams as more furry bodies brushed against her. She waded to the chest of drawers and took out her spare underclothes, all wet, and took them up the stairs to the dry landing. As an afterthought she went back for the marble clock which had come from Eden Hope.

Shivering, she lay down on a strip of carpet on the landing, pulling the blanket over her. Her mind was numb. She was past worrying about anything, even managed to doze a little. When she awoke, the light of morning was creeping on to the landing from an open bedroom door. The rain had stopped. Someone was moving about downstairs. Molly stood up, pulling the blanket round her.

'You can give us a hand here, if you like,' said the landlord. He had a yardbroom in his hand. As she watched he opened the front door and began sweeping water out. It cascaded over the steps, brown river water, dark with peat and full of debris. The rats had disappeared or perhaps were still in the basement.

The grass in front of the house was bedraggled and sodden, bits of debris caught in patches of nettles and ground elder.

'We get flash floods like that every time it rains up the

dale,' the landlord said, making conversation. 'It soon goes down, though. But mebbe you should look somewhere else for lodging. The basement will be flooded for days now. I knew I shouldn't have let it.'

Chapter Twelve

'Just get out of here, will you?' Mr Bolton said. Molly gazed at him. His face was as hard as nails, she realised. He obviously wasn't going to change his mind.

'But it wasn't my fault! I've told you, we had a flood,' she protested. What was she going to do? She had had to spend the last of her reserve money to buy a second-hand dress and jacket on the market, she'd had nothing dry. She had got to the factory as soon as she possibly could and only to be given the sack. And at the back of her mind was the ever-present fear that she would not find any place to stay tonight, and she couldn't stay out on the street, could she?

'Aye. You'll tell me anything but your prayers, won't you?' Mr Bolton said. He picked up some papers from his desk and flipped through them. 'Go on now. I told you, I don't want you back. I'll say nothing about it, that's fair enough, isn't it? I'll even give you a reference if that'll get rid of you.'

Molly gave up. She might as well save her breath, he wasn't going to believe anything she said anyway. She felt utterly defeated. 'All right, I'll go,' she mumbled.

'Hang on,' said Mr Bolton. He picked up a piece of
headed notepaper and wrote on it, slipped it in an envelope
and handed it to her. 'Mind, you're lucky I'm doing this,
do you realise? I told you, didn't I? Just one slip and you're
out.' It was a pity, he thought, she was a tasty piece. Maybe
if he'd kept her on . . . No, it was tempting but better leave
it alone, that way only trouble lay. Molly Mason was bad
news. Look at that fellow in Adelaide Street . . .

Outside Molly took the sheet of paper from the
envelope.

'*Miss Mason proved to be a good and efficient worker,*'
it said. What good was that? Any prospective employer
would wonder why, if she was so good at her job, she had
lost it. Putting the reference away in her bag she walked
out on to the street, hesitating over which way to turn. She
was drawn towards West Auckland where the only woman
to give her a kind word in recent months lived. She
wondered whether Cathy's attic bedroom was still for rent.
No, it would have been snapped up months ago. Sadly
Molly turned in the opposite direction.

The Eden bus passed her, making her think of Eden
Hope. She felt a sharp longing for her home village, the
rows, the Chapel, the colliery winding wheel and chimney
towering over everything. Even the slag heap where, in the
depression, miners who were out of work had searched for
small coal. The bad old days had turned out to be the good
old days for her.

She had to stop thinking about it, she told herself, setting her face for Bishop Auckland and the Labour Exchange. She would walk the couple of miles, it was a nice day and anyway she couldn't afford the bus fare.

In spite of her troubles her spirits lifted a little. The sun was shining. A group of pit ponies galloped about in the field by the side of the road. Their pit must be on holiday, she thought. They jumped and kicked up their sturdy hind legs in play, charged playfully then stood and blew gently on each other's necks. Little ponies, Shetlands, for the seams in the South-West Durham coal field were small.

Molly thought sadly of the contrast between their lives in the pits and what they would have been on the islands. She tried to rub the nose of one who came close but it backed away, no doubt fearful it would be caught and taken back down under the ground.

Fanciful, she thought, that was what she was, too fanciful. Her dad had always said so. Molly walked on, to the old road which had first been built by the Romans and led straight as a die to the centre of the town.

'They want girls at the Royal Ordnance Factory,' the man behind the counter at the Labour Exchange said. He gazed disapprovingly at her. 'I don't know, you don't seem to be capable of keeping a job, do you?' he commented.

Molly lifted her chin and stared back at him. Little tin gods, her dad had called the men at the dole office.

Thought they were better than most just because they had
good jobs.

'Was it my fault there was a flash flood on the Wear?
I'm supposed to go to work in wet clothes, am I?'

Something about her direct gaze, the glint of defiance
in her eyes, made him smile in spite of himself. Here was
a lass who had been through the mill. He knew her history,
it was all down on her file. And even if she had done
wrong, she had had an awful lot of provocation it was true.
He struggled but couldn't help softening his tone.

'Well, we'll say no more about the past,' he said. 'Now,
about this job at the Royal Ordnance Factory.'

Molly fairly danced down the stairs of the Labour
Exchange, the precious paper which she was to present to
the manager of the factory clutched in her hand. Workers
at the munitions factory were well paid. She could make
thirty shillings a week, maybe more. She would be able to
afford a nice room somewhere fresh. It was a new
beginning for her, she knew it in her bones, the bad times
were past. Hope sprang up in her, she fairly bubbled with
it, smiling brightly and standing aside to let a bent old
miner go past. The factory would take her on, she thought.
They must be going full pelt now, what with the war
coming and everything. Not that she wanted the war to
come, not when Harry and Jackson were in the army . . .

'Jackson!'

As if by magic, as if he had been conjured up by her
thoughts, there, in the bright sunlight, was Jackson

Morley, just turning into the entrance of the Labour Exchange.

They both stopped dead in their tracks. Molly blinked. After the comparative darkness of the stairs and entrance the sunlight was blinding. Perhaps it wasn't him, maybe she was fooled because she'd wanted it to be so much. She closed her eyes and wished.

'Molly.'

Jackson sighed, stepped forward, took her in his arms. He was hungry for the feel of her, couldn't believe that after all their efforts in the last few days he had actually found her by accident. He was filled with a profound sense of thankfulness. They stood quietly in the doorway, holding each other. Molly was drowning in the sweetness of the moment. After all that had happened, all the longing, here was Jackson. She clung to him as though he might disappear into thin air if she let go of him.

'Howay then, put her down, man, there's a time and a place for that sort of thing,' a man's gruff voice said. 'Come on, let a bloke in. You're blocking the doorway, man!'

'Sorry, mate.'

Jackson drew Molly outside. They stood to one side, her face radiant, eyes glazed with happiness. She looked about her eagerly.

'Where's Harry? He's not hiding, is he?'

Harry had often teased her when they were small. He

would hide behind a bush or the furniture, jumping out at her when she least expected it.

'He's not here, he . . . he had to go back to barracks,' said Jackson, a shadow falling across his face. So the welcome hadn't all been for him, he thought with a sense of loss as he saw the disappointment on her face.

'Without coming to see me? You mean, he was here and he didn't come to see me?'

Molly couldn't believe it, Harry had been here and she had missed him. She looked up at Jackson, her brown eyes wide, waiting for him to tell her why.

'We didn't know where you were. We were looking for you, we only had a few days.'

'But I wrote to him – I wrote twice.'

That had been an age ago, before she went into *that* place. As usual she couldn't even think of prison, her mind shied away from it. She hadn't written since, she'd been too ashamed.

'Look, come into Rossi's, we'll have a cup of tea and talk about it.'

They walked down to South Church Road, turned the corner back into Newgate Street and went into Rossi's ice-cream and coffee shop. It was practically empty at that time of day. They took the booth furthest away from the counter so that they could talk in peace. Of course Molly was disappointed because her brother wasn't here, Jackson chided himself, she hadn't seen him for years and in the meantime she had lost her father in the pit. She was only a child when they went away, of course she was, she couldn't have been so excited just to see her brother's friend. That was it, he was her brother's friend. He'd been a fool to believe she thought any more of him. Still, now she was older . . . and so bonny, he mused as he stirred sugar into his tea.

'I'm that glad to see you,' Molly said simply, and his spirits lifted. She smiled at him. His face was lit up by a beam of light coming in from the high window. By, he was like Harry, yet different too. The same colouring, the same dark eyes, but Jackson had a look of his dad, that was it. But the two lads could have been brothers, she mused.

'Seen enough?' he asked softly, and Molly blushed and looked down at her tea. She took a sip. Ugh! You could tell Mr Rossi was Italian, his tea tasted funny.

'Tell me what happened, Molly?' said Jackson, and her heart dropped into her shoes. She didn't want to have to tell him, not Jackson, it was so humiliating. Maybe he wouldn't believe her.

'You can tell me, Molly. I already know some of it. We asked about in St Helens and West Auckland. You poor kid, what was it like in that place?'

He meant prison, she realised, and her mind closed up as it always did when she thought about it. Oh, she would never tell anyone what it had been like! No, she would not.

He put a hand across the table and took hers. She stared down at their two hands, his so brown, hers white.

'Tell me, Molly?'

'I got a place in St Helens when I had to leave the house,' Molly began, her tone expressionless. 'It was cheap at Bart Jones's and I couldn't afford any more.' She paused and he waited quietly. 'It was all right when his daughter was there. Betty was a nice kid, we got on. But she had to go to the sanatorium, she got TB. And then he began to pester me.'

'Don't go on if you don't want to, I can imagine the rest.' Jackson's grip on her hand tightened. It was firm and comforting. 'Why didn't you go to my mother's when you had to leave your place? She would have taken you in, I know.'

'I didn't like to ask. Not when she had your dad the way he is.'

'But you should have gone back. The folk at Eden Hope would have helped you. Anyone who had known you all your life would know you couldn't have stolen anything.'

Molly thought about Joan Pendle. She would have told the tale *her* way, poison dripping from every word, oh, yes, Molly was sure of that. She stared at Jackson and sighed. 'I was ashamed,' she said simply. She drained her cup and got to her feet. 'Now I have to go after this job, I can't afford not to.'

'But Harry was arranging to make you an allowance out of his pay, if he'd only had your address . . . Come home with me, I'm sure Mam will welcome you with open arms. She's been worried about you an' all.'

'No, I can't do that. Not yet. Not until I have a job and can make something of myself.'

'Well then, come on, I'll go with you. You'll get that job and I'll help you find a room. Where is it you're going?'

'The munitions factory.'

'The train then, that'll be the fastest way.'

They walked up to the station, caught the Darlington train and settled into a shabby compartment. Jackson held her hand like a lover and it felt so good to have someone with her, someone on her side. He meant no more than that, oh, she knew he didn't, but she could pretend, couldn't she? At Shildon other passengers got on. A couple looked into the compartment, saw the soldier and his girl, and went further down the train. That pair would have to part soon enough, they told each other, the way the news was going on the wireless.

They alighted at Aycliffe. The factory was easy to find it was so big. The gatekeeper wouldn't let Jackson in.

'I'll wait here, don't worry. Then, when you've got the job, we'll go looking for lodgings.'

He strolled backwards and forwards along the perimeter wall. Pulled a packet of Players from his top pocket, took out a cigarette and lit it with the flat lighter his mother had given him for Christmas. As soon as he had Molly settled he would catch the next train from Darlington, he thought. It was only forty-eight hours he had been AWOL. Surely he wouldn't be in too much trouble? Probably lose a stripe but it was worth it. He was so relieved to have found Molly, he felt relaxed for the first time in ages. Leaning against the wall, he crossed his feet at the ankles, blew out a cloud of smoke into the air which was already tinged with a touch of autumn though it was still August. Autumn came early in the North East. He wasn't complaining, though, not after the torrid heat of India.

Jackson glanced idly at the army truck coming up to the gates of the factory. He was so relaxed he failed to notice the red caps of the Military Police which the soldiers inside it were wearing.

'That's him, lads,' said the gatekeeper, nodding towards Jackson about fifty yards away. 'Durham Light Infantry. I know the badge, of course. My lad was called back a couple of days ago, they all were.'

Molly came out of the Administration building and ran towards the gate, past the keeper who stared straight-faced at her as he unlocked it for her.

'Jackson!'

She looked around eagerly. 'I've got the job, Jackson –' she went on before trailing into silence. Two redcaps had him by the arms, were frog marching him towards the truck. Molly ran towards them. 'What are you doing? He hasn't done anything!' she shouted at them. 'Leave him alone!'

'He's AWOL, miss,' the redcap nearest to her said. He looked down at Molly. Her face was flushed, her eyes flashing. Beneath her thin dress he could see the outline of her breasts, rising and falling rapidly as alarm took hold of her.

'Mind, looking at you, I can't say as I blame him,' he commented admiringly as his eyes raked up and down her.

'Don't worry, Molly, it's nothing,' said Jackson, talking over his shoulder as they hustled him into the truck. 'I'll be back soon as I can, me and Harry, we both will. Look after yourself, pet. Don't forget, if you need to, go to my mother.'

'Jackson! Jackson!'

But the redcap who had spoken to her closed the door of the truck. It was moving away, turning smartly and going off down the road. Molly was left gazing after it, the euphoria which had been with her all morning draining away. Tears rolled down her face unheeded. Jackson was gone.

'He didn't do anything,' she said to the gatekeeper, who was standing just inside the gates from where he had been following the proceedings with interest.

'He should have been in barracks,' snapped the man. 'Absent without leave – it's just another name for desertion. In my day they shot deserters.'

'He's not a deserter! Any road, there isn't even a war on yet!' Molly shouted at him.

'Not yet mebbe,' said the gatekeeper. 'Any day now, though. An' if my lad had to go, so should that one. Just trying to get out of it . . . scared to death likely.'

Molly turned to him furiously. 'He's not! He's not!' But the gatekeeper grinned and went inside his hut, well satisfied with the results of his telephone call.

Chapter Thirteen

Molly went on looking for somewhere to live, preferably near the factory, in a sort of daze where everything seemed unreal. She trailed about the surrounding villages all afternoon, gazing in newsagents' windows, chasing after the few notices which said 'rooms to let'. She couldn't allow herself to think of anything else. Not Harry, not Jackson. She used her search for a room as a buffer against such thoughts.

'Nay, it went last week, love,' was the usual reply she got as she stood on yet another doorstep. Or sometimes a man was wanted or the rent was far too high. There was a hostel but it was full to bursting.

It was hopeless, she knew it was hopeless; making her way to the train station Molly tried to think logically. What was she going to do? But somehow the fact that she had found Jackson only to have him snatched away before she had even found out where he and Harry were stationed was an agony which insisted on filling her mind, making even the necessity of finding a bed for the night seem of little importance.

The day was already turning to twilight and the trials and emotions of it had wearied her so much she sat in a stupor on the platform, moving like an automaton on to the train when it finally came.

She had bought a ticket for Bishop Auckland though she had no idea where she was going to sleep in the town; her money was practically gone. But what did it matter? Nothing was going to go right for her, she knew it now. She must have offended God somehow, Molly thought dully.

At Shildon a young mother came into the compartment with two children, a tiny boy sucking a lollipop and a girl of about six, holding him tightly by the hand, her face anxious. The woman was heavily pregnant, her abdomen sticking out in front of her, forcing open her cheap coat to reveal a cotton smock.

The boy sucked on his lollipop, staring gravely at Molly with big blue eyes. His nose began to run, the mucus shining in the light of the dying sun. Molly watched as it ran down his upper lip to meet the lollipop.

'Wipe Eddie's nose, Alice,' the mother said, noticing Molly's stare. She herself sat listlessly, legs apart, hands curved under her belly, as the little girl pulled out a grubby rag and wiped it across the boy's face. Eddie took the lollipop out of his mouth to protest loudly.

'Noaw, noaw, noooaw!' he screamed.

Suddenly Molly jumped to her feet. She had to get out into the fresh air. Nausea rose in her. Gagging, she flung herself on to the platform just as the station master came along, banging the doors closed.

'Hey, you want to watch it, miss,' he shouted, but she didn't hear. She was running to the side, gagging, gulping air. Gradually the nausea subsided, her vision cleared, her heartbeat slowed.

'Are you all right, lass?' the station master asked and Molly nodded, forced herself to smile, he looked so concerned.

'I . . . I just forgot I wanted to be off here,' she lied.

'Well, be a bit more careful in future,' he warned, clicking his teeth in disapproval. 'You could have had a nasty accident, you know.' He stumped off towards the barrier and looked expectantly back at her. She walked over and handed him her ticket. 'This is for Bishop, there's no refunds, you know,' he remarked.

Molly nodded without really registering what he had said and walked off up the path which led to Shildon town. She would just walk home from here, she thought, it wasn't all that far. She felt calm and peaceful now, going home. As the twilight turned to black night she trudged along, turning off at the stile which was the beginning of the shortcut to Eden Hope Colliery. The dark didn't matter, she knew all the footpaths around. She was thinking of nothing now, nothing at all, it was better that way. She was simply going home.

'Eeh, Mrs, will you come round our house a minute?

There's somebody says she lives there. She asked me what I was doing in their house, the cheeky monkey!'

Mrs Hardy had knocked on her neighbour's door and walked straight in. The Pendles were having their tea. Ann had made a meat pudding and the gravy oozing from the suet crust gave off a wonderful smell, rich and meaty. She put down her knife and fork and got to her feet.

'Sit down, Mam, it can't be that urgent,' said Joan sharply. 'Eat your dinner first!'

'No, lass, I'll go now,' she replied mildly. Jim, her husband, looked up but went on eating his tea calmly. 'I'll put it in the oven, it'll keep hot,' Ann decided.

Molly was standing just inside the door of the house in which she had been brought up, looking around her in bewilderment. She must have made a mistake was her first thought, this must be the wrong house. Where was her mother's press, the marble clock? She felt as though she was in the middle of a nightmare. She swayed with tiredness, slumped, pulled herself together as the door opened behind her and Ann Pendle and the woman who had been in the house when she arrived came in.

'Eeh, Molly pet, what's the matter?' asked Ann. Somehow she was not surprised. She had heard from Joan how Molly had lost her job yet again and as usual had felt a twinge of guilt.

'Hello, Mrs Pendle,' said Molly. Memory was flooding back to her. What a fool she had been! How could she have thought she still lived here? Was she going out of her mind? She had to take a hold of herself, had to. That woman behind Ann was gazing at her as though she were a candidate for Sedgefield Asylum. 'I'm sorry, I don't know what came over me, I'll go –'

'Howay along o' me, Molly,' said Ann. 'Mrs Hardy did the right thing coming for me. I bet you haven't had your tea neither? There's a bit of meat pudding left, we're just having ours. Come on, pet.' She put an arm around Molly's shoulders and drew her to the door.

'I'm all right now, I am,' said Molly. Looking over her shoulder, she apologised to Mrs Hardy, who was standing open-mouthed. 'I'm sorry, I was so tired, I just forgot –'

'Howay now,' said Ann.

Next door Jim Pendle had finished his meal and was sitting by the fire in the act of lighting a cigarette. He paused, the piece of paper which he had torn from the edge of his newspaper and lit from the fire still black and smoking in his hand. He raised his eyebrows at his wife.

'What's this? Young Molly Mason?'

'Mam!' Joan snapped. 'What's *she* doing here?'

'Aw, shut up, will you, the pair of you,' said Ann. 'Can't you see the lass is at the end of her tether? I'm just going to give her a bite to eat, that's all.'

'You know she got the sack again the day? I told you, didn't I?'

'Aye, you did. Strikes me you took a delight in telling me an' all,' said Ann.

She took a clean plate from the press and spooned on vegetables from the pans still standing on the fender then scraped the last of the meat pudding on too. 'Come on, love,' she said to Molly, 'get that down you.'

'It's all right, Mrs Pendle,' said Molly, blushing bright red as she caught the venomous look which Joan was giving her. 'Really, I'm not hungry.' But the smell was wonderful. Her stomach rumbled as if in direct contradiction of her words.

'Don't be daft, pet,' said Ann. She took her own out of the oven and picked up her knife and fork. 'Come on, tuck in.'

Molly sat at the table and began to eat. The meat was tasty and tender, the suet crust delicious. Though she hadn't felt hungry before, she now realised she was. After all, she had had practically nothing to eat all day. She cleared her plate, wiping the last piece of pudding around it to mop up the gravy.

'Eat the plate, why don't you?' said Joan. Molly looked up, startled, to see the other girl glaring at her with open animosity. Molly blushed yet again and put down her knife and fork.

'Thank you, Mrs Pendle,' she said quietly, 'I enjoyed that.'

'That's all right, pet,' said Ann. 'I'll make a nice cup of tea now. Then we can sit on the settee and have a long talk about what you've been doing all this while.'

'Huh, we know what she's been doing! Probably spent

the day thieving, gaolbird that she is,' Joan commented.

'That's enough of that,' Ann said sharply. 'Leave the lass alone. Do you not think she's had enough to put up with?'

'Leave her alone after what she did?' Joan demanded, her voice rising so that Jim Pendle, who had been buried in his newspaper and appeared to be taking no notice of the women, suddenly flung it down and jumped to his feet.

'If there's to be no peace in this house, I'm off out!' he roared. Striding to the door, he took his coat from the hook and pulled it on. 'I'm away down the club,' he snapped over his shoulder.

'There now, look what you've done,' said Ann. 'If he comes in with a skinful I'll never get him up for fore shift then me wages'll be short again. I don't know, our Joan –'

'Oh, aye, it's all my fault, it always is,' she said while Molly sat embarrassed, studying her empty plate. 'I suppose you'll want the gaolbird to stay an' all, share my room? Why don't you give her my bed an' be done with it?'

Molly got to her feet. 'No, I can't stay. I have to go now. Thank you very much for having me, Mrs Pendle.' She moved towards the door. 'And for the supper, it was really good. Me mam always said you made the best meat puddings and she was right.'

'You don't have to go, Molly,' said Ann, but she

glanced at Joan as she said it and Molly, intercepting the glance, thought she saw a touch of relief in it.

'Yes, I must. I only came to Eden Hope to . . . to see Jackson's mother.' It was said on the spur of the moment but, as Molly said goodbye again and walked down the yard and out on to the street, she realised that that was what she was going to do. Oh, not to stay, she wouldn't impose on Mrs Morley for the world, but just to look in, enquire after Mr Morley. Now she had eaten she felt better. She could visit Jackson's parents and not be too ashamed, for hadn't he and Harry been home and spoken for her?

'Eeh, lass, I'm that glad to see you! Father! Father! Will you look who's here!' Maggie called through to Frank.

It was heartening to stand at the door of the Morleys' house and be ushered in by Jackson's mother, her face wreathed in smiles. Molly allowed herself to be divested of her coat, to sit in a chair by the fire. It was such a luxurious novelty to be made a fuss of, to accept a cup of tea from the pot which stood on the hearth. It was black, strong, and laced with sweet condensed milk. So reminiscent of the tea her mother used to make that Molly almost broke down. She watched as Mr Morley was wheeled through to the kitchen in one of those long carriages she remembered seeing occasionally in her childhood, the ones which carried men who had had their backs broken in pit accidents, and her heart went out to the couple. But Mr Morley was smiling broadly, alert and happy to see her.

'You've just missed our Jackson and Harry, they've been on leave. Eeh, what a shame! Just by a day or two,' Maggie said, full of regret for what might have been.

'I saw Jackson, Mrs Morley, this –' Molly broke off. She couldn't tell his mother of the circumstances in which she had last seen him. It would worry her to death to think that he had been carted off by the military police because he had overstayed his leave. 'I saw him just before he went back,' she said instead.

'Did you? In Bishop? An' did you not see Harry?'

'No, he was already on the train, but I had a quick word with Jackson.' Molly looked down at the cup in her hand. She moved it slightly on the saucer, embarrassed that she'd had to lie, and not very convincingly either. It was her fault Jackson was in trouble, she thought guiltily, and she couldn't tell his mother that.

'Aye, well, that would relieve their minds any road.' Mrs Morley looked puzzled for a minute though she didn't question the tale.

'Now then, lass, we've heard all about your trouble,' said Mr Morley. 'You got yourself into a right pickle, didn't you?'

Molly's eyes prickled. He sounded so kindly, so concerned for her. 'I didn't do it, you know. I didn't rob that man.'

'No, we never thought you did,' Mrs Morley put in quickly. 'Not for a minute. But I wish you'd come to us, lass. I couldn't come looking for you, not with Frank the way he was, It must have been hell on earth for you in that prison. I've heard tales . . .' She broke off as she saw the expression of acute distress on Molly's face. 'Never mind, you're here now,' she said. 'I'm right glad you came an' all. So tell us what you're doing now?'

Molly almost lost her composure as a picture of the prison rose in her mind. She pulled herself together, back from the horror. 'I've got a job at the munitions factory. I start Monday.'

'Well, that's all right then, if you're working,' said Frank. Like a lot of pit folk after such a long depression he thought that to be working at least was halfway to paradise.

'Where are you staying?' Maggie asked. 'In Bishop, is it?'

'I was. Down by the Wear. But my room was flooded when it rained last night, and I can't go back there.'

'You mean, you haven't got a place?' Maggie glanced at her husband and he nodded slightly. 'Well then, you'll have to stay here. No, don't say a word, I insist. You can have our Jackson's room.'

'Oh, can I? Are you sure? I mean, I know you have a lot on –'

'It's settled. You bring your things tomorrow, pet. It'll make me feel a bit better an' all, I know I should have looked for you before.'

'I can help you when I'm home from work,' Molly said

eagerly. 'An' I'll pay for my board, of course. I've got a good job now, I can afford to.'

'We'll talk about that later,' Maggie said comfortably. 'You can stay here tonight, go get your things the morn. I'll lend you a nightie.'

Molly could hardly believe it. How could so much happen in one day? As she lay in Jackson's bed, a double bed for it had once held his brother Harold too, long since emigrated to New Zealand, she felt that at last her luck had changed. She snuggled down under the patchwork quilt, wrapped in Maggie's voluminous flannelette nightie, her feet on the warm oven shelf wrapped in an old sheet. Oh, her mam had done that always, put the solid oven shelf in the bed to air it. The pillow slip smelled of Sunlight soap, just as the pillow slips had always smelled at home. But there was also a faint something else there, a male smell, the smell of Jackson.

Oh dear, Jackson. How selfish she was. She had actually forgotten the trouble he was in, she had been so happy to be here, in his house, with his family. And they'd actually believed her when she'd said she wasn't a thief. By, she was so grateful to them, she was. Molly closed her eyes tightly and prayed as she hadn't prayed in months. That Jackson wouldn't be in too much trouble. That he would be all right. And most of all that if the war came – and there was nothing so certain but that war was coming, everyone knew it, it was just a matter of how soon – please God, let nothing happen to Jackson. Or

Harry. 'Look after them both, God, I beg you,' she cried in her heart, her whole being concentrating on the prayer. And then, as suddenly as walking off a cliff in the dark, she was asleep.

Chapter Fourteen

Molly was happy for the first time since her father had died. Even though the war had finally begun, and even though she was working in a room by herself filling trench mortar bombs with explosives. Her hair was tied up in a turban, her face smothered in face cream to protect it and her slim body wrapped in an enveloping overall. Yet still the all-pervasive yellow powder dyed the roots of her hair at the front, got under her finger nails, put a mustard-coloured 'V in the neck of the thin jumper she wore underneath the overall. She couldn't wear a hair grip or slide to hold her hair back in case friction caused the powder to ignite so wisps escaped and yellowed too. But she was happy.

Today, 1st December, 1939, was a red-letter day. Today was going to be Christmas and New Year and all her birthdays rolled into one, for today, when she went home from the day shift, or back shift as her dad would have called it, Harry and Jackson would be home. They were coming for a week, a whole week! Maggie and Frank were beside themselves with joy, had been talking of nothing else since the letter came. Jackson had only been away a few months this time but the dangers of war made them deeply anxious for him. Now they were going to have him home and that anxiety was eased for a short while at least.

'We can have Christmas early,' Maggie had said to Molly. 'By, isn't it a good job I have the cake and pudding all ready? 'Cause I don't suppose they'll get home for proper Christmas, not this year.'

'No, nobody thinks it'll be over by Christmas this time,' said Frank. 'Only silly buggers thought so last.'

'Less o' that swearing, Frank Morley,' said Maggie automatically. But he had made her wonder how long it *was* going to go on. She thought of the carnage of the last war and shuddered. Please God, not that again, not four years of it.

Molly was going to have their bedroom while Maggie slept in the front room beside Frank. Harry was to share with Jackson. They were going to be a proper family, almost like it had been at home, Molly thought happily as she stopped the stream of powder going into the bomb and sent it on its way into the next room to be fused.

Music came over the radio: '*We're going to hang out the washing on the Siegfried Line*'. Molly sang along with it under her breath. It wasn't so bad working here, even though she was on her own. No one knew much about her past. Thousands of girls worked here, bussed in from all parts of the county, and those in her group were friendly to her. She'd even joined the fledgling concert party.

Someone had heard her singing to herself in a sweet soprano she hadn't even realised was good before, no one had ever commented on it. But then she hadn't had much occasion to sing for a year or two, she thought, without self-pity.

The buzzer went and the belt slowed to a halt. It was four o'clock already, Molly realised with a tiny surge of elation. Were the boys home now? Sitting at the kitchen table eating parkin made yesterday with Golden Syrup and some of Maggie's precious hoard of powdered ginger?

By, she hoped they were. It would be grand having a natter tonight, all of them round the fire in the kitchen. Maybe the lads would go out for a drink at the club but they would be coming back for supper and she and Maggie would have it ready for them, they would do it together. There was tomorrow, of course, and Saturday morning too when she had to come to work, but she had the evenings and the whole of Saturday afternoon and Sunday with them.

Dreamily Molly went through to the changing rooms, took off her overall and turban, shook her hair out and washed her face and hands in the basins provided. Her street clothes were in her locker. She changed quickly and rummaged around in her bag for her comb and the slide which held back her thick brown hair from her forehead. She combed it before the mirror on the wall, turned her head this way and that to get a better view of it. It was all right, she supposed. She'd washed it last night with green soft soap and rinsed it with vinegar water to make it shine.

'Got a date, Molly? You're not usually so particular.'
Mona, the girl with the locker next to hers, gave her a
friendly grin. She was a small blonde girl, no more than
five feet, with plump, round breasts and hips. She worked
in the fusing room next to Molly, and told comic
monologues with the concert party. *Me Mother's Duck
Eggs* was Molly's favourite, Mona was a scream telling
that one. They rehearsed for the Christmas show in the
dinner hour.

'My brother's home on leave,' said Molly. 'Just back
today.'

'Eeh, I thought it must be your lad and it's just a
brother! I wouldn't bother just for a *brother*,' teased Mona.
'Got a sweetheart have you, Molly?'

Most of the girls talked all the time about their
boyfriends, about the boys they would like to be their
boyfriends, or, failing that, about Clarke Gable or Ronald
Colman or whichever heart throb was on at the pictures
that week.

Molly felt the heat rise in her cheeks but said nothing
as she turned for the door.

'You're blushing! Hey, girls, Molly has a sweetheart!'
called Mona.

'No, I haven't!' said Molly as she turned for the door.

'Ooh, is it a secret?' Mona kept pace with her then
relented as she saw Molly's face. 'Oh, go on, I was only
kidding,' she said. 'Take no notice of me, pet.'

'I don't, you daft ha'porth!' Molly smiled and ran for the gates, taking out her pass to hold aloft as she joined the inevitable crush to get through. The train was already standing at the station. She pushed her way through the crowds of girls and men queueing to get on the buses which would take them home. Luckily the railway line went to Shildon and Bishop Auckland. It was faster and easier to get a bus from there to Eden Hope. Or sometimes she walked from Shildon.

Tonight she would have to go all the way to Bishop, it was too cold and wet to get off at Shildon and take the footpath home. The train was crowded too, as it always was. And they had to stand in the station as a troop train went through. All the girls cheered as the soldiers went past though truth to tell there was little to see of them through the blacked-out windows. Molly wondered if Harry and Jackson were on the troop train. She felt thrilled to think they might be. Well, Harry was her brother, wasn't he? She kept telling herself it was because of him. But the picture in her mind was of Jackson: that lopsided grin on his face, the dark wave of hair falling over his forehead when he took off his cap, the way his left eyebrow lifted sometimes. She smiled secretly and stared out at the dark countryside, relieved only by the blue lantern of the station master as he waved it and their train chuntered slowly out of the station, following the troop train. And the tiny wink of the green light up the line.

The bus from Bishop was full too. It halted at every stop

until Molly could alight at Eden Hope and run along the row and up the back yard. And at last she could open the back door, closing it quickly behind her in case the air raid warden saw the light. And then she was overcome by sudden shyness so that she stood rooted there, just inside the door, smiling foolishly as the two tall figures in khaki got to their feet and came towards her. Harry got there first and, taking hold of her under the arms, whirled her off her feet so that her gas mask fell to the floor unheeded then put her down, dizzy and laughing, before planting a kiss on her cheek.

'Mind, our Molly, you've gone and grown up while I had my back turned,' he cried. 'You're a sight for sore eyes, pet.'

Then it was Jackson's turn and he held her tight, her head against his chest so that she could feel the imprint of a brass button against her cheek. He turned his broad back to the others and she was hidden from their gaze as he kissed her, swiftly, but not at all as her brother had kissed her.

'Molly!' he whispered. 'Molly, my love.' At least that was what she thought he said but it was so low a whisper it might only have been wishful thinking on her part.

'Put her down, Jackson,' said his mother. 'Let the lass get in. She must be fair clamming for her tea and half frozen an' all.'

The table was set with Maggie's second best table-cloth which had unlikely-looking roses embroidered round the edges. The best one was reserved for Christmas Day. There was smoked haddock, poached in milk in the oven, and mashed potatoes and cabbage. For afters there were fairy cakes with the wings stuck on with real butter icing.

'It looks grand, Mrs Morley,' said Molly. 'An' you're right, I am starving.' She was too, she realised. It was a long time since pie and chips in the canteen.

'I'll just mash the tea, pet. We were waiting for you.' Happiness lit Maggie's face, spilled over and softened her voice and movements. She kept looking at Jackson then smiling at Frank as he lay against his pillows and smiled back, his carriage drawn up to one side of the big square table.

'What happened to your other stripe?' he asked suddenly, his brow knitting. Jackson looked up quickly, a forkful of haddock halfway to his mouth, but before he could say anything Harry butted in.

'He got lost on his way back to camp, didn't he? No sense of direction your Jackson, man. I'm sure if I wasn't going with him he'd never find a German to fight.'

'You lost a stripe for being late back?' Frank asked, incredulous. 'You hadn't been drinking, had you, lad?'

'No, no, I never had a drink,' said Jackson, 'it was nothing really.' He concentrated on eating his meal. Molly stole a glance at him but his expression betrayed no emotion. He chewed on. She had a vivid picture in her mind of him with a military policeman to either side of him as they pushed him into the van.

'He'll soon get it back, man,' Harry was saying. 'Good sergeants like Jackson are hard to find. An' this lot coming into the regiment now – by, they're keen but green as grass! They need someone like Jackson and me to knock them into shape, look after them, wipe their . . .' Hurriedly he changed what he had been going to say. 'Tuck them up in bed at night an' all.'

Molly kept her own head bent but the awkward moment soon passed and Maggie was telling the boys about the number of young miners who had joined up the minute the war had broken out, even some of the girls.

'I had a letter from Lancashire an' all,' she said. 'After all these years! That woman I went to work for when I was but a lass of fourteen wanted to know could I recommend anybody?' Maggie shrugged and pulled down the corners of her mouth. 'As if I would if I could, the stuck-up bitch! Won't hurt her to get her own hands dirty. Any road, the lasses are all off to the factories, nobody has to skivvy nowadays.' She nodded in satisfaction. It might have been a while ago but she remembered it well. 'That woman thought she was better than honest Durham folk, she did.'

'Now then, lass, Christian charity,' Frank admonished.

'What about the Pendles?' asked Harry, remembering the time he had gone to see them on his last leave. 'Did they not help you at all, Molly?'

'Ann wasn't too bad,' she said. 'But . . .' Her voice trailed off as she remembered Joan's bitter dislike, the way she'd seemed to delight in Molly's troubles. It still hurt after all this time.

'Aye, I know,' Harry said quickly. He couldn't understand how he had once thought Joan attractive, even gone out with her. Spiteful, that was what she was.

'Never mind, everything's all right now,' said Frank, thinking it high time the subject was changed before anyone mentioned prison. He couldn't bear to see the haunted look in Molly's eyes if the talk ever went anywhere near *that*.

'Molly's fine with us, isn't she, Mother? The past's best forgotten. When are you expecting to go to France then, Jackson? Chase the Hun back to his own country?'

'We can't tell you that,' he said solemnly. 'Walls have ears, you know.'

'Fifth columnists all over the place,' said Harry. He lifted the table-cloth and bent to look underneath.

'Aw, go on, you daft ha'porth!' Molly exclaimed.

'No, we mean it,' Jackson protested.

'Aye, well. I'll make a fresh brew to have with the fairy cakes.' Maggie put her knuckles on the table and heaved herself to her feet. 'You get them, Molly.'

'Nice and strong, mind,' said Frank. 'I daresay we'll be drinking it like dishwater soon when it has to come all the way from India. Blooming rationing! We saw enough of that in the last war.'

Later Maggie took her husband away to ready him for the night. Molly brought out the enamel washing-up dish

and tray and washed the dishes while the two men dried.
Later still they sat around the fire, listening to Tommy
Handley on the wireless. When the programme was ended,
Jackson got to his feet.

'I think I'll take a walk,' he said. 'I feel like some fresh
air. Anyone coming?'

'Going to the club?' asked Harry.

Jackson looked at Molly. She couldn't go to the club.
'No, I don't think so. Just along the lane, around the
village, like.'

'Well, I think I'll have a quick one at the club,' said
Harry. He glanced from his little sister to his best mate. It
was plain to see what was happening there. Well, he
couldn't wish a better lad for her. And not so little now, he
reminded himself. Molly was growing up.

'I won't be long, just a quick half, see if any of our old
mates are in.'

Outside the wind was rising but it had stopped raining.
Molly didn't feel the cold. She walked between the men,
each holding one of her arms, huddling in together,
laughing and joking. At the club Harry left them and Molly
and Jackson went on up the lane, away from the houses
and the colliery, dodging the dark street lamps, the only
lights their flashlights, the dimmed beams bobbing along
in front of them. At the top of the bank Jackson stopped.
They were in the lea of the old engine house which had
once housed the standing engine which hauled the corves
of coal up the hill and down the other side to the railway.

'We'll stand a minute,' he said. 'Come here, Molly, we'll keep each other warm.' He opened his greatcoat and pulled it round her so that they were both enveloped by it. She could feel the beat of his heart as he held her and for a minute felt panicky. She wasn't ready for this, no, she wasn't.

But he was sensitive to her feelings and said quickly, 'Don't worry, I'm not trying anything on. I wouldn't do anything you didn't want me to, petal.'

'Oh, Jackson, I do love you.'

Surely she hadn't said that? Overcome, she hid her face in the rough serge of his tunic. Mam had always said never to tell a man you liked him, not until he'd said it first. Had he said it in the house or had she imagined it? Any road, here she was standing in the dark with a man, even if it was Jackson and she'd known him all her life. But not like this. Not standing breast to breast, her head on his shoulder, his arms around her, making her feel warm and safe. Eeh, what would he think of her? She tried to move back, away from him, but his hold was unyielding, he wouldn't let her.

'Say it again,' he whispered, his lips against the nape of her neck, just below the brown beret she had pulled over her hair.

'I don't think I can.'

'Oh, Molly!' He laughed softly, caught her tighter in his arms and lifted her off the ground until her face was on a level with his. He kissed her lightly on her cheeks,

her chin, her lips last of all, and small tremors of delight
ran through her body. A new and strange excitement began
somewhere deep inside her and rose up, threatening to
engulf her. It was so dark she couldn't even see his eyes
but she knew he was smiling. He moved his hand. His
thumb brushed against her breast and her nipple sprang
erect in response. She closed her eyes and leaned further
into him, completely bewitched. But the next kiss never
came. Instead she found herself back on her feet, he took
a step back away from her, she knew he was no longer
smiling.

'Come on,' he said, his voice suddenly rough. 'I'll get
you back home. It's going to rain. And anyway, you have
to go to work in the morning.'

The shock was like a slap in the face. She'd been too
forward. Oh, aye, she could almost hear her mother's
voice: 'A man won't respect a lass as is too free with her
favours, you mark my words!' She had been talking about
a girl from the other side of the village at the time. Molly
had only been twelve and had puzzled about what was
meant by 'being free with favours'. Now she knew. Her
face burned. She had offered herself and Jackson had
backed away. Not altogether, though. As she stood deep in
misery a bus went past and in its dim lights he saw her
downcast face. She saw his expression change from a
frown to a grin. He stepped forward and pulled her beret
on straight, her collar up around her neck.

'Howay, our Molly,' he cried, grasping her hand and

pulling her after him in a run down the lane. 'We'll dodge the drops, eh?' As he had cried so often when they were children and she'd trailed after Harry and him, 'making a proper pest of herself', as Harry would tell her.

They arrived at Eden Hope, breathless and laughing, running past the pit yard to the rows of houses thrown up by the mine-owners at the smallest cost possible to house the workers for their new mine.

Harry was already back from the club as they went in. There was a faint smell of Federation Ale in the air. He looked from one to the other knowingly.

'Where've you two been then?' he asked, but didn't wait for an answer. 'There's tea in the pot if you want a cup. Your mam's gone to bed, Jackson.'

'No, thanks, I'd best get up. I've to be out by six in the morning,' said Molly. She could hardly look at her brother. Suppose they'd done more, her and Jackson? 'Gone all the way' as folk said. Would Harry have known and despised her for it?

Long after she'd gone to bed she could hear the soft murmur of the men's voices downstairs. Molly tossed and turned on the deep feather mattress which had been a wedding present to Maggie and Frank. Eventually she dropped off and dreamed confused dreams of Jackson and her going into Bishop Auckland to buy a ring. They stood before the counter in the jeweller's and she was ecstatically happy, so brimful of joy she couldn't contain herself. And then she looked down through the glass top and there, among others, was the bangle. The one which had put her in prison.

'You brought that bangle in,' the jeweller said accusingly. 'I'm going for the bobbies.'

'No, I didn't!' Molly shouted. 'I didn't, Jackson!'

But he was stepping away from her, looking at her with accusing eyes, hard as nails. 'The man should know,' he said. 'Oh, Molly, how could you do it?'

She woke in a sweat, still murmuring denials. Her head ached, her heart pounded with fear. There was a terrible noise. Molly turned on her back and took a deep breath. She reached over to the bedside table and pushed down the button on the cheap tin alarm clock she had bought in Woolworth's. The horrible noise stopped and after a moment or two the pain in her head lessened. It was morning, time to go to work.

Molly climbed out of bed and lit the gas jet on the wall above the fireplace. These dark mornings were a bane. She put on her overcoat in case one of the lads should wake and get up. Then, gathering her clothes together, crept downstairs.

The privy was across the yard. Slipping out of the back door and running across with her shoes unlaced on her bare feet, she shivered in the nagging, bitter cold. Back in the kitchen, still warm as the fire had been banked up the night before, she washed in a ladle of water from the boiler in the range and dressed hurriedly. She hadn't time to make a cup of tea. The fire was sluggish, reluctant to come back to life. Never mind, she'd get one in the canteen during her break.

Soon she was speeding down the road to where the bus was just pulling up at the stop on the end of the rows. Jackson would be there when she got back tonight, she thought, a warm glow suffusing her so that she hardly felt the cold. And Harry too, of course.

Chapter Fifteen

Saturday morning went on and on until Molly thought it would never come to an end. She was filling cordite bags for the navy, bag after boring bag, except that she couldn't be too bored, couldn't let her mind wander much. This stuff was dangerous.

George Formby was on the wireless singing 'Mr Woo' and Molly sang along with him softly, her voice sounding hollow in the small room on her own.

This afternoon she was going only as far as Bishop and Jackson was coming into town to meet her. The whole lovely afternoon stretched before her. They were going to have something to eat at the King's Hall cafe. Then, if the weather was cold or wet, and she couldn't really tell where she was working, they would go to the matinee at the King's Hall picture house. Or, if it was nice, they would walk in the Bishop's park. She didn't care which, she was going to be with him. There was happiness bubbling inside of her at the thought of it.

They could do exactly as they liked because Harry had

a date. He was going out with a girl – was being evasive about who she was exactly.

'Fast work that, mind,' Jackson had said last night when her brother told them he had a date. 'You haven't been home two days yet.'

'Can I help it if I'm irresistible to women?' Harry had grinned and put on what he called his Clarke Gable look. He'd taken out his comb and combed back his dark hair with exaggerated care, pushing it back slightly at the front to make a quiff.

Molly smiled at the memory. Tonight they would worm out of him who the girl was. So far all they'd got was his hands describing curves in the air and a long wolf whistle.

For the thousandth time she wondered what time it was. Surely it must be twelve o'clock by now? She started on another bag but at last the buzzer went, George Formby was cut off in the middle of asking Mr Woo what he could do, and Molly was free to go.

They ate pie and peas and chips at the King's Hall. Jackson had half a beer and Molly had a shandy, pale amber and sweet from the added lemonade. It tasted like nectar.

'Now what?' asked Jackson as they finished their meal and the waitress brought the bill. 'You choose, I'll do whatever you want to do.' He delved into his pocket and brought out a pound note and gave it to the waitress. 'Sixpence for yourself,' he said and smiled at her. She blushed and walked away hurriedly to get change at the desk. 'Some girls have all the luck,' she commented to the cashier, who followed her glance to the dashing soldier and his girl.

'I see what you mean,' she replied. 'It makes your heart flutter to look at him, doesn't it?' She held a hand dramatically over where she thought her heart to be and they both giggled.

'The sun's shining, we'll go for a walk,' Molly decided.

'Walking in December? Folks'll think we're off our chumps.' Jackson raised an eyebrow but she knew he was joking. He took hold of her hand and drew her out and down the stairs to Newgate Street, busy with Saturday shoppers.

'The park it is then.'

They walked slowly down the street, looking in shop windows, not exactly hand in hand but close enough to be touching each other sort of accidentally all the time. Jackson paused by the jeweller's window. 'Look, Molly, what sort of ring would you like? Always supposing, of course, that we were going to get engaged, you'd like a ring, wouldn't you? Or if you don't want to get engaged, we can pretend, can't we?' He was laughing but his eyes were serious, watching her.

Suddenly she was short of breath. Her hands fluttered in front of her, she couldn't keep them still. She bit her lip. Was this a real proposal? No, she told herself, he's joking, he doesn't mean it. If I said yes and picked out a ring he would run a mile, of course he would. She stared up at him.

'Oh, Molly, if you're not ready we'll wait,' he said, the smile gone from his face. They stood close together in the middle of the pavement as people pushed past them on their way to the market.

'You're having me on,' she said, forcing herself to look away. 'Come on, let's walk, it's too cold to stand about.' She made to walk on but he caught hold of her shoulders, his firm grip holding her still.

'No, Molly, I've never been so serious in my life,' he said, and suddenly a great elation filled her, shining out of her eyes.

'You're asking?' she said, for all the world as though they were at the church hall hop and he had come over for a dance.

'I'm asking,' he said. And it didn't matter at all (or just a little bit) that they had to come down to earth when they saw the prices in the window. Seven pounds ten shillings for a ring with three minuscule diamonds set on the slant on a golden band!

'You like it, don't you? I can't buy it today,' he said regretfully. 'But I will, now I know what you want, I promise you, my love.'

'Are you going to stop blocking the blooming pavement or have I to batter me way through with this pram?'

A strident voice cut into their dream. A tired-looking woman with dull untidy hair was trying to get by, pushing an enormous old pram with two toddlers hanging on to the handle on either side. They sprang into the shop doorway to clear the pavement.

'Love's young dream, eh?' the woman said as she passed.

One of the toddlers started to wail, 'Can I have a ride, Mam? Me legs're tired. Howay, Mam, lift us up, I won't sit on the babby's legs.'

She stopped and lifted him on to the bottom of the pram, glancing again at Molly and Jackson. 'Aye, well, just you wait a year or two an' see what happens,' she said to Molly. 'I'd think twice if I was you.' But Molly wasn't looking at her any more, she was gazing through the window at the glass counter just inside the jeweller's with a sense of *déjà vu*. It was just like in her dream, the nightmare she'd had the other night when the jeweller had accused her of bringing in the bracelet. Oh, dear God! Suddenly all her old terrors rose to the surface.

'Molly?' Jackson took her arm, pulled her to him. 'What's the matter, Molly? You're not that upset because I haven't got the money with me to pay for a ring now, are you?'

She shook her head, shaking away the terrors. It had just been a nightmare, she told herself firmly.

'Nothing. Nothing's the matter,' she said, and smiled brightly up at him. She tucked her hand in his arm, feeling the warmth and strength of him beneath the rough khaki cloth. 'Come on, let's go to the park or it'll be dark before we get there.'

The market place was filled with stalls and thronged with shoppers hoping for bargains. Late Saturday afternoon was the time for those, the traders dropping their prices before packing up to go home. 'Now then, missus, two cauliflowers for the price of one . . . three pounds of carrots for the price of two . . . a proper bargain. Why, man, I'll be out of pocket . . .'

Jackson and Molly strode on to the gothic archway and the gate which led to the bridle path past the castle and on to the deer park. There were few people about though the sun still shone, slanting its rays through the railings of the castle gardens and pointing up the ancient battlements. But the lovers weren't interested in the castle, they were in a world of their own, going through the cattle gate at the end and on up the grass to the square deerhouse then back down into the valley where the Gaunless ran, hurrying to meet the Wear, brown and peaty and swollen now in winter time.

A wind had sprung up, keen and promising a frost later on, but here, in the small valley, they were sheltered from it though it soughed and whined through the high, bare branches of the trees. Molly felt as though they were the only people in the whole world. They could stay here, hidden away from everyone else, the war and all its dangers.

They paused beneath the branches of one of the oaks

which had given the town its name, a thick, ancient tree with branches low and spreading, its carpet of dry brown leaves rustling under their feet. And it was all so perfectly natural, so *meant* to be, as Jackson's arms went around her and Molly lifted her face for his kisses. He loosed her coat and his, undid the top button of her blouse and kissed the swell of her breast. She sighed in ecstasy, feeling the two of them cocooned in the warm blanket of their love.

'You will marry me, won't you, Molly?' he asked urgently.

'I will,' she replied, and to her it was a dedication as binding as if she had said her vows in church.

'My next leave? Even if I have to get a special licence?'

'Your next leave.'

For a while she could think of nothing but the feel of his hands on her body, the surge of her response taking her by surprise at the strength of it. She was filled with the need to sink down on to the carpet of leaves with him and make love, full, total love.

An aeroplane went by overhead, then another. She heard them only as part of the background: the waters of the Gaunless rushing over stones, a lorry going up Durham Road in the distance, the wind. But for Jackson the engine noise brought him back to reality. He lifted his head, moved his hands back to the comparative safety of Molly's waist. She moaned softly with her need, leaned even closer in to him.

'We have to be sensible,' he whispered. 'You're so

young.' That wasn't really what he meant. He meant that he was going to war and couldn't just make love and leave her. Suppose she was expecting a baby? Suppose he didn't come back? What would she do then? She was just a girl herself, nobbut a bairn. When she opened her eyes they were dark with the want of him and his resolve almost went. But another flight went past. Five, no, six planes this time. He looked up to the sky. Hurricanes they were, flying low enough for him to see the roundels on their sides. The war was real and where would he be in a couple of weeks' time?

'Come on, Molly, it's getting dark,' he said and fastened her buttons again, then his own. They walked out of the park against the stiffening wind, apart now, not touching. He didn't think he could bear to touch her without making love, not yet, not until his blood had cooled down.

The aeroplanes had had their effect on Molly, too. She didn't know whether they were fighters or bombers but it had suddenly occurred to her that there were factories in Germany with girls filling bombs just as she was doing, and the thought of them dropping on Jackson and Harry and the rest of the Durham Light Infantry, and all the other soldiers going over there to Belgium or France or wherever they were going, filled her with unspeakable dread.

They caught the bus back to Eden Hope and sat close together on the narrow seat, holding hands. The bus filled up with people they knew; housewives with full baskets, men running to join the queue from Kingsway Football

Ground, talking loudly of the match, arguing about the results. It had been a local derby, Shildon versus Bishop, and there were supporters of both teams. The bus was packed, men standing in the aisle, shouting across the heads of those sitting down. 'The ref wants his eyes tested!' being the mildest of the comments. Some of the men, young miners, looked at Jackson in his uniform with a mixture of envy and respect. Some spoke to him: 'Good luck, lad.' Or, 'On leave are you, mate?'

A few of the women gave Molly peculiar looks and whispered to each other but she didn't care, not now, not when she had Jackson beside her. Most of the folk in Eden Hope had accepted her back among them anyway. The scandal had been a nine days' wonder. There were more important things to talk about now.

Alighting at the end of the rows, most of the women joined the men in calling 'Goodnight!' to them. It was already black dark as they walked down the back street, bumping into each other between the blacked-out houses for both of them had forgotten their flashlights. Jackson took her arm and led her into the yard and she felt cherished and looked after. Something of a novelty for Molly.

'There's a dance at the church hall the night,' said Harry after they had got in and were eating their tea. Sausages and mash it was, with brown sauce, and dire warnings yet again from Maggie about how these would probably be the last they saw before the meat rationing came in.

'There's them that's hoarding tins as fast as they can get a hold of them, but not me,' she said self-righteously. Then had the grace to add, 'I haven't the money to do that any road.'

'We'll go, won't we, Molly?' Jackson said in answer to Harry. 'A military two-step'll go down a treat, eh?'

'Oh, man, don't be so old-fashioned,' said Harry. 'A nice why-dance is what I like.'

'Why-dance?' said Molly, puzzled.

'Aye, you know, a slow waltz and a crowded floor and me just to say moving, me arms round a girl . . .' He held his arms in front of him as though round a girl, his head on one side, his eyes half-closed, and they all laughed.

'You haven't got a partner,' said Molly.

'Who needs a partner? They'll be falling over each other to dance with me, our Molly.' He paused. 'Any road, as it happens I'm meeting a lass inside. Wait till you see her an' all. A blonde, just as high as my heart, curves in all the right places . . .' His hands drew a figure of eight in the air.

'Well, we'll have to go now, pet, if only to see this beauty.' Jackson grinned at Molly.

'Aye, go on. Me an' your dad are going to have a night by the fire listening to the wireless,' said Maggie. Time was when Frank was down the club every Saturday night with his mates but things were different now.

The church hall was filling up nicely when they arrived. Molly left her coat in the cloakroom and combed her hair in front of the looking glass, surprised at her own reflection. Her eyes shone, her cheeks glowed. Why, she was almost pretty!

'Well, look who's here!' a familiar voice said and there was Mona from the factory, standing beside her as she applied poppy red lipstick to her pert mouth.

'Mona! What are you doing here? You live at Ferryhill, don't you?'

'Visiting me auntie,' said her friend, pressing her lips together then inspecting them critically in the glass. 'I'm here for the weekend, did I not tell you?'

'You at the dance on your own?' asked Molly. If she was, then in all civility she had to let her friend keep them company.

'No, I'm with a fella.' Mona grinned triumphantly. 'Fast work, eh? A soldier an' all, home on leave. I met him last night. By, he's lovely an' all, Molly, I think I've fallen for him. He likes me too, I can tell.' She put a hand to her nape and flicked her long blonde hair back from her shoulders, arranging the front so that a lock fell forward in the manner of Veronica Lake. Her eyes twinkled up at Molly. 'Right, let's go. We'll knock 'em dead, eh?'

Molly laughed and followed her out of the cloakroom to see her walk straight over to where Jackson and Harry were waiting by the side of the stage where a five-piece band, most of whom were members of the colliery brass band, were striking up the first dance. Jackson's face was a study as Harry seized Mona round the waist and took a whirl round the floor, completing almost a whole circuit before other couples joined them.

'You dancing?' asked Jackson, and took Molly in his arms. They too began quickstepping to 'Dancing Cheek to Cheek'. The hall was crowded, mostly with miners and their girls but there was a sprinkling of khaki and Air Force blue, a couple of sailors standing out in their navy blue.

Molly was in heaven with Jackson's arms around her. They danced a Boston two step followed by the quickstep and then a waltz and a veleta, and then it was a ladies' excuse-me quickstep. Molly hardly heard the announcements from the stage, she was in a world of her own, dreaming away, not wanting the evening to end, she was so happy. So it was a bit of a surprise when she felt a tap on the shoulder.

'Excuse me!'

Jackson's arms loosened reluctantly and Molly found herself left at the side of the floor while he whirled away with a girl with long black hair hanging down her back over a bright red dress which swirled out as they spun round. Feeling bereft she watched the dancers until she was caught up herself by a tall gangly youth who took her round the floor with more enthusiasm than skill. But it was not the thing to refuse to dance with anyone when you were without a partner, and anyway, she was so euphorically happy she even smiled when his foot descended with some force on hers.

'Hey, watch what you're doing!'

They stopped abruptly as the boy cannoned into another couple, knocking the girl from the arms of her partner.

'Sorry, did I hurt you?' the lad mumbled, his face bright red.

'What do you think, you clumsy oaf?' snapped Joan Pendle, rubbing her shoulder and wincing theatrically. For that was who it was, Joan Pendle, and she was dancing with Harry. Molly gazed up at him in surprise. He looked stiff and uncomfortable.

'No harm done,' he said. 'Come on, Joan.' He pulled her away and set off dancing again. There were only a few bars of the music left and Molly and her partner didn't get started before it came to an end.

'Blooming cheek, hasn't she?' Mona was at Molly's elbow, gazing at Joan. 'Who is she any road?'

'Nobody,' said Harry, hearing her as he came up. 'She's nobody. It's the interval now, how about lemonades all round?'

Chapter Sixteen

'That lass has her sights fixed on you,' Jackson commented. He didn't say which lass, he didn't have to. They were sitting at the kitchen table having breakfast and for once the two of them were on their own for it was Monday morning and Maggie was out in the wash house in the yard, the rhythmic thumping of her possing the clothes in the zinc tub loud and clear.

'Aye, well, she's wasting her time,' said Harry. He picked up the *Daily Herald* and glanced through it, quickly put it down again. 'Funny war this, man,' he said. 'Nothing's happening.'

'It will soon enough,' said Jackson. 'Aye, but you want to watch yourself, Harry, she's a determined sort. Look how she butted in for that excuse-me quickstep. Brass-faced I call it after all she's said about your Molly.'

'Well, it'll do her no good, will it?' asked Harry. 'Any road, I've a fancy for little Mona, she's promised to write to me.' He grinned at Jackson and changed the subject.

'You going down to Bishop to buy that ring?'

'Yes.' He glanced at the clock on the mantelpiece and

got to his feet. 'I'd best be off, catch the bus.'

'I'll come with you, I've nothing else to do, not 'til Mona finishes work. We're going to the pictures after.'

The girls were on first shift and Mona was still staying with her aunt in Eden Hope. She'd only known Harry for four days yet they were going steady. It was happening all around them, for a lot of young miners had been in the territorials before the war and had recently been drafted. There was a sense of urgency somehow, a feeling of time being short.

The girls had travelled in to work together on the train, gravitated towards each other during the break.

'I wish we were getting engaged the night,' Mona said as they drank lukewarm tea and ate currant buns in the canteen. 'By, you never told me you had a dream boat for a brother!' She grinned, eyes sparkling over the rim of her mug.

'Well, I can't let everyone know, I might get knocked over in the rush,' said Molly, laughing before turning serious. 'Aw, come on, you've only known him four days. You can't get engaged to a fella when you've just known him four days.'

'I could!' Mona said fervently. 'If he asks me, I could. We're going to the pictures this afternoon. I'm going to take him to see a love story if I can. Do you know what's on at the Majestic or the Hippodrome?'

'Can't say I do,' said Molly as the buzzer went and they joined the crowd going back to work.

If anything the rest of the shift dragged by even more slowly than the one on the Friday before. Molly's hands were busy but the work came to her automatically now. Her mind was left to wander happily on thoughts of Jackson and the future. Because, she told herself, nothing was going to happen to Jackson or Harry. They were experienced soldiers, weren't they? Just occasionally Joan Pendle came to her mind, the way she'd butted in on Harry and Mona in the dance. Why had she done that? Probably it was just an urge to make mischief, thought Molly, Joan was a nasty piece of work all right.

There was a surprise for the two girls as the train pulled into Shildon. There were Jackson and Harry on the platform, running up and down, looking for them through the windows. Neither girl saw them at first. Mona was still talking about Harry. It seemed as though every other sentence had to be about him.

'Are those soldiers waving at you?' someone asked, and the two girls just managed to jump down from the train before the guard's flag went down and the other girls cat-called and wolf-whistled, emboldened by their numbers.

Harry grinned, not at all put off, and swept Mona into his arms. He gave her a smacking kiss then bowed to his audience on the train as it pulled away from the station.

'You daft ha'porth!' cried Mona when she could get her breath, and he swung her round and off her feet before putting her down again. 'Now we'll have such a ragging when we go in tomorrow!' But she loved it and so did

Molly as Jackson took her hand and kissed her gently, his lips brushing against hers.

They walked down the path to Eden Hope, not noticing that the distance between the two couples grew longer and longer until they disappeared from each other's view. Skirting a wood by the corner of a ploughed field, brown and with dank dead grass sticking up in tufts in places for this had been a meadow before the war but now was needed to grow crops, Jackson drew her to a halt. It was sheltered here, halfway down the bank side, the sun shone, it could almost have been spring.

'I've been to Bishop this morning and bought you something,' he said softly, and drew a small box out of the breast pocket of his uniform. A ring box. Molly was speechless. She hadn't expected it yet. In fact, she'd thought it would be during his next leave.

He opened the box and put the ring on her fourth finger. The tiny diamonds sparkled and shone in the sun looking twice as big as they were. She gazed at it and it was the most beautiful ring in the whole world. Oh, yes, it was, it was!

They ambled along, arms around each other, sometimes stopping to cuddle closer. Molly couldn't help thinking that in three days he would be gone away, out of England even, to that menacing place the continent. It was a shadow on her happiness, one which took more and more of an effort to push to the back of her mind. She couldn't let him see how much it upset her.

The winter sun had disappeared by the time they reached the end of the rows at Eden Hope, the pit hooter had sounded and the back shift men were coming out of the pit yard making for home and a bath and hot meal. Smoke curled up towards the sky from the chimneys, visible in the star light. But the houses themselves were already blacked out, shutters up, blackout curtains drawn together.

'Where the heck have you been?' asked Maggie as they went into the kitchen. 'Harry was back hours ago. They've gone to the first house pictures. I've kept your meal hot in the oven but . . .'

Molly held out her hand, holding it under the gas mantle so that it caught the light. 'We're engaged.'

'Eeh, will you look at this, Frank! A ring – our Jackson's given Molly a ring! By, I'm right pleased for you both,' Maggie cried and flung her arms around them both. 'Congratulations, son,' she whispered into Jackson's ear, 'you've got a good 'un in Molly. An' you an' all, pet,' she nodded to the girl. 'Now, come on, sit yourselves down an' I'll dish up or it'll be kizzened to a cinder.'

As she turned to the oven she wiped her eyes with the corner of her apron. If she could have wished her lad had picked someone without the shadow of prison hanging over her, even if it had been a big mistake, she was wise enough to hide it.

Later, Jackson and Molly had the front room to themselves as befitted their engaged status while Maggie and Frank listened to the wireless in the kitchen. They sat on the imitation leather chesterfield in front of the fire and made plans for what they would do when the war was over. For both of them had decided they had to live for the present, it was no good meeting trouble before it happened. The Germans would be sent back to their own country, and Jackson *would* come back. How could it be any other way when men like him were there to make it happen? With his arms around her, Molly felt safe, confident, optimistic. The war might have just begun but her own bad times were over.

Somehow she was not so sure the day before they had to report back to their unit. The reality of the impending separation hit her. There were twenty-two hours left, twenty-one, nineteen. And she had to spend precious hours at work filling bombs, the sharp smell of the TNT getting up her nose, shrinking from the knowledge that the two men she loved most in the world could be killed. They were *soldiers*, for goodness' sake. But somehow she had to batten the dark thoughts down, show a cheerful, loving face to Jackson and to Harry.

Mona was cheerful enough when they met in the canteen, giggly in fact.

'We went to the King's Hall pictures – you know, those seats made for two in the back row? Eeh, it was lovely. Deanna Durbin it was. She's gorgeous, isn't she? Harry wanted to go to see a cowboy but I told him this was a gangster picture. Well, it was set in the twenties, wasn't it?' Mona sighed. 'She's got a gorgeous voice an' all, hasn't she, Molly? Molly, are you not listening to me?'

'I am, yes, I am,' said Molly but soon went back to studying her mug of tea. The buzzer went and she still hadn't drunk it. She put it down and went back to her work room and the band started up again and she worked away for the rest of the shift, trying hard to keep her mind a blank and succeeding to some extent.

At the end of the shift Mona was waiting for her in the changing room. She was going back to Eden Hope to stay with her auntie again, just until Harry went back from leave. 'Auntie June doesn't mind,' she had said to Molly, 'she likes me to stay, only she wants to know all about everything.' Molly knew Mona's auntie by sight. She lived on the other side of the village, her husband was a postman.

'Harry and me, we're going into Darlington this afternoon. There's a tea dance on at the Grand, very grand it is an' all.' Her eyes twinkled at Molly but then, all of a sudden, the grin left her face as Molly took her engagement ring from its hiding place at the back of her locker and put it on, saying nothing.

'Aw, Molly,' said Mona. 'Don't look so worried. They'll be all right, I know they will. I'd go mad if I didn't have a laugh. I can't stand the glooms, I can't.' Molly glanced at her. Mona's normally bright little face was pale, her eyes frightened.

'I'm all right, really,' she said. 'You're right, the glooms never did anyone any good. Come on, let's run for the train, see if we can get a seat for once.'

By the time they were sitting in the carriage, breathless from the race through the crowds, Mona was her old self, looking as though she hadn't a care in the world. 'Blondie and Dagwood!' she cried, and the whole compartment burst into laughter.

And then it was the last afternoon. Molly and Jackson had the house to themselves. Harry was round at Mona's auntie's: 'Getting his feet under the table,' as Maggie put it. And she herself had gone with Frank in the ambulance to Durham County Hospital where he was going to be re-examined by the surgeons to see if there was any sign of improvement.

The whole family was excited about it, swinging between hope and resignation. Not many men with spinal injuries such as he had suffered ever walked again.

'But if he could just sit up, you know,' Maggie had said to Molly the evening before. 'Sit in a wheel chair, get out a bit in the fresh air – by, it would do him the world of good.' And when he went out of the door, the stretcher manoeuvred expertly by the ambulance men, Frank had had such a look on his face, a look of desperate hope which Molly prayed wouldn't be dashed before the day was out.

In the street men and women stood at their yard gates to see him off, calling out to Frank as he was lifted into the ambulance. 'Good luck, Frank!' 'All the best, lad!'

Maggie climbed in beside him and waved her thanks to the well-wishers before the door was closed and then the ambulance was off, down the street and round the corner, on its way to Durham.

So Molly and Jackson were left alone in the house. Neither of them felt like going to the pictures and there was a wind outside sharp enough to cut a person in two. Molly jobbed about, changing the sheets on Frank's carriage, tidying the kitchen. Jackson carried in coal for the fire in the front room, and then they were free to sit together on the chesterfield, the doors closed, cocooned in a small world of their own.

The sense of urgency, of time fleeting, was in both their minds as Jackson took her into his arms, his kisses all the sweeter for it, her response all the stronger. Everything outside his arms faded to insignificance for Molly, the touch of his hands so unbearably exciting, the feel of his body sweet against hers. And for all their good resolutions, Jackson's in particular, they were carried away on the strong tide of their love, sinking to the thick clippie mat which lay in front of the fire. Somehow her dress was open, discarded, the straps of her satin camiknickers down from her shoulders until her breasts were bare, the rosy tips standing firm and erect. And then they were lost completely, drowning in such a depth of feeling that nothing mattered except the two of them together, expressing their love, taking it to its limits.

When he entered her the sharp pain gave her only

momentary pause before it was forgotten in the triumph of fulfilment. Molly held him to her, her love for him heightened if that was possible, such a feeling of contentment as she had never experienced before washing over her, filling her with peace and a quiet elation.

'Oh, God, I'm sorry,' Jackson said brokenly. 'I am, Molly, I'm so sorry. Did I hurt you? I never meant to go that far, not when I'm going . . .'

'Shh, don't say it,' Molly whispered in his ear, 'don't. Not now. Don't spoil it, this is our time.'

Jackson was quiet. He lay by her side as his blood quietened, his breathing returned to normal.

'I'm not sorry,' said Molly, her voice soft with love. 'I'm glad, I am. So glad.'

She could be pregnant now, Jackson thought, what had he done? He was going to war, God only knew when or even if he would get back to Eden Hope, hadn't she had enough trouble in her short life without him going and adding to it? He groaned and Molly rose on one elbow and looked down at him. His face was lit by the firelight. Outside on this short winter's day it was already dark. The firelight lit the strong planes of his cheeks, the straight brows above the dark eyes, hidden in shadow now. A coal flared in the grate and she caught a glimpse of the uncertainty and pain in those eyes. Oh, she didn't want him to feel pain, she did not!

'Don't be sorry, please don't be sorry,' said Molly.

The firelight made her skin glow with a rosy light,

glinted on her hair which hung down over her shoulders and glorious breasts, and in spite of his resolution he felt himself responding again, the blood rising in him.

Abruptly he sat up, kissed her lightly on the tip of her nose, forced himself to look away. 'I'm not sorry, Molly, not if you're not. But we have to be sensible, my love. Come on, Mam and Dad will be back soon. And if we don't draw the curtains the warden will be knocking at the door. The firelight will be showing through the window.'

Feeling slightly rejected, Molly stood up, pulled on her underclothes and frock, keeping her back to him as he too dressed, unsure of herself. Until she felt his arms around her as he turned her to face him.

'I love you, Molly,' he said. 'More than anything in the world. You know that, don't you?'

She sagged against him. 'I love you too.'

'It's just, well, suppose you were to have a baby and me not here to look after you? I don't want you to be in trouble because of me, Molly, you've had enough of that.'

She thought of having his baby. The prospect didn't frighten her, she longed for it in fact. But she knew she had to be sensible. When they were married would be time enough, she told herself. When they were married. By, those four words sounded grand. But when?

'My next leave,' said Jackson. 'I'll get a special licence. Everything will come right, you'll see. Then when this war is over . . .' He stopped, thinking of the war. It was hardly begun, never mind being over.

Chapter Seventeen

It was almost six o'clock when the ambulance returned with Maggie and Frank. Molly and Jackson were back in the kitchen by now. She had the tea all ready, the mince cooking nicely in the oven just waiting for the dumplings to go in for the last ten minutes, vegetables coming to the boil on the fire. They had worked together, Jackson peeling potatoes surprisingly expertly, something he said he had learned in the army, not mentioning that it was when he was in detention after being absent without leave.

The table was set and Molly was just beginning to worry that the meal would be ready too soon when the door burst open and there was Maggie, her face wreathed in smiles as she almost danced into the kitchen.

'Come and see! Come on, you two, come and see!' And she took hold of both of them and dragged them out, down the yard to the back street, not even noticing or caring that the back door was left open and light was spilling out into the yard. The ambulance men were just opening the doors and putting down the step and then, instead of a stretcher with Frank laid flat on it, they were lifting out a wheel chair and he was sitting up.

'Dad!' cried Jackson. 'Dad, what's happening?'

'Hey, lad, let me get in the house first,' said Frank jovially as he was wheeled down the yard and over the step through into the kitchen. 'Thanks, lads, you've done a grand job,' he said to the ambulance men. 'How about a cup of tea now?'

'No thanks, mate, we have to get back,' one said. 'See you next time.'

It wasn't until they were gone and his wheel chair settled by the fire in the place where his old armchair used to be, Maggie by his side, still beaming all over her face, that Frank spoke.

'Me back's getting better! There now, what do you think about that, eh? A bloody miracle it is! I thought it was, I could feel me toes. I wiggled them a bit when I was on me own but didn't want to say anything 'til I'd been to see the specialist. Why, man, I might even get back on me feet – mebbe not digging coal just yet, but you never know!'

'That's grand, Dad, grand,' said Jackson. He didn't go so far as to throw his arms around Frank or kiss him but his grasp on his father's arm was eloquent enough. Molly, though, did bend and kiss and congratulate him, and Maggie stood back, content as a queen.

In the excitement Molly forgot to put the dumplings in among the mince but no one minded that the tea was late. It gave Jackson time to go down to the Miner's Arms in the village and bring back a jug of brown ale and a bottle of lemonade, and they all toasted Frank's health, and when Harry came in with Mona they celebrated all over again.

They sang songs from the old war and 'Roll Out the Barrel' from this one and then there was a knock at the door and their neighbour walked in to complain that her man was on first shift and could they have some quiet, please? Then she got him out of bed to come and join the party when she saw Frank in a wheel chair, the hated long carriage pushed into a corner of the room, abandoned.

Jackson and Molly didn't have another minute to themselves. She was called from making sandwiches to sing 'When I Grow Too Old to Dream', and the applause brought the neighbours in from the other side, and so the party went on until the air raid warden came to complain that the back door was opening so often it was almost like a light flashing and were they *trying* to signal to the Germans? Frank said there wasn't a cloud in the sky when he came in and not a German either but the party broke up then and Molly went to bed for a couple of hours until it was time for her to catch the bus into Bishop station and another day's work.

Before she went she slipped into the bedroom to whisper cheerio to the men. Jackson got out of bed and went downstairs with her. He pulled her into his arms and kissed her. 'Watch yourself, kid,' he said. 'Don't get into any sort of trouble 'til I come back. And I promise you, I will be back. We'll be married, you'll see.'

Mona was at the gate calling softly to her and reluctantly Molly went out.

'I love you, Jackson Morley,' she said softly as she went.

'Me an' all,' he replied. 'I mean it.'

The girls were quiet as they hurried down the road for the bus, both of them deep in their own thoughts. Mona had lost her sparkle, there were no jokes on the bus, none on the train.

'War is hell,' was her only comment as they separated to go to their work stations. 'Who would have thought it, eh? Me mooning over a fella I've only known a week.'

'We're beginning to look like Chinese,' said Mona, gazing critically into the mirror on the wall of the changing room.

'We're all turning a bit yellow, it's true,' said Molly. 'They say they're going to supply a special cream to stop the powder affecting the skin. It'll form a sort of barrier.'

'I can't see it meself,' said Mona gloomily. 'The powder might just mix with it and soak in all the more. Harry won't know me when he comes back.' She still hadn't returned to her usual bouncy self, Molly thought. Mona's brows were usually knitted nowadays; her smile wasn't to be seen so often as it once had been. She was worried about Harry, Molly supposed, but then she was herself. Most of the girls were worried about the brothers and sweethearts who were in France.

No, Belgium they were now, if the wireless was to be believed. The British Expeditionary Force was in Belgium anyway and the DLI were part of it, weren't they? She looked up at the poster on the wall:

KEEP IT DARK,
FOR THE DURATION!

And the other one alongside it:

WALLS HAVE EARS!

There was a picture of a brick wall with an ear growing grotesquely out of the bricks.

Everyone talked about fifth columnists or spies. Maggie had been saying only last night that she had heard it as gospel in the doctor's waiting room where she had gone to collect Frank's tablets, for his slow recovery wasn't all a bed of roses, she told anyone who would listen.

'No, he has terrible pain and you would think in this day and age they could give him something strong enough to help him sleep through the night at least,' she had remarked to Molly. Anyway, she' d heard that Hitler had sent hundreds of spies with the refugees who had come from Germany and all over. No, she had nothing against the poor souls, they'd lost their homes and some had lost their families, but it made you wonder, didn't it? Molly was brought back to the present by Mona.

'If you don't get a move on you'll miss the train,' she said as she went out of the door. Mona herself was going on the bus to Ferryhill. She had no reason now to go back to Eden Hope to see her auntie, not when Harry wasn't there.

'Righto,' Molly replied. 'See you tomorrow.' She went out and set off for the gate, not noticing that someone was walking by her side until he spoke.

'Molly?' he said and she looked up in surprise, seeing it was the foreman on the band, a man in his thirties, she supposed, no taller than she was herself and podgy with it. He was sometimes sharp with some of the girls but had always been civil to her, smiling when he asked her to do something and adding, 'If you don't mind, Molly?'

'Oh, hello, Mr Dowson,' she said, wondering what he wanted with her. The next minute she found out.

'I was thinking, Molly, how about going to the pictures, on Saturday? We could go to the Hippodrome in Shildon, or if you like we could go to . . .' He stopped speaking as he saw that she was shaking her head. His eager smile slipped a little.

Molly was taken aback. For a minute she couldn't think of an answer, simply shook her head.

'We can go somewhere else, if you'd prefer,' he said, recovering. 'How about a dance? There's one on at –'

She stopped walking. 'No, I'm sorry, Mr Dowson, I can't. I'm engaged to a soldier, didn't you know? I have to catch my train now.'

She set off at a smart pace, leaving him standing frowning after her.

Mona needn't have worried. The train to Bishop Auckland was held up on a branch line. There was a munitions train standing by the platform of the tiny station and it was still being loaded. By the time the workers' train actually got moving it was thirty minutes late and the tired passengers were low and dispirited.

Molly found a seat in a corner and stared out of the window at the dark shapes as they rushed by. The train was unlit although once they were through Shildon tunnel and away from the munitions factory a tiny blue light came on, giving an eerie glow.

Snow had begun to fall earlier in the afternoon, a desultory sort of fall, starting and stopping and not lying except in small patches near the side of the line. But now it suddenly thickened until the windows of the compartment were blotted out with white.

'Oh, heck, I hope the buses aren't stopped before we get home,' someone moaned. 'It can snow as much as it likes tomorrow, maybe we won't get to work in the morning and can have a day off. But not tonight, please, I have a date the night.'

When the train arrived in Bishop Auckland it was a slipping, sliding struggle to get down to the bus stop. The bus was crowded, the conductor shouting to the queue, 'Workers only, please, workers only!' Somehow Molly managed to squeeze on and it lurched off on its way round the mining villages to the east of the town.

'Sorry, folks, we're going no further tonight!' the driver called, sounding quite cheerful as he climbed the steps into the bus. 'I'm not going to chance it any road.'

There was a chorus of groans from the passengers who only a minute before had been congratulating themselves that no one had been hurt when the bus had skidded and slithered to a sudden stop in a snow bank at the side of the road. At least there'd been no standing passengers by this time, the bus was only a few stops from its terminus.

Those left sat and looked at one another until the driver, sounding impatient, went on, 'Let's be having you, you'll have to walk the rest of the way. Come on, it cannot be far. Got your flashlights, have you? Well then, you'll be fine. Worse things happening to our lads, you know!'

Molly got to her feet, thankful that she had invested in a pair of rubber over-shoes to go over her shoes only last Saturday. Outside the snow was driving down, freezing cold. It stung her face and drove under her collar, flung open the bottom of her coat, needled her knees.

She set off up the dark hill, one of a crowd which gradually grew thinner as people came to their homes. Eden Hope was the last village in the string. Down into the valley she trudged, where there was at least some relief from the biting wind, up the other side and at last in to Eden Hope, past the colliery to the end of the rows.

'Eeh, come on in, lass,' said Maggie when at last Molly

reached the house and pushed her way through the drift of
snow which the wind had blown against the back door. It
came over her rubber over-shoes, and soaked wet and cold
through her already wet stockings. 'A rotten night. Eeh,
did you have to walk? You look like Nanouk of the North!'

'We had to walk the last bit, the bus was stuck.'

There was a letter propped on the mantelpiece, Molly
saw with a sudden lift of her spirits. The warmth of the
blazing fire filled the kitchen together with the smell of
liver and onions cooking in the oven. She took off coat and
scarf, both encrusted with snow, sat and undid her shoes
and only then did she walk over to the fire, to see that it
was Harry's handwriting.

Not that she was disappointed, she told herself. Only
last year she would have given anything to hear from her
brother. But it wasn't from Jackson.

'Oh, aye, a letter from your brother,' remarked Maggie
as she opened the oven door and took out the steaming dish
of liver and onions. 'We haven't heard from Jackson
either,' she added as she read Molly's expression. 'There'll
be a reason, pet. But mebbe Harry has some news of him.'

'Nothing much,' said Molly as she tore the envelope
open and scanned the single sheet. 'Most of it's been
crossed out by the censor. He says the two of them have
become attached to something, but what that something is
has been blotted out. And he says they're both in the pink.
Jackson is a sergeant again. He says . . .' She looked up to
see both Maggie and Frank watching and listening eagerly.

'I knew he'd get his stripe back,' said Frank. 'Can't keep a good soldier down, can they?'

'Here,' said Molly, handing over the letter. 'You read it, if you like.' She attacked her meal, feeling the heat of the fire seeping through to her chilled bones, her feet aching as the circulation returned to normal.

At least there had been a letter from one of them and both were fine when it was written, she thought. That was a bit of a relief. Finishing her meal, she got up to clear the table and wash up, which had become the accepted routine since she came to live at the Morleys'. Maggie did the cooking, Molly the washing up.

Afterwards she sat with them round the fire, listening to the wireless, Maggie knitting a pullover and Molly darning the elbows of one. At nine o'clock there was the BBC News. Both women's hands stilled as they listened.

There was fighting in Belgium, near the border with France, the news reader announced. Was that where Jackson and Harry were? Molly stared into the fire, her mending forgotten.

Maggie rose to her feet afterwards, lifted the kettle to see if there was enough water in it for the cocoa and settled it on the fire. She went to the window and lifted a corner of the blackout curtain, peering out.

'It's stopped snowing any road,' she remarked. 'I reckon you'll be able to get to work the morn, Molly.' She made the cocoa, put a careful spoonful of sugar in each cup and handed it round.

'In the Co-op today I heard that women with more money than sense were coming round from the towns and asking to buy folk's sugar ration.'

'No one sold, did they?' Molly looked up from her cocoa. Sugar rationing had begun just after Christmas, other foodstuffs in January.

'Well, one woman was going to, but they soon put her right according to Mrs Wright. You know, her from the top row. Sent the lah-di-dah one off with a flea in her ear an' all.' Maggie grinned at the thought. The men were all working now, women had a bit of money in their purses, no need to give up their precious sugar to the better off, nor anything else, neither. Why, she remembered a time just before the war when a woman had come to the village and bought up the whole stock of sugar in the shops, filling a car with the stuff. The miners' wives had been up in arms over that.

'In a motor car an' all, she were, Mrs Wright said.' Maggie reverted to the present. 'How did she get the petrol, that's what I'd like to know?'

Molly drained her cup. 'I'll just wash these up then I'll be off to bed,' she said. 'At least I'm on second shift, the roads will likely be cleared by then.' She smiled at the older couple, feeling a surge of affection for them. With all their troubles they had taken her in, treated her as one of the family. She would always be grateful to them for that. She touched the ring on her finger with the other hand, looked down at the stones glinting in the gaslight.

When this war was over . . . Her eyes were alight with dreams.

Next morning, as Maggie had predicted, the roads were fairly clear. The bus grunted and groaned its way into the town then Molly easily caught the train to work. The snow covering fields beside the line shone in the pale sunshine, the cleared track snaking out before the train.

Even the sprawling mass of the factory buildings looked clean and attractive under the snow. It was so big now that there was a bus to the Administration building at the far end. Eight square miles, Mona said it was, though how she knew Molly hadn't an idea.

'Hello, Molly,' a man's voice said as she came out of the clean room, once again swathed in an overall, her hair tied up under a turban.

'Hello, Mr Dowson,' she replied and quickened her pace. As she turned to go into the room where she was working, she glanced back. He was still standing where she had left him, gazing after her. He smiled and gave a little wave. Molly wished he wouldn't, he made her feel so uncomfortable.

'I think he's smitten with you,' one of the girls walking past in a group said, and they all burst into giggles.

'Don't talk so daft,' said Molly. Even if he was, she thought as she started work, she'd told him last night she was engaged, hadn't she? She dismissed him from her thoughts, humming along with the Andrews Sisters on the wireless. Today was a good day, she told herself. Today there would be a letter from Jackson sitting on the mantelpiece when she got home. It was lovely, getting a letter from him, almost as good as actually seeing him. Almost but not quite.

Chapter Eighteen

Refugees streamed along the country road. Jackson watched one grandmother with a baby in her arms, the mother pushing a baby carriage filled with clothes and household goods wrapped up in bedding and dragging a toddler with the other hand.

'Hell's bells, I wish they would get off the road,' said Harry feelingly. 'It's bad enough trying to get the lads moved along without fighting your way through this lot.'

Next minute the whole column were fleeing for the ditch at the side as a twin-engined ME110 German fighter plane swooped out of nowhere and began strafing them. Harry grabbed the old woman and screaming baby and dived with her for safety, Jackson close behind with the mother and little boy. They huddled together in the scant cover and after what seemed an age and another couple of runs by the plane, the pilot tired, or perhaps his fuel was running low, and turned to go back where he came from. The sound of the engine died away in the distance. It was very quiet except for a baby crying and someone moaning a few yards away.

'Come on, we can't help them.' Before the refugees could gather themselves together Jackson was back on the road, shouting for the men of his patrol. 'Fall in! Come on, lads, we have to make the river by nightfall.'

They had been seconded to a French Army unit which was defending a small hamlet on the River Dyle. The roads were choked with refugees. The only way through was on foot. Why they were going to aid the French neither Jackson nor Harry knew, but they had had their orders and were determined to carry them out. Even more determined now even though they had to pass by a group of crying children clustered round a woman lying on the ground, wounded if not dead. Surely others among the refugees would help?

Setting off at a quick march the soldiers of the DLI moved down the road, at times detouring into the fields beside it to overtake a group of refugees. They were silent mostly, grim-faced after what they had just witnessed.

'I keep thinking, Jackson,' Harry said after the first mile, 'if that lot should get to England it could be our Molly on the run with your parents. My God! They could be being strafed by . . .'

'Neither Hitler nor the Luftwaffe nor his bloody army is going to get to England,' snapped Jackson roughly. 'I don't want to hear that sort of talk.'

Harry glanced quickly at his set face and away again. He was right, it couldn't happen. It didn't bear thinking about.

They reached the French position by seven o'clock. It was a warm May evening, the sun casting long shadows on the fields surrounding the cluster of houses. The French soldiers welcomed them quietly, gave them bread and slices of Belgian sausage, spicy, with lumps of fat in it, and completely alien to the lads from Durham.

'I'll be up half the night with this lot,' one of them grumbled though he went on ploughing his way through it, washing it down with rough red wine. 'What I wouldn't give for a bit of meat pudding and a glass of Newcastle Brown!'

'Get away, man,' said Harry. 'This is nothing to what we had to eat in India. The food there was hot enough to take the roof off your mouth. Why –'

What he had been going to say none of them discovered because at that precise moment three German dive-bombers, the noise of their engines muffled at first by the hill which they came over, zoomed down on the hamlet and strafed everything in sight. There was only the one run and after it Jackson picked himself up from under the bush where he had dived and looked around to assess the damage.

A few yards away a French ack-ack gun had opened up from its cover behind a clump of bushes. Now the gun barrel was lifted to the sky, waiting for the return run which never came.

'Harry!'

Jackson ran to his friend who sat slumped against the

trunk of a tree, a lump of French bread still in his hand, his mouth hanging open slackly. Even as Jackson got to him, a dark red stain showed through the rough khaki of his battledress, spreading, turning almost black, beginning to drip on to the bare earth under the tree.

'Harry!' Jackson cried again. He was rifling through his kit, searching for a field dressing. He found one at last and the man who had been grumbling about the food barely a minute before was helping him get the battledress open.

'He's not dead, Sergeant,' the soldier said. 'Look, he's breathing.'

Jackson had control of himself now. He found the place, the entry wound deceptively small considering the amount of blood Harry had lost already. But it didn't look as though it was anywhere vital. He managed to put on the dressing, binding it tightly, and the flow of blood slowed.

'What the hell was that?'

Relief flooded Jackson as he looked up quickly to see that Harry's eyes were open. He was pale but his eyes were focussing properly. He tried to sit up and winced, his hand going to his side.

'It's all right, just a nick in your side. You were lucky that time, Harry,' he said. 'Help me get him inside, Private, will you?'

'Aye, Sergeant. That lot will be back, nowt so sure.'

Behind them was a cottage, its windows dark, the owners long gone. Probably they had passed them on the road earlier in the day. They got him inside, Harry walking at least though supported on either side by the other two. As soon as he could, Jackson would get him back to a First Aid post. It would have to be a French one, they were too far away from their own lines.

'I'll see the French officer, Harry.' Jackson got to his feet. 'Get you back to the –'

He broke off at the sound of gunfire, not in the distance but close, too close, coming nearer all the time, on the other side of the hill.

'Go on. I'll be all right,' said Harry. But Jackson and the Private were already at the door, rifles at the ready. The Germans were coming.

The concert party, mostly girls with a sprinkling of men, were rehearsing for the first works concert. Molly and Mona were there. They had rushed their dinner to allow as much time as possible for the rehearsal, though even then half an hour was about the most they had.

'Now then, lads and lasses.' Mr Dowson banged his baton on the music stand importantly, calling them to order. There was some giggling and a few remarks made in undertones but most of the concert party turned to listen.

Mr Dowson had surprised them all, turning up for the first rehearsal in response to a leaflet pinned on the notice board asking anyone interested to join the party. Not only could he sing in a fine tenor voice, he had a talent for acting which transformed him. When he was on stage everyone forgot his short stature and podgy figure. His voice rang out pure and true, mesmerising all who listened. He could play the piano too with an impressive ability so that straight away he was voted in as leader of the concert party.

Today they were rehearsing 'Kiss Me Goodnight, Sergeant-Major'. The girls were going to be dressed up in battledress, the Sergeant-Major would be Mr Dowson, sporting a large false moustache. He strutted up and down the stage as they danced, not exactly like the Tiller Girls as yet but they were getting there.

'The thing is, it's hard to sing *and* dance,' Mona complained. 'I can't get me breath, I'm like a stranded trout.'

'Shouldn't smoke so much,' said Molly. But she grinned at Mona. Most of the girls smoked. She herself had tried it once or twice but couldn't understand what they saw in it. Anyway, it seemed a shame to start when there weren't enough cigarettes for the men as it was.

'They're getting so scarce we'll all be cutting down,' Mona said gloomily.

'Will you two girls at the back there stop gossiping and get on with it?' enquired Mr Dowson.

'*Kiss Me Goodnight, Sergeant-Major,*' the girls sang, in a line, kicking their legs in unison, arms along each other's shoulders.

'Just like that picture that's on at the Majestic. You know, *Ziegfield Follies of 1938.*'

Molly hadn't seen it, she didn't get to the pictures much.

Usually she was doing jobs for Maggie when she was on the right shift.

The half hour sped by and she was soon back in her little room, filling shells with TNT from the hopper once again. Her movements were automatic by now but she had to concentrate, it was too dangerous not to. Nevertheless thoughts of Jackson sneaked into her mind. She wondered where he was, what he was doing, had he written to her?

There was a letter when she got back to Eden Hope. As always her eyes went straight to the mantelpiece and there it was. And Maggie and Frank were both smiling, they too had had a precious letter.

'He doesn't say much, lass, not about where he is. But according to the wireless, they're fighting in Belgium. I tell you what, our lads'll soon see the Huns off, you mark my words.'

'The main thing is, he's all right. Harry an' all, he reckons,' said Maggie.

Molly kept the letter beside her as she ate her tea. She kept looking at it, a warm glow suffusing her whole body. When she had finished she left the washing up and went up to her room. Jackson's room, it still was really, his things were still about, comforting to her.

'*My love . . .*'

Molly was lying on her bed, gas jet turned up high so she could see to read by its flickering light. (The mantle was about done, it had two holes in it and the flame hissed and licked at it. Gas mantles were getting scarce along with everything else. The houses had been about to be wired for electricity but the war stopped that.) She kissed the words. She was his love, she thought. *'As soon as this campaign is over, I'll get some leave and we'll be married . . .'*

There was no real information. Harry was well, so was he. There might not be a letter for a while because he was going . . . The rest was blanked out by the censor, the only bit in the letter which was. Jackson was always careful what he wrote.

But at least it was a letter. He had held it in his hands, written the words. It was the only link Molly had had with him for weeks. She closed her eyes and imagined the feel of his lips on hers, him lying beside her.

Oh, well, she'd best go down and see to the washing up. And she'd promised to turn the pantry out for Maggie who had little time to spare now she took Frank out in the wheel chair every day. Up to the pit yard where he could meet the men coming off shift and have a few words with them. Or down to the Miners' Welfare, where there was a ramp for the chair and the chance of meeting some of his old mates for endless talks of wet seams and cavils and, nowadays, how the war was going.

'I had a letter from Harry yesterday,' said Mona. 'I think he wants us to get wed when he comes home.'

'Me too.' Molly smiled at her friend. 'I mean, I had a letter too.'

'Hurry up, girls, there's another rehearsal,' a voice said behind them and they looked at one another. It was getting difficult for Molly to hold off Mr Dowson. He was always about when she came out of her work room, always next to her in the queue at the canteen somehow.

'We know, Mr Dowson,' said Mona, and gave Molly a meaningful grin. 'He's here again,' she whispered loudly.

'Shh!' hissed Molly.

'Call me Gary,' Mr Dowson said affably, and Mona could hardly control her giggles.

'Now then, our Mona, stop messing about. Do you want cabbage or not?'

Mona's mother was behind the counter, her hair done up in a net, a voluminous white overall wrapped round her. Mrs Fletcher was a widow. Mona's father had died only three months before the war started and his wife had been just under fifty so didn't receive a widow's pension.

'Quite right, Mrs Fletcher,' said Mr Dowson primly. 'Go on, girls. As I said, we have to rehearse.'

'OK, Mam, give us a spoonful,' said Mona. 'It looks all right, you cannot have cooked it, eh?'

Her mother made a threatening gesture with her serving spoon and Mona ducked, laughing. The girls took their trays to one of the long tables and settled down to eat fish and chips and cabbage followed by spotted dick and custard.

The days were getting longer. When Molly left the factory and walked along by the perimeter wall to where the buses were lined up near the station the sun was still shining; in the trees across the road birds were twittering as they got ready to roost for the night. She felt a surge of optimism. Summer was almost here. Surely it would be a good summer after the cold snows of winter? Was the sun shining on the boys in Belgium, or wherever they were?

Jackson and six of his men were lying just under the brow of the hill above the hamlet, watching the column of approaching Germans. The French Lieutenant was further along the hill, staring at the advancing column, looking as though he couldn't believe what he was seeing. But Jackson didn't wait for his orders. As soon as the column was within range he ordered his men to fire. The column slowed, halted for a minute or two, and then came on inexorably.

'Fall back!' called the Lieutenant. 'Fall back!' he cried in English to Jackson, but Jackson didn't hear. Rifle fire in his ears drowned out all else. When he looked across at where the Frenchmen had been, they were gone.

'I think we're on our own here, Sergeant,' said the Private who had helped him with Harry earlier in the afternoon.

'You're not supposed to think,' snapped Jackson. 'Keep firing!' Suddenly there was a deafening explosion as one of the leading tanks in the column fired at the hill where they were concealed. Three of his men were thrown into the air and fell heavily, to be covered in a rain of grass tufts, soil and stones.

'Bloody hell!' the Private said. Jackson glanced at him. He was white and shaking with shock. He had dropped his rifle but picked it up quickly and turned back to face the Germans.

'Fall back to the gun emplacement,' said Jackson. 'Now!'

Only two of the men got to their feet. As the dust cleared, Jackson crept closer to the others. They were all dead.

Harry . . . He had to get back to Harry. What would Molly think if he let her brother fall into the hands of the Germans? With its even occurring to him how ludicrous the thought was when they were all likely to be taken by the enemy at any minute, Jackson picked up one of the dead men's rifles and carried it along with his own down the hill to the cluster of houses near the bottom.

Thank God there was a French ambulance standing there, they must be taking away the wounded. There were bodies all around, the German fire had taken a heavy toll of the French infantrymen.

'Harry?'

His friend was being brought out of the cottage, leaning heavily on the arm of a Red Cross man. He was white from loss of blood, but he was on his feet.

'I'm fine, Jackson, don't bother about me. I reckon this lot'll get me a nice fortnight back in Blighty.' He looked over his shoulder and winked at his friend as he was helped into the ambulance which was already crowded with wounded.

'Lucky beggar,' said Jackson. At least Harry was getting out of it, he thought as he turned away and began to climb back up the hill to the clump of bushes where the French ack-ack gun was, barrel trained on the skyline where the Germans would appear. The thing was to hold them back as long as possible, he told himself.

The French were falling back, only the gun crew were still there. But even as Jackson slid behind the sandbag barrier the Germans appeared on the skyline, inexorably moving nearer. The French were shouting to each other. The soldier manning the gun left it and moved back. Jackson realised they were going to abandon the position. But if they did, the Germans could easily overrun the ambulance, take them all prisoner, and then what about Harry?

'*Allez! Allez!*' he shouted, and took hold of the gun. With a quick glance behind him he waved them away, a gesture they understood more easily than his terrible French. He began firing at the enemy, succeeded in halting the first car, then the tank behind. He didn't pause but carried on firing until the ammunition was exhausted. When he looked behind him the French were gone, all of them, men and vehicles, including the ambulance carrying Harry, thank God.

Now was the time to get away himself, while the

Germans were momentarily halted. Jackson slid away from the gun emplacement on his belly, got almost to a clump of trees by the now roofless farmhouse when an explosion rocked the earth once more. The gun he had been manning was flung into the air like a child's toy and he sank into oblivion.

Chapter Nineteen

'Middlesbrough bombed!'

The news spread fast around the Royal Ordnance Factory.

'Bloody hell,' the guard on the gate said as Molly showed him her pass to get in. 'Middlesbrough! Not a kick in the backside away from here, is it?'

Molly agreed. All of them felt a surge of disquiet at the news. It wasn't the fact that Middlesbrough was the first industrial town to be bombed so much as the thought of what would happen if a bomb dropped on this factory. Half of County Durham could be blown to smithereens.

'What the heck?' said Mona when they met during the break. 'They'll never find us, not with the fog down most of the time. Any road, we have to go sometime, haven't we?'

They were getting used to the feeling of danger, all of them. At the beginning of the war they'd all carried their gas masks everywhere but now fewer and fewer people did, though more might well after this latest event.

'No letter from Harry,' Mona said as they walked down

to their places. For once she was solemn-faced. It had been on the radio that the Germans had broken through, were streaming into France. She looked at Molly questioningly.

'I haven't had anything either.'

Mona sighed. 'Oh, well, let's get on with it.'

Today at dinnertime they were to give their first show to the workers. Gary Dowson was full of himself, they moaned to each other.

'Don't forget, girls, straight in and go to the head of the queue. I've arranged it,' he said, hurrying past them. Though even then he still had time for an ingratiating smile at Molly, followed by a look which drank her in from head to toe, though her figure was hidden under the enveloping overall. Instinctively she folded her arms over her breasts.

'My Lord, Molly, you're going to have to watch him,' Mona commented as they paused outside Molly's door. She watched the foreman disappear around the bend in the corridor.

'Not so easy when we're singing a duet,' she replied.

They were singing 'The Indian Love Song' from *Rose Marie*, and Gary Dowson gave every indication of revelling in it. He was only acting, Molly assured herself. Don't be a fool, he knows you're engaged.

'Bring your heel down on his instep,' Mona advised. 'Or there are other moves I could teach you which will make him reach high C.'

'Oh, Mona!' said Molly. She was smiling as she went in to begin work.

The concert was a success, the canteen packed with their fellow workers. Everyone cheered and clapped with enthusiasm for the dancers, now not quite so ragged in their performance as they got into the swing of it. They cheered Gary Dowson and Molly when they sang their duet, Gary looking deep into Molly's eyes until she discovered she could fake rapture in return by staring fixedly at the Brylcreemed lock of hair arranged carefully on his forehead.

They fell about laughing when Mona recited her comic monologue, but it was when Molly stood on the improvised stage and sang the 'Love's Old Sweet Song' that they clapped and cheered the most. Her heart beat fast and her palms sweated so she had to rub them with her handkerchief and then keep it there, twisting it between her fingers as she began the song. But then the image of Jackson appeared in her mind's eye, his dark eyes smiling into hers, one eyebrow lifted quizzically, and she sang to him. It was so quiet in the canteen that she could have been all alone but for her dreams. And then the applause began.

Afterwards, brought down to earth by the need to get back to her work, she stood by the hopper filling shells, one after the other. Her workmates actually liked her, she thought. They did. A few of them had come up to congratulate her, clapped her on the shoulder. This was a new life for her in spite of the dangers of the war and the fact that her brother and Jackson were in France fighting. She felt that everything would turn out well, her bad times were surely over.

She was smiling softly to herself when there was a loud bang and the alarm sounded. For a second she was disorientated. She looked around at the door as the belt stopped its progress and the music halted on the wireless.

'Evacuate the building! Evacuate . . .' Molly rushed for the door, turning to see if Mona was there before realising that she wouldn't be. She had been transferred to the detonator section at the beginning of the week.

Joining the stream of people as they hurried for the emergency exits, Molly tried to ask what had happened but those around her had been working in closed-off rooms themselves, and were as mystified as she was.

'Have we been bombed?' She caught sight of Gary Dowson standing by the door, but he was busy ushering them out and for once not willing to talk to her.

Outside groups of workers were talking in hushed voices as they went to their emergency stations, away from the danger. One of the First Aid team came out of a door and hurried down the street and everyone watched as though that would give them the answer to what had happened.

'What was it, do you know?' Molly asked Violet, a girl from her group.

'You know as much as I do, Molly,' she replied.

'Fifth columnists, I bet,' one of them said. 'Sabotage.'

The girls fell silent as they reached the perimeter wall

and lined up by the emergency exit. The idea that a saboteur could get into the works and cause mayhem was sobering to say the least.

'It was the detonator shed,' a new voice broke in. 'I was working right close. I was deafened by the bang, I can tell you.' She put her fingers in her ears and wiggled them about, frowning. 'I never ran so quick in all my days.'

'Are you sure? I mean, that it was the detonator shed?' asked Molly anxiously, an awful dread creeping over her. She began looking round for Mona, her gaze going from group to group, but her friend was nowhere to be seen. A fire engine went by along one of the internal roads, followed by an ambulance.

'Was anyone hurt, do you know? Mona was working there, has anyone seen her?' Molly's dread was mounting. Her heart beat so fast it threatened to choke her. She went from group to group, asking if they had seen Mona but no one had. But it couldn't be true. Mona couldn't be dead. She was so alive, always laughing. Molly had a vision of her flicking her long blonde hair back from her forehead. Oh, she was so *pretty*. She couldn't be gone, blown to smithereens, of course she couldn't, the idea was ludicrous. Mona was her friend, her very best friend. Please God, not her.

Molly struggled to keep a hold of herself, fighting down the panic, the feeling that it was true and that it was all her fault. She had a jinx on her. Mona was her friend, ergo Mona had to die.

The group looked at one another, shook their heads. Molly chewed her lip. It seemed like an age before they could move away from the emergency exit. The ambulance drove away, not using its siren. Was that a good sign or was it a bad? The Tannoy crackled and everyone looked up expectantly.

'Everyone to the canteen. Move to the canteen in orderly fashion, please,' a tinny voice ordered and the girls started to move away, quiet now, all of them wondering the same thing.

In the canteen Molly searched the faces behind the counter for Mona's mother. If anyone knew what had happened to Mona she would. But Mrs Fletcher wasn't there. Perhaps she was working in the kitchen, Molly thought. No, of course, she was probably not back yet. Even the catering staff would have had to go to their emergency stations.

There was tea from the urn but Molly couldn't face it. She sat at the table with the others while they drank and lit cigarettes. For the first time Molly wished she smoked, it seemed to release tension. Then the word went round the room, coming from nobody knew where: a girl had been killed working on detonators.

It still didn't have to be Mona, thought Molly, but where was she? The next minute her worst fears were confirmed as Mrs Fletcher was led out of the kitchens, supported on either side by members of the First Aid team. Head bent she was taken out, looking neither to left nor to right as she went. Molly was on her feet and pushing her way through the crowd to reach her but by the time she got to the door Mrs Fletcher was being helped into a car.

'Mrs Fletcher!' Molly called, and the woman looked up, her face white, her eyes staring. Molly ran to her.

'Is it –' But she couldn't say it, she couldn't. Mrs Fletcher merely nodded and began to get into the car.

'Are you a friend of hers?' someone asked, and looking up Molly saw it was the works doctor.

'A friend of her daughter's,' she said. And it was because of her that this had happened, she thought again. The numbness of grief crept over her, mixed with guilt. It was because of her own bad luck. It had rubbed off on her friend.

'You'd best go with her then,' he said. He was a middle-aged man with heavy jowls and thinning hair which was parted in the centre of his large head and plastered to either side with some sort of dressing. His eyes were dark brown and sympathetic. He had been a local GP for twenty years. Now his list was twice as big with the advent of this sprawling factory amid the green fields of central Durham.

Molly hesitated. 'I'll have to ask . . . get permission.'

Five minutes later she was sitting in the back of the car with Mona's mother. They didn't talk, there was nothing to say.

'I'll leave her with you,' said the driver. 'I'll be outside.' Not until they were inside the little terraced house in Ferryhill did Mrs Fletcher speak.

'Our Mona's not usually careless,' she said. 'I mean, she wasn't.'

'No! I'm sure she wasn't,' Molly answered. 'It must have been an accident, you know.' She looked around, hardly knowing what to do, or what to say. 'Would you like a cup of tea? I'll get you one, shall I?'

'No. I've had enough tea to sink a ship. Well, if she wasn't careless, how could it happen?'

'It does, these things do,' said Molly helplessly.

Mrs Fletcher looked at her. She seemed to accept Molly's assurances and changed tack. 'I mind when her dad died,' she said. 'It's funny, it doesn't seem real at first.'

'No,' said Molly, thinking back to the time when her own father was killed. Her heart ached for the older woman.

'I was that pleased when she got on with your brother. A nice lad, yes, a nice lad.'

'Yes.'

Molly looked about the neat kitchen-cum-living room. The linoleum on the floor was scrubbed and polished and covered with oblong clippie mats, just like most of the houses she'd known. The windows gleamed. Cheap cotton curtains hung there, lined with thick blackout material, the same as Maggie had at her windows, bought at the Co-op no doubt. A cinder fell to the enamelled plate covering the hearth. Automatically Mrs Fletcher got to her feet and scooped it up with the steel-handled brush and shovel which hung on the companion set by the side of the grate.

'Will you be writing to Harry?'

Molly looked back at Mrs Fletcher. Mona's mother sounded so polite. She sat on the edge of her chair, smoothing her skirt over her knees as though she had unexpected company.

'Yes. Yes, of course,' Molly said. The clock on the mantel ticked loudly. 'Are you sure I can't do anything for you?' she asked. 'Is there a neighbour I should call? Anyone else that I could get in touch with?'

'No, no, that's fine, you've been very good,' said Mrs Fletcher. She got to her feet. 'I'd like to be on me own now. It's not that I don't appreciate . . .'

And Molly found herself outside on the street, ushered out. She needed to be allowed to mourn, with Mona's mother, oh, she did. But she couldn't push herself forward, she wasn't wanted. Mrs Fletcher closed the door behind her, leaving Molly staring at it for a moment. A minute or two later the curtains closed too, leaving the windows looking strangely blind as the black cloth gave back her own reflection through the glass. The sign of a death in the family, a sign for the neighbours to walk past quietly, the children not to play too close, show some respect. It was always done.

Molly was surprised to find the car still waiting. She had supposed that she would go straight home from Ferryhill. As she approached it the driver got out and opened the door for her.

'All right, is she?'

'As all right as she's going to be,' Molly said shortly. 'Are we going back to the factory?'

'Those are my orders. To take you back to Administration.'

The Administration building was on the opposite side of the complex from where Molly had been working and when she came out it was only five minutes to the end of her shift. Instead of taking the internal bus she walked across to the station, glad of the fresh air.

The manager had asked if she was a friend of the family, told her the funeral would be taken care of, all in very business-like tones. He made notes on a piece of paper in front of him, looking up at Molly from time to time.

'Mrs Fletcher has a sister in Eden Hope,' he commented. 'Her only relation. She will have to be notified. Well, I think that's all.' He put down his pen and sat back in his seat. 'May I say how sorry I am about the death of your friend? By the way, how was Mrs Fletcher when you left her?'

'Shocked,' said Molly. 'I don't think it has hit her yet.'

'No, of course not.'

He looked uncomfortable as Molly stared at him, but what could he do? How was he supposed to act?

'Well, goodbye then, Miss Mason,' he said finally, standing up.

The funeral was small. There had been nothing in the

paper about the explosion and workers weren't encouraged to take time off to go to the funeral. The powers that be didn't want a fuss made, nor did they want the public to think the works were unsafe. Molly did get the afternoon off. She went with Maggie, Mona's aunt and uncle to the Methodist Chapel at Ferryhill. A few of the girls from the concert party who were off shift went too. But it was a low-key affair.

What on earth was she going to write to Harry? How could she tell him that Mona had been blown up and the inquest returned a verdict of accidental death? They sang the twenty-third psalm and then the minister began to talk about Mona as a child in Sunday school, or telling jokes to the back row of the choir as a fourteen-year-old. And now she was buried in the wind-swept cemetery, only twenty-one years old.

Molly travelled back to Eden Hope with Maggie, Mona's aunt and uncle going back to the house with her mother. As soon as she got in, Molly resolved, she would sit down at the little table and write that letter.

It took a few sheets of spoiled paper before she felt reasonably satisfied. She told the bare facts and expressed her sympathy and in the end didn't try to write anything else. She put the letter in an envelope and addressed it care of the regiment. It would be forwarded to wherever Harry was from there.

'I'll just go to the post with this,' she said to Maggie. 'I'll be back in time for tea.'

As she walked past the newsagent's to the post office she saw the chalked notice on the billboard:

FRANCE CAPITULATES

The first thought which came into her head was that at least it meant Harry and Jackson would be coming home soon.

'They will, won't they?' she asked Frank when she got home and told them the news.

'Nay, lass, how would I know?' he replied. Seeing the look on her face and hearing her sigh, he went on swiftly, 'I'd say they stood a good chance of getting leave any road, when they get back this side of the Channel. We'll get it on the news.' He wheeled himself over to the wireless which stood on a table in the corner and began twiddling with the knobs, causing bursts of static before the voice of the BBC announcer came on.

Chapter Twenty

There was an epidemic of diphtheria in Eden Hope. The summer days were fine and hot. While there were often planes droning overhead, sirens wailing, dog fights in the sky, and the excited cries of bairns on the ground searching for bits of shrapnel for souvenirs, ambulance sirens were wailing too as they took small children to the fever hospital.

The panel doctor went to the schools to vaccinate the ones who were well while their teachers harangued them about the dangers of collecting shrapnel and of drinking from each other's cups.

In their houses people sheltered under the stairs or built underground shelters in the gardens. Others used the entrance to an old drift mine, putting in chairs and emergency supplies, a door across the opening made out of pieces of wood. That was until a bomb was dropped too close for comfort, the German pilot obviously mistaking it for a working mine.

The fumigating team was in the street as Molly came home one morning from night shift. They usually followed the ambulance after a diphtheria victim was sent to hospital.

'Little Annie Sutton,' said Maggie in answer to her query. 'There was an allowance of oranges the day at the Co-op store. One for each ration book. I sent them up for the other Sutton bairns. You don't mind, do you?'

Molly assured her that she didn't mind at all. She looked up at the mantelpiece but there was no letter. She sighed. She had even resorted to the old child's game of adding up the numbers on her bus ticket and dividing them by seven. It all depended on how many were left over.

> One for sorrow,
> Two for joy.
> Three for a letter . . .

The rhyme went on and on endlessly in her mind, she had to make a conscious effort to stop it. It was just too childish altogether to think it might work. It showed how much she missed him, missed them both. Harry was on her mind a lot. She couldn't bear for anything to happen to him, he was all she had left of the family.

Men were filtering back from Dunkirk. It was on the wireless all the time about the army of little boats bringing them home. A triumph, they said, when the Germans thought they had had them trapped.

'They just don't know us British,' Frank said proudly. 'Just like in the last war. The Kaiser called our lads "that contemptible little army". But we showed them, didn't we, Mother?'

'Aye,' said Maggie absently. She had her baking things out on the table and was about to make a meat and vegetable pie, though it wouldn't taste like one of her usual pies, she told Frank crossly. 'Not with only half the fat, like.'

Most folk didn't care that they had lost their main ally. They'd manage better without the French, they told each other. There was an air of relief almost, they were on their own now.

'Well,' said Frank, who had been occupying his time reading history books from the library, 'we've been on our own afore now.'

'If I only had word of our Jackson I wouldn't care,' Maggie said wistfully. Frank was fiddling with the wireless, hoping for the racing results. He had a sixpenny bet on a horse in the one-thirty at Sedgefield. The bookie's runner still came to the end of the rows on racing days, slyly taking slips of paper wrapped round coins while keeping an eye out for the polis. To Molly it was amazing that racing and football or any kind of sports should go on just as though the war wasn't happening, as though Jackson and other mothers' sons weren't in danger.

'You're all strung up, lass,' said Maggie, seeing her exasperated expression. 'But folk like Frank have to have something to take their minds off the war.'

It was true, Molly thought, as she ate her porridge

sugarless, like the Scots did, and drank her tea sugarless too. Frank had a sweet tooth and they were saving sugar to make bramble jam in the autumn. It was strange coming in from work in the mornings to eat breakfast and getting up in the evenings to eat dinner before going out again. But she couldn't ask Maggie to cook things separately just for her.

Afterwards she took a few turns at the poss tub, thumping the stick up and down in the soapy water, watching the clothes twist and turn. It had a strangely soothing effect and when, later on, she washed and changed into her nightie and climbed into bed, the curtains drawn against the bright sunshine outside, she fell easily into a deep sleep.

It was still light when she woke but the sun's rays had left the front of the house, showing it must be afternoon. At first she didn't recognise the noise outside. It took a minute or two to realise it was the pit blowing the air raid siren. Soon there was a plane droning overhead. Molly wondered if it was British or German, if she should get up and investigate, even look for shelter. But her limbs were heavy with sleep. Instead she simply lay there. In the end the noise faded away, the plane evidently heading home, its bombs already dropped.

The chapel had been full on Sunday, people turning back to God who hadn't seen the inside of a church for years apart from weddings and funerals. Molly's thoughts wandered back to it. She had prayed for Jackson and Harry but all the while she couldn't help thinking that there must be women in Germany praying for their sons and sweethearts too. Ah, well. She sighed and climbed out of bed. She would go downstairs and see if Maggie needed a hand with the ironing. If only there was a letter when she came home tomorrow, if only she had some news.

Downstairs, Maggie was extricating Frank and his wheel chair from the cupboard under the stairs.

'I'm going in there no flaming more, woman,' he growled. 'If a bomb drops on us, we'll go any road, I've told you before. Besides, I want you to push me up to the corner, I have some winnings to collect.'

'I'll do it, if you like?' offered Molly.

'No, I'll go. I could do with a bit of fresh air,' Maggie replied.

After they had gone, Molly covered the table with an old blanket which Maggie kept for ironing and connected the gas iron to the outlet by the gas ring. Soon she was working away at the pile of clothes which she brought in from the yard, filling the overhead line which stretched across the kitchen.

It was hot working in the glow of the gas and the fire which had heated the oven for Maggie's pie. Molly paused and rubbed her brow with the back of her hand, then hung up the shirt she had just finished and turned to pick another from the pile. And through the open doorway saw the telegraph boy just coming to the door, raising his hand to knock.

Her heart dropped into her shoes. She felt sick and faint with dread. The telegraph boy meant only one thing nowadays, especially if you had a soldier in the family. Carefully she turned off the gas at the outlet, turned her back on the boy and stood for a minute or two, trying to tell herself it wasn't happening. Dear God, she'd prayed for a letter, not this. The boy interrupted her frantic thoughts.

'Missus?'

Molly turned slowly. The boy was holding out a yellow envelope. 'I'm sorry, Missus.' His face was solemn. He had done this before, of course he had, he must have done it countless times over these last few months. Molly took the envelope. It was addressed to Frank. It wasn't Harry then, she thought. Suddenly she tore it open, not able to bear the suspense any more.

'. . . *regret to inform you that Sergeant Jackson Morley is missing, believed killed.*'

'There'll not be a reply, Missus?' asked the boy. No one wanted to reply to the War Office.

Molly shook her head and he went off up the yard. He started to whistle in his relief to have it over, realised what he was doing and stopped, looking guiltily over his shoulder.

It wasn't true, of course it wasn't true. Missing he might be but he wasn't killed. Anyone as full of life as Jackson couldn't be dead. Molly was still standing there, the telegram in her hand, when Maggie came back with Frank.

*

Jackson's name was read out in chapel on the following Sunday along with half a dozen others. Molly stopped going to the services then. After all, she thought dully, they did no good. All these years of Christianity, all the centuries even, and there were still wars. If there was a God, He didn't care.

About a week later, there was a letter from Harry.

I got your letter today. It had followed me around for weeks. Little Mona, I can't believe it. This bloody war. And you, Molly, you be careful, I don't want to lose you too. Can't you get a transfer or something? It doesn't seem right, lasses getting blown up, doesn't bear thinking about. I don't know where Jackson is, we got separated. But he'll be all right, Jackson knows what he's doing.

He didn't say much more, except that he was expecting leave and would try to get up to see her and the Morleys. Molly told Maggie but she didn't know whether the older woman had taken it in. She and Frank had withdrawn into themselves since the telegram came, sitting for hours in silence. Frank didn't even listen to the wireless now except for the news. In vain Molly told them that it wasn't definite. She felt in herself that if Jackson were dead she would have known, have felt it in her heart. But the next minute she was telling herself not to be a superstitious fool.

There was no way, no way at all, she would be able to tell. And then Harry came home.

When Molly came back from the factory he was waiting for her on the corner of the rows, a tall, rangy soldier, a lock of dark hair falling over one eye, his forage cap stuck in his epaulette. He was leaning against the end wall of the last house and there was a ring of lads surrounding him, firing off questions, asking about the battles, about Dunkirk. When Molly saw him he had his back to her and was describing something, using his hands to draw in the air. For a moment she thought it was Jackson. Her heart leapt, her pulse raced, she could hardly see. But then her vision cleared and she saw it was her brother. And a surge of gladness and a wave of sorrow washed over her at the same time.

'Harry!'

He picked her up and swung her round then grimaced as he put her down. 'Oh, heck, I shouldn't have done that,' he said, putting a hand to his side.

'Why? What's the matter?' She gazed anxiously at the place.

'Nothing, just a nick, it's better now.'

Molly was desperately wondering if he knew anything at all about what had happened to Jackson. He had said nothing and she couldn't ask him in the street for fear of his reply.

They went into the house arm in arm. Maggie and Frank were by the fire in spite of the warmth of the day. They looked more alert than they had since the day the telegram came. Maggie had even made the tea, a salad with lettuce and scallions from next-door's garden, tomatoes and cucumber from the cold frame.

It was Frank who brought up the subject which was uppermost in Molly's mind. 'Harry thinks Jackson might be still on his way back. He might even be a prisoner-of-war, the lists haven't all come out yet,' he said. For the first time for days there was an air of hope about him.

Molly glanced quickly at her brother. 'You saw him?'

'We were attached to a French platoon,' he said. He dropped her arm, looked guilty somehow. 'I was wounded, came away in an ambulance while Jackson was left behind.' He was looking at the floor as he spoke. Suddenly he lifted his head and looked at them. 'I couldn't help it, honest!' he exclaimed. 'I was hit in the side, I would never have left him otherwise, I wouldn't.' He sounded on the defensive and the others stared at him.

'Nay, lad, of course you wouldn't,' said Maggie. 'We never thought it was your fault, not at all.'

At the weekend Molly took him to Ferryhill to see Mona's grave and pay his respects to her mother. It was an uncomfortable interview. Mrs Fletcher seemed surprised to see them and politely glad to see them go. There was simply nothing to say, thought Molly sadly.

Harry went back to barracks the following Monday. Molly was on fore shift and so she could go in with him to the station at Bishop Auckland. She smiled and waved as she stood on the platform and the train pulled away, but behind the smile she felt desperately alone. More alone than she had ever been in her life, even after her dad was killed in the pit. She went back to Eden Hope where Frank and Maggie had relapsed into sad apathy, hardly noticing her coming or going, not even listening to the news.

'He got away then?' Maggie did manage to say as she came in the door.

'Yes,' Molly replied. She went upstairs to toss and turn in Jackson's bed, getting up once to take his old coat off the hanger in the closet and lie cuddling it, breathing deeply, catching the essential scent of him. She slept fitfully, waking with a headache and that deep sense of loss which wouldn't go away.

Her days and nights were filled with the factory. She began working in the sewing room. Mrs Fletcher came back to the canteen, thinner and older-looking but as efficient as she had always been.

The battle in the air faded or moved away. The RAF had beaten off the Luftwaffe, people said, the threat of invasion was not so imminent. But Molly felt as though she was in a fog, it was all so unreal. Her wage packet became lighter. For the first time she had to pay income tax of eight shillings and sixpence in the pound.

'It's a flaming disgrace!' Jenny Johnson said when she sat down beside Molly in the canteen. She ate her Cornish pasty and chips rapidly then lit a cigarette. 'Fags going up an' all. They're making us workers pay for the war, all right.' She sat back in her chair and took a long drag on her cigarette, blowing out smoke through a round 'O' of bright red lipstick. Jenny was on Molly's band in the sewing room. They were sewing cordite bags for the navy today.

'Yes,' she said absently.

Jenny regarded her thoughtfully. 'You're going to have to come out of it, you know.'

Molly looked up in surprise. 'Out of what?'

'Look, there's more than you lost somebody in this war. I know it was rotten losing your friend *and* your boyfriend, but you have to pull yourself together. You've not been to the concert party rehearsals for weeks and we could certainly do with you. Most of us can't sing for toffee. We just go for a laugh and a bit of fun.'

'I can't. Anyway, rehearsal's after the shift and I have to get home.'

'Want to see if there's a letter? You're not still thinking your lad might be in a prisoner-of-war camp, are you?'

Anger bubbled up in Molly, rousing her from apathy, stinging her to a reply. 'You shut up! What's it to do with you anyway? Mind your own business!'

Jenny got to her feet. 'Suit yourself.' She shrugged. 'I was only telling you for your own good.'

And Jenny was right, Molly admitted to herself as she ran the bags under the needle back at work after the break.

She would go to rehearsals. She had to face the fact that Jackson wasn't coming back, he was never coming back again.

Chapter Twenty-one

Jackson tried to fight his way through the cotton wool clouds which enveloped him, but they were too thick. As fast as he thought he was getting out, the clouds thinning so that he could see shapes moving about, they closed in on him again. There was something he had to do . . . what was it? He had to watch out. There was danger, terrible danger, he knew it even if he didn't know what the danger was.

There were voices close by. He tried to listen but they were incomprehensible. He couldn't even make out what language this was. Where was he? His mind struggled with the problem. He had no time to waste, the sense of urgency was overwhelming. He tried to hold his thoughts together. The voices droned on. Then there was a prick in his arm and suddenly sleep, taking away the urgency. He fell into nothingness.

When he woke he was in a strange bed in a strange room. He moved his head to get a better view and winced as pain darted through him, searing in its intensity.

'Don't move,' a man's voice said, heavily accented, 'be

still.' A face swam into view, a strange face with a black beret atop it.

'Where am I?' Jackson asked.

'Never mind,' said the man. 'You were hit in the head. Go back to sleep.'

'Hit in the head?' Who'd hit him?

'We're going to try to get you back,' said the man. 'You are a very brave man.'

Jackson looked blank. What was the man talking about? But thinking hurt too much, he was weary to death, thought slid away and he was asleep once again.

The Frenchman called to someone through the door, an older man perhaps in his sixties. He brought in clothes, a rough fisherman's jersey, baggy trousers and beret, and they dressed Jackson in them. He moaned once or twice as they moved him but didn't open his eyes.

'We'll have to go tonight, there's no moon,' the older man said. 'Do you think he'll be able to stand it?'

The younger one shrugged. 'We have no choice,' he replied.

A few minutes later the door of the cottage opened and the older Frenchman came out. He looked around and beckoned and the other followed him quickly down a path to a narrow beach. They were carrying Jackson wrapped in a blanket. They laid him in a small boat, similar to the cobles the fishermen of the Durham coast used when the mackerel were running, and climbed in beside him. They did not start the engine but rowed out to sea with long, sure strokes which carried them through a channel they knew well, away from the dangerous undertow which could so easily tip and sink a small boat like this one.

In the bottom of the boat Jackson stirred. His eyes fluttered and his lips moved. He was in a nightmare again, one where danger was drawing nearer and nearer and he had to help . . . but who he had to help, he didn't know.

Some time later, it could have been days or even weeks, he woke up and his mind was clear. He turned his head, and though the movement made him wince it wasn't unbearable. He was in a hospital ward, he recognised it as such, two parallel rows of beds with pale green counter-panes, a screen around one of them.

'How are you today? Feeling more yourself, are you?'

A doctor was standing by his bed, an open file in his hands. He looked down at it and made a quick note.

'Fine,' said Jackson. 'Where am I?'

'This is a military hospital in Essex,' the doctor replied. 'Now, can you tell me your name, rank and number?'

Jackson tried to remember, it was there on the edge of his mind but oddly elusive. 'I don't know,' he had to admit in the end.

'Don't worry, it will come back to you.'

'But how did I get here?'

'As I understand it, you were smuggled out of France. The Frenchmen who brought you said only that you had held off a German assault virtually on your own. They insisted you were a hero.'

'I don't feel like one.' Jackson gave a small smile at the thought.

The doctor looked at his head, shone a light in his eyes and nodded with satisfaction. 'Well, you are definitely on the mend. Don't worry, it will come back to you,' he repeated. 'This often happens after a head injury. Don't push it, it will come.'

After he had gone, Jackson relaxed back on to his pillow. France . . . There was something about France . . . what was it? He puzzled and puzzled and then was seized by a violent headache and had to give up.

Molly was late coming out of rehearsal. They were practising for a *Workers' Playtime* programme for the wireless, and Mr Dowson had made them do the last song over and over again. She was bone weary. It was the end of a very long and hard week and she was looking forward to her free weekend.

Though she didn't have anywhere to go, she thought. But she would at least get out of the house in Eden Hope, she had to. The atmosphere there just made her more depressed than ever. Perhaps she would go the pictures in Bishop, she thought. Take in the matinee at the Majestic, do a bit of early shopping afterwards for already things suitable for Christmas presents were growing scarce in the shops. There was talk of bringing in ration coupons for clothes.

'That'll be the next thing,' Maggie had reckoned in a

rare moment when she came out of her sombre mood and talked to Molly.

'Best get a move on if you want to catch the train,' said Mr Dowson. As usual he had contrived to be by her side as she came out of the gates. Sometimes she wished he would just leave her alone; other times it didn't matter, nothing mattered. She quickened her pace, however.

'Are you doing anything tomorrow night?' he went on, increasing his pace to match hers.

'I don't go out much in the evenings.'

'We could go to the dance at –'

'No, thanks,' said Molly, beginning to run up the platform, jumping on the train and leaving him behind. Why couldn't he take a hint?

The following afternoon as the lights went up in the cinema and they all stood to sing 'God Save The King', she saw him standing on the end of her row. Almost as though he felt her gaze upon him he turned and smiled at her, his hopeful, ingratiating smile.

When she came out he was waiting in the foyer, just as she had feared he would be. Molly sighed. She had sat through the film, one with Greer Garson and Walter Pidgeon being heroic against all the odds and setting a fine example to the lower orders, though she couldn't remember much more about it than that. During the newsreel, with the cheerful voice of the news reader booming out over the audience, she had scanned the faces of troops whenever they came on, hoping against hope that

Jackson would be there among them. But he was not and she was once more filled with melancholy. Hope was gradually draining away from her.

'Hallo, Molly. Did you enjoy the picture? I thought you might like to go for a bite. Maybe a cup of tea? My treat. We could go to the King's Hall, what do you say?'

He wouldn't be snubbed, she realised. He stood before her, smiling so hopefully, so persistent! Did he really feel for her as she felt for Jackson? Molly wondered as people milled around them and the foyer began to empty. No, of course he couldn't. Or was that a sort of arrogance on her part?

'All right,' she said at last.

They sat in the cafe at the King's Hall, eating toasted teacakes and drinking milky tea. The cafe was half empty, most of the afternoon shoppers had already gone home, Molly thought. And that was where she should be as well. She could stay in her room, keep out of the way of Maggie and Frank if they wanted to be on their own.

'I think I'd best be going now, Mr Dowson,' she said suddenly, picking up her bag and making as though to get up from her seat. 'Or I'll miss my bus.'

'No, no, there's no hurry. You don't have to catch the bus,' he exclaimed anxiously. 'I've got my car, I've enough petrol to take you home.'

She looked at him in surprise. 'You've got petrol?' she asked.

He winked and nodded. 'You can get the coupons if

you're in the know,' he said. 'Any road, let's just say I've got it. I thought we could go for a spin.'

Molly was shaking her head and he looked crestfallen.

'Aw, come on, it won't hurt. You could do with some fresh air after breathing in that powder. We both could. What do you say, just a little run up the fell? Please, Molly, I promise to get you home early.'

She considered it, tempted. She thought of the sharp moorland air. It was ages since she'd been up the dale. And there was nothing to rush home for, nothing to hope for, there wasn't another post until Monday. And Maggie and Frank were so quiet, so wrapped up in each other and their grief just now, they hardly noticed if she was there or not. They had given up and she was beginning to feel the same way. Her thoughts shied away from that, she couldn't bear to think it.

'Righto.'

The car was a Morris four-seater with dark blue paintwork and leather upholstery, all polished to a high gleaming gloss. There were few cars in Eden Hope and those there were belonged to the management of the pit and the doctor. None of the ordinary people owned one. Once she was sitting in the front passenger seat with Gary Dowson pulling away from Newgate Street and heading for the ancient stone bridge over the Wear which a fourteenth-century bishop had had constructed to take him to his hunting grounds in Weardale, Molly couldn't help being shaken out of her apathy a little and started showing interest in her surroundings. The little car climbed gradually out of the valley and soon they were out in the open with great vistas of fields and tiny villages and woods. Down below them on their left she caught glimpses of the Wear, running back to Bishop and Durham and beyond. The war seemed to be an irrelevance as they caught glimpses of farmers gathering in the harvest. They were held up by a tractor chugging along the road with a load of straw, then an old cart pulled by a horse, straining forward, its muscles rippling as it hauled its load.

'We'll stop here, I think. I don't want to waste too much petrol,' said Gary. He pulled into the side along a winding track. They were past the fields now, close by huge swathes of heather, some of it still purple with summer flowers.

He sat there, not moving, and the tiny frisson of alarm which Molly had felt faded away. He didn't mean anything, he wouldn't do anything, no, of course he wouldn't. Anyway, she could look after herself, couldn't she? She was a woman now, an experienced woman.

She made herself relax too, staring out over the fells, wondering what it would be like to live in a remote place like the tiny farm she could see half hidden in a fold of the moor some distance from the road. Gary offered her a cigarette from a gunmetal holder, lighting one for himself when she refused. He wound down his window and the sharp air came into the car, the muted baa-ing of sheep audible amongst the heather.

Molly relaxed into her seat, put her head back and

closed her eyes. She let the evening sun play on her eyelids. Just for a moment, she told herself, just for a moment she would pretend it was Jackson sitting beside her in the little car, Jackson's warmth she could feel beside her.

'Molly?'

Her eyes flew open as Gary flung the cigarette end out of the car and turned to her. He put a hand to the nape of her neck and stroked it gently. She stiffened, didn't move. She could feel his fingers on her neck. She lifted her head to protest but his arm slid around her shoulders and he drew her towards him.

He kissed her on the lips, a soft, gentle kiss, becoming more insistent. Molly sat there, feeling the warmth of his lips, not thinking, just feeling.

'I love you, Molly,' he murmured against her ear, and her eyes flew open. She struggled upright. What was she doing?

'Gary,' she said, against his restraining arm. 'Gary! Let me up!'

'Why? Don't you like it?'

'You know I'm engaged to a soldier – he's away in France, I can't do this.'

Gary sat up and lit another cigarette. He shook the match out, threw it out of the window. 'I've heard all about it. So he's away in France, is he? Molly, the soldiers are all back from France – all those who are coming, any road. The man's dead, he has to be. If he was in a POW camp you'd have heard by now, you know that, don't you?'

She stared at him. She wanted to shout, to tell him it wasn't true, Jackson *would* be coming back, there could be a letter any day now. What was she doing sitting beside this horrible, self-important little man on the moor where nothing else moved but sheep, where the sky was already darkening to night and they were miles from home? She fumbled with the door catch, managed to get it open, fling herself out of the car and to begin walking back towards Woodlands, the last village they had come through. The road was pot-holed and stony and she stumbled once or twice but kept on, tears streaming down her face, his words echoing in her mind.

For it was true, everything he'd said, she knew it. Jackson wasn't coming home, she wasn't going to feel the sweetness of his love-making ever again, never again, no. Blinded with tears she stumbled once more, fell against a snow pole and clung on to it as she lifted her foot and rubbed her ankle. It wasn't really hurt, the pain was lessening already, she could make it down into the village. Maybe there was a bus.

'Molly, don't be silly, pet.'

Gary had turned the car round. He pulled up beside her, got out and came to her. 'Are you all right? Have you hurt yourself?'

'Just turned my ankle, it's OK,' she managed to mumble, keeping her head down. She felt so foolish now, he sounded concerned and kind. Why on earth had she run away from him, thought she could get home on her own when she didn't even know if there was a bus? She turned to him, allowed him to put his arm around her, take her back to the car. She felt so confused.

'Sit in the back, pet,' he said, 'then you can put your foot up. It'll be better.'

There you see, she told herself, he was only concerned for your welfare. He *was* a nice man, no matter if all the girls scoffed at him. She was safe with him, he hadn't any dark designs on her, of course he hadn't. All men weren't like that horrible Bart Jones. And it did feel better to put her foot up.

'Comfortable?' He smiled at her, patted her arm as he bent over her. It was quite accidental that his hand brushed across her breast as he straightened up, she was sure.

'Yes, thank you,' she said, and managed a small smile.

'I'm sorry about your lad, Molly,' he said softly. 'But it's best you face facts.'

This almost started the tears again but she managed to hold them back. What a fool she was being!

He got into the driver's seat, switched on the blue-shaded headlights and drove carefully downhill to where a small bridge led over a stream. Then he pulled off the road on to a patch of gravel and took a clean handkerchief out of his pocket.

'I'll just wet this in the water,' he said. 'That's what they teach us at the First Aid post at work, isn't it? Cold compresses for sprains.'

'Oh, I don't think it's much of a sprain,' said Molly, startled. 'Why don't we just get on home?' But he was already scrambling down the little bank and dipping the hankie in the water.

The cool wet cloth against her skin was soothing, she had to admit when he came back and climbed on to the seat next to her and laid it against her ankle. She sighed, laid back against the window. Yes, he was a nice man really, thoughtful too. The feel of his fingers against her leg was pleasant. It was almost completely dark in the car now. He leaned over to her and kissed her on the lips and for some reason it felt like . . . it could almost have been Jackson. Oh, Jackson! Gary kissed her so gently, his lips fluttering over her eyelids, his hands touching her breasts, cupping them in turn, easing her blouse from her waist band, finding the warm flesh beneath.

Suddenly Molly was kissing him back, her body responding to his, remembering that other time.

'Oh, Jackson, my love,' she breathed, and Gary's hands stilled but only for a moment. The next minute he was pulling her cami-knickers aside, adjusting his position in the cramped back of the car, thrusting into her. And her treacherous body responded to every sensation. The pain in her ankle forgotten, she clung on to him and breathed her lover's name.

Chapter Twenty-two

Afterwards Molly couldn't believe it had happened, that she had acted like that. What sort of a girl was she? Were those who had called her terrible names after that night in West Auckland right? She remembered how she had felt only too well: the excitement in her blood, being swept along on it, helpless to stop. She couldn't bear to think of it. *Gary Dowson*? Dear God, it had to be just a terrible nightmare.

Afterwards she sat beside him as he drove down the dale. There were no twinkling lights from the villages along the banks of the Wear, only a slight glow from the chimney of Townhead colliery, a gust of sparks now and then to show that the black bulk further down was the town. Into it and out again, she sat looking dumbly out of the window. Even if there had been anything to see she would not have seen it. It was cold and Molly shivered involuntarily.

'You cold, pet?' asked Gary Dowson. Even now she couldn't think of him as Gary without giving him his surname, even after doing the most intimate things with him. Her mind shied away from the thought. He put a hand on her thigh, squeezing the flesh with a proprietorial air. Molly pulled away from him as far as the seat allowed.

'I'm fine!' she snapped.

He glanced across at her but of course there was nothing to see but the outline of her head. Perhaps he had imagined it. He didn't think she could be turning hoity-toity on him now, not after what she had let him do.

'You can let me out at the bus stop,' said Molly.

'Don't be daft, lass,' he said easily. 'I might as well take you all the way, it's practically on my own way home.' She opened her mouth to demur but he was accelerating out of Newgate Street, sailing past the bus stop, ignoring her desperate need to get out of the car and away from him. For how could he not feel it? The need was so strong she had to restrain herself from opening the door and jumping out while the car was moving.

The car drew up in Eden Hope, right on the end of the rows. At last she could get out and run up the back street to the gate.

'See you, pet,' Gary called after her, and Molly mumbled something in reply. She was never so thankful as when she had the back gate closed behind her and could lean against it, panting heavily as though she had run all the way from Weardale. After a moment she managed to gain some control over herself and walked up the yard and in at the back door.

'Mind, you've been a long time, lass,' said Maggie. But

she didn't ask where Molly had been, why she was late. Maggie and Frank were still in a world of their own. There was no room for curiosity about anyone or anything, they were mourning their son still.

'I . . . I don't want anything to eat,' said Molly. 'I think I'll go straight up, if you don't mind?'

'Aye, lass,' Maggie answered, the tiny spark of interest she had shown dying away as she turned to stare into the fire as she had been doing when Molly came in. Frank hadn't even looked up.

Molly stripped off her clothes and poured cold water from the jug into the china basin which stood on the wash stand. She took the piece of flannel which hung over the rail and rubbed it with Sunlight soap, dipped it in the water. Then she scrubbed at herself, never minding that it was cold and her skin stung with the harsh rubbing. She scrubbed at the sensitive skin of her breasts and between her thighs, rinsed off the flannel and did it again. She pulled on her long flannelette nightie and climbed into bed, lying shivering, filled with self-loathing. She had betrayed Jackson. Her body had betrayed him. She was like a cat on heat, she told herself savagely. She couldn't understand why she had done it, she could not.

But gradually warmth seeped through her, her mind closed down, she fell asleep to dream of Jackson. He was calling her and she was running after him but somehow she couldn't reach him, he was too far away. She called after him, 'Don't go, please don't go, I didn't mean to do it!' But he went anyway and she woke up desolate. And somehow the reality of being awake was worse than the terror of the nightmare.

Molly dreaded going to work the following Monday. All day Sunday she wandered the lanes around Eden Hope avoiding anyone she knew, slipping into the fields if she saw anyone coming. The weather was turning cold but dry and the hedges still afforded some protection from the gaze of anyone on the road, still held some leaves. She ate very little, couldn't think of it.

'You'll be in for your dinner?' Maggie asked as she was going out of the door.

'No . . . I expect to be eating with my friend in Shildon,' Molly replied.

'You might as well take your ration card there,' Maggie said acidly. 'I mean, how does her mother manage?'

'Er . . . we'll eat in a cafe,' Molly replied.

'Aye, well, some folks cannot afford to eat in cafes,' was Maggie's parting shot. Their relationship hadn't been the same since the telegram came about Jackson.

Jackson, Jackson, Jackson. She could still hear his name over and over in her mind. Sometimes she had talked to him there but now she couldn't. Not after what she had done. On Monday morning Molly went into work, managing to avoid *him* all morning for now she was in the sewing room he was no longer her foreman. But she had to go to the canteen at dinnertime, had to pass the table where he sat with the other foremen. As she passed he looked up at her.

'Now then, pet,' he said. 'Will I see you outside when you've eaten?'

'I . . . I haven't time today,' said Molly, and he shrugged and turned to the other men, said something and laughed. The others laughed too, one or two grinning slyly at Molly. She blushed and hurried to catch up with Jenny, holding her tray high as she squeezed past tables in the crush.

'I said that Gary Dowson liked you,' Jenny observed as she sat down. 'You want to watch him.'

'Don't be daft!' said Molly, but she blushed vividly and bent her head over her plate to hide it. The talk turned to other things: how there were hardly any air raids now, the Germans giving them a rest.

'Me mam does her turn fire watching down at the school,' one girl was saying. 'It's just an excuse to sit in the headmistress's study and have a natter with her pal, get away from me dad for a bit, have a sleep on the job.'

'Well, they were kept well awake in the summer, though, weren't they?' said Jenny.

Molly listened with half an ear but she was still preoccupied with memories of Saturday. What would she do if Jackson came back now? Could she pretend it hadn't happened? Many another woman had. She heard the talk in the factory about what some of the married women got up to. But not her, no, never again. She would tell Gary

Dowson the first time she was able to talk to him alone.

The chance came as she walked back to the station one night the following week, a few yards behind everyone else for she had been last out of the sewing room.

'What's the matter with you, Molly?' Gary asked with no preamble. 'Why are you keeping out of my way? I thought we were going together, you and me?'

'Going together? No, we're not, of course we're not. You know I was engaged to a soldier.'

'Aye, I did. But you seemed to forget it that night up on the fells, didn't you? I didn't force you, you were willing enough. Any road, the fella's dead, you can't hanker after a dead man.'

Molly stopped walking and turned to face him. 'The telegram said missing, believed killed. It didn't say he was definitely dead. He could be anywhere – lying injured in a French hospital maybe or perhaps a German camp. He could . . .'

'Oh, don't talk so daft, Molly! We've been over all this before. And besides, if you feel like this, why did you go with me? An' don't say you didn't enjoy it, because you did!'

'Oh, go away, Gary Dowson, and leave me alone, will you? I tell you, I don't want to go with you!'

Molly marched off towards the train, leaving him standing on the track. 'You'll come looking for me afore I ask you again!' he shouted and turned on his heel and stomped off. Molly was the last to get on the train so she had to stand all the way in the corridor of the last carriage. The others there looked curiously at her but they were not people she knew and at least they left her alone.

A couple of weeks later Molly went into work and sat down at her machine, turning to take the thick, densely woven material from the box beside her. It was quiet in the sewing room, the wireless not as yet switched on, so that the sound of the new girl's voice rang out loudly and Molly turned to look at her.

'Well, would you believe it, it's Molly Mason!'

Molly's heart plummeted. She looked incredulously at the girl who had been on her way to the furthest machine but had stopped right opposite her.

'Joan,' Molly said faintly.

'That's right, it's me, Joan Pendle,' the girl said, and gave a smile which didn't quite reach her eyes. She looked around at the other girls. 'We know each other well. We should do, we were brought up next door to each other, me and Molly.'

'What are you doing here?' she whispered.

'Same as you, what do you think I'm doing here?' demanded Joan. 'I got a transfer from West Auckland. Well, it's more money, isn't it?'

Suddenly the wireless came on, the music drowning out what she was saying. The other girls were bending over their machines. Joan grinned, came closer to Molly so that she could speak into her ear. 'I'll see you in the break, will

I?' Her voice was heavy with meaning. Then she laughed and went on to her own machine.

Molly sewed automatically. Picking up the cut out material, sewing and oversewing, dropping it in the basket, picking up more material, repeating the process over and over. The Andrews Sisters were singing a popular melody, the other girls singing along with them, but it might as well have been a dirge for all it meant to Molly. Her mind was busy with what it might mean if Joan were to tell everyone about her past, the fact that she had been to prison. Well, she would just have to face up to it, she told herself when the whistle blew and the machines fell silent. Face it out. By this time she was almost past caring.

She got to her feet, squared her shoulders and followed the other girls on their way to the canteen. She queued at the counter and got her meal. Sausage and mash it was, two pale sausages and a pile of mash with a spoonful of processed peas. Jenny was sitting halfway down the room but Molly didn't go to sit beside her, instead taking a place at an empty table in the corner. Stolidly she began to eat, though for all she tasted it might as well have been cotton wool. She kept her eyes on her plate. Perhaps Joan would not see her, she thought dimly.

She did. 'Now then, Molly Mason,' she said as she slipped into the empty chair beside her. 'How've you been getting on then? Managed to keep quiet the fact that you're a thief and a gaolbird?'

Molly put down her knife and fork and sat up straight,

squaring her shoulders. 'Just leave me alone, will you?' Joan laughed and began to eat her own meal, grimaced and put down her knife.

'Pass the brown sauce, will you?' she asked, and Molly handed it to her silently. 'That's not very friendly, is it?' Joan went on, shaking a dark stream of sauce from the bottle.

'You've not exactly been a friend to me!' she was stung into replying. Suddenly she was sick of talking. If Joan expected her to plead, she wasn't going to. Rising to her feet, Molly picked up her bag and turned for the door, feeling an urgent desire to get out into the fresh air.

'See you later then,' Joan called gaily after her.

Outside Molly had to skirt round a group of men lounging against the wall of the canteen. At least Gary Dowson wasn't among them, she thought. She walked along the road between the sheds, up to the top and back again, and then it was time to go back into work. Gary was waiting at the door, in spite of what he had said the last time they met.

'Don't forget there's a rehearsal tomorrow dinnertime. I thought we could meet tonight an' all, run through that duet . . .'

'I can't tonight. Anyway, I'm thinking of dropping out of the concert party,' Molly said, backing away down the corridor as she spoke. She felt panicky. She'd almost let herself be caught and dreaded the thought of his putting a finger on her now. She couldn't bear that.

Gary frowned. 'What do you mean, drop the concert party? You can't do that,' he called after her. He made as if to follow her but the whistle had blown for work to start, he halted and she ran, making good her escape.

Somehow she managed to elude both Gary and Joan for the rest of the day. She didn't see Joan on the train back to Bishop Auckland but that wasn't too surprising, there were so many people working at the munitions factory now. But the day's bad news wasn't finished for her yet. When she got in from work, Maggie was waiting for her.

'You look a bit peaky, lass,' she said, gazing intently into Molly's face.

'No, I'm all right, I'm fine,' she protested. 'I just had a hard day at work, that's all.'

'There were none of your monthly clouts in the wash,' observed Maggie. 'I wondered about it, that was all.'

Dear God, no! It was like a shout in Molly's mind. In fact, she couldn't believe she hadn't spoken it aloud. It couldn't be . . . could it?

'I'm not due 'til next week, Maggie,' she managed to say.

She folded her arms. 'I think you are.'

For goodness' sake, how could she know? thought Molly.

'I tell you, I'm just not myself. I think I'll go to the doctor tomorrow. Maybe I need a tonic or something.'

Maggie pursed her lips but said no more. Instead she began to ladle broth from the iron pan on the bar. Molly watched her. She couldn't understand the older woman. One minute she was showing not a bit of interest in her lodger and the next she was saying she knew when Molly's periods were due. Why was she so suspicious? She couldn't think that Molly might be having Jackson's baby, it was too long since that last time he had been home. It was almost as if she was jealous on behalf of her son, could that be it? But Molly was too tired even to think about it. She looked at the broth which Maggie put before her, saw the globules of yellow fat floating on the top and jumped out of her chair. She ran for the outside sink where she retched and retched. Bile came into her mouth, sour bile which stung the back of her throat.

'Aye, I think you should see the doctor all right,' Maggie sighed as she turned away and flopped into her chair.

Next morning Molly waited her turn to see the doctor in a waiting room full of women with pale children. Though the cold weather had seen off the diphtheria epidemic, the children who had survived it were debilitated and prone to other infections. In the yard leading to the waiting room a few men clustered, some sitting on their hunkers, wheezing and coughing. Cigarette smoke curled up into the damp air.

'You haven't been doing something you shouldn't, young lady?' was the first question Doctor Hardy put to Molly when it was her turn to go in and she'd stammered

out her symptoms. His gaze was penetrating and she
lowered her eyes as she replied.

'Yes, Doctor.'

The examination was brisk and brief and when she
came out she knew her worst fears were realised.

Chapter Twenty-three

Molly felt numb with shock as she left the surgery, stumbling blindly through the waiting room. Outside she leaned against the wall for a few minutes with her eyes closed until she heard a woman's voice.

'Are you all right, hinny?'

'Yes, thank you, just dizzy for a minute,' Molly managed to reply and hurried off down the street and along past the pit to the open country beyond. What she was going to tell Maggie she had no idea. She shrank inwardly from saying anything at all to Jackson's parents. In the end she walked all the way to Shildon and went into a cafe in Church Street and bought a cup of tea and sat with it in a dark corner, not even drinking it, just moving the spoon round and round in it, hardly knowing what she was doing.

The day wore on. The woman behind the counter kept looking at her. In the end she walked over to where Molly sat.

'Do you want anything else?' she asked. 'Because I'll be closing in a few minutes.'

It was four o'clock, Molly suddenly realised, and she

had to go to work on the night shift. She left the cafe and caught the bus back to Eden Hope.

'Where the heck have you been?' Maggie demanded in an injured tone as she walked through the door. 'Here I've been, worried to death about you!'

'Sorry, I went for a walk . . . to see a friend in Shildon,' said Molly.

'You didn't think about me and Frank, did you? Of course, I'm just your landlady . . .'

'Oh, Maggie, of course you're not, you know I'm fond of you both. It wasn't like that, really. Only the doctor said I need to get more fresh air so I thought I'd take the opportunity, that's all,' Molly protested.

'Hmmm. Well, what else did he say?'

Maggie stood with her hands on her hips, her expression showing only too plainly her suspicions, and Molly quailed before her.

'He said I was anaemic,' she lied on a quick inspiration. One lie begat another, she thought miserably, that was what her mother used to say. 'He gave me an iron tonic.' He had. She took it out of her bag now, showing the bottle of dark brown fluid to Maggie.

'He gives that to all them as has fallen wrong.'

'Does he? Well, that's what he said to me anyway,' Molly replied, and escaped upstairs to change for work.

'I'm doing some tatie hash for the tea. Only you'd best look sharp. It's nearly ready,' Maggie called after her.

'No, thanks, I'm not hungry. I had a bite in Shildon, at . . . my friend's.'

'Well, I'll keep it to warm up for you the morrow,' said Maggie. 'We can't afford to waste food. There's a war on, you know.'

Even the thought of warmed-up hash made Molly feel nauseous. She could feel the bile rising in her throat and made a desperate effort to keep it down. She sat on the bed and closed her eyes and after a minute or two felt better, able to finish changing her clothes. She stayed upstairs until it was almost time to go for the bus then went down, drank a cup of tea with Frank, asked about the day's news and escaped thankfully as soon as she could.

'You're going to be early for the bus,' Maggie observed, her face grim and expressionless, implying she hadn't been fooled one little bit.

'Well, sometimes it comes early,' Molly replied. She hated the atmosphere in the house now but didn't know what to do about it.

She stood at the bus stop, the only one there until a queue began to form behind her. The line chatted and laughed behind her but Molly heard nothing. Being first in the queue she got a seat and sat still and quiet though her thoughts were still whirling. She knew she had to tell Gary Dowson. He would surely offer to marry her, that's what always happened in this situation, but her mind shied away from the thought in horror. How could she possibly marry Gary? After all her hopes, her love for Jackson, all their plans. Oh, Jackson, she cried inside herself, why did it have to happen?

'I'm only sitting here because it's the last seat left on the bus.' Joan Pendle sat down beside her.

Molly jumped. Dear God, she thought, what did I do? What did I do to deserve this? She barely looked at Joan but stared out of the window instead.

'By, you're a stuck-up madam, you,' said Joan. 'I don't know why I bother to talk to you.'

'Well, don't then,' Molly was stung into replying.

Joan ignored that. 'But I wanted to ask you if you'd heard from Harry?'

'Harry?'

'That's what I said, Harry. Your brother, remember him?'

Molly was so surprised by the question that Joan's attempt at sarcasm went over her head. 'Why do you want to know?'

'I'm interested, that's all.'

Molly's attention was diverted. For a few seconds she forgot about her own trouble. 'I haven't as it happens, not since he went back last time. But I didn't really expect to. He said he was going on some sort of special duty.'

Joan sat quietly as the bus drew into Bishop Auckland, got off it with Molly and walked beside her to the station platform where the train was standing. They had joined the queue of workers before she spoke again.

'I could make it pretty hard for you at work. If I told

them about you being in prison, and why.'

Molly waited for her to go on. Obviously Joan had more to say. Molly had been worrying about her past getting out ever since she'd come to the factory but her present trouble loomed even larger, more threatening. She felt quite detached as she waited. In a few months she would have to leave work anyway.

'You could write to Harry, you must have his address.'

'Come on, Joan, just say what you mean,' said Molly, though she was beginning to get the idea.

'You could tell him about me, say how we're friends now that we're working together.'

'Friends?' Molly's eyebrows rose. She couldn't believe what she was hearing.

'Yes. Say how I didn't tell on you, how I admitted I was wrong about you. Maybe say I was asking after him?'

Molly started to laugh. She couldn't help herself, the laughter bubbled up inside her. She laughed as she climbed on to the train so that people turned to gaze at her in astonishment; laughed until tears came to her eyes and she had to fish out a handkerchief to wipe them away. The compartments were full so she walked on, not looking behind to see if Joan had followed her. When she did stop at the end of the carriage she leaned against the window, blew her nose and smiled at those around her.

'Sorry, just a fit of the giggles,' she said. There was no sign of Joan. She must have found a seat. Joan was the sort who usually did, Molly told herself. She couldn't believe the girl. Oh, she had known that Joan still had feelings for Harry even though she went the wrong way about expressing them. But after all that had happened . . . Yes, Molly would write to Harry, through the regiment, tell him about it. He would have a good laugh and no doubt he could do with one. Especially now that Jackson wasn't there with him as he'd always been, ever since their schooldays. But for the minute Molly had other things on her mind.

When the dinner break came she sought out Gary at the table where he was sitting with a few of the other men.

'Can I have a word with you, Mr Dowson?' she asked. The other men looked at one another with knowing amusement. They obviously thought she was chasing the foreman. Had he said anything to them? she wondered.

Gary Dowson had finished his meal. He paused to light a cigarette, making a show of keeping her waiting. The men smirked. 'Oh, all right,' he said at last. 'Come on, we'll take a walk outside.'

They walked between the buildings, along the road to Admin, round the corner and back in a circle. They walked in the dark, no flashlights allowed in the grounds in case they attracted the attention of a stray bomber. Molly glanced sideways at Gary; there was nothing to see but the dark shape of him. Now they were out on their own she couldn't get the words out. This was the wrong time anyway, she thought.

'Can I see you when the shift is over?' she asked at last.

'I don't think I have anything to say to you,' he said carefully. She could feel the change in him and was bewildered. She stopped walking and peered at him in the dark, trying to make out what he meant. A shaft of moonlight caught his face. His eyes glinted coldly in it.

'Why? What's the matter?'

For answer he pulled her round the corner of a building and slammed her against the wall, holding her there with his body.

'Here, is this what you want?' he asked roughly, grasping her breast in his hand and pushing his knee hard between her legs so that she cried out at the sudden pain of it.

'Don't! Gary, don't!' she cried.

'Oh, come on, don't act the innocent with me, I know you better than that. You were panting after it the other week and then you pretended to hold me off. What do you take me for, a neddy?'

'No, no! What do you mean? I haven't done anything!' Molly cried.

'No, not lately you haven't. Though you thought you could string me along, didn't you? Well, I've been hearing a thing or two about you from that lass what used to work with you at West Auckland. You never told me about what you did there, did you? About taking that poor fella for his dead wife's jewellery and landing up in prison.'

Too late, Molly realised what a fool she had been. She remembered Joan's venomous expression when she had laughed so uncontrollably on the train. Already she was spreading her poison around the factory.

'Whatever she's told you, it wasn't true,' Molly said at last.

'No? Then you haven't been in prison for leading your landlord on and robbing him?'

'No! Yes, I was, but I didn't do it! I didn't, really I didn't.'

'No. Well, they all say that, don't they?'

The buzzer went for the return to work. Automatically they turned and began to walk back. The words to tell him were in her mind, on her tongue, but somehow Molly had trouble uttering them. It wasn't until they were practically at the door of her building that she said them aloud and even then she wasn't sure whether she had or not.

'I'm expecting.'

Gary halted and caught hold of her arm, pulled her into the building and whirled her round to face him. The entrance was deserted, they were the only two who had gone out into the night.

'Say that again?'

'I'm expecting. Fallen wrong. Pregnant.'

'All right, all right, I know what it means. Are you trying to say it's mine?' His tone was hard, his pale eyes narrow.

'Of course it's yours. You're the only one . . .'

'Oh, aye? You'd say that any road, wouldn't you?'

Molly wrenched her arm away from his grasp and

walked rapidly away to her own section, the sewing room. As she turned into the doorway she caught a glimpse of him still standing where she had left him.

Molly felt numb and just for the minute nothing else. This was a day for surprises all right, she thought as she took her seat at the machine, switched on the power, placed the bag she was sewing under the needle and began sewing. It was indeed . . . All of a sudden she had an urgent need to throw up. She left her work and rushed for the toilets, knocking over a basket of material as she went.

Afterwards she wiped her mouth with a piece of hard toilet tissue and leaned against the wall. There was a strong smell of Lysol so after a moment she went out into the corridor before she started gagging again. One or two people walked past and looked curiously at her but Molly hardly noticed.

It was no longer a question of whether she could bring herself to marry Gary Dowson, she thought. He didn't *want* to marry her. The idea that this might happen had simply not occurred to her. So much for that. She wasn't good enough for Gary Dowson. Well, at least that made her decision easier. Molly stood up straight and went back into the rest room, washed her face in cold water at the basin and dried it on a clean bit of the roller towel hanging in the corner. Then she went back to her machine and bent her head over her work, not lifting it until the buzzer went for home time.

'Were you not well earlier on?' asked Jenny, coming to

walk by her side out of the gate before crossing towards the buses which took girls back to the eastern end of the county.

'Something I ate, I think,' said Molly. 'But I'm all right now.'

'You're not talking to her, are you?' Joan was close by, a hard grin of contempt fixed on her face as she glanced at Molly. 'Did you not know she's a gaolbird, a convicted thief? Oh, aye, I could tell you a few things about that one there,' she went on to Jenny, who looked bewildered.

'What's she talking about, Molly?'

'You may well ask,' said Joan. She drew closer to Molly and took hold of her arm, pinching. 'I'll show you, you bitch!' she said in an undertone. 'You won't laugh at me again in a hurry.' She smiled and nodded to emphasise her words then went on ahead to the station platform.

'Molly?'

Jenny was gazing at her, waiting for an explanation. 'It's true. I was in prison but it was a mistake, I didn't do anything,' said Molly. It sounded lame even in her own ears.

Chapter Twenty-four

'I am looking for my friend, Captain. His name is Sergeant Morley. Sergeant Jackson Morley, I understand he may be a patient here, sir?'

The middle-aged Captain pushed his chair a little way back from the desk and crossed his left leg over the right, swinging it once or twice. He put his hand up to his moustache and studied the soldier standing before him, a tall, upright man, obviously regular rather than enlisted.

'Ask my Sergeant to look through the lists,' he drawled. Why had the man been allowed to come in here pestering him? It had been a long hard day and it wasn't finished yet. Though no longer crammed with wounded from the Dunkirk evacuation as it once had been, the hospital was still full.

'He's not on the lists, sir, but still . . .'

'What are you talking about, man?'

'I think he may be the unidentified man brought in by the French a few weeks back. My friend was seconded to a French unit, sir, we both were.'

The Captain sighed. 'Evidently a few men were. How

did you find out about him?' he demanded. 'Hell's bells, I'm sick to death of being pestered by people who think they might know who he is! I won't have him disturbed again –'

The Captain stopped, got to his feet and turned his back on Harry to stare out of the window.

'Sir?'

'Did your friend have any identifying mark?' The officer turned back to him.

'Like a birthmark?' He had been asked this question before. There were lists of unidentified men, both living and dead, and most had a mark – a mole, a birthmark, even a bad vaccination mark – somewhere on their bodies. 'Sergeant Morley had a mole on the back of his calf, sir.'

The Captain picked up a paper from his desk, scanned it quickly. He sighed again. 'OK, Sergeant.' He took a chit, scrawled something on it and handed it to Harry. 'My Sergeant will show you where to go.'

Fired with hope, he went out to the wards. This time perhaps it would be Jackson. He was in a fever of excitement. Had been ever since he had heard about the French fishermen who had rowed across the Channel in a tiny fishing boat which had never been out of French coastal waters before. They'd brought with them a wounded Englishman whom they insisted was a hero, nominated for the Croix de Guerre. A man who had held off a German attack with a French machine gun while its crew escaped over the border from Belgium.

There were three men in the side ward, two of them sitting in armchairs facing the windows which looked out on to sodden grass and dripping trees. They glanced up when Harry entered the room with little interest, then turned back to their contemplation of the landscape. Another man was lying in bed, his face white in startling contrast to his bright red hair.

None of them was Jackson. The disappointment was crushing. Harry stared at them each in turn in disbelief. He had been so sure Jackson would be there.

'You looking for someone, mate?'

The voice was of the North Country, and not just North Country but definitely County Durham. Harry whirled around and there he was, standing by the door.

'Jackson!'

Harry covered the few yards between them in two strides. His arms went out and he grasped his friend by the shoulders as though to embrace him, then saw something in the eyes and changed the gesture. He took hold of Jackson's hand and pumped it up and down in a fervour of recognition and joy.

'I knew it would be you! I knew you wouldn't let the bloody Jerries get hold of you. Too fly for that, you are, Jackson!' he cried, words falling over themselves in the emotion of the moment. At first he didn't realise that the hand in his was still not reciprocating. In fact, Jackson wasn't even smiling. He was looking at Harry as at a stranger, a polite half-smile playing around his lips.

'Who are you?'

Harry dropped his hand, stood back a pace or two and gazed into his face. For some reason it hadn't occurred to him that Jackson might not recognise *him*. After all, they had been mates since they were bairns together at school.

'I'm Harry, man, don't you know me?'

Jackson looked puzzled. 'I should do, shouldn't I?' he asked hesitantly.

'You should that,' agreed Harry. 'By, I've been looking all over for you.'

'You know who I am then?' Eagerness lit Jackson's face. 'For God's sake, tell me, man!'

Suddenly, it was Harry who was hesitant. Jackson looked so different. He had lost weight, his cheeks hollow, his uniform hanging slackly on him. And his dark hair, though as thick as ever, was flecked with grey now. Harry glanced at the door. A male nurse had appeared and was standing silently watching them. He stepped forward.

'Don't get too excited,' he warned Jackson. 'You know it brings on your migraine.'

Jackson threw him a look of contempt. 'I'm not a bairn!' he said, and turned back to Harry. 'Tell me, man. If you don't, I think I'll go stark staring mad!'

The two men sitting in the window had turned from their study of the garden and were watching Harry and Jackson, even showing interest in what was happening. One leaned forward to hear what Harry had to say.

'I'm your friend Harry,' he said simply. 'And you are

Jackson Morley – and I'm that glad to see you, lad, I could eat you! They'll be dancing a jig back home in Eden Hope tonight when I ring the post office to tell them!'

In Eden Hope Maggie and Frank were sitting as usual around the fire in the kitchen. They were on their own again for Molly had gone. That morning she had packed her straw box and left.

'You don't need me now, with Frank so much better. And I'll find somewhere nearer the factory where I don't have the travelling to work. It's hard sometimes, especially on first shift when I have to go in the dark.'

Molly could hardly look at Maggie and Frank as she made up all the excuses she could think of to get away. But how could she stay? What would her life be like when Maggie found out that what she'd suspected was true? Shame flooded through Molly as she stood by the door, her box in her hand, her new utility coat buttoned up to her neck against the December cold.

'But why, lass? Where are you going to stay?' Frank knitted his brow and looked from his wife to Molly and back again. He couldn't understand what was happening, in the way of most men hadn't even noticed any tension between the two women. But he could see there was something now. Maggie wasn't half so upset as he'd have thought she would be.

'Have you two had a row? Has the wife upset you, pet?'

'No, I haven't, Frank Morley, and I'll thank you not to

blame me every time anything goes wrong,' Maggie snapped. She was knitting a striped jumper from odd pieces of wool which would once have ended up in her darning bag. Her needles clicked away fast and furious, cheeks flagged with bright patches of red.

'No, we haven't.' Molly shook her head in agreement with the older woman. 'It's like I said, I could do with living closer to my work and when an empty place came up at the hostel . . . Anyway, I'll always be grateful to you both for giving me a home when I needed one, I really will.' She paused, unable to go on. Was it only a few months since they had been so happy here, both she and Harry? He meeting Mona and falling for her, and she and Jackson . . . It seemed like a lifetime ago.

'I'll keep in touch,' she said. 'I've written to Harry to tell him.'

'Aye, well, *Harry* will always be welcome to a bed here,' said Maggie, and Molly flushed and turned away.

'I'll be going then,' she said. 'I don't think there'll be any letters but if there should be, you can send them to the factory.'

The conversation went round and round in her head as she sat on the bus to Bishop Auckland, then the train to the factory. When she arrived she put her box in the cloakroom. She would take it to the hostel after she had worked her shift.

It was almost as bad as the first time she had had to leave Eden Hope. Once again she was going to live among

strangers only this time it was entirely her own fault. 'You
deserve everything you've got!' she whispered fiercely to
herself as she bent her head over the machine, stitching
away at the tough cloth which left calluses on her fingers
and broke her nails. She felt a sort of perverse satisfaction
in that. When her working day was over she sat on the only
chair in her tiny room at the hostel or lay on the bed, not
reading or even relaxing, just in a kind of stupor. When a
girl asked her to go down into the communal sitting room
to listen to the wireless Molly refused, making weak
excuses. After a few days the other girls stopped asking
her and left her alone.

'Old misery guts,' she heard one of them whisper at
work. 'Does she think she's the only one to lose her man
in this damn' war?'

'She was always the same,' Joan Pendle assured them.
'Ever since I've known her.'

Mrs Fletcher called her to the end of the serving counter
one day at lunchtime, a day when Molly was feeling sick
and dizzy and had had trouble sewing a straight line that
morning.

'I heard you were living in a hostel now, Molly,' the
older woman said. She hesitated before going on, taking
time to tuck a stray lock of grey hair up under her turban.
Molly watched her. Surely Mrs Fletcher hadn't been so
grey before? Poor woman, she thought compassionately,
forgetting her own troubles for a minute.

'Yes, that's right, Mrs Fletcher.'

'Well, I just wondered . . . how would you like to stay with me? I have plenty of room in my house.' She bit her lip as she gazed at Molly, trying to gauge her reaction.

'Well . . .' For a moment Molly was unsure what to say, she was so taken by surprise. Since Mona's death her mother had been quiet as a mouse at work, simply getting on with what she had to do and keeping herself to herself.

'Like I said, I have the room and could do with a bit of rent coming in to help out with the rates and that,' Mrs Fletcher went on. 'It cannot be very nice in a hostel.'

Molly was shaking her head. 'I don't know, really I don't. I might be having to leave the factory anyway.'

Mrs Fletcher nodded, unsurprised. She cast a quick glance at Molly's stomach though she was sure there was nothing to see, not with the enveloping overall.

'Aye,' she said, 'I thought so. And you won't be able to stay at the hostel, will you?'

Molly didn't know what to say. She looked at the floor, at the food on her tray. Food she certainly didn't feel like eating.

'You'd be doing me a favour, it's lonely on me own,' Mrs Fletcher said. She put a hand on Molly's arm persuasively. 'And Mona would have liked me to help you out an' all.'

'Are you going to give me a hand or are you going to stand there all day gossiping?' the woman serving along the counter called.

'Sorry! I'm coming now,' Mrs Fletcher called back.

Turning to Molly, she said, 'Look, come along of me home tonight, will you? I'll give you a bite of supper and we can talk. It'll be better than going back to that hostel, won't it? You can get the Ferryhill bus, can't you?'

She was already walking back along the counter so Molly nodded her agreement before carrying her tray to a table where she could sit on her own. She was even avoiding Jenny these days.

Why was Mrs Fletcher offering to help her? she wondered. She picked up her fork and forced herself to eat a few bites of Woolton pie, drank the cup of sugarless tea. As she walked back to the sewing room, Joan Pendle fell into step with her.

'I don't suppose you've heard from your Harry?'

'By, you're bold as brass, aren't you? After the lies you've told about me.' Molly could hardly believe Joan would come and talk to her. 'No, I haven't heard from him lately. He's off somewhere training for some new thing as far as I know.' She could hardly bear to think about her brother. What would he say if he knew how she had let the family down?

'I wondered, that was all,' said Joan. Molly glanced at her. The other girl wore such an expression of longing on her face Molly could almost feel sorry for her in spite of her meddling.

'If I hear from him, I'll let you know how he is,' Molly surprised herself as well as Joan by saying. She sat down at her sewing machine and began the monotonous work of sewing powder bags yet again. At least she had reason to look forward to the evening, she thought. Going to Ferryhill on the bus and having supper with Mona's mother was better than going back to her bare room in the hostel. Anything was.

It was a dark and stormy night when Molly got off the bus in Ferryhill market place and walked along the end of the rows of terraced houses until she came to George Street. Sadness flooded through her as she walked halfway down its length to the house where Mona had lived for all her short life. Molly was glad of her flashlight for the street was very dark, not a chink of light from the windows and of course not a street light lit. She played the beam of the torch on the number of the house to make sure she'd the right one and a passing air raid warden growled: 'Keep that light down!'

Hastily she lowered it and knocked at the door. 'Sorry, warden.'

Mrs Fletcher had been waiting for her. The door opened in a trice and Molly was ushered into the kitchen where there was a delicious smell of meat and onions.

'Sit yourself down, it's all ready,' the older woman said. She was bustling about from oven to table, cloth in her hands as she took out a shepherd's pie which even had a crust of cheese on the top.

'I don't want to take your precious meat ration,' said Molly, though in truth her mouth had begun to water embarrassingly. It was a long time since the canteen meal she had been unable to finish.

'Nonsense, get it down you, it's a pleasure to have you,' said Mrs Fletcher. She served the meal and sat opposite Molly. 'Tuck in,' she said. 'We can talk later. No use letting the food get cold.'

Later they sat by a blazing fire and drank tea from a pot which Molly suspected held at least two days' tea ration. Mrs Fletcher was putting herself out to be friendly, she thought. Completely different now from the silent woman who served them in the canteen at dinnertime. She had a look of Mona, thought Molly as she sipped her tea. And, yes, her hair had gone completely grey, she could see that now the turban Mrs Fletcher had to wear at work was removed. But the thing was, if she was to take up this offer, Molly had to tell her the truth, she owed her that.

'Mrs Fletcher –'

'Call me Dora, dear.'

'Dora . . . I would love to come and live here, I really would, but you should know I won't be at the factory for very long. I'm expecting a baby.' There, she'd said it. Molly hung her head in shame.

'I know. I can tell. There are signs, you know. That wet streak of nothing Gary Dowson, was it?'

'How did you know?'

'We hear things in the canteen, you'd be surprised.' Dora leaned forward and gazed earnestly at her. 'You can come here, I told you you could. Our Mona would have wanted it. And any road, I have the spare room now, don't I?'

Molly felt tears spring to her eyes. The back of her throat swelled up, thick with those unshed.

'But if I lose my job . . .'

'Why, there's nowt so sure but you'll do that,' said Dora calmly. 'Look, lass, you're not the first this has happened to, not by a long chalk. Many a lass has been taken down by a good-for-nowt. Aye, and let down after an' all. Now, I think we should be making a few plans, don't you?'

Molly could only smile tremulously and nod her head. At least her immediate worries were over, she told herself. Though a small voice within her said that *she* had not been taken down, she had been as willing as Gary Dowson though she still couldn't understand why. Oh, if only the father of her baby had been Jackson, her own dear Jackson, though she hadn't the right to call him that now. But if only! The two most poignant words in the language.

Chapter Twenty-five

There was another telegram from the War Office. Maggie gazed at it as the new telegram boy, a young lad of sixteen years whose one fear was that the war would end before he had a chance to register for the Royal Air Force, proffered it.

'That cannot be for us, lad,' she said.

'Aye, it is,' he said. 'Look you here. Mr F. Morley – it says, plain enough.' He hadn't been in the job long enough to know the hatred the sight of a lad in Post Office uniform with a yellow envelope in his hand could generate, so he was surprised by Maggie's joyful reaction.

'Frank! Come here, will you?' she cried and Frank rolled towards the door in his wheel chair.

'Who is it, lass?' he asked testily. He glanced at the boy, still holding the telegram. 'Aw, give it here, man,' he said. 'How do you expect to find out what it says if you don't open it?' he asked his wife. Tearing the envelope open with his third finger because the tip of his index finger and thumb had been chopped off in the pit, he drew out the thin sheet.

'Why, yer bugger! Yer bugger!' he said, over and over,

before handing the sheet to his wife. 'Our Jackson's not dead at all, Maggie, now what do you think of that?' This last was a shout of triumph which made the telegram boy back away down the yard.

'There's no reply then?' he asked, before diving out of the gate and on to his bike.

Maggie and Frank didn't even hear him. They were clinging to one another, tears streaming down their faces.

'I told you he wasn't dead,' she asserted, though she'd told him nothing of the sort. 'I told you!'

'Eeh, lass, isn't it grand?' asked Frank, not bothering to contradict her. Maggie dried her eyes on the corner of her apron and ran down the yard and into the next where her neighbour was hanging out clothes.

'Our Jackson's not dead!' she cried, waving the telegram at the woman who stood, forgetful of the couple of clothes pegs sticking out of her mouth. 'He's in a hospital down south. Look, here's the name of it here.' She pointed to the piece of paper. 'He's not dead!' she shouted aloud.

'Mind, I'm right glad for you, Maggie,' the neighbour said after removing the clothes pegs and dropping them on top of the basket of clothes. 'Eeh, who'd have thought it, eh?' But Maggie was off down the row, calling her news out to anyone else who was there.

When she finally calmed down a little and returned to her own door, Frank was still sitting there. 'Give us another look at that, woman,' he said. 'I've been waiting for you.'

Taking the telegram, he read it again. 'It doesn't say what it is that's the matter with him, does it?' he muttered. 'Just that he's been injured.'

The delight died from Maggie's face as she stared at him, visions of her lad being brought home in a wheel chair like his dad's filling her mind.

'I wonder, like,' said Frank soberly, 'why it's been so long? I mean, it's months since the lads got back from Dunkirk, isn't it?'

'What can we do, Frank?' She sank down on the rocking chair by the fire, the chair where she had sat for so many unhappy hours contemplating the fact that, barring miracles, they weren't going to see Jackson again, not in this life.

The pit hooter had gone for the first shift. Men were coming out of the mine when there was a second knock at the door.

'Mrs Morley, me dad says will you come? There's a telephone call for you,' the little boy from the post office said. 'An' he said will you hurry? It's long distance.'

Maggie raced down the street after him and into the little shop at the bottom of the rows. The man behind the counter looked up as he saw her.

'Mind, I wouldn't allow this if it wasn't for the fact it's long distance and about your lad,' he said. 'It's not allowed, really.'

'Oh, thanks, Mr Dunne, thank you,' Maggie said humbly, still breathing hard from her exertions.

'Aye. Well, he said he'd ring back in ten minutes,' said
the postmaster and looked up at the clock, kept on time by
a phone call every morning from the exchange. On cue the
bell rang and he picked up the receiver, handing it over to
her.

'Mrs Morley? Is that you? This is Harry Mason here,
I'm speaking from a hospital in Kent. I've seen Jackson,
Mrs Morley, he's going to be fine! A knock on the head,
that's all. Did you get a telegram from the War Office?'

'We did, lad, not long since. Are you sure now? I mean,
are you sure he'll be all right? We wondered why it took
so long . . .'

'I'll write and explain, Mrs Morley. Come home if I can
next leave. Have you told Molly, Mrs Morley?'

'No, I haven't. She's –'

'At work, is she? Well, I bet she'll be pleased as punch.'

The pips sounded, an operator's voice cutting in. 'Your
time is up, caller. Three minutes only for civilian calls.'
The line went dead and Maggie handed the receiver back
to the postmaster.

'Good news, eh?'

'By, it is, Mr Dunne, it is. The best news there is.'

'Aye, I thought as much.'

Maggie practically skipped up the rows, her head in the
clouds, but as she neared her own back gate she slowed.
Molly . . . She had to get in touch with Molly. In her
euphoria she was prepared to forget her suspicions of her
lad's fiancée. There were lots of things stopped a girl's

courses. That blasted powder for one, the stuff which dyed all the lasses' necklines.

Maggie nodded to herself as she turned in at the gate. Jackson wouldn't thank her for losing touch with Molly again, indeed he would not. She would write now, catch the four o'clock post.

Frank was waiting, a thin white line of strain around his mouth. 'Well?' he asked.

'It's fine, Frank, really it is. That was Harry on the phone. He says our Jackson has nowt but a bump on the head!'

'When will he be able to travel home, Doctor?' Harry had waited at the door while the doctor examined Jackson, heard him pronounce approval of the way the patient had recovered physically. 'Good,' he had said, testing Jackson's reflexes. 'Yes, the wound has healed nicely. I think we should leave the bandages off now.' There was a vivid red line above Jackson's brow and disappearing into his hair, a puckering of scar tissue on his right temple and a patch where the hair had had to be shaven above his ear. The hair was grown again now, of course, except in one stubborn part about two inches long.

The doctor frowned at Harry, his expression forbidding. 'Patience,' he pronounced.

Harry had managed to get down to see Jackson for at least a short visit every week, but he knew this wouldn't be able to carry on. He was being posted shortly. He wasn't supposed to know where but the fact that he and his fellow paratroopers had been given an intensive course in Norwegian was a good pointer. And he dearly wanted to get Jackson home before then. Harry felt his friend looking gravely up at him and he smiled, his quick lopsided smile, his teeth gleaming white against a face still brown after so many years in the Indian sun. Just as Jackson's was. This visit he had been sure that the past was coming back to his friend. Sometimes he started to say something then stopped, wearing a frown of puzzlement.

'I will speak to you in my office, Sergeant Mason,' the doctor said now, and Harry had no choice but to go out into the corridor and along to the door marked 'Dr West'. He stood by the window of the office, staring out at the garden, waiting for the doctor, wondering how he could convince him that Jackson would be better among his own people. Surely there in Eden Hope, with the people he had known all his life and the familiar accents of home, Jackson would remember, wouldn't he?

'I wish to keep him under supervision,' Dr West said when Harry put this to him. Did he think that there were no doctors experienced in head injuries in the north? Harry clamped his lips tight together; he was a soldier and used to doing what his superiors told him to, no matter how wrongheaded.

'I know what I'm doing,' Dr West said, and smiled in perfect understanding of what was passing through Harry's mind.

'Well, couldn't he go north anyway? There are hospitals there too and he would be safer from the bombing, wouldn't he, sir?'

'That's true,' said the doctor, 'and don't think I haven't thought of it.' He sighed. 'Look, I'll make enquiries, see if there is a place for him. But I'd have to travel with him. Hmmm . . .'

Harry watched him as he sat down at his desk and picked up a pencil, began to doodle on his blotting pad. Suddenly he threw down his pencil and stood up.

'Right, Sergeant. I'll see what I can do. Now, I have other patients to see to. I'll let you know of any developments.'

Harry had to be content with that. He wrote to Maggie and Frank, and also to Molly through them for he still hadn't had word of where she was staying. But he was sure that Maggie would see she got the letter.

Don't worry, Jackson is in good shape physically. Evidently he must have been caught in some blast or something and it has affected his memory so the doctors want to watch him. You know what they're like, over cautious mostly. But he'll be fine. He's coming back up north as soon as there's a place for him. I'll try to get leave so I can come with him.

But Harry's own orders came through before Jackson got his place. Early one morning he and his men were driven

to a quiet air strip where they boarded a plane and headed
north themselves. They skirted London and the Midlands,
flying over the West Riding and turning north-east over the
North Riding and County Durham. If there had been a
porthole Harry would have seen the broad sweep of
Teesdale and Weardale, Wear Valley and its clusters of
villages with pitheads standing proud above them. And
then the city with its ancient cathedral, majestic above the
curve of the Wear in the early-morning light. Then they
were out over the grey North Sea, heading for the fjords
of Norway.

In hospital in Kent, Jackson was dreaming. He was on
a parade ground in India, one of a company of men, and
they were marching forward in a perfect straight line, right
to the end of the enormous, dusty ground, left turn and one,
two, three, four, and about turn, two, three, four, forward
again, back and forth over the ground. The heat was
tremendous, the sun beating down on them. He could feel
the sweat trickling down his back. The sun was so bright
it made his eyes water, heat struck through the soles of his
boots and still they marched, one, two, three, four. Until
he felt himself falling. He was going to disgrace them all,
he thought, and sank into a deep, black, bottomless hole.

'Howay, Jack, man,' said someone, and he knew the
voice. He couldn't open his eyes because the sun was so
bright if he did it would blind him, but he knew who it was
only the name eluded him for the minute. Think, Jackson,
bloody well think! he told himself. You're just not thinking

hard enough. And then the name came to him.

'Harry, is that you?' he asked hoarsely. But there was no answer, only another voice then, a woman's voice like Harry's but not his. She needed him, he could tell. There was distress in her voice, panic even.

'Molly?' he called. 'Molly?'

With a tremendous effort of will he opened his eyes, braving the light from the sun, defying it. Only it wasn't the sun, it was an electric light directly above his bed where the sheets were damp with sweat. Jackson blinked and a face swam into view but it wasn't Harry's or Molly's, it was a woman in a nurse's cap that sat over her ears, covering all her hair.

'Now then, Sergeant,' said the nurse, 'stop shouting, there's a good boy. You must have had a nightmare. Why, you're sweating like a bull. Here, have a drink. It's nice cold orange juice.'

Jackson drank thirstily, thanked her and lay back on his pillow. He knew who he was now. It had come to him. 'My name is Jackson Morley,' he said.

Molly went into Winton Grange mother and baby home in June, 1941.

'Well, if you must,' Dora Fletcher had said, though it was not what she had wanted. 'You can have the baby and bring it back here afterwards. I'll look after the poor little mite, give up me job in the canteen, it'll be all right. You can go back to work, you've no need to worry.'

'I'm not,' said Molly. Not about having the baby she wasn't, not now. She sat in Mrs Fletcher's best armchair and put one arm protectively across her swollen abdomen, waiting to feel the slight movements the baby made. Ever since she had first been startled by the fluttering in her belly she had begun to think of the baby as real, a little person, one she was responsible for. 'I love you, baby,' she said beneath her breath.

'What? What did you say?' demanded Dora.

'Nothing, nothing at all,' Molly replied. She watched as Dora cast on a white matinee jacket. Molly had got the wool with the extra clothes coupons she was allowed for the baby; there was enough for three jackets. And a ball of pink which Dora had bought herself, using her own coupons.

'How do you know it will be a girl?' Molly had asked.

'I know, I just know,' Dora replied confidently.

Molly watched her now, feeling a slight sense of disquiet. Sometimes it seemed that Dora was taking over this baby. She seemed much livelier and happier these days. For the first time since her own daughter's tragic death she was putting on weight, her pale face showing a hint of colour high on the cheekbones. And she was always busy. She had brought down an old wooden cradle from the attic, cleaned it up, given it a coat of varnish. Now it stood, wood shining in the light, an old soft blanket cut down to fit, a muslin-covered quilt fashioned from Molly knew not what.

It all looked very nice, she had to admit, and everything Dora had prepared for the baby was good and sensible. She had even begged a wooden fruitbox from the greengrocer and padded it with the remains of the blanket, covered with a muslin frill.

'It'll hold the bairn's bits and pieces, talcum powder and such,' she had said to Molly, displaying it with an air of triumph. Working in the canteen, she got home earlier than Molly and had fitted up the box in the interval.

'Very nice,' said Molly, sniffing the air for any smell which would indicate a meal was being cooked, but there was none. And she felt empty suddenly, dizzy with hunger. It was a feeling that came on her often these days, ever since she had been carrying the baby.

'What's for tea, Dora?' she asked, sinking down into the armchair.

'Well, me being busy, I thought I'd just pop along to the fish shop when it opens.' Dora put the box down, frowning slightly. It was evident she was disappointed with Molly's reaction, had expected more enthusiasm.

'I'll go, if you like?' said Molly, though she was weary and all she really wanted to do was snuggle down in the chair.

'No, I'll do it. It's about time now any road.' She gazed keenly at Molly. Now that her attention was diverted from the baby box she noticed the deep shadows beneath the girl's eyes, her white face.

'You want to look after yourself better,' she reproved

Molly. 'There's more than yourself to think of now. Goodness knows I do my best for you.'

'Yes, I know, Dora, and I'm grateful. I don't know what I'd do without you.'

'Aye, well, I'll just go along the fish shop now, see if I can get you a nice bit of haddock.'

After she had gone, Molly rested her head back against the cushion and gazed into the heart of the fire, one which was on every day no matter what time of year it was for it was the only means of cooking and heating the house. There was a small fireplace in the sitting room but it was never lit. Though Dora had plans for Molly to be confined in there, in which case it would be. She was uneasy still; it was as if every decision about the baby was being taken out of her hands.

As ever when she had a few minutes to herself Jackson came to the forefront of her mind. He was always there, of course, but pushed to the back, waiting. She could feel his presence no matter how busy she was, what else she had to worry about.

What am I to do, my love? she cried silently. What else can I do? If Molly left Dora's there was nowhere to go except the mother and baby home and she shrank from that. There had been so many whispered stories about those places, how awful they were, how the girls were made to work and not allowed to go out, slept with no wireless, nothing. A girl had come back to work at the factory after having her illegitimate baby there and she was changed out of all recognition. From a lively, outgoing girl she had become a silent, solemn-faced one, someone who rarely spoke to anyone, just sat like a frightened rabbit and got on with her work.

She had had her child adopted, Molly remembered. Oh, poor lass, she had thought at the time, how could she do it? She would never do that, no, she wouldn't, she vowed to the baby inside her. 'It's you and me, petal,' she whispered now, stroking her distended belly. And Dora was her best hope. She was the mother of the only real friend Molly had ever had, she wouldn't fail her, no, of course she wouldn't.

Molly got to her feet and filled the kettle, settled it on the fire. She spread a checked cloth on the table and laid out knives and forks, brought the milk and sugar from the pantry, spread margarine on bread. Her stomach rumbled and she took a slice of bread and ate it. There, she felt better for something in her stomach.

Dora was just excited at the prospect of a baby in the house after so many years, that was it. Of course she wasn't trying to take over the child.

Chapter Twenty-six

Molly had told no one at work that she was leaving. Of course she had had to hand in her notice, secure her release, for no one was allowed to leave for no good reason. But the manager had said nothing. So many girls were working at the factory now that one more or less made little difference. He simply took the doctor's note which Molly handed him, perused it briefly, didn't even look at her again and the following Friday she received her severance pay. As a pregnant woman she was exempt from war work.

It was strange handing in her pass and walking away from the factory gates. The other girls chattered and laughed among themselves. Jenny called goodnight to her, waving cheerily as she went off to meet her soldier who was home on leave. Molly watched them, a strange feeling of melancholy sweeping over her. She had been happy here, she thought, most of the time at least.

Joan went past, sniffed and looked away. Molly drew her loose coat around her, turning away, dreading that Joan would find out and tell everyone in Eden Hope about the baby. It was just as well she was leaving. Her loose overall had served her well up to now but it wouldn't cover her condition much longer, Molly was well aware of that. At least Gary hadn't told anyone, or she didn't think so. He had gone out of his way to avoid her lately. If he met Molly at all he looked away, embarrassment plain on his face.

What an escape she'd had from him, she thought. She would manage without him all right. Why, it was coming up to the middle of the twentieth century and what with the war and soldiers going away all the time there were many girls in her position. Though with more excuse, she told herself, feeling the by now familiar pang of guilty shame.

She had another job to go to, cleaning a school at Ferryhill. Then as soon as the baby was old enough she would go to another Royal Ordnance factory, the one nearer Darlington. It was easy to get to from Ferryhill. Oh, yes, she had everything planned. And when she had the baby she would have someone to love, someone who would be totally uncritical of her, a child of her own.

The work was hard at the school for the caretaker had gone to war and his replacement was a retired man. The hours were awkward too, early morning and evenings, but Molly didn't care. She went through her days scrubbing and polishing until the classrooms shone. If she worked hard she would be tired enough to sleep without dreams or nightmares of a future without Jackson. Sometimes the dreams were worse than the nightmares for she was happy in her dreams. Jackson was always there. Sometimes they were in the woods or on the path from Shildon, and it was summer and the sun was shining, and Jackson would have his arm around her and it was one of the magical times again, like the time he was home and they were planning to marry. Then she would wake up and be filled with devastating despair for those days gone forever.

'I have the baby to look forward to,' she told herself aloud in the empty classrooms. But she wouldn't have Jackson or even her brother Harry. She couldn't bear to think that he might find out about the baby. Oh, if only it had been Jackson's . . .

'You don't need to pay me any board, Molly, not now, not until after the baby comes,' Dora said one Friday night. It was only three weeks before the baby was due and Molly had given up work at the school. She would have worked on, but the headmaster had insisted she leave.

'After all, Miss Mason,' he had said, looking away from her rather than at her noticeable bulge, 'you are not a good example to the children, are you?'

'Oh, go to hell!' Molly had replied. It was a Friday afternoon and she was bone tired. She had worked late the evening before and this morning had come in early rather than lie in bed sleepless. She had gone to sleep in the armchair in Dora's kitchen after scrubbing the place out and dulling the itching of the skin on her hands by rubbing them with olive oil and sugar. It was one of Dora's remedies.

'It's the soda as does it,' she had asserted. 'Me mam always rubbed olive oil and sugar into hers, it never fails.'

Dora came in from the canteen and found Molly asleep, slumped in the chair, legs sprawled out before her.

'Wake up, lass,' she had cried and Molly jumped up, her mind in a whirl, hardly knowing where she was. She hadn't been dreaming this time but in a deep, deep sleep and her head thumped with the sudden awakening.

'You'd best be away down for your pay,' said Dora. 'It's close on half-past three and the school will be empty if you don't.'

Out in the fresh air, birds singing and bright dandelions glowing from every little patch of grass, Molly began to feel better. Until the headmaster handed her her notice along with her pay.

'Go to hell,' she said again. 'Do you think they don't see their mothers like this most of the time?'

'That is irrelevant, Miss Mason,' the headmaster said stiffly. 'You are unmarried.'

'You're a bit of a bastard yourself, headmaster,' Molly replied and walked out, amazed at herself. It was the first time she had ever used such a word.

'It doesn't matter,' said Dora when she got home. 'You'll get dole or sick pay or something, won't you?'

'I'm not going down the dole office,' Molly said flatly. Not letting those mealy-mouthed clerks look at me as though I'm a whore, she thought. I'll starve first.

'Mind, you're in a mood with yourself, lass, aren't

you?' said Dora. She sniffed. 'How am I supposed to keep you and the bairn when she comes?'

Molly was just in the mood all right, ready to kick against the world and Dora in particular.

'I don't expect you to keep me,' she snapped, 'an' what's more I'll keep my own child, thank you.'

'Getaway! What will you do without me, eh? You're having the baby here, in *my* front room, and it's me is going to see to her an' all.'

'I'll see to her myself, I told you. I'm sick of you trying to take over. And anyway, what makes you think the baby will be a girl?'

'Of course she'll be a girl, it's the way you're holding her. Me mam always said –'

'An' that's another thing. I'm sick to death of what your mam used to say! And don't think I'm relying on you either. I'll go into the mother and baby home. In fact, I've decided that's what I'll do.'

'Molly! After all I've done for you. You wouldn't, would you?' Dora blanched.

'I will. I'll go into a home, I'm telling you, then I'm not beholden to anyone. I'll see the doctor tonight, ask if he'll arrange it.'

'Oh, Molly, don't! Please don't,' said Dora. She sat down heavily, looking stricken. But Molly was determined, though when she saw the effect on Dora she felt a pang of compunction. But she had been uneasy for a while about the way the other woman was taking over.

Sometimes you could swear the baby was hers or at least that she was the grandmother. It would be best to get away for a while. And in the home there would be other girls like Molly.

'Look, Dora, it'll be for the best,' she said. 'I'm not saying I won't come back to see you, I will.'

'You won't,' Dora sniffed.

Molly sighed. 'Well, I'm away to the doctor's now, the surgery starts at five and I'll get a good turn.' Dora said no more and Molly put on her coat and went out in silence.

It was a beautiful day when she walked up the drive to the home. Dora had offered to take the day off and go with her but Molly had refused. At least Dora had accepted her decision to have the baby there, thought Molly. She had apologised for losing her temper and Dora had accepted gracefully. Only too pleased to, Molly realised. In the back of her mind she suspected Dora wanted the baby as a substitute for Mona, but what could she do?

She winced as the gravel from the path pressed through the thin leather of her shoes. Her feet were already slightly swollen and aching. The path undulated between what had once been lawns and were now potato patches. DIG FOR VICTORY said a poster seen everywhere, and most people obeyed. So instead of grass and roses there were yellow potato flowers, promising a good harvest of King Edwards in the autumn.

The baby in her belly moved and kicked. Molly winced,

her bottom rib sore. This child would be a footballer, she thought wryly as the large redbrick house came into view. She rang the bell and waited. After a few minutes a tiny girl in an all-enveloping overall, like the one Molly herself had worn at the factory, opened the door and peered at her through thick-lensed spectacles.

'Aw,' she said, opening the door wider. 'You're the new lass. Howay in then.'

Molly followed her into the hall of the big house. The great curving staircase with the large window at the first bend testified to the former magnificence of the place, but now it was bare with the floorboards scrubbed and a great, empty stone fireplace. A damp cold struck Molly in contrast to the warmth of the summer's day outside.

'I'll tell Matron you're here,' said the girl, and scuttled to a door at the side where she knocked.

'Enter!' a voice boomed out, and something about that imperious command made Molly's heart plummet in despair. For some reason it reminded her of prison. She put a protective arm around her stomach though she hardly knew why she did it. Standing waiting in the hall, she told herself it was just something else to be got through. 'What can't be cured must be endured' sprang to her mind, a cliche often repeated in Eden Hope.

Molly was to repeat it to herself often before her baby was born. When she was on her knees scrubbing down the great staircase with her belly sometimes rubbing against the treads. Or mangling sheets in the ancient laundry where washing machines hadn't been heard of, or if they had were not considered necessary in this place. After all there was the free labour of the pregnant women or new mothers.

Vi, the girl who had answered the door to Molly on her first day, was a new mother though she hardly looked big enough to have carried a baby, let alone delivered one. In fact, she hadn't. Not a live baby that is.

'My baby was born dead,' she confided in Molly as they rubbed the banister with vinegar water before polishing it. Her little face was screwed up and her eyes invisible behind the thick lenses of her glasses.

'I'm sorry,' Molly said, pausing in her brisk rubbing of the mahogany rail, knowing her response was inadequate.

'Aw, I'm over it now, it was two months ago,' said Vi. 'But I was that pleased when Matron said I could stay on. I haven't got no mam or dad, like.'

'Me neither,' said Molly, feeling an instant kinship with this diminutive girl. 'How old are you, Vi?'

'Fifteen, I think.'

'What did your boyfriend say when you started the baby, Vi?'

She looked at Molly with transparent innocence. 'Eeh, I haven't got a boyfriend,' she said, and giggled. 'That's what Matron asked me but I told her the same as I'm telling you – I never did have a boyfriend, the lads don't look at me.'

Yet somebody, some man, had taken the girl down,

thought Molly, and when she was just a kid. She herself felt only a weary resignation at the ways of the world.

'Well, me and you can adopt each other as sisters, what do you say? We can be family.'

Molly didn't know why she said it, she had enough problems of her own without taking on Vi's, hadn't she? But somehow the girl's simple tale had pierced the protective shell she'd adopted since the telegram came.

The regime at the home was hard and unremitting but Molly welcomed it. They were wakened at six o'clock every morning except Sunday when they were allowed to lie in until seven. Before breakfast they all had their allotted tasks; those not actually in labour or lying-in, that is. For Molly and Vi it was to the laundry where the bloody sheets and cloths from the labour ward which had been soaked overnight had to be put through the mangles, a task Molly found more and more exhausting. Vi, for all her small size, was surprisingly strong and turned the mangle with a will but Molly couldn't let her do it all herself.

At eight o'clock the gong went for breakfast and the girls, looking like maids from a bygone age in their overalls, with faces scrubbed clean and hair tied back 'like little orphan Annie' as one described it bitterly, went in to their porridge and fried bread. On Sundays they had their ration of one slice of bacon and a small pile of scrambled egg, which was really dried egg reconstituted.

The rest of the day was filled with housework, with a

free hour in the grounds after tea, rain or shine. The obstetrician on call to the home believed in fresh air. Some of the girls grumbled but Molly was glad of it. She and Vi would stroll around, inspect the progress of the potato patches, go round to the back to the kitchen gardens where the girls who had already had their babies and were over their lying-in period looked after the carrots and cabbages, peas and sprouts growing there.

It was nice in the gardens. There were high walls that reflected the evening sun and blocked out the chill winds.

'You'll be working here soon, Molly,' Vi said to her wistfully. It was a day in July and pods of green beans were swelling on the thick stems.

'No, I'm going as soon as I'm allowed out,' said Molly absently. She was watching a late bee busy in a clump of hollyhocks that had escaped being dug up in favour of vegetables. She wandered on up the path, at first not noticing that Vi hadn't followed.

'We'd better go in now,' she said as she reached the end of the path. 'Vi?' For she hadn't answered and when Molly turned round she saw the girl standing by the hollyhock clump, her shoulders hunched. She was crying.

'Why, what's the matter?' Molly asked, and went back to her.

'I thought you would be here another three months like the rest of them,' Vi replied, between sobs, hiccuping a little. 'What will I do when you've gone? You'll forget about me.'

'No, I won't, Vi, I promise I won't,' Molly tried to assure her, but the girl nodded her head.

'You will,' she asserted. 'Everyone does.'

'Well, I won't,' said Molly. She put an arm around the other girl's thin shoulders. 'You're the only sister I've got, aren't you? Didn't we adopt each other? I won't forget you. You can come and see me on your afternoon off. Come on now, pet, dry your eyes and blow your nose and we'll go in. We have to look after each other now.'

Looking only partly reassured, Vi did as she was told. Goodness knows, thought Molly, the lass has had few reasons to trust anyone so far. She would never let Vi down, she vowed silently, never.

That same night Molly woke with a deep, nagging ache in her back. She lay for a few minutes, unsure what to do. The baby wasn't due for another week. Perhaps this was another case of that false labour the other girls talked about frequently. But the ache deepened into a pain that made her gasp and at the same time she felt a gush of wetness between her thighs.

There was a bell at the head of the bed, there for just this sort of emergency, and Molly struggled to reach it. The pain was holding her in a tight clamp and at first she couldn't move. But reach it she did in the end and the bell rang out, loud and clear, so that the other girls in the ward, which was converted from the upstairs drawing room of the old house, stirred, a few lights went on and they came to crowd round the bed to see what was wrong.

'Get out of the way this minute, girls!' an authoritative voice snapped from the door and the crowd backed away to let the midwife on duty through. A capable woman, she was middle-aged with iron grey hair under a starched white cap and a bosom like a platform under her apron.

'Now, what's all the fuss about?' she said to Molly. 'Turn on your back and let me have a look at you.'

'Right, it's the labour ward for you,' she said after she had examined Molly. 'Though I've no doubt it will be hours yet before we see junior.'

In fact it was not the next morning when Molly made her final, desperate push but the morning after. And when the baby girl did arrive, crying with rage no doubt at the delay, Molly was a quivering wreck and all she felt was an enormous thankfulness that at last her ordeal was over. Half an hour later, when the child was washed and put into her arms, 'Only for a minute mind,' the midwife admonished, Molly looked down at the red face of her daughter and fell instantly in love.

Chapter Twenty-seven

'But why did she leave Eden Hope, Mam? I mean what possible reason could she have had?'

Maggie Morley gazed at her son, biting her lip. She couldn't voice her suspicions of Molly, not to Jackson, not when he was so obviously worried about her. She was aware that he had trusted her to do her best for his girl this time and she had failed him. And Molly too. She and Frank had shut her out from their private grief, not admitting she might have been hurting as well. What's more, Maggie was only too aware this wasn't the first time she hadn't spared enough thought for the lass. And it was only a suspicion she'd had that Molly had fallen wrong. Maybe she had been wrong. In fact, surely she would have heard by now if she'd been right? That spiteful cat Joan Pendle would have seen to it.

'She said she wanted to be nearer the factory so she could save money on fares. Time an' all. It wouldn't take so long to get there, especially when she was on nights.' Even as Maggie said it she turned away. He'd know they were only excuses.

Jackson shook his head in disbelief, automatically putting a hand up when the movement caused him a spasm of pain.

'Don't, lad, be careful,' his mother warned, forgetting about Molly. She put a hand out to him then took it back as he turned away and pulled a chair out from under the table.

'I'm all right, Mam,' he said, and sat down. Putting an elbow on the table, he leaned his aching head on his hand, using it as a prop.

'Eeh, you're not right yet, are you, son?' asked his mother, her face creasing in anxiety.

'I tell you, I am. I'm just upset about Molly.'

No, she definitely couldn't say anything to him yet, Maggie decided. If at all. Maybe she *had* been wrong about Molly, maybe she hadn't been expecting after all. Maggie sighed. She had had enough on her hands when Jackson was missing all that time. Oh, she never wanted to go through that again. No, indeed. And worrying about the way Frank had taken it. She had hardly been able to look at the lass, never mind take an interest in her. Molly had reminded her too much of Jackson, her lovely lad.

Then, when she had had the good news, she had told Joan Pendle to tell Molly and to give her the letter Jackson had sent. Well, Joan saw her at work, didn't she? Surely the girl would have done it? She wasn't as spiteful as all that, was she?

If in the back of her mind Maggie had wondered why Molly hadn't come straight back to Eden Hope to wait for Jackson, she hadn't had time to do much about it, she had been so busy turning the house out, getting ready for his return. She'd even saved the precious fat and meat rations so that she could make him a real old-fashioned steak and kidney pie. And now he wasn't eating it. It lay ignored on the table while he went on about Molly Mason. Maggie felt a niggle of jealousy. It was enough to make a saint swear, it really was.

Jackson had picked up his letters to Molly, two of them, both unopened. 'If I had her address, I'd go through. But I only have a few days, I have to report to the hospital on Monday.'

Maggie felt a pang of disappointment and dismay. Monday! And it was already Thursday evening. And if he was going to spend the little time he had chasing after the lass, what time did that leave for his mother and father?

'You're not going to rush off straight away, lad, surely not?' she protested.

'No, of course I'm not,' he said quickly, noticing the hurt expression his mother wore. 'But I'll have to try tomorrow. I'll go to the factory, I think. After all, the weekend is coming up and she won't be there then.'

He couldn't understand why Molly had gone off without even leaving her address. Of course, she hadn't known he had survived and got back from France. But still, Harry might have been coming home on leave and she wouldn't have wanted to miss him. Though perhaps she had written to her brother? Goodness knows, he thought unhappily. Harry was off somewhere on a 'hush-hush' operation he had been told, when his friend didn't come back to see him at the hospital. There was no way he could get in touch with Harry just at the present. Poor Molly, she must think that she had no one at all. What good were he and Harry to her, always away at war?

'Howay, lad, eat up the pie. Your mother made it especially for you,' said Frank. He wheeled his chair up to the table next to his son. 'Don't blame her, lad,' he said in a soft undertone. 'She was at her wit's end about you, she was.'

Jackson smiled at him, tried to throw off his melancholy mood. 'No, Dad, I'm not blaming her,' he replied and looked across at his mother. He smiled at her and suddenly his face lit up, eyes crinkling at the corners, twinkling at her. And Maggie saw she had her lad back again and felt again the joy she had known when the news of his miraculous return from the dead reached her.

'Aye, lad, tuck in now,' was all she said, however. 'There's the best part of a week's ration of meat in that lot.'

Of course, Jackson couldn't get into the factory when he went in search of Molly. He couldn't get past the gate.

'But I want to see the manager,' he protested to the guard. 'I only have a couple of days before I have to go back to my unit. I must get in.'

'Not without a pass you don't,' the guard said stolidly.

'Well, ring the manager and ask him to come down here, will you?'

'No, I can't do that, not if it isn't urgent,' the guard replied.

'But it *is* urgent! I told you it was.'

'You told me nothing, Sergeant,' said the guard.

'It's my girl, she's in there . . . she thinks I'm dead.'

'If I did it for you, I'd have to do it for every soldier as comes looking for his lass, wouldn't I? Write a note and I'll give it to her when she comes out.'

'But it's only eleven o'clock in the morning. She won't be coming out until the end of the day, will she?'

'No, likely not,' the guard conceded. 'But you don't expect her to come out when she's supposed to be working, do you? The work here's important, like. There's a war on, you know.'

'Aye, I do,' said Jackson in exasperation. 'I'm a soldier or haven't you noticed?'

The guard bristled. 'I see you're wearing a uniform, but then any fifth columnist could get hold of a uniform, couldn't he?'

Jackson controlled his rising temper and dug into the breast pocket of his battledress for his identity card. 'There! Now will you get her?'

The guard took his time about examining the card then handed it back. 'Aye,' he said. 'Well, all right, you're a soldier on sick leave. Wounded in France, were

you? Whereabouts?' The guard saw Jackson's look of
exasperation and his voice hardened again. 'But like I said,
I still can't bring her from her work. What's the lass's
name, any road? I'll see where she's working and try to
get a message to her. I can do no more.'

'Well, thank God for that,' breathed Jackson, who was
getting to the stage where he was ready to punch the man
in the nose. And that, he well knew, would get him
nowhere.

'Molly Mason.'

The guard went back into his cubbyhole and began
sifting through lists. He came back out, shaking his head.
'She's not here the day,' he said. 'Not any Molly Mason
on this list. Mind, she might be on night shift.'

Jackson groaned. He hadn't thought of that. There was
more time wasted until the night shift came on. After
leaving a note for the guard to hand over to Molly, he
walked back to the station and caught a train back to
Bishop Auckland.

He was back at the factory gates when the night shift
was going in. There was no sign of Molly though he was
sure he hadn't missed anyone. He saw Joan Pendle coming
along in the crowd from the station and managed to push
his way through the throng to her. She turned as she heard
him calling her name.

'Jackson Morley! Well, fancy meeting you here. I heard
you were back.' She looked over his shoulder. 'Is Harry
with you?'

'No, sorry. He's in the paratroopers now, I don't know where he was sent.'

Joan's face dropped. She started to walk towards the factory gate. 'Any road,' she said, 'where've you been? We all thought you'd been killed.'

He fell into step beside her. 'Well, as you can see, I wasn't. I was injured but I'm all right now. Is Molly on this shift? Did you give her Mam's letter?'

'How could I? She hasn't worked here for months,' said Joan. Jackson stopped and stared at her. The disappointment was shattering. For a minute he could think of nothing else and Joan walked on, almost disappearing into the crowd. He ran after her, caught hold of her arm.

'She doesn't work here?' he asked incredulously. 'But where's she gone? And why didn't you tell my mother?'

Joan shook her arm free. 'How the heck do I know where's she gone? She's no friend of mine. Do you think I keep company with gaolbirds, like?'

Jackson grabbed hold of her again. 'Don't you speak of Molly like that,' he growled, glaring down at her menacingly. 'What about the letter Mam gave you? I said. What did you do with it?'

'Aw, I can't remember now. Do you think I've nowt else to do but run messages for your mother?' But Joan's voice was rising; she felt a tremor of fear.

'Hey, you, leave that lass alone!'

It was the gatekeeper, a different one from the morning. Jackson looked up, realising they were right by the gate and the streams of workers had slowed to a trickle.

'He's hurting my arm,' cried Joan, appealing to the gatekeeper over her shoulder.

'Leave her alone, I said,' shouted the man. He even left his post and came out the few yards to where they stood. Jackson stared at him, his lips a thin line in his angry face. He had never hit a woman in his life but he realised he had come very close to doing that. His grip reluctantly relaxed and Joan pulled herself free once again.

'Don't you ever touch me again!' she shouted, retreating through the gate. 'I'll have the law on you, I will.'

'Get along then, Sergeant,' said the gatekeeper. 'You'd best be off.' Now the girl had gone he felt quite sorry for the young soldier. Some of these lasses got up to all sorts of devilry while their men were away fighting for their country, he knew that. He'd seen them throwing themselves at the Canadian airmen who were stationed out Darlington way.

'You're better off without her, lad,' he said kindly.

Jackson stared at him a moment or two before comprehension dawned. 'She's not . . .' he began and stopped. No point in trying to explain, he thought. In any case he hadn't the time. He might as well catch the train back to Bishop. He turned on his heel and strode off to the station.

'Cheerio, then,' called the gatekeeper. 'Watch theeself, mind.'

Jackson half-turned and waved. 'Thanks. Cheerio.'

*

Back home in Eden Hope he sat around the house for the rest of the weekend, trying to think how he could get in touch with Molly, or at least find out what was happening to her.

'She'll be all right, lad. Likely she just got transferred somewhere else,' Frank said. He watched Jackson's pale face with the livid scar just showing under his hairline.

'I don't know whether the lad's so out of sorts because he cannot find Molly or because he still feels badly,' he confided to his wife.

She sighed. 'Aye, well, time will tell. Eeh, we were that glad when we found out he was alive and coming home, weren't we? I tell you, there's always summat to worry about. At least he's going to get a transfer to that convalescent hospital near Sunderland. We'll be able to go and see him there, won't we? And looking on the bright side, the war might be over before he has to go back, mightn't it?'

Molly had been directed to a munitions factory nearer Ferryhill. It was easier for her to get home now. Her life was centred round Beth, her little daughter, and work. Because she had a child she wasn't allowed to work where the bombs were filled or anywhere near explosives.

'I wouldn't anyway,' she said. She was sitting watching Dora bathe the baby, her own hands itching to take over.

In fact she had already offered to but Dora had shrugged it away casually.

'You're tired after work, I'll do it,' she had insisted.

Molly watched as Dora lifted the tiny, plump and perfect little figure from the water, laughing and talking baby talk to her, Beth gurgling and laughing back. Dora had been the first one to see Beth smile; she had met Molly at the door to tell her. Beth followed Dora everywhere with her eyes, her smile disappearing when Dora went out of her line of vision.

'Let me hold her,' Molly said suddenly. 'I'll dry her and get her ready for bed.'

'No, it's all . . .' Dora stopped as she saw Molly's stubborn expression. 'Righto, then,' she said, and handed the baby over with obvious reluctance. Immediately Beth started to whimper.

'It's all right, baby. Look, it's your mammy,' Molly said softly, trying hard to smile though anxiety lurked in her eyes. If only Beth wouldn't cry, if only she would smile back at her then everything would be fine, of course it would. Beth was *her* baby, wasn't she?

Dora had got to her feet and picked up the kettle to fill it for the tea and Beth's bottle. But she was hovering about, watching Molly and Beth anxiously, making Molly more nervous. The baby sensed it and her whimpers turned into full-blown crying. She arched her back and yelled at the top of her lungs with rage.

'Don't cry, Beth. Please, please, don't cry,' Molly

whispered. Dora put down the kettle and bent over Molly's shoulder and clucked and chattered to the child. Beth wriggled more than ever, and being still wet was slippery so that Molly had to grasp her firmly. The baby was screaming loudly now, her little face red, the eyes screwed up, her fists waving in the air with frustration.

'Go on then,' said Molly, defeated. 'Take her, she likes you the best.' Dora stepped forward eagerly and held out her arms and Molly put the child into them.

'Howay, my bairn,' said Dora fondly, and gently patted Beth dry. The baby stopped crying immediately and leaned against her, snuffling now with just the occasional hiccup. 'You're a naughty girl, aren't you?' said Dora in a tone of voice which implied the exact opposite of what she was saying. 'Now just wait until Auntie Dora has your clean nappy on and your nightie and then you can have your bottle, can't you? Are you hungry, my flower? Of course you are, petal.' Her tone changed to a normal one as she turned to Molly. 'Put the kettle on, will you? This one will be shouting for her bottle next.'

Molly picked up the kettle and took it to the tap in the pantry. She felt like crying herself, she was so tired and frustrated and filled with resentment of Dora because the baby obviously preferred her to her own mother. It wasn't natural, really it wasn't. She settled the kettle on the fire and brought out the tin of National Dried Milk and sugar and began preparing it for the baby's evening feed.

'Put a bit more sugar in, Molly,' Dora ordered.

'No, I don't think she needs extra sugar.'

'Go on, she's growing that fast she needs it for energy,' said Dora. 'If you're thinking about the ration, I'll do without mine.'

'Of course I'm not thinking about the ration!' Molly exploded, tears pricking the back of her eyes. 'I –'

'Shh, never mind, you'll upset the bairn,' said Dora.

'Anyway, I always put a bit of extra sugar in, she's used to it now.'

'I should have been breast feeding her,' said Molly fretfully. 'It's more natural.'

'Well, you can't, can you? Not when you have to go to work at all hours an' all. No, it was much better to start bottle feeding her.'

Molly sighed and made up the bottle as the kettle boiled. She cooled it under the tap and brought it back into the kitchen.

'I'll feed her now.'

'Best not disturb her,' said Dora comfortably. 'She'll be asleep as soon as she's finished her milk and then we can have ours. There's a nice hotpot in the oven.'

Chapter Twenty-eight

'At least it's more money at the munitions factory,' said Dora. She had a proprietorial hand on the pram as though Molly couldn't really be trusted with pushing it, not when it held the baby. The bubble of resentment that seemed always to be present in her these days swelled a little more. Dora glanced up at her.

'You're not listening to me,' she accused.

'I am, really I am,' said Molly. 'You were saying how I made more money at the munitions factory.'

'Aye. Just as well when I had to leave work to look after my little princess, isn't it, petal?' The question was addressed to the baby who turned her head sideways to smile at Dora. A milky sort of a smile but one of delight that Dora was speaking to her. Her first word will be 'Dora', Molly thought sourly.

It was a Sunday morning, the time when Molly usually took the baby out on her own, a time she looked forward to all week. Only today Dora had declared her intention of coming with her.

'It's a nice crisp morning, just the sort I like,' she had said. 'Autumn is so lovely, isn't it?'

'It's still September,' Molly had replied shortly. But she couldn't say to Dora that she didn't want her company as she strolled down the lane away from the village and between the fields where the corn was being harvested. The fact was she needed Dora and she couldn't afford to antagonise her.

They strolled in silence for a few minutes then Dora started again.

'I mean, a house like mine has a big mouth,' she said. 'The winter coming on and coal to buy and the electric. A baby has to be kept warm in the winter, you know.'

'You mean, I don't give you enough money? Is that what you're saying, Dora?'

'Well, like I said –'

'I can raise it to four pounds a week, I suppose,' said Molly doubtfully. It was practically the whole of her pay, she thought. But she didn't need much for herself and if she did she would have to try to get more overtime, that was all she could do.

They called at the newsagent's on the way home, Dora buying the *News of the World* and Molly the *Sunday Sun*, the local North Eastern Sunday paper. Because the weather had taken a turn for the worse they didn't even look at the headlines, simply rolled the papers up and put them under the pram's storm cover before making a dash for home as the rain began coming down in earnest.

It wasn't until the dinner was cooked and eaten and the dishes washed and put away that the two women sat down before the fire to read their papers, Beth asleep in her pram.

It was the photograph that caught Molly's attention first, a grainy photograph on the inside page of a soldier with dark hair under his forage cap, dark eyes and an unassuming smile. A lop-sided smile like her brother Harry's but it wasn't him, oh, no, it was Jackson Morley. LOCAL HERO, it read in big letters beneath the photo.

Molly sat straight in her chair with a sharp intake of breath. It couldn't be, not after all this time!

'What's the matter?' Dora had noticed her agitation and leaned forward, full of curiosity. But Molly didn't hear her; her heart was beating so fast she felt as though she was choking. There was a mist before her eyes so that when she tried to read the text she couldn't, it merged and blurred before her eyes. Dora got to her feet and came round to the back of Molly's chair. 'What is it?' she asked again. 'By heck, you've gone as white as a sheet, you have.'

She leaned over Molly's shoulder to see what it was. 'Do you know that lad, like?'

'No,' said Molly, only half-attending. 'I mean, yes.'

'He comes from Eden Hope, I see,' said Dora. 'The Croix de Guerre, eh? That's French, isn't it?'

'Yes.'

'Eeh, why, fancy. I wouldn't have thought they'd have been giving out medals, not now, not when they gave in.'

Molly wanted to jump to her feet and scream at Dora,

tell her to shut up, stop looking over her shoulder, go to hell or anywhere, she didn't care where. But mainly just to *shut up*!

Her vision was clearing now after the initial shock. Oh, yes, it was Jackson. My love, my love, my love is alive, her heart sang. A great thankfulness enveloped her whole body. 'Thank you, God,' she said aloud. 'Thank you, God.'

'What for?' asked Dora, mystified.

'It's Jackson, don't you understand? He . . . we are engaged to be married.'

Molly began walking about the kitchen with quick, jerky steps, over to the window, stopping, turning around and walking back.

'For goodness sake, lass, stand still, you'll have me dizzy,' said Dora. Molly picked up the paper again, stared hard at it as though she might have been mistaken the first time. Her fingers trembled so much the paper rustled. But it was still Jackson's face looking out at her. Blurred as it was, definitely him. And didn't it say so anyway? She read the text properly this time.

. . . Sergeant Jackson Morley of the Durham Light Infantry, presented with the Croix de Guerre by General De Gaulle for bravery when seconded to a French unit in Belgium, in that he manned a field gun against a German advance so allowing the rest of the unit to escape with the wounded. In the action Sergeant Morley was wounded . . .

Molly dropped the paper. Oh, she had to go to Eden Hope, she had to find out where he was, write to him . . .

'I have to go to Eden Hope,' she said to Dora, and started towards the stairs. 'If I hurry I'll catch the bus to Bishop. Or maybe Merrington to catch the Eden bus. That'll be the best, I think.'

'An' what will he have to say about the bairn then?' asked Dora. She gazed at Molly, head on one side, an ironic half-smile playing around her mouth.

Molly looked blankly at her. 'The bairn?' She stopped in her tracks and turned slowly round. 'I . . . I . . .'

'I bet he doesn't know about our little Beth, does he? Innocent little babe that she is, he's not going to like it, is he?'

Molly looked piteously at her and Dora nodded her head.

'Aye, I thought as much,' she said. 'Oh, go on then, you go. I'll see to her. At least it'll put your mind at rest. But mind, don't build your hopes up because it takes a saint of a man to accept another man's bairn, I'm telling you that for nothing.'

'I have to go, Dora,' said Molly. She crossed to the pram and touched her child's face briefly; Beth slept on. Molly ran upstairs to change into her best costume, a grey flannel cut on the new utility lines with a short skirt and only one pleat and square military shoulders to the jacket. She brushed her hair until it shone, looked into the mirror and

frowned slightly, added a touch of colour to her lips and
ran back downstairs again.

Dora had abandoned the papers and was sitting with her
feet propped up on the fender, staring into the fire.

'That didn't take you long,' she said, and sniffed.

'No, well, I have to catch the bus, don't I?' said Molly.
'I'll see you when I get back.'

'Oh, don't hurry on my account,' said Dora. 'Nor Beth's
neither. We'll be all right, don't you worry yourself.'

'Dora –'

'Aye. Well, go on then. An' don't forget to close the
door properly. It's getting cooler by tea-time now.'

It was only as she stood at the bus stop by the triangular
green in Kirk Merrington that Molly allowed herself to
wonder what Maggie's reception of her might be like. Had
word got back to Eden Hope that she'd had a baby?
Perhaps not, she thought. After all, no one knew her in
Ferryhill apart from Dora and the immediate neighbours.
And these days there were often strange folk about,
especially young mothers and children evacuated inland
from Sunderland or Hartlepool, even Middlesbrough. As
far as she knew no one in Ferryhill had asked who she was.

There was fifteen minutes to wait for the Eden bus.
Molly, filled with excitement, couldn't stand still. She
walked up and down, up and down. Gazed at the corner
from which the bus would appear as though she could
make it do so by the power of her will.

'I'm not going to tell her,' she said aloud on the corner. A door opened in one of the houses bordering the green. A young woman came out, glanced at Molly, startled, then decided she couldn't possibly have been talking to her and disappeared round the corner. Talking to yourself was a bad sign, thought Molly, and turned the other way and walked to the opposite corner.

She wouldn't tell Maggie about Beth, she decided. At least not before she told Jackson. Jackson . . . Would he be there, in Eden Hope? In his mother's house? Her pulse leaped at the thought and panic rose into her throat. She would have to tell him, wouldn't she? And she wasn't ready yet, oh, no. He would send her packing, he would too. Oh, God, if he should look at her with contempt, she wouldn't be able to bear it.

The sound of an engine impinged on her anxious thoughts. The bus was coming. She couldn't go, couldn't face Jackson with what she had done, not now. She needed more time.

What a fool she was, Molly told herself as she climbed on to the bus, she had to go, had to see him one more time even if he did reject her. The bus set off, winding its way round the farming communities and colliery villages, coasting down hills and creaking slowly round corners, drawing nearer and nearer to Eden Hope and her own personal Judgement Day. All the time Molly's thoughts whirled chaotically. One minute she was filled with wild elation that she could see Jackson at any minute and the next plunged into despair, sure he would cast her off. She alighted at the top of the rows, her stomach churning, and walked the short distance to the Morleys' house on trembling legs.

'Molly! Well, who would have believed it? Frank, Frank – here's Molly come to see us.'

Maggie stood in the doorway, one hand on the door, her face breaking into a smile of surprised welcome. 'Why, yer bloke, we were just talking about you, wondering where you were. Why the heck didn't you keep in touch?'

'Hallo, Maggie, Frank,' said Molly as Maggie took her arm and drew her into a kitchen still redolent of Yorkshire pudding and boiled cabbage. 'Eeh, who would have believed it? We were just talking about you, wondering where you were . . .'

'Is it true? Is he alive?' Molly butted in, unable to wait any longer to ask. She gazed anxiously round at Frank in his chair by the fire; an ordinary chair now with crutches propped against the wall beside it, not his wheel chair she noted with one part of her mind. No Jackson, though, he wasn't here, she thought, and slumped in disappointment.

'He is, lass,' said Frank. 'And out of his mind wondering what happened to you. Where the hell have you been, any road? There's been no word from you in all these months, you never even told us you'd changed your job.'

Molly heard what he said, the words were there in her head, but for a second or two she was incapable of understanding anything but the first three. It was true,

Jackson was alive, it wasn't some cruel trick the *Sunday Sun* had played on her. It wasn't some other Jackson Morley, it was *hers*.

'Where is he?' she whispered as Frank fell silent.

'A place out Sunderland way. A convalescent place.'

'He's hurt?'

'He was. Getting better now, though. He'll be back with his unit soon.'

Frank had instinctively answered her questions as tersely as they were given. Molly sat down again for she had risen to her feet when she had thought Jackson was hurt.

'You never even wrote, lass,' said Maggie reproachfully. But she was affected by Molly's obvious agitation, as was Frank.

'Put the kettle on, Maggie, make the lass a cup of tea,' he said now. 'She looks as though she could do with it.' She did an' all, he thought. By heck, she must love their Jackson all right. Well, mebbe this time there would be a happy ending to it. They deserved one, that was for sure.

'Near Sunderland?'

Molly looked as though she was ready to go there now, this minute. She sat on the edge of her chair, looked at the clock on the mantelpiece. Her clock it was, she thought suddenly. The clock that had come from her dad's house, the marble clock, still ticking away. Beside it stood a wooden clock from around 1930 that had stopped.

Maggie saw her glance. 'You don't mind, do you? But

ours stopped and yours was upstairs doing nothing, so I thought . . .'

'No, of course I don't mind,' said Molly. She looked at Maggie, really looked at her for the first time since she had entered the house. Jackson's mother looked well, better than she had done for ages. The dullness had left her eyes, the corners of her mouth turned up as though she was ready to smile at any minute and there was a healthy colour in her cheeks. Very different from the last time Molly had seen her, when they had both thought Jackson was lost.

Maggie lifted the kettle and felt its weight before settling it on the fire. Then she began bustling about from the pantry to the kitchen table, laying a cloth and bringing out the best cups from the press.

'I'll help you,' said Molly, moving to do so.

'No, I can manage,' said Maggie. Then, realising she must sound short, she paused and smiled at Molly. 'Look, like I said, we'll forget the past, will we? I know I likely said things I shouldn't but I was near out of my mind about the lad. You an' all, I shouldn't wonder. I just didn't have room in me to consider how you were feeling.'

'It's all right, I know.'

'An' if I should have had suspicions I shouldn't, I'm sorry about that too,' Maggie went on.

'What the heck are you on about, woman?' Frank demanded.

'Nothing, it was nothing. I'm sure I took no notice,' said Molly hastily.

How could she say it like that? she asked herself. How could she take a forgiving tone when Maggie had been right all along and it was she herself who was in the wrong? By, she was a right bad 'un, she knew that. But she would tell Maggie the truth, she would really, after she had had a chance to explain to Jackson. If he forgave Molly, his mother would. But it was a blooming big if, indeed it was.

Suddenly the need to see him for herself, even if it meant he couldn't bear the sight of her after what she had done, was paramount, an all-consuming desire.

'How far away is it? The convalescent home, I mean?' Perhaps she had time to go there and see him tonight.

Maggie looked up from setting out a raspberry sponge filled with jam from the canes that grew wild on the old disused railway embankment. She saw at once by her expression what Molly had in mind.

'Eeh, you can't go there tonight, man, it's thirty miles or more. You have to get a bus to Sunderland from Bishop and another out to the place. No, don't be so daft. There's time for you, he'll likely be there a while yet. It's two or three weeks before he goes back to his unit.'

Molly's eyes dimmed. 'You'll give me the address, though?'

'Oh, aye.'

'We have some letters here from your Harry,' said Frank. 'Maggie, fetch them out for the lass.'

Molly looked at the writing on the envelopes. There

were two of them, one written weeks ago and one just the previous week. 'I'll read them on the bus home,' she said, and stuffed them into her bag feeling guilty once again. She should have told Harry, she knew that. After all he was her only kin.

In spite of all her feelings of guilt and worry and foreboding for the future, Molly enjoyed the couple of hours with the Morleys before she left to catch the bus back to Ferryhill. For whatever her troubled thoughts there was one big underlying truth which shone in her mind. Jackson was alive. He was even in the county. He had been hurt but he was better or at least recovering. And he still loved her. He had come looking for her, hadn't he? Surely he would still want her, no matter what she had done? She would forgive him anything, anything at all, of course she would, because her love was big enough for it. And his too, she told herself. His too.

Chapter Twenty-nine

'Was he there then?' asked Dora when Molly arrived back in Ferryhill that Sunday evening. Dora looked agitated even though she was sitting in a chair knitting away furiously. She didn't lift her eyes from the work.

'No. He's in a convalescent home up Sunderland way,' Molly answered. 'But, oh, Dora, isn't it marvellous? He's alive!'

'Marvellous,' she agreed. Her knitting needles clicked busily on to the end of the row. She changed the needles round and straightened out the tiny garment she was making before relaxing her hands into her lap and looking hard at Molly.

'He might not want you back, you know, not with the bairn.'

The light died from Molly's eyes. Oh, she didn't need Dora to tell her that. She was unbuttoning her coat but now slumped down on a chair without taking it off.

'I know.'

Dora resumed her knitting, making the steel needles click hard like a tattoo. 'Not many men will accept another man's baby.' She nodded her head to emphasise her words.

'Dora, I know that, don't go on about it.'

'Aye, an' if he does, what then?'

'What do you mean?'

'What about me? What do you think I mean? After I stuck by you, gave you a home, looked after Beth like she was my own?'

Molly gazed at her. Dora's face was red, she had obviously been crying. As she knitted, her lips worked continuously.

'I love Beth like she was me own an' all,' she burst out angrily before she stopped knitting abruptly and rolled the garment up, stabbing the ball of wool viciously on the end of the needles.

'I'll put the kettle on. We'll have our cocoa. You have work the morrow.'

'I'm on nights,' Molly reminded her gently. She didn't know how to deal with Dora's pain and fear. Surely the woman must have known that Molly and the baby might move away one day? After all, Beth was her baby, not Dora's.

'I'd like to go to see him one day this week. I could go during the day . . .'

'Best go tomorrow,' said Dora. She was mixing cocoa and sugar with dried milk; half a pint of fresh milk a day didn't allow for such luxuries as cocoa. 'You want to go tomorrow, don't you?'

'Yes.'

'Well then, I take it you don't want to take Beth?'

'No. Not this time at any rate.' Molly looked at her. 'Look, I'm sorry, really I am. But I don't know what's going to happen, do I? Or even if anything is. In any case you would still be able to see Beth, of course you would. I'll always be grateful to you, Dora.' She tried to put out of her mind all the times when she had not been grateful, those occasions when Dora seemed to be taking over Beth.

'There she is now, I'll go,' said Dora, and it was only after she'd said it that Molly could hear the baby whimpering. Either Dora had especially acute hearing or she was so attuned to the baby that she heard her almost before she started to cry. She rushed upstairs and Molly could hear her crooning softly, the baby's cries stilled. Sometimes Molly thought Dora was trying to put Beth in Mona's place. But perhaps she was reading too much into it.

Next morning Molly caught the eight-thirty bus to Durham and a connecting one to Sunderland. Her first glimpse of the town shocked her and she was surprised at the amount of bomb damage. There were great holes in some of the streets, single walls still standing even to third- and fourth-floor level. It was raining and water stood in exposed cellars; wind blew at a pair of green curtains hanging at a third-floor window with all the glass blown out.

A twinge of anxiety went through Molly. Surely the

soldiers' convalescent home wasn't near this place where there was so much danger from air raids? She rummaged in her bag for the address: Barton Lodge, Washington Road. There was a post office nearby and Molly went in and asked for directions.

'Why do you want to know?' the postmaster asked with suspicion. 'How do I know you're not a spy?'

'My boyfriend is there. Do you want to see my identity card?' She wasn't a bit affronted, it was good that people were suspicious.

'Number 23 bus will drop you at the gates,' the postmaster said after looking at her identity card. Molly thanked him and hurried back to the bus stop. Her feelings were so mixed up by now, elated anticipation uppermost one minute then dread at what Jackson would say the next, that her stomach was churning. No matter what, though, she told herself, she had to see him, touch him. If he rejected her after that she would die; she couldn't bear to think of what she would do if his reaction was contempt.

'I would like to see Sergeant Morley,' she said to the young girl in mobcap and apron who opened the door.

'Who?' asked the girl, and Molly could have screamed at her. But instead she said again.

'Sergeant Morley. Jackson Morley?'

'You'll have to ask Matron.'

The girl pointed to a door at the side of the hall and Molly walked over to it and knocked.

'This is not visiting time,' said a thickset woman with

hairs on her chin and an incongruous lace-edged cap tied under her chin with a large bow.

'I know, I'm sorry. But I have to work tonight. I'm on night shift at the munitions factory.'

'Well, all right. Sergeant Morley is in the garden. The girl will show you where. He is expecting to be discharged today, after the doctor's rounds. Now they're at twelve o'clock sharp so you haven't got long.'

The clock on the wall stood at half-past eleven. Molly went with the maid around the corner of the house to where there were long lawns running down to a stream. There were only one or two soldiers visible, one sitting on a bench in the shelter of a wall, another walking along by the stream. His head was bent, shoulders hunched. He stared at the brown, peaty water bubbling along over the stones as he walked.

'Jackson!'

Molly took one look at him and all her doubts, all her misgivings, were forgotten as she ran down the slope to him. He lifted his head, gazing at her, opening his arms as she ran into them, holding her close. Her arms were round his neck, her face buried in his shoulder. She could feel the beat of his heart through his tunic, only a little slower than the fast wild beat of her own.

'Molly . . . Molly,' he whispered in her ear. 'Oh my God, I was beginning to think I would never find you again.'

Tears were dropping from her eyes unheeded. She lifted

her face and he kissed each eyelid, her cheeks, her chin, and at last her lips. A deep, satisfying kiss which yet conveyed all the loneliness of the last months, years even. He took out a handkerchief and wiped her face gently, gazed down into the deep brown pools of her eyes. She clung to him, never wanted to let go, could not even if she had wanted to.

'Jackson . . .'

'Whisht, my love, hush. Don't talk, not now.'

Holding her close against him with one arm, he began walking her to the edge of the garden, a secluded corner where a large laurel bush screened them from any prying eyes that might be looking from the windows of the home. There he took her in his arms again, stroked her hair and held her against the lean, hard length of him. She lifted a hand against his brown cheek, twisted a lock of dark hair in her fingers, felt faint with love of him. She pressed closer to him, her breasts tingling, the tips hardening; felt the answering hardness of him against her belly.

'I want you,' he whispered in her ear. 'I want you now!'

'Sergeant Morley? Sergeant, where are you? The doctor is here, come in at once!'

They didn't hear it at first until the soldier who had been sitting on the bench by the wall, and had watched with interest as they took cover behind the laurel bush, added his voice to that of the nurse.

'Jack? Put her down and come out of there, you're wanted,' he called. 'Can't you hear the nurse?'

Jackson sighed, loosed his arms from Molly, though retaining her hand in his, and kissed her on the tip of her nose. 'Wait for me,' he said softly. 'I won't be long.'

As he walked back to the house, the soldier on the bench grinned at him. 'Lucky devil,' he said. 'How did you manage to get a girl like that?'

'Never you mind, Don,' Jackson replied. 'You find one of your own.'

They went to a hotel overlooking the beach at Roker for the need to hold each other, to touch and make love, was overwhelming. Molly hung back a little, sure the bored-looking woman behind the desk would guess they weren't married and tell them to go. But she didn't, merely reached behind her for the key to the room. She had lots of soldiers coming in with their girls or wives, she didn't care which.

'After all, there's a war on, the poor lads have to go somewhere,' she said to her husband as she went through into the office. 'And any road, we need the money.'

'I'm not saying nowt, am I?' he asked.

The room was fairly basic but clean, and in any case they weren't really interested in their surroundings. They undressed each other, carefully at first then with increasing haste, pulling off the inhibiting clothes, dropping them on the floor where they lay unheeded. Her arms were around his neck, her mouth on his. He lifted her up and she wound her legs around him and they fell on the bed, both lost in an ecstasy of pounding blood and rising excitement until

Molly at least thought she would die of it. And when release came it was in such a crescendo of feeling that both of them cried aloud and collapsed in each other's arms. And a few minutes later it all started again.

It was Molly who woke first from a deep contented sleep. Her head was resting in the crook of his shoulder, his arm across her breasts. She felt herself deeply wrapped in his love, so bewitched that all her worries were as nothing compared to it. This was the real world, this was what mattered, nothing else in the whole world.

Jackson stirred, opened his eyes and smiled at her. His smile was perfect, eyes shining into hers so that she smiled back adoringly.

'We could stay here tonight,' he said softly. 'We'll stay in this bed until tomorrow. If we're hungry later I'll order a meal sent up. Will I do that?'

'Yes. Oh, yes,' she breathed into his ear, took the lobe between her teeth, nibbled gently at it. But then an image of Beth rose before her eyes, intruding on her Eden.

'No,' she said, moving away from him so that he protested and held on to her arm, trying to stop her. 'I have to get back, it's important.'

'Stay,' he insisted. 'What could be more important than this?'

It's not a what, it's a who, thought Molly. She tried to say it aloud, now, when it was a good time to say it, but she couldn't, not when they were so happy.

'I have to go to work,' she said lamely.

'Take a shift off,' said Jackson. 'Surely at a time like this you're entitled to a night off? Oh, come on, my love, stay with me.'

'I can't. I have to go,' Molly said, a catch in her voice. Oh, God help me, she thought, what am I going to do?

Jackson took his arm away, sat up in the bed. 'Then if you have to go, I'm coming with you.' He swung his legs out of bed, stood and went to the window. She watched him, loving his long, lithe body, the powerful shoulders, and the line of his hair on the strong column of his neck. Then his words echoed in her mind, she realised what he had said and sat bolt upright.

'No!'

He turned, raised an eyebrow in surprise. 'Why not? I have to know where you're living, I don't intend losing you again.' He strode to the bed, took her in his arms. 'Not ever again, do you hear me?'

Molly leaned her head into the curve of his shoulder and closed her eyes. She felt drunk with the proximity of him. It became harder and harder to think, but she had to.

'Why?' he asked.

'It's just that I'm living with a widow and she doesn't like men callers,' Molly said lamely, and Jackson put back his head and shouted with laughter.

'She doesn't like men callers! Which century is she living in? Is this the twentieth or not?'

Molly pulled away from him and got out of bed. She began picking up her clothes from the floor where they had been discarded in the urgency of their need. She went to the wash basin which stood in a corner of the room, ran water and began washing herself.

'What's wrong?' asked Jackson, watching her. He pulled on his underpants and uniform trousers, looked around for his shirt.

'Nothing. At least . . . I can't go back there now, I'll have to go straight to work or I'll be late.'

'All right, I'll come with you there,' he said. 'You can give me your address on the way. Or, better still, I'll meet you tomorrow morning at the factory gate and we can go back to Eden Hope, how's that?'

'No, I can't. I'll be altogether too tired, I will honestly. No, I'll have to go home myself in the morning.'

Jackson said nothing. He washed and finished dressing and was ready when she was. But the smile had left his eyes. He kept glancing at her with a puzzled expression which gradually hardened into resolve.

As they walked away from the hotel he took her arm and put it through his but the closeness of before was missing and Molly was acutely and miserably aware of it. They caught the Darlington bus which wound its way through the coastal villages before turning inland and sat close together, he holding her hand, saying little. He did not ask for her address again, but simply watched her with that questioning look.

The bus stop was about a quarter of a mile from the factory and they got off together and walked the rest of the way. Molly was more than an hour early for her shift so they found a cafe and drank weak tea and ate toasted teacake with plum jam. No butter, of course.

'I'll pick you up tomorrow,' said Jackson in a voice that brooked no argument. 'And I will go home with you. We'll tell your battleaxe of a landlady that we're going to be married next week before I go back to duty. If she says anything, anything at all, you'll come back to Eden Hope with me. Now, is that understood?'

Molly nodded, looking down at the half-eaten teacake on her plate. She was going to have to tell him, she thought.

Chapter Thirty

'We can't, you see,' said Molly, thinking: God forgive me, I'm lying through my teeth. 'Dora, that's my landlady, has gone to see her sister. So we might as well just go to Eden Hope. Did you tell your mam and dad?'

'Of course I did. And I told them we'd be coming to see them. I thought tomorrow, but we can go today. Did you ask for next week off work?'

'Yes,' said Molly. The morning was bright and sharp with that touch of frost that seems to clear the air so that the trees and bushes stood out against the pale blue sky. Strangely Molly felt not a bit tired even though she had worked all night, concentrating on the straight seams as she sewed the stiff cloth together into powder bags. She flexed her fingers at the thought; they were stiff and slightly painful.

The management of the factory was understanding, that was one good thing. Especially if you were marrying a member of the fighting forces. And in any case, she was owed the time off. Molly glanced up at Jackson and her heart melted within her. She couldn't lose him now, she told herself, forcing down the panic which threatened to rise and overwhelm her. No, she couldn't. But now was not the time to tell him about Beth.

Jackson looked down at her, took her hand, and they began walking towards the bus stop for Bishop Auckland.

'Don't look so worried, my love, nothing is going to go wrong this time. I won't let it, I love you too much. Howay now, smile. I promise I won't lose you again.'

Molly smiled, enveloped in his love. Surely it was too strong for any revelation to break it? She would tell him tomorrow, she resolved. Yes, she couldn't marry him without confessing. And when he saw Beth he would be captivated by the baby, of course he would. She was so beautiful, he couldn't fail to be.

On the bus they sat close together, Molly leaning on Jackson's shoulder.

'That's right, pet,' he said. 'You have a snooze, you must be tired out. This afternoon you can have a couple of hours while I go to see the registrar about a special licence. We have arrangements to make.'

'I must go back to Ferryhill,' she said quickly. 'For clean clothes if nothing else.'

He frowned. Their time together was so short, he begrudged any of it being spent apart. 'Righto,' he said, 'of course. And I'll see you tomorrow morning and soon it will be the weekend and we'll be together.'

*

Molly walked up the yard of the Morleys' house.

'Come away in, love,' Maggie cried. 'I'll soon knock you up a bite of breakfast. And we've got a surprise for you . . . look who's here!' There, rising from the rocking chair by the fire, was Harry. He held out his arms and Molly went to him with a surge of delight and affection. He lifted her off her feet and swung her in the air.

'Now then, sis,' he cried. 'Where the heck have you been this time? I tell you, I can't take my eyes off you in case you disappear again!'

'Not any more,' said Jackson firmly, coming up behind Molly as her brother put her back on her feet and clapping his friend on the shoulder. 'You made it back then, mate,' he said. 'How much leave have you? A week?'

Harry pulled a face. 'No such luck,' he said. 'Seventy-two hours, that's all.'

'Still you'll be here for the wedding. I'm going down to Bishop for the special licence today. Fancy coming with me? We haven't a lot of time to waste.' Jackson glanced at the marble clock which still stood on the mantelpiece though Molly noticed that Maggie's own was keeping good time now. She must have had it mended.

Harry followed the glance and grinned at Molly. 'You've still got the old clock, eh? Still going an' all.'

'Of course I still have it. It's all we've got left from the old house.'

Harry sobered for a minute. 'Aye,' he said. Then he smiled the lop-sided smile which was so like his father's.

'Well, we have to look forward now, haven't we? Soon you and Jackson will have a place of your own. When this flaming war is over, eh?'

'Time you settled down, Harry,' said Maggie. 'Have you not met a nice lass yet?'

'Lots of 'em.' He grinned and felt in the pocket of his battledress. 'By the way, here's me ration coupon. It's for three days.'

'Eeh, thanks, lad. I can't deny it'll come in handy.'

Molly listened with half an ear to the talk around her. Jackson was discussing the course of the war with Frank, who was wondering when the Americans would come in: 'For they will, late, just as they did the last time,' his father said.

'If only,' said Molly, surprising herself. She hadn't realised she was thinking aloud.

'They will,' Jackson insisted. 'But if they don't, what the heck? We've been on our own, backs against the wall, before now and come through. We can do it again, don't you worry.' And everyone nodded agreement.

Molly hadn't been thinking about the war, she had other things to worry about. By, she thought, leaning back in her chair and closing her eyes wearily for a few seconds, if it wasn't for Beth I would be so happy, I'd be out of my mind. With Jackson home, and Harry. Dear Lord, what was she thinking of . . . if it wasn't for Beth? What sort of depraved mother was she even to think such a terrible thing? Her lovely, lovely Beth! Molly sighed and tears pricked the back of her eyelids.

'Come on, love,' said Jackson, taking her hand and pulling her to her feet, 'I think you'd best go and lie down for a couple of hours. I have to go into Bishop anyway, there's arrangements to make.'

'No, I'll go back to Ferryhill. I have things to see to as well, you know.'

'You're going to eat this first, though, aren't you?' asked Maggie. She had a pan of scrambled dried eggs in her hand; Frank was toasting bread before the bars of the grate.

'Thank you,' Molly whispered. They were so kind. Her eyes were wet with unshed tears.

'Sit down at the table, lass,' said Maggie. 'You'll feel better when you've got this inside you. You're tired, that's all. It's all been a bit much for you.'

Later, on the bus to Ferryhill, Molly felt almost too tired to worry about the situation at all. She dozed off time and time again, woke up with a start whenever the bus slowed to a halt at a bus stop, dozed off again when it lumbered into motion once again. When it turned into the market place at Ferryhill, she woke to hear the conductor calling, 'Terminus! Everybody off!' At least she couldn't go past her stop.

'What sort of a time is this to be coming home, that's what I want to know?'

Dora was sitting at the table with Beth in her arms,

feeding the baby with a bottle in one hand and eating her own meal with the other.

'I'm sorry, Dora, really I am. I know I shouldn't have left you with Beth. I wouldn't do it with anyone else but I know I can trust you with her. But, oh, when I saw Jackson again I couldn't believe it, and you know how difficult it is to catch a bus these days. The time simply flew by –'

The baby was smiling at her, waving her fists in the air with excitement, and Molly's heart melted. How could she have gone all day yesterday without seeing her baby? She held out her arms and took her, cuddled her in, kissed the top of her head. Dora watched, unsmiling.

'Give me her back, will you? You'll make her sick, squeezing her like that. And if she doesn't finish her feed, she'll be fretful for the rest of the day.'

'I'll give it her, will I? Then you can eat your own meal in peace.'

'Hmmm. You never thought about how I was managing when you didn't come home, did you?' said Dora, but she didn't really sound angry. 'Oh, go on then, take her. I tell you, the poor bairn doesn't know who's her mammy. You don't, do you, my petal?' Her voice changed to a warm and loving tone as she spoke to the baby. And Beth looked at her gravely as she handed over the bottle to Molly. The child opened her mouth to receive the teat and recommenced the serious business of sucking.

Dora watched for a second or two and then resumed

eating her own meal. 'I suppose you'll have to go to bed now an' all,' she said. 'I reckon you must be dead tired.'

'I am. But I'll stay up and watch Beth while you go to the shop, if you like.'

'Mind, that's blooming good of you,' said Dora, casting her a sarcastic glance. But Molly could see she wasn't anything like as angry as she had expected her to be.

Dora laid Beth down and went out to the shops. Molly bent over the baby, stroked the soft, downy cheek with a forefinger, smoothed the silky hair back from her forehead. By, she was a bonny bairn, she was. The baby stirred, whimpered slightly, and it was all the excuse Molly needed to pick her up, wrap a shawl round her and sit down in the rocking chair, cuddling her in. Beth slept on, a sweet, heavy bundle on her arm. She was growing fast, no longer a very tiny baby. Her eyelashes curled down on to her cheeks, dark and becoming thick. A beauty she would be, Molly thought proudly.

'I won't leave you, petal, not for any man in the world,' she whispered. And at the same time another voice was saying in her head, *But what about Jackson?*

'Eeh, Molly, put the bairn down, will you? She'll be sore with so much handling and then she won't sleep the night.'

Dora had come in without Molly even noticing. She came swiftly over to the rocking chair and took Beth from her; laid her back in the pram that was still used as a downstairs cot.

'Go on to bed, lass, you'll be no good for work the night if you don't get some sleep at least.'

Molly went upstairs feeling so tired she was past thinking any more about Jackson or Beth. She would be able to think better, she thought, when she had a clearer head. But when she woke it was with a headache and leaden limbs. Now she had to tell Dora she was getting married on Saturday.

'Saturday? Did you say Saturday?' Dora's voice rose. She stared at Molly with a shocked expression.

'Yes. Jackson was applying for a special licence today and he'll get one, him being a soldier and going back on duty.'

'An' what about me? What about this canny bairn?'

'I'll tell him, Dora. It'll be all right, I'm sure it will. Anyway, he'll be going off to North Africa won't he? That's where they're fighting now. Goodness only knows when he'll come back.'

Molly was looking down at her plate as she spoke, overcome almost by the prospect of Jackson's going away again. So she didn't realise that Dora was crying until she raised her head. Molly dropped her knife and fork and rushed over to the other woman.

'Oh, Dora, are you worried you won't see Beth any more? You will, I promise. Of course you will. I'll never forget what you did, you were such a friend when I needed one.' She put an arm around Dora's shoulders and hugged her.

'Aye, you say that now, an' you mean it, I know. But you'll take the poor little mite away and you'll forget all about bringing her back to see me, I know what it'll be like. I'll be losing another daughter, won't I?'

Dora sniffed, pulled out a handkerchief and blew her nose. She shrugged off Molly's arm and squared her shoulders.

'Oh, don't mind me, you'll go off with your soldier lad and he'll forgive you and keep the bairn. You're a bonny lass, you know. You'll look at him with those big brown eyes and he won't be able to help himself, that's the top and the bottom of it all.'

No matter what Molly said Dora wasn't to be persuaded that she wouldn't be forgotten. In the end Molly had to leave her to get ready for work.

Molly and Jackson were married at the Register Office at Bishop Auckland. It was ten o'clock in the morning, a cold, damp day when the mist hung about so that the Methodist Chapel just along the road was partially obscured by it. She and Dora came in on the train without Beth, who had been left with a neighbour for a couple of hours.

At first Dora had refused to come, saying she couldn't leave the baby. And Molly had misgivings about her coming, too, dreading that she would say something to Jackson before she herself got a chance to explain about her little daughter.

She would have liked to have asked Vi to come to the wedding too. But Vi would almost certainly give her secret away to Jackson in all innocence. In fact when Molly thought of Vi she felt guilty; she had seen her only twice since she left the home, the last time weeks ago. But she dare not ask her to the wedding.

For she had not as yet told him. Throughout the last couple of days before the wedding she had set out to see him with every intention of telling him, but each time when it came to it she had not.

'You dither on much longer, my girl,' Dora remarked grimly, 'and you will really be in trouble. It's not right, marrying a chap and keeping a secret like that from him. It's bound to come out, you mark my words.'

But she was not angry or woebegone as she had been when Jackson first came back. Most of the time she had a faraway look in her eyes, or Molly would look up suddenly and find Dora gazing speculatively at her. She did not complain when Molly spent time with Jackson but looked after Beth as though she were her own. In fact, Molly sometimes had the uncomfortable thought that Dora did think of Beth as her own.

'I could adopt the bairn,' she had said abruptly the night before the wedding. 'That would be an answer, wouldn't it?'

Molly was horrified. 'No, of course you couldn't!' she cried. 'No, Dora really, everything will be fine, you'll see.'

In her heart Molly had grave doubts about everything being fine. But it just had to be, she told herself fiercely. And when she was with Jackson he was so loving towards her she began to believe it would be.

'I'll do anything for you, my love,' he'd whispered in her ear. 'Anything at all.' And Molly was beginning to believe it.

So she walked along Newgate Street towards the Register Office, past the Chapel where another wedding was in progress. She could hear the choir singing Charles Wesley's great hymn 'Love Divine All Loves Excelling' and knew it was a wedding. A chapel wedding, that was what she had always dreamed of, Molly thought with only a faint twinge of regret. The important thing was to marry the one you loved, she told herself. And she loved Jackson. Oh, yes, she did.

He was waiting for her on the pavement outside the office, he and Harry. They kissed and made introductions, and Harry looked sadly at Mona's mother who glanced at him and looked away rapidly at a couple walking past on the opposite side of the road, then up the road, anywhere but at him. Harry had forced himself to smile, to laugh at something Frank said, and then they had all gone into the Register Office.

The ceremony was short, the office bare and dingily brown, and they were outside on the pavement again before Molly was properly aware she was at last married to Jackson. And she still hadn't told him about Beth.

Jackson had booked a photographer from Taylor's in Newgate Street and they stood together for the wedding photographs. But the photographer didn't take long; the other wedding party was emerging from the Chapel and he rushed along to it. A grand wedding it was, Molly could tell. The guests were laughing and throwing confetti which she could see was made up of chopped bits of newspaper for of course confetti was not available because of the war effort.

Harry had brought some too and Molly's heart swelled with affection for him, her brother in his red paratrooper's beret and khaki battledress. God keep him safe.

'All right, sweetheart?' Jackson had hold of Molly's arm and was bending down to whisper in her ear. He had noticed the look of anxiety which had flashed across her face as she studied Harry. Then they were laughing and trying to dodge as he threw the newspaper confetti.

They were going to the Wear Valley Hotel for a celebratory drink and walked along the road in a small group, the men with late roses from Frank's garden in their buttonholes and Molly with a spray of carnations from Hardisty's flower shop. The wedding party were moving away from the Chapel too, she saw, going towards the schoolroom where no doubt there was a spread from the Co-operative Store acquired with the special food points allowed for weddings and funerals.

At the Wear Valley Hotel they paused and Dora stepped away from them. Molly watched her; unconsciously her grip tightened on Jackson's arm so that he looked down at her, momentarily surprised.

'I'd best be getting back home,' said Dora.

'Won't you stay and have a drink first?' Jackson asked politely. He didn't press her, though, still thinking she must be something of a termagant after what Molly had said about her.

'No, I have to get back. I have the baby to see to.'

Molly felt faint. The dark day turned darker. A cold wind whistled down the neck of her grey utility costume. 'Dora?' she whispered, her brown eyes large in appeal.

Dora let her eyes roam over the company: Harry, holding on to Frank's wheel chair with Maggie beside him. Jackson in his Sergeant's uniform. He was smiling at her though his eyes were watchful. And lastly she looked at Molly.

'No, I'm sorry, I have to go. I'm minding a bairn for the neighbours. I promised, you see. I'll see you soon, will I, Molly?'

'Yes, soon.' It was all she could do to get the words out. The party stood and watched as Dora hurried over the road to Station Approach and disappeared into the station.

'Molly, you look fair nithered,' pronounced Maggie. 'Come on, you two, shift yourselves. Let's get in the warm.'

Chapter Thirty-one

The newly-weds wandered hand in hand through the park at Cockton Hill and along Etherley Lane until they came to the banks of the Wear. The clouds had thinned at last and the sun kept peeking through as they walked on to the path alongside the river. They didn't speak much, they were too happy just to be there together, forgetting the war and the fact that Jackson had to return to his unit by the following Tuesday morning, when Molly would also be back at her machine in the arms factory.

It had been a muted celebration in the Wear Valley Hotel where they had reservations for two nights, all the honeymoon they had time for. Now Frank and Maggie had gone back to Eden Hope while Harry had returned to camp. He was due back that evening, Jackson and Molly had seen him off at the station.

'Watch yourself, mate,' said Jackson. 'Though how you'll manage without me to look after you, I don't know.' He grinned and dodged Harry's mock blow. 'Anyway, I reckon I might join you in the Airborne Division. It's more money, isn't it? Aye, I thought that's what must have tempted you.'

'What else?'

Harry turned to his sister. 'You'll have to stand up for yourself with this one,' he said to her. 'Don't take any lip from him, mind.' He put out his arms and pulled her into a bear hug. 'Look after yourself in that factory, won't you?' he whispered, and she knew he was thinking of Mona. Poor Mona, killed so soon after she'd met her love.

Now as Molly and Jackson wandered by the river, which was brown and peaty after its run through the dale high in the Pennines, her brother was uppermost in her thoughts.

'I wish Harry would meet a nice girl and settle down,' she said to Jackson, who laughed.

'Married all of two hours and already you like it so much you want it for Harry,' he said, and put his arm around her to draw her to a fallen log by the side of the path. He kissed her lingeringly on the lips and small boys walking past whistled and cheered.

'Go on, soldier, give it to her!' one cheeky urchin cried. Jackson made a threatening move after them and they scattered and flew along the path and round the bend in the river.

Jackson smiled and turned his full attention back to Molly. 'I'll give you everything you've ever wanted, you'll see!'

Molly took a deep breath. Now was the time, she thought. He would forgive her, of course he would. He loved her. She wished she had told him straight away but she had not and now she couldn't let it go on any longer.

'Even your forgiveness?' It didn't sound like her own voice asking. She could hardly believe she had finally found the courage.

'Forgiveness? What could I possibly have to forgive you for?' Jackson laughed, his arm tightening around her. With one hand he tilted her chin, looking deep into her eyes. Oh, it was too hard. Molly coughed slightly, pulled away a little, looked in her pocket for a handkerchief.

'Well?'

'Dora had to go back to see to a baby, do you remember?'

'Yes?' Jackson was looking puzzled now.

'She said it was a neighbour's baby, but it wasn't.'

'No? Surely Dora hasn't got a baby at her age, has she? Has she had a secret love affair, is that it? The baby is hers? I don't believe you, you're joking!'

'No, I never said that. Oh, just listen to me, Jackson, and let me tell you.'

He sat back on the log, leaning against the low branch of an oak tree, a remnant of the forest that had given the town its name.

'You know, Jackson, when you were posted missing, believed killed, I nearly went mad, I think.' Molly sat forward, picked up a stick and began scratching in the dirt at their feet with it. Anything to occupy her hands, keep them from trembling. Anything to stop her heart from jumping up into her throat and threatening to choke her, the way it was doing now.

'I know it has been hard for you, love. But I'll make it up to you, I promise.'

'I was so low,' Molly went on. She was speaking deliberately now, the terror rising within her. She had to make an enormous effort to force her voice to work at all. 'And your parents . . . well, they were grieving so much, too, they closed in on themselves, didn't want me. Oh, I don't mean that in a grumbling sort of way. And I'm not making excuses for what I did either –'

'What you did?' Jackson sat forward suddenly, put his hands on her shoulders and stood up, taking her with him. 'What are you saying, Molly? Are you telling me the baby is yours?'

He held her away from him, the grip of his hands on her shoulders like iron. She couldn't bear to look at his eyes; they were so changed, so cold.

'Jackson, you're hurting me,' she whispered, but he didn't appear to hear. His relentless grip on her shoulders tightened.

'Whose is it?'

'No one's. Nobody important.'

'Nobody important? Are you telling me you went with some bloke but it wasn't *important*?'

'Yes! No . . . Oh, God. Jackson, let me go!'

'I'll let you go all right – you can go to hell! Or go back to your *unimportant* lover!'

'Jackson, it wasn't like that. I was out of my mind . . . I thought you were dead.' She tried to explain, her words falling over themselves in her hurry to get him to understand how it had been.

'Don't make excuses, Molly,' was all he said. She looked up at him. There was a white line around his nostrils, his mouth was pinched and his eyes glittered.

'I'm not! I'm not making excuses . . . I'm just telling you how it was . . .'

'You couldn't tell me yesterday, though, could you? You couldn't tell me when I first came back, could you?'

Jackson released his grip, pushing her away from him violently so that she staggered and almost fell over the log they had been sitting on. The place where he had whispered so lovingly in her ear, where he had told her he would do anything for her. He turned and walked away, not even pausing to see if she had been hurt but striding along the path in the direction of the town.

'You all right, pet?' a kindly voice asked. It was a man returning from his allotment, a basket of vegetables in his hand. He paused on the path and looked at her with concern.

Swiftly Molly turned away, found her handkerchief and blew her nose. 'Yes, I'm fine, thank you. Just a cold, I think,' she said, her back to him, her head bent.

He regarded her doubtfully for a moment. 'Aye, well,' he said. 'If I were you I'd go home to bed, lass, you look terrible.' He went on his way.

Molly walked in the opposite direction, then paused to study the turbulent waters of the dam head. She was deeply shocked, in a kind of daze. The waters were dark, deep and rushing, and for one brief moment she thought of ending it all, throwing herself into the depths, at last finding some peace. She couldn't believe Jackson had said what he had. He hadn't even asked why or how, had simply condemned her out of hand. His features had been transformed with hatred and jealousy. And now he never wanted to see her again. She swayed, dangerously close to the edge, almost hypnotised by the river, her eyes closing. Then a picture of Beth flashed before her eyes. Beth, her innocent baby, smiling at her as she had done that morning before Molly went out to her wedding. But maybe she would be better off with Dora . . .

'Come here!'

Molly turned, her heart suddenly fluttering for Jackson had come back! He was going to forgive her, he really was. But the hope died in her as she saw his face, still that of a stranger. He took her by the arm and marched her along with him, back down the path to the town and the hotel. He got the key to their room from a mystified receptionist who gazed after them curiously as they mounted the stairs, the soldier pushing the girl in front of him. A bedroom door banged shut above. The receptionist glanced at a waiter, who was hovering in the dining-room doorway, her eyebrows raised.

'By heck,' she said. 'Those two have soon started fighting, haven't they?'

Inside the room Jackson flung Molly on to the bed. He pulled at her suit buttons, sending one flying into the corner of the room so that she tried to undo the rest herself only to have her hands thrust away. Then she let him finish undressing her. He pulled off her blouse, pulled down the straps of her bra so that her breasts were exposed, the nipples proud and the contours fuller since she'd had the baby. He pulled her skirt up around her waist and held her down with one hand while he pushed the wide-legged cami-knickers to one side.

Molly lay there, the roll of her clothes around her waist hurting her back, her legs spread-eagled so that the elastic of her suspenders stretched hard against her skin. His hands were rough on her breasts, squeezing, digging into the soft flesh. He has a right, she thought dimly. I married him under false pretences. Tears ran down her face and she didn't even know she was crying. She was nothing, less than nothing, she was worse than a whore, she knew it now, saw herself through Jackson's eyes and shrank from what she saw.

He was unbuttoning his flies; he wasn't even going to undress, she thought dimly. She wasn't worth it. She turned her face away and closed her eyes. Suddenly he stopped in the very act of pushing her legs wider apart. His hand was on her breast but he was still. Molly opened her eyes and looked up at him.

Jackson was staring at her reddened face, at the tears, with an expression of disgust. But the disgust was not for her, she realised as the next minute he was climbing off the bed, adjusting his clothing, pushing his hair back from his forehead.

'Cover yourself up,' he said, his voice ragged. He turned to the window and looked out at the darkening street, filled with shoppers making their way home. He couldn't do it, she thought. When it came down to it, he couldn't do it. A flicker of hope stirred within her to be instantly quashed as he spoke again.

'You can stop here tonight. The room's paid for. I'll go back to camp early. I don't want my mother and father to find out about this, do you hear?'

'Yes.'

Jackson turned and looked at her. She saw the suffering in his eyes and it was because of her and she couldn't bear it.

'I wanted to tell you, Jackson. Oh, dear God, I thought you were dead, don't you understand?' She sniffed, looked around for her bag, found it and searched inside for a handkerchief. A tiny blue lacy handkerchief which Dora had given her for luck. It was completely inadequate. He threw her a large khaki square and Molly wiped her eyes, blew her nose.

She pulled down her skirt and buttoned up her blouse,

still conscious of the marks of his fingers on her breast, squeezing and twisting. She shrugged into her costume jacket and winced.

'I'm sorry if I hurt you,' he said. 'No, I'm not, what am I saying? Dear God in Heaven, you've done for me today, Molly. I was going to treat you like the whore you are, but when it came to it I couldn't.' Jackson sighed heavily and turned to the window, his back straight and unforgiving.

'I'm sorry,' she said, and he laughed mirthlessly.

'What was it, Molly? I gave you a taste for it, did I? Was it my fault, all of this?' She was shaking her head in denial but he wasn't looking at her, talking to himself. 'I know it's been happening a lot in this blasted war, I hear of it often enough. What's it going to be like by the end, whenever that might be? Oh, God, I never thought it would happen to me!'

His voice was full of anguish and bitterness and Molly couldn't bear it. She moved towards him, to comfort him; put a hand out to him. But he shrank away from her touch as though it burned him. She moved quickly away, sat down on the only chair in the room and clasped her hands tightly together in her lap.

'I love you, Jackson,' she said. 'I'll never love anyone but you.'

'I know that really,' he replied. 'I know you thought I was probably dead. But you didn't know for sure, did you? So soon, Molly, it was so soon after I'd gone!'

'I was half-mad with grief.'

'Yes, I'm sure you were,' said Jackson heavily. He sounded so sad, so resigned, and Molly knew that he had decided, he wasn't going to change his mind, not now.

'I'll have to go back to my baby,' she said and rose to her feet.

'I don't want my mother and father to find out what has happened, not yet,' he said again. 'They've had enough grief. You'll have to pretend.'

'I can't stay there, Jackson. I have my baby. Dora looks after her when I'm at work, that's all.'

'Yes, well, you'll have to concoct a story, won't you? You're good at lying.'

There seemed nothing more to say. Jackson had been going straight from the Wear Valley to the train in any case; he did it now instead of a few days later. She knew he didn't want her to go with him to the station, of course he didn't, but she watched through the window as the train steamed away and felt as though her heart was being cut out of her body.

Molly stayed in the room that night, sitting sleepless in the chair, staring at the wall. She didn't eat; couldn't face the curious eyes of the women working in the hotel. On Monday, she packed her bag and went downstairs, said a dignified goodbye and went out to catch the bus to Eden Hope.

'I thought you weren't coming back until tomorrow,' said Maggie, surprised when she came in.

'I wasn't, but Jackson was called back early so I might as well go to work.'

'You'll be bringing your things here, will you?' Maggie studied her; Molly looked so white and there were huge shadows under her eyes.

'It's easier to travel from Ferryhill,' she said. 'Jackson sends his love and says he'll be seeing you.'

'By, I hope he doesn't have to go abroad again,' said his mother. 'In my opinion he's done his bit, it's somebody else's turn.'

'I'd like to take the marble clock, is that all right?'

'Oh, aye, it's yours, isn't it? I bet you're fond of it, what with it coming from your mam's house.' Maggie lifted the clock down from the mantelpiece and dusted it with the corner of her pinny, spotless and gleaming though it already was.

Oh, Mam, thought Molly. If you could see me now you'd be ashamed of me, and that's a fact.

'I'll be back to see you, you know that,' she said aloud. 'But, you know, we're going to be working overtime . . .'

Back in Ferryhill, the clock wrapped in newspaper under one arm, her going-away case in the other hand, Molly walked down the street to Dora's door, knocked and went in.

'You've told him, then?'

'Yes.'

'And he left you. Well, I could have told you what would happen. You should have let me have the bairn and kept quiet.'

'I couldn't do that, Dora.'

Molly walked over to the sofa where Beth lay propped up between cushions. She was smiling and waving her arms, chirruping away to her mother to attract her attention.

'Hallo, my precious,' said Molly. She cuddled the baby tightly until Beth began to struggle and protest. Molly sat down on the sofa with her, jiggling her knees and turning the cries of protest into chuckles.

'You're all I've got now, petal,' she said softly. The baby burped and a dribble of milk ran down her chin and dripped on to Molly's skirt. Dora ran over with a cloth and began wiping it.

'Oh, leave it alone, Dora.'

'But it will spoil! It'll smell an' all. Clothes aren't that easy to come by these days,' she protested.

'I don't care. I'll never wear it again,' said Molly. 'Coupons or no flaming coupons.' She bent her head until her chin touched the soft curls of Beth's head and wept. The tears ran down and mingled with those of the baby who began to cry also, frightened by her mother's emotion.

'Give her here,' Dora commanded. 'You're tired out. Get away up to bed and get some sleep. I'll bring you a nice cup of cocoa. Once I've got Beth to sleep, that is.'

As Molly climbed the stairs she reflected that Dora looked happier than she had done since Jackson came home.

Chapter Thirty-two

It seemed to Molly that she was living in a kind of limbo. The weeks dragged on, one after the other, filled with going to work and sewing and coming home and sewing. The only bright spots, the only times she came alive at all, were when she was with Beth, her baby, watching her grow, sit up unaided, begin to crawl. The war passed her by apart from the fact that rationing tightened and the news was all of the Tunisian campaign with little maps on the front page of the *Northern Echo* illustrating the position of the troops; the line sometimes moving forward, sometimes back towards Egypt. Was Jackson among them? she wondered, anxiety for his safety rising in her.

'You look tired out, lass,' Dora greeted her one evening, a dark, cold evening with sleet slanting down the street as she walked home, drenching her skirt and bare knees for her last pair of stockings had 'gone home' as Dora put it. She should have worn her one pair of slacks, Molly thought dully, but the morning had been fine and sunny.

'I am tired, Dora,' she admitted. 'And I promised Mrs Jones that I would finish her skirt tonight.'

Molly took in sewing now. She had bought herself a hand-operated sewing machine and specialised in making over clothes from others bought before the war. Mrs Jones's skirt was cut out of a full-skirted coat, which had been her mother's. The style looked as though it could date from the last war. Still, it was a warm tweed and when the material was turned it looked quite good.

'Tell her you'll do it the morrow, lass,' Dora advised. 'Go on, have a night off.'

Molly shook her head, smiling. She couldn't, she needed the money. She received a small allowance from Jackson's pay every month but she didn't use it, of course. The slips were all in the top drawer of the chest in her room. Sometimes she opened the drawer and looked at them. They were the only link she had with him now. She thought back to the last time she had seen Harry.

He had come to see her on his last leave. He'd met her out of the factory and insisted on going with her to Ferryhill. He had nodded to Dora gravely and said hallo before going over to where Beth was lying on the couch, waving her arms in the air and cooing. Molly waited for his condemnation. He sat down beside the child, put out a finger and she clasped it tightly.

'Well, will you look at that?' he said admiringly. He put out his hands and lifted the baby in the air and she gurgled and tried to grab at the badge in his red beret. Obligingly he settled her on his knee and gave her the beret. The badge twinkled in the firelight and Beth smiled in delight, touching it with her tiny baby fingers.

'Mind, you're a bonny bairn, aren't you?' her uncle asked, and she chuckled and tried to pull off the medal ribbon.

Molly relaxed. Oh, he was the best brother anyone had ever had, he was indeed. 'Thanks, Harry,' she said, and he smiled at her, before turning his attention back to the baby.

'Well,' he said finally. 'We Masons have to stick together, haven't we?' He stood up with the baby on one arm and put the other round Molly's shoulders, kissed her on the cheek. 'You have had a hard time of it, little sister,' he said without looking at her. 'I don't blame you for anything. Mind, that bloody Joan is spreading her poison all over Eden Hope. Jackson's parents are bound to have heard.'

Molly nodded. Well, she thought, she couldn't keep Beth a secret forever and she wouldn't want to.

He tickled the baby under her chin and she gurgled, wetly, making a damp patch on his khaki shoulder.

Now, as she took out her sewing machine and set it up on the kitchen table, Molly thought back on that day fondly. She would always be grateful for Harry's love and support, but he had refused to talk about Jackson.

'I don't see him now,' was all he had said. Had she caused a rift between the two men or was it simply that they had been separated by the war?

'Are you going to Eden Hope on Saturday?' Dora

asked. ''Cause if you are, I'd like to know now. I thought I might go to the pictures if you're here to look after Beth.'

Molly thought about it. She tried to go to see Maggie and Frank whenever she could but she was sick to death of pretending to them that everything was all right. Still, if Joan had been talking she wouldn't have to pretend. She would have to face them sometime. She quailed at the thought of going again, though. Sometimes she saw a letter from Jackson propped up on the mantelpiece and itched to take it down and devour it. But she couldn't, of course. She found it harder and harder to conceal the fact that he never wrote to her. She had to guard her tongue at all times, in case she should let slip something about the baby, so she always made an excuse to leave early.

'I don't think I'll go this weekend, Dora,' Molly said now. 'I have some jobs to do.'

It was true, she had half a dozen orders waiting for her in a pile in the corner of the sitting room. She glanced up at the marble clock and frowned. It had stopped, she couldn't think why. She had dragged it all over the place with her since her father was killed and it had never stopped before but now it didn't seem to run for five minutes after she had wound it before stopping again. She would have to take it to the clock mender's on Saturday morning, she thought.

Dora went off to the pictures on Saturday afternoon to see *Pride and Prejudice* with Greer Garson and Molly got on with her sewing. But her head ached for some reason and she was glad to have a break when Beth woke from her afternoon nap and demanded attention.

'We'll go for a walk, shall we?' she asked the child and Beth crowed with pleasure as her mother struggled to put on her siren suit. She had made the suit the night before from a remnant of cloth she'd found on the market; an all-in-one suit in yellow with a hood which she had trimmed with white. Siren suits had become all the rage since Churchill began to wear one, even for babies.

She pushed the pram along the road to the park that looked strangely denuded with its railings chopped off at the base and gone to make tanks or something. The trees were bare, the only bird about a dejected-looking robin pecking beneath an elm. Molly shivered. She was wearing her slacks under her coat and a headscarf over her head but the wind was cutting. Only Beth looked cosy and warm, sitting up in her pram in her siren suit with an old quilt that had been Mona's over her. She chuckled and talked in her own personal language to the bird, the trees, anyone who happened to pass. But Molly's headache was becoming more insistent, like a hammer pounding in her temples. She longed for a hot drink and a couple of aspirins.

Back home she was surprised to find Dora had returned from the pictures. Surely the big film wasn't over yet?

'I've got a headache,' Dora explained as she blazed the fire and put on the kettle for tea. 'I expect I'm getting that 'flu which is going around the village.'

'Is it? I hadn't heard.' Molly gazed anxiously at Beth, dreading the thought that she might get it. There had been an epidemic the month before but it had passed by their house, thank the Lord. Beth looked back at her, her smiles turning to howls of indignation for it was time for her tea too. She held up her arms to be taken out of the pram, pumping them up and down when Molly didn't immediately rush to do her bidding. But her yells were loud enough, her eyes bright, her cheeks flushed with health as well as temper. No, she wasn't sickening for anything, not Beth. And Molly herself was probably only suffering from eyestrain. She had sewed on late last night, trying to finish the siren suit.

'I'll tend to her. You make the tea, will you, Molly?' asked Dora. 'I have to stop her making such a noise, I feel my head might burst with it.'

Eventually the child was settled and peace reigned again. Dora and Molly sipped their tea and ate corned beef hash and cabbage, took some aspirin each. But it didn't seem to work as it should and in the end Molly stopped sewing and folded her work away.

'I think I'll have an early night,' she said to Dora.

'That makes two of us,' the older woman replied.

Jackson fingered his weekend pass and even now, after all that had happened, his pulse quickened at the thought that if he wished he could be on a train in half an hour and on his way to see Molly. He didn't want to see her, though, did he? Not after what she had done. It was what all the married and engaged men in his unit feared, and it had happened to him.

'Well, Sergeant?' The middle-aged Captain sitting behind the desk looked up at him impatiently. 'Do you want a travel warrant or not? Come on, make up your mind, I have men waiting.'

If he did go north he would see Molly, Jackson knew that, he wouldn't be able to help himself. And how was he going to tell his parents? Or had they found out already? He shied away from the thought. But he should see his parents, he told himself, there was no telling when he would get back to England. Not that they had been told where they were going but there had been a short, intensive course in everyday French.

'Sergeant?'

'Yes, sir. A travel warrant to Bishop Auckand, sir.'

Even as he boarded the crowded train with only minutes to spare and threaded his way through the troops sitting on their kitbags in the corridor until he found a space just large enough for him to dump his own small bag and stand beside it, he still wasn't sure if he was going to go to Ferryhill. He took off his red beret and folded it, buttoned his epaulette over it and turned to gaze out of the window. Not that there was anything to see. The night was dark and soot from the engine smeared the window anyway. There was only the reflection of him standing grim-faced and those reflections of the other soldiers and airmen lounging about in the crowded corridor. It was of course impossible to get into any of the compartments with seats, they had been taken up at King's Cross.

Jackson flexed his shoulder muscles. They had stiffened slightly since the morning when they had practised their jumping over and over again. He could still feel the pull of the harness as the parachute opened, the rush of air against his legs as he floated down to earth. He wondered if he would be posted anywhere near Harry this time.

The last time he had seen his friend was when he had told him he was going to volunteer for the Airborne Division. And about Molly and her baby. Jackson had watched Harry's face for his reaction. Condemnation of his sister perhaps.

'Do you think they're managing?' he had asked. 'Oh, why didn't Molly tell me?'

'Who knows?' Jackson replied. 'And don't worry, she'll be getting a wife's allowance, I haven't stopped that.'

'Poor Molly. She's had a hard fight of it since Dad died.'

'Yes, well, so have a lot of women and they didn't go completely off the rails, going with men, acting like a . . .'

'Don't say it, Jackson,' warned Harry. 'It's not true. Molly loved you, you know she did.'

'Only a few weeks after I was posted missing?' said Jackson. 'Oh, aye, I'm sure she must have loved me then.' Bitterness welled up in him; it was like bile in his throat. 'Well, I'm finished with her.'

'Poor kid. All on her own. What it must have been like for her.' Harry bit his lip, gazing at Jackson. 'I'll have to see her, first chance I get. I'll go up, seek her out.'

'She lied to me, Harry,' said Jackson. He felt almost on the defensive, as if it had been he who had done the unforgivable, not Molly. 'Well, not exactly lied but she married me without telling me about the baby.'

'She must have been desperate,' said Harry. 'We let her down, Jackson. At least I did. I should have been there to look after her better. This isn't her fault, it's the fault of this bloody war.' He sighed. 'She must have been convinced you were dead. She was all alone, don't you see?'

'No, I don't,' Jackson replied.

'For God's sake, Jackson!'

He said nothing but turned on his heel and walked away.

The train was pulling into York where the platform was awash with people even though it was past midnight. Next stop Darlington, Jackson thought, and had to make up his mind what to do. Maybe he should go to see that Molly was all right, he told himself. He needn't even look at the baby, just find out how Molly was, see if she was in need. Then he would go home to Eden Hope and tell his parents that his marriage was over. That was his best course.

After all he would be away fighting by this time next week, he expected. He had to have his domestic problems sorted out by then.

In his heart Jackson knew he was fooling himself as to his reasons for taking the Durham train from Darlington and alighting at Ferryhill station. But he couldn't seem to help himself.

He walked down the street to the house, stood irresolute before the door, his heart beating as hard and as painfully, perhaps more so, than on the occasions when he had faced the enemy. Squaring his shoulders, he knocked. And knocked again. There was no answer and he felt incredibly let down. In the distance a pit hooter sounded, signalling the end of a shift, the beginning of another. Fore shift, he thought, it must be just after twelve o'clock. Jackson knocked again, louder this time. No response. A straggle of miners in their pit black began walking down the street. One of them flashed his light over Jackson, inspected his uniform, saw the badge gleam on his red beret.

'Now then, mate,' he said respectfully, and a few of his marras spoke too. 'Wotcher.' 'Good luck, lad.' There was a lot of respect for the paratroopers among the miners. They wandered away down the street, talking to each other in low voices. A shaft of moonlight illuminated the group, which was thinning out as the men dropped away on reaching their homes. Jackson turned back to the door and raised his hand to knock.

Suddenly there was a cry from inside. At first he thought it might be a cat. It came again, not a cat but a baby. Well, that would wake Molly at least. He waited, listening for movement, but there was none. The baby's wailing was louder now, a continuous, furious crying out that no one was taking notice.

Jackson tried the door handle with little expectation of the door opening but to his surprise it did. He pushed it open and stood in a narrow passage leading to a kitchen-cum-living room. Closing the door after him because of the blackout, he struck a match and looked around. There was a light switch on the wall; there was electricity then. Upstairs the baby's wailing had subsided a little, was almost despairing.

'Molly?' he called. 'Molly? It's Jackson.'

The baby cried afresh. There was a thud as though someone had fallen. Jackson took the stairs two at a time and opened the first door he came to. A woman, it must have been Dora he thought, lay there, breathing heavily. Why hadn't she woken? But he hadn't time to think of that. He opened the other door and switched on the light. Molly was lying half in and half out of bed, her arms moving weakly as she tried to pull herself up.

Jackson's heart filled with dread. Running over to her, he picked her up in his arms, laid her back on the bed and pulled the covers over her. The atmosphere in the room was freezing, her face was blue-white with the cold. Oh, God, she wasn't dying, was she?

'Molly? Molly? Wake up, please, wake up!' he cried, laying his face alongside hers, cradling her in his arms. She opened her eyes and tried to move.

'Beth,' she said, her voice faint and faraway. 'I must get to her.'

'No, no, you can't! You're not well enough,' said Jackson. 'Oh, Molly –'

She looked at him properly for the first time. 'Jackson? Oh, Jackson!' she began to sob. 'I prayed you would come.' Exhausted, she lay back against the pillow, her breathing fast and shallow. She closed her eyes then opened them immediately. 'See to her, please . . .'

Reluctantly he stood up, adjusted the covers over her. 'I will, I will, don't fret.'

Going over to where an old brown-painted cot stood in the corner, he looked down at the bright red face of the baby. She had stopped screaming and was now sobbing quietly, looking up at him with Molly's dark eyes. The bedclothes had been kicked off; her feet were like ice. She lifted her arms to him and he picked her up.

Beth was wet, very wet. She must have been lying there for a long time. Jackson looked helplessly around, he had to do something. Beth hiccuped, waved her fist at him, and where it touched his cheek it was so cold he realised he had to do something. He laid her down again, found the safety pin in her nappy and released it, drew the sopping nightie over her head. 'Give her to me,' said a wavering voice he hardly recognised as Molly's and he took the baby over to the bed and laid her beside her mother.

'Warm milk,' said Molly, and closed her eyes as though the effort to speak had been too much for her.

'I'll get it,' he said and ran down the stairs. He chopped sticks from an off-cut of pit prop he found in the coal house, built a fire in the cold grate and fanned it to life by propping a tin blazer on the top bar. Milk now, he thought, and found a baby's bottle in the pantry and a saucepan on the shelf. He picked up a bottle of milk then saw the National Dried can of baby's milk beside it. He heated water, read the instructions on the side of the can, found two cups and Beth's boat-shaped bottle, and soon was carrying a tray up the stairs. He even had time to be amazed at how well he had managed.

Molly took a cup and drank thirstily then sank back on the pillow as he took the baby in his arms, wrapped her in a large towel he had found on the rail over the kitchen range and offered her the bottle.

'It's not too hot?' croaked Molly anxiously.

'Do you think I'm daft?' he asked. But all the same he shook a few drops on to his hand before Beth took the teat in her mouth and sucked with the serious expression of a dedicated drinker.

It was when the baby had finished her bottle and pushed it away and was smiling up at him that he caught sight of the other cup of milk. Giving Beth back to her mother, he took the milk into the next room. But Dora couldn't take the milk, she was deeply unconscious.

'Dora's very ill, Molly,' he said as he went back into the other room. But she didn't hear. She was sound asleep, breathing noisily, her mouth open slightly.

'Oh, God,' said Jackson aloud. 'Don't die, Molly, please don't die!'

Beth started to cry. She held out her arms to him and he picked her up and rushed downstairs and outside to bang on the door of the neighbouring house. A miner just returned from the pit answered. He was in his stockinged feet, braces hanging down. But he was quickly galvanised into action when Jackson gasped out his story.

'I'll fetch the doctor, lad.'

''Flu, that's what it was, followed by double pneumonia,' said the doctor. It was half an hour later and Jackson and he were in the kitchen waiting for the ambulance that was to take Dora away to hospital. 'A lot of it about, I'm afraid. I'll write you out a prescription for . . . the young lady.'

'My wife,' said Jackson firmly. He held Beth lightly to his chest with one hand and the baby tried to reach up to the shining badge in his cap. She seemed to have recovered already from her cold night. She chuckled and grabbed at the beret and, like Harry had a few weeks earlier, he took it off and gave it to her to play with.

'A shame about Mrs Fletcher,' said the doctor. 'I've had a few similar cases after this 'flu.' He paused and wrote something on his prescription pad. As he handed a torn-off sheet to Jackson he added, 'Don't worry, your wife will be fine in a few days. And it looks like your little daughter has escaped it though she'll be to watch for a while. When are you due back?'

'Monday evening. But I'll ask for compassionate leave. It should be all right for a few days at least. Then there's my mother.'

The doctor sighed. 'So long as proper care can be arranged if you have to go.'

After he had gone and Jackson had dispatched a neighbour's son for the prescription, he started up the stairs with Beth on one arm. Sitting down on the edge of the bed, he took Molly's hand. Already she was looking more her old self.

'Mind, you gave me a heck of a shock,' he said. He bent and kissed her on the forehead, squashing Beth a little so that she protested loudly and he sat up straight.

'You're not going to come between us all the time, young lady,' he said to her, and Beth smiled and crowed and held out a hand to him. Obviously she was taken with him and by the look on his face the feeling was reciprocated.

Downstairs, the marble clock suddenly chimed. It must be going again, Molly thought, startled. Her hand beneath the bedclothes, she crossed her fingers.

'Is it all right now, Jackson?' she asked, holding her breath in case she had misread the signs. Was he being nice simply because she was ill? Oh, she couldn't bear it if it was that.

'I don't know. I don't know how I feel.'

In truth his emotions were in complete chaos. He looked at the baby and she gazed back at him, with Molly's eyes.

She even tilted her head in the way Molly did. He couldn't hate her, of course he couldn't. None of this was her fault. In the back of his mind he knew it was nobody's fault. It was the war, the flaming war.

Molly said no more, she was afraid to. Instead she stared out of the window at the row of chimney pots opposite. But a spark of hope had been ignited and it was still flickering.

'Well, at least Dora is going to get better,' said Jackson. 'Though you won't be in a fit state to look after her when she comes out of hospital.'

He had been down to the telephone box to ring the hospital to enquire after Dora. Now he sat on the edge of Molly's bed again, dandling Beth on his knee. She was gurgling and smiling for all the world as though she had known him all her short life rather than a few hours. Molly, already feeling a little better, was propped up on pillows, a doting smile on her face as she looked from her man to her daughter and back again. She refused to think about tomorrow.

'At least she'll be all right. I'll manage somehow.'

'No, you won't, my love.'

Had the endearment just slipped out? Molly wondered.

'I know you're used to managing but I won't have you doing too much. You have this one to see to.' Jackson lifted Beth up in the air and jiggled her about and she crowed with pleasure.

'There's my mother . . .'

'But she has your dad on crutches,' Molly reminded him.

'I'll ring up, ask for extended leave,' said Jackson. 'But I'm not sure . . .' After all, Molly was not in any danger now.

She suddenly sat bolt upright, her weakness forgotten. 'I know! I'll ask Vi.'

'Vi?'

'A girl who worked in the maternity home. I got friendly with her when I was there and I've felt guilty ever since that I hadn't asked her here at all. She has no family of her own and she loved Beth. Oh, I know she'll come! I'll ask Vi. Send her a card now. It'll catch the post, won't it?'

It was the following morning at nine o'clock, just half an hour after the post was delivered at the home, that Vi presented herself before Matron.

'I have to leave,' she said, her smile stretching from ear to ear. 'I'm going to help my friend, live at her house.'

'Are you sure of what you are doing?'

Matron gazed at the diminutive figure before her. She would be sorry to lose Vi, she thought. The girl was a good worker. Vi handed over the card from Molly.

'Molly Mason, is it?' asked Matron and Vi nodded. Matron sniffed. Molly Mason was a strong-minded girl. She had refused to put her baby up for adoption which was the only sensible course for a girl in her position. Still, she had been kind to Vi, Matron remembered that.

'Very well,' she said, handing the card back. 'You can take a week's notice.'

Vi lifted her head and gave Matron a determined look. 'Eeh, no, Matron. I'm going now,' she said.

'*The funny thing is*,' Molly wrote to Jackson a fortnight later, '*that Dora and Vi have taken to each other really well. Dora is thinner and still weak but Vi couldn't look after her better if she was her own mother . . .*'

Molly stopped writing and looked over to where Beth lay on the rug. She rolled over on to her stomach and tried to push herself up, her head wobbling a little as she grunted with the effort. Her hands slipped from under her and she whimpered before trying again. Her mother went over to her and picked her up and sat down on the rocking chair with her. She crooned as she rocked back and forwards, the baby laid against her shoulder, and eventually Beth fell asleep.

Molly was supremely happy. She felt that she had never been so happy in her life. There was Maggie, of course, and Frank. They weren't nasty to her when they found out about Beth, not at all.

'They are my family now,' Jackson had said to them. 'Both Molly and Beth. I don't want to hear a word against them.'

'I wasn't going to say one,' said Maggie. She and Frank had exchanged a glance, each understanding what the other was thinking. They didn't want to lose Jackson again and were definitely not going to say anything to risk it.

'Any road, she's a fine bairn,' Frank had said.

Molly stood up and put the baby down in her cot and went back to her letter to Jackson.

''*Til we meet again*,' she wrote. '*Watch yourself, my love.*'

Things might seem OK between them but she wasn't so soft as to think everything was as it had been before Beth. There were bridges to build still. And it was difficult to do it by letter. But when the war was over . . .

A Daughter's Gift

Elizabeth Nelson is only ten years old when her mother dies in childbirth. With her father gone, the siblings are separate; her Aunt Betty takes baby Kit. Elizabeth and her brother, Jimmy, are sent to a children's home and Alice and Jenny are sent into foster care.

Life in the home is hard, but Elizabeth is determined to look after her brother and make a better life for them both. Working as a nurse gives Elizabeth a purpose but she risks everything by falling for local mine owner, Jack Benson. Wounded at Gallipoli, Jack is far above her in wealth and station. Elizabeth cannot marry him and she risks losing her nursing place if there is any hint of impropriety about her conduct.

Then Elizabeth learns that her sister, Jenny, has been adopted by an abusive farmer. Torn between her hopeless love for Jack and her sister, must Elizabeth make an extreme sacrifice to reunite her family?

A Mother's Gift

Taken in by her grandparents to ease the pressure on her poverty-stricken family, Katie Benfield knows she's one of the lucky ones. Even so, she dreams of a better life and of pursuing a nursing career. Despite many hardships, Katie achieves her goal, but tragedy strikes Winton Colliery when both her grandfather and childhood sweetheart are killed in a mining accident. Shocked and distraught, Katie finds herself vulnerable to the advances of the owner of the mine, Matthew Hamilton, a married man who wastes no time in taking advantage of her.

Thrown out by her grandmother, her reputation and career in tatters, Katie finds herself facing a home for unmarried mothers. Only Matthew Hamilton offers her a way to keep her baby, but only if she forgoes her principles and becomes his mistress...